BENEATH THE SAND

KATHERINE L. BICHLER

For my parents, for teaching me to read

PROLOGUE

ANCIENT ROME

The morning's execution was set to be spectacular. The crowd was one of the largest the colosseum had seen in the last three hundred years. Thousands of Rome's people were packed into the stands, awaiting what was promised to be unlike anything anyone had ever seen before.

People of all classes were jammed into their respective seats. Even the servants had managed to worm their way into any standing-room available on the highest level of the five-story colosseum. Down in the arena below, the stage was set. Countless crews had been working to bring the emperor's vision to life. On what was usually a dusty, plain, sand-filled arena floor stood the complete opposite: a jungle. Hundreds of bushes, trees, and other shrubs had been planted throughout the arena, making it look lush and exotic. The greenery filled out the floor, with the less dense areas in the middle so the spectators could get a better view. There was so much vegetation that a fresh, rain-like aroma wafted throughout the stands, enhancing the already once-in-a-lifetime experience. On most of the perimeter of the arena, a moat had been dug and filled with water, ensuring there would be no escape for anyone unfortunate enough to be down there.

But what most of the crowd came for that day was not to witness the execution, but to see the many beasts the emperor had imported from exotic lands far and wide. For the jungle-clad arena now teemed with these animals. Camouflaged in the dense trees and swimming in the moat were beasts no one had ever seen or heard of before. These were much more than the occasional elephant the emperor had brought in, but what people could only imagine in their wildest dreams. Tigers, boars, ostriches, stags, lions, and many more were now scattered throughout the jungle, awaiting their imminent death —not to mention the hippos and crocodiles lurking in the dark waters of the moat.

The roars and screeches were near deafening. The captors had labored tirelessly to transport the animals into the arena from the stables at first light and were now working to prevent the animals from escaping before the start of the execution. The anticipation and excitement of the crowd could be felt throughout the entire arena as they watched the predators kill some of the weaker beasts.

Some wondered why the emperor was going to such extreme lengths for an execution. No one knew for sure. To question the emperor was a one-way ticket to your own execution.

The beat of the drums from the emperor's parade to the colosseum was now within earshot. He had his own private tunnel from his palace so as not to be bothered by the public, although on this particular day he was making a spectacle coming in the main gates with more pomp than normal. The emperor was a fat, quirky shell of a man with one of the most wicked tempers the empire had seen in centuries. He was strange and unpredictable, with a thirst for adventure and grandiose gestures. Rome's citizens feared him, but knew if they obeyed the law, they could live a satisfactory life.

Trumpeters announced his arrival as he approached his decadent throne, clad in a too-tight royal purple toga. He sat, looked down into the jungle, and smiled as he reveled in his achievement. Behind him, off to the side but still on his private platform, sat his most trusted advisers, his wife, and his current concubine. With one wave of his hand, the crowd was silent and only the beasts could be heard. A shackled and bloodied prisoner emerged from one of the large arched doors below. Cheers erupted throughout the arena; it was finally time for some action. Two guards forced the man into the edge of the jungle and onto his knees into the dirt. As the prisoner fell to the ground, he took in his surroundings and hung his head in fear and dismay. The guards removed his shackles and provided him with a small dagger and a spear, tossed next to him in the sand. This was the emperor's idea, of course. It would make it more exciting if the prisoner could put up a little fight. The emperor silenced the crowd once more. He stood and addressed his subjects.

"Today marks a momentous day," he announced. "By my decree, I hereby sentence this man to death. He has forsaken our empire, culture, and people. As punishment, he must face my beasts." With that, he sat back down on his gilt throne and the crowd erupted once more. They did not care much about the reason for the execution.

The guards then shoved the prisoner farther into the arena and closed the giant gate, locking him in. At first, the prisoner did not move. He was frozen in fear. He stayed that way for a full minute and probably would have never moved if not for the beast. A large ram came charging across the arena. Dirt whirled up behind it as it ran toward the prisoner. He just barely jumped to the side in time to avoid being gored. Snorting in anger at its failure, the ram slowed down and reversed to take aim at him again.

The prisoner, looking defeated, was on all fours in the dirt, crawling as fast as he could to distance himself from the beast. The ram regrouped and began another charge. As it lowered its head to deliver a blow with its horns, the prisoner did something surprising. Just as the ram was about to tower over him, he rolled to avoid being trampled and raised the measly dagger that had been provided, expertly slicing open the ram's underbelly from its neck to its tail. The beast stumbled and fell to the arena floor, its innards pouring out in a pool of steamy blood as it took its last shallow breaths.

Meanwhile, all eyes were on the emperor, the crowd unsure how to react to the prisoner's success. The emperor's face was stoic, and then a small grimace appeared as he started to clap slowly with long

3

dramatic pauses in between each clap. The crowd immediately joined in, hooting and hollering. The prisoner, unfazed, locked eyes with the emperor, as if daring him for more. His demeanor had changed from that of a weakling just moments ago to a fierce hunter. Instead, he lay in wait in the middle of the arena, head moving in a swivel, spear and dagger in his hand waiting for whatever was coming for him next.

With roars and grunts from all directions, it was difficult to see where the animals were in the midst of all the dense greenery. The smell of blood from the ram's carcass began to draw other beasts out from the cover of the bush to investigate. A few hyenas had begun dismantling the carcass, not paying any heed to the man who remained like a statue in the middle of the arena. It was taking too long for something to happen. Everyone could sense it. The whole colosseum held its breath.

The emperor stood again, motioning to his gamesman in disgust at the lack of progression. Immediately, some of the trap doors around the arena flew open. Workers began slinging meat at the man, some pieces hitting him where he stood. This got the attention of some beasts. A few boars charged out from the far side of the arena, emerging from their hiding place under a large pile of brush. The prisoner turned in anticipation of the charge. He was able to dodge the first three, diving and rolling past each. However, the last boar was coming right for him. With no more room to duck and roll, he crouched and launched his spear, connecting right between the boar's eyes above its tusks. The other boar flew past him, too busy enjoying the meat scraps that had been tossed on the arena floor.

Again, the prisoner stood unscathed. The emperor did not even need to signal the gamesman this time. All thirty-six trap doors encompassing the arena opened at once, releasing what seemed like every large predator the colosseum could house. Numerous tigers, lions, bears, panthers, leopards, cougars, and jaguars ran out into the jungle in search of prey. The crowd was in awe of the beasts, pointing every time they caught a glimpse of one through the trees.

The man was sure to have no chance of evasion now, but no one could have been prepared for what happened. Instead of going after the prisoner, the beasts became threatened by each other. Different powerful species all trapped in the same arena sparked an internal struggle to establish dominance. The roars and grunts began bellowing from each species, an almost deafening sound. Fighting erupted, some of the beasts hunting the others, leaving many dead throughout the jungle. The man all but disappeared into the jungle while the crowd refocused its attention on these never-before-seen creatures. The pace was fast and because of all the trees, it was difficult to see the animals. Jaguars leapt from limb to limb clawing at the leopards and panthers as they each tried to claim the high ground as their own. Cat-like screams rang throughout as the fighting intensified.

All eyes were on the treetops, a bonus performance no one could have planned or coerced. Beasts with razor sharp nails clawed at each other, just yards away from the crowd. The wealthy and distinguished patrons of the first few rows could almost reach out and touch the beasts, they were so close, though they would not dare for fear of losing a limb. The bodies of the animals not as fortunate to survive began littering the arena floor. Torn up carcasses with their entrails laying in the sand and dirt were everywhere. The animals fought each other for what seemed like hours, the chaos of the initial charge winding down as the dominant beasts prevailed. The crowd could not get enough of these magnificent creatures. What was once a prisoner execution had turned into a full-on exhibition of animal slaughter. The panthers had taken over the tree tops, exploring their new domain. At some point a large panther must have finally noticed the spectators because it made a flying leap toward the arena wall from a tree leaning slightly over the moat. Its jump carried it to almost the edge of the spectator section where its front claws gripped the ledge while its back claws fiercely tried to run up the wall.

The false pretense of security overcame most of the spectators as they leaned over the edge to get a better look. The panther caught a hold in the wall and was able to scramble to the ledge where it expertly balanced, taking in the scene of its new position in the crowd. The spectators who did not run in fear stood there half wondering if this was part of the show. A young boy tried to cling to his father, but was no match for the panther who swiped at the boy, grabbed him with its claws, and dragged him back down into the arena. The boy's father tried to jump over the wall after his son, but other men held him back. People were screaming and looking down through the trees to get a glimpse of the boy whose terrified yells could be heard.

The emperor just sat there on his throne, not even a look of panic on his face. His crooked smile made it seem like he was enjoying the tragedy unfolding before him.

The crowd started to quiet, mostly due to shock and also because they were trying to follow the boy's screams to see where he was. The screaming stopped after a few long minutes. The father was inconsolable back in the stands, as he knew what that meant. The emperor could be seen whispering something to his adviser, not at all concerned about the ill fate of one of his young citizens. Then, from the opposite side of the arena where the boy was taken, the crowd suddenly began to point and whoop. For coming out of the trees toward the north side of the arena was the prisoner. He was covered in blood, running as fast as he could toward what looked like the emperor's podium with the young boy on his back. Miraculously, he wasn't being chased by any of the beasts—yet.

The crowd was on the edge of their seats, hollering for the boy. The prisoner made it to the north wall where the moat ended. Jamming his knife into the wall, he made a quick foothold which he used to launch the boy from his back into one of the cutouts in the walls of the arena, halfway up from the ground. From there, the man propelled himself into the cutout, quickly grabbing the boy and tossing him up over the wall directly onto the floor of the emperor's podium where he was immediately attended to by the emperor's servants. The crowd cheered for the boy's safe return, the father knocking people over trying to reunite with his son. Meanwhile, the beasts had caught on to the prisoner's whereabouts and begun pacing underneath the cutout in the wall. Inching to the edge of the cutout, the man propelled himself into the start of the moat, splashing down into the murky water avoiding the predators waiting for him. His luck ran out in the moat, for he did not anticipate the beasts lurking in it. Within seconds of his plunge, a fight erupted between the man and a large crocodile. Only glimpses of them could be seen through the splashing water.

Eventually the splashing ceased, and the murky water turned a dark crimson as the prisoner's body floated face down in the water while whatever other beasts were in the moat feasted on his fresh corpse. If it wasn't for the boy, the prisoner might have been forgotten about all together and survived his execution by staying hidden. Instead, he chose to save another's life and end his own, a feat that was sure to be rewarded by the gods in the afterlife. The emperor could not have dreamed up an outcome such as what had just happened. Romans would be talking about this day for centuries to come and that was just what he desired.

As the crowds of people filed out of the arena to go about their day, underneath the arena floor *she* was there waiting—as she was every day—for the injured and the dead. She had seen it all.

1

NOEMI

"Come on, Noemi," her sister, Livia, said. "Try this one on. You have to like one of these tunics."

Noemi rolled her eyes again. "It really doesn't matter to me. They all look the same. You pick one." Now it was Livia's turn to roll her eyes. "You are impossible. You are getting married, for god's sake. Can't you at least pretend to care? This is one of the most important days of your life," Livia said as she spun around their room holding a white muslin tunic to her body.

Noemi laughed. "Why does it bother you so much that I am not like every other girl in Rome, anxiously waiting for her betrothal?"

"*Sic, Sic*, we know, you would much rather be mucking out the stalls in the hypogeum than gods forbid act a little bit girly," Livia said, pretending to gag. "Personally, I cannot wait until father announces my betrothal."

"Oh, you can't? I never would have guessed," Noemi said sarcastically. "And I don't muck stables, for your information. I train beasts with father. Something you would not understand, considering it might cause you to break a nail."

"If that's what you want to call it," Livia said annoyed.

Noemi could not take one more minute of her nagging sister. It wasn't that she didn't want to get married. It was all the pomp and circumstance that came with it that was not for her. Tying her long brown hair back, she left Livia to sort through all her wedding details and headed to the hypogeum. If she was lucky, she might be able to watch the execution before she went to work with her father.

Underneath the colosseum, Noemi sat at the entrance to the tunnel known as the Gate of the Dead. She couldn't see much, but by the sounds of the crowd, she knew the execution was over. Although it wasn't her job to tend to the dead, Noemi couldn't help but bid one final farewell to the animals heading into the afterlife; the same animals she knew so well and had helped her father train.

She watched as the *mortams*—or the dead gatherers, as they were called—loaded the carcasses onto wooden carts to be wheeled out through the tunnel. Before being disposed of in mass graves located outside the city, the bodies were first offered to the people of Rome. At the tunnel's exit, the empire's poorest gathered in ill formed lines in the hopes of getting their hands on pieces of meat to feed their families. Others gathered with the promise of gaining a souvenir from an exotic beast, like a tusk or a hoof. Noemi felt good about this part of their journey because she could see her work ultimately gave back to the empire, and for that she thanked the gods.

As the carts began their ascent, Noemi whispered one final prayer for her fallen friends and scurried off to help her father. For the animals that had survived the emperor's jungle experiment extravaganza needed to be dealt with and transported back to their respective stalls and stables.

"Noemi!" her father Jovian yelled. "What is taking you so long? These beasts won't move themselves! Let's go!"

Hundreds of men had already begun the process of corralling the animals above in the arena, moving them down the ramps into the various stalls and rooms below. Organized by species, the two levels of the hypogeum were home to hundreds of animals. Each floor accessible by various ramps and stairs to accommodate the movement of the animals and workers.

By the time Noemi got to her father, the beasts from the jungle execution had already been triaged. The sick and lame were the first to be moved. If they needed immediate care and attention, they were transported to the central medical area right there in the hypogeum itself. If they were deemed able to make the journey to the stables for a long-term recovery, they were caged and carted through the tunnels to be rehabilitated. The more dangerous beasts were netted or lassoed or captured by whatever means necessary to move them to the stall on either the first or second level.

Noemi knew she shouldn't have taken so long to help out her father, but she had been glued to the grandiose execution like every other person in the empire.

"Help Felix with the lions, please. We need all these beasts cleared out before the afternoon battles or it will be my head," her father instructed her while wrangling a tiger himself. Her father, Jovian, ran the hypogeum as the emperor's chief operator, a very demanding job.

She could see the exhaustion in her father's face from the endless nights of preparation for today's execution. He had pulled it off somehow, as he always did.

She found Felix waiting for her near the long line of lions ready for transport.

"Would you look who decided to show up? I was beginning to think I needed to send out a search party for you," Felix teased as he exaggerated tapping his foot in fake frustration.

Noemi rolled her eyes at him and grabbed a long spear that was hanging on the wall. "Sorry, Livia bombarded me with wedding stuff again this morning. She doesn't seem to get that it's our wedding and not all about her."

"Oh, leave her be. If it was up to you, you would marry me in your filthy work tunic," he teased.

"Fair enough." She laughed. Dropping down into a crouched

stance holding the spear out in front of her to mimic a gladiator, she joked, "Okay, I'm ready for the lions."

Felix grinned back at her as he untied a large lion from its post. He pulled on the rope attached to the spiked collar around the lion's neck, prodding it to follow him. The lion, exhausted from its work in the arena, did not put up much of a fight as it walked in the direction of Felix's lead.

Noemi walked next to the lion, her spear inches from its side, ready to strike if the lion were to attack. They had done this countless times together, only ever having to use the spear once.

"Slow down, Nomee," Felix said using his nickname for her. "That lion might still be hungry, I don't want to be its next meal," he half joked.

"Would be a shame for such a good-looking guy like yourself to end up eaten by a lion," Noemi teased.

"I would at least hope to make it to our wedding day before you throw me to the lions, Nomee," Felix teased back.

They stopped in front of a large square stall built out of limestone and tuff, one of forty in a long row of lion pens. The lion perked up, wet drool dripping from its mouth as it smelled the meat waiting for it in the stall.

Felix tightened up the lead, halting the lion and allowing Noemi to open the heavy wooden door to the stall. The lion pulled on the tether, desperate to get to the meat.

Noemi moved out of the way so Felix could release the lion into the stall. It wasted no time barreling into the pen, diving on its meal while paying the two no mind as they slid the door closed, securing it with a wooden board.

Noemi then used a piece of white chalk to write the date on the wall next to the pen, marking when the lion was last used. It helped to rotate the lions, giving them a greater longevity, just one of the many of Jovian's protocols for keeping the hypogeum organized.

Certain that the lion was locked in, Felix pulled Noemi into a warm embrace. She nuzzled her face into his chest taking in his unique smell of sweat and leather. He gently kissed her on the top of the head and said, "Come on, love, the rest of the lions won't pen themselves."

Noemi had been penning lions and other beasts since as long as her father would let her. At first it had just started out as something fun to do, instead of being cooped up with her mother and Livia doing household chores. A few days here and there turned into every day, watching and learning everything about the beasts that she could from her father. Finding she was more than capable, and added value to his work, Jovian started pairing her up with Felix, his top handler, to work with the beasts. In turn, Noemi became the only female trainer in the empire.

So, it was no surprise when her father announced their betrothal months ago. Truth be told, the two had been in a relationship for a while, realizing they were more than just friends after many a long day in the hypogeum together.

They had tried to sneak around, not wanting to disrespect their families, but it was obvious to everyone they were in love. Plus, there was nothing that went on in the hypogeum Jovian did not know about.

Noemi and Felix made quick work of penning the rest of the lions. Jovian's men had taken care of the hard part, wrangling them from the arena floor above in one piece and tethering them to the posts.

Last one, Noemi thought. As she went to close the final stall, the door stopped moving halfway, stuck on an uneven piece of raised limestone from the ground. "Felix!" Noemi screamed. "Help! The door! It's stuck."

The lion, sensing something was off, stopped eating its meal inside the stall and turned back toward the half-opened door.

Noemi tried everything she could to get the door to move again, between throwing herself into it and pushing as hard as she could, but it wouldn't budge. The lion pounced at the open door sensing an opportunity for escape. Her heart was beating so fast, trying not to panic.

Felix dove in front of Noemi and jammed his spear at the lion's side. A loud whine could be heard from the beast as it fell. The two then pushed the heavy door shut together and sank down to the ground in relief, their backs leaning against the door.

Noemi's nervous laugh broke the silence between them. "I guess maybe I spoke too soon about you being a lion's snack today," she said as she picked her head up off of Felix's shoulder where she had been resting it. "Thanks for having my back," she said as she playfully tapped him on the chest.

"Anytime," Felix replied. "Anytime."

Looking in on the lion through the bars of the stall door, the two could see that the spear had only caused a shallow cut on its side. Its breathing had slowed a little, but nothing extreme enough to mention it to the healers. Noemi marked the wall next to pen with a large "X," indicating an injured beast.

She hated to be the one to cause an animal's pain, especially for a silly accident like that. Per Jovian's protocol, the animal was strong enough to make it through the night, so they would leave it in the stall. In the morning if it was still alive, it would be used in the execution of a prisoner or slave tied to a post in the arena. The weakened beast could then eat the stationary prisoner while still maintaining its look of ferocity to the audience. Most likely it would be the lion's last feat in the arena before it would die and make its way to the Gate of the Dead.

Jovian had many protocols in place. He had to if he wanted everything to run smoothly, thus keeping the emperor pleased. The hypogeum was a well-oiled machine. Beneath the arena, the amount of people and moving parts on any given day was impressive to say the least. There was a whole world below the arena floor that most in the city had no idea existed. A city under a city. It literally took a small army to meet the emperor's demands. The amount of manpower alone just to work the trap doors in the arena floor totaled in the hundreds, not to mention the many other jobs involved in a single day in making the events run. Noemi's father was in charge of the entire operation, the head puppeteer, so to speak. She would never understand how he kept it all straight. Things like which trap doors needed replacing, or when the sand on the arena floor needed to be cleaned, were all up to him.

"I have to go assist some of the wranglers in the arena getting the rest of the beasts underground," Felix said, turning to head up the ramp.

"Okay, I'm coming with you. You could use the extra help," Noemi said.

"Uh..." Felix paused for a second knowing she was not going to like his response. "As much as I know you could handle it, it is not the job for my future bride, nonetheless a woman."

As expected, Noemi's face hardened. "Felix, don't tell me what I can and can't handle. I am coming with you and that is final," she said as she followed him up into the arena.

Knowing enough to pick and choose his battles, Felix took a deep breath and said, "Fine, you can come as long as you stay behind me the entire time."

Noemi smiled, knowing she had won.

"But don't think that this will continue once we are wed," Felix continued. "I will not have my wife and mother of my future children risking her life day in and day out with these beasts. And *that* is final."

Noemi did not even respond. She had had this argument with Felix way too many times to count. She knew he believed this was all going to change once they were married, but there was no way she was ever going to give up working with the animals. *He will just have to get used to it,* she thought.

What remained of the jungle was surprising, even for Noemi. Men were working to drain the water from the moats, while others were filling it in with gravel. The vast amount of greenery was mostly dug up, laying in heaping piles waiting to be removed by Jovian's team. The bloodied sand was being replaced and being raked into a crisp circular pattern. By the time the gladiators fought later that afternoon it would be as if nothing had ever happened. A feat of almost sorcery that Noemi still couldn't get over no matter how many times she saw it being done.

The beasts that remained were being pushed into a corner by the wranglers for capture, and by the looks of it, it was not going smoothly. Noemi was not sure which was in worse shape, the animals or the men, both with their fair share of injuries.

Felix made his way to the wranglers, dodging the props and carcasses strewn around the arena, still needing to be cleaned up.

As they neared the wranglers, Noemi started to think this really was no place for her. These beasts had had no training and were clearly virulent, doing anything they could not to be captured again. A bloodied panther lunged at Felix who barely knocked it down with a pike, saving them both while the other men quickly bound the beast once it was down.

Once she realized she would not be much help, Noemi wanted to change her mind, but did not want Felix to know he was right. There were just too many wild beasts she was unfamiliar with for her to be useful. Instead, she stayed behind him as close as she could without hindering him, watching as the wranglers took whatever means necessary to collar the beasts.

When all the animals were roped, Felix handed Noemi the lead to an ocelot that could probably have been carried without any danger. She knew this was Felix's way of trying to make her feel useful, but she only felt diminished, proving this was no work for a woman. Suddenly, the idea of playing dress up with Livia was not seeming so bad to her anymore.

Noemi avoided Felix for the rest of the afternoon. It wasn't his fault she felt so defeated, but working with him was a reminder that despite knowing everything about how the hypogeum ran, she would always have limitations just because she was a woman.

If anything could take her mind off of things, it was the gladiators. To Noemi, their lives were fascinating, with their strict rules and lifestyle that could all be over in a split second with the end of a sharp sword.

Navigating the poorly lit cavernous maze beneath the arena, Noemi made her way to the far end of the hypogeum near the Gate of the Dead. Growing up under the colosseum, she knew the dark passages like the back of her hand. For years, she had taken each opportunity to explore every single corner of the place, every sound and smell ingrained in her mind.

She stopped at the farthest corner where the light from the lanterns barely reached. There in the shadows was a small alcove, an old storage room, long forgotten about as it was too small to be of any real use anymore. It was here Noemi had collected and put together a small bedroom of sorts, her own private hideout that not even Felix knew about.

In one corner, she had made herself a bed from straw she had collected from the stables and pens. Next to the bed she had scavenged an old shipping crate one of the beasts had been transported in. To the unsuspecting eye, the crate appeared to have been discarded and thrown in the small alcove after one of the shows years ago, long since forgotten about. At least that was what Noemi wanted people to think in case anyone ever stumbled upon her hideout. Not that it was likely anyone would ever wander into her room because the only people below the arena were prisoners, wounded gladiators, or workers too busy to pay any attention to anything other than their tasks. It was what the crate was blocking that was what was important to her.

Moving the crate to the side, Noemi pried out a loose stone block from the wall. Behind it was a small space she had carved out to make a secret compartment where she hid some clothes and a few of her valuables.

Pulling out a disguise, she quickly changed from her simple stable tunic and put on a lavish ivory silk robe. Next, she wrapped the large pale blue *palla* over her shoulders and draped the excess fabric around her head. The more fabric, the wealthier the woman, but in Noemi's case the excess fabric was a welcomed addition in helping conceal her face. She also had one piece of jewelry, a metal arm band in the shape of a serpent, all the rage in the forum these days, or so she was told by Livia.

The last, and probably Noemi's favorite part of her disguise, was lip rouge, a piece of red wax she had stolen from her father's chambers back at the stables. She rubbed her finger over the soft wax and pressed it to her lips smacking them together to evenly distribute the red color. For a wealthy woman always wore makeup as it was very expensive and hard to come by in the empire. Once her outfit was complete, she hid her plain stable clothes in the compartment in the wall, replaced the stone and put the crate back in its place messing up the dirt around the crate so as to hide any footprints or signs of activity.

On the opposite side of the small room was a ladder propped up against the wall. Noemi expertly climbed the ladder, the bulk of her tunic in one hand to keep her from stepping on it. Once at the top of what seemed like nowhere to go, she gently pressed both her hands on a large stone block in the ceiling and pushed it up out of place. She then slid it over to make room for herself to crawl up into the passage.

Noemi had created this passage when she had first found the room, chipping away at the mortar around the stone block with a broken piece of an old bronze nail she had found in one of the animal pens. She had gotten the idea from stone robbers. Workers were constantly having to replace stone blocks around the colosseum because people would pry the stones loose, steal and sell them. She thought, why not make the stones movable, gaining her secret access to nooks and crannies throughout the colosseum only she knew about.

Climbing up into the dark hole in the ceiling, being careful not to snag her silk robe on anything, she came up behind the stone benches in the back of one of the wealthier box seating areas for the arena. Silently, she replaced the stone block back into its place so no one would be suspicious of her comings and goings. Dusting herself off, she emerged from the shadows and found an empty seat behind an older wealthy couple deep in conversation recapping the morning's execution. They did not even bother to turn around at the approach of someone sitting behind them. She found that as long as she dressed the part and acted like she belonged in the wealthy section, no one paid her any attention and she was free to enjoy the gladiator combat. Worst case, she had a forged pottery shard with her box and seat number chiseled on it in case anyone questioned her.

Because of the excitement of this morning's execution, the stands were not nearly as crowded as they normally were for the gladiators; possibly because the emperor was not in attendance or possibly because spending all day in the stands of the colosseum was no picnic.

The sounds of the clanging swords drew Noemi's attention away from the crowd and to the arena below. Two gladiators were centered on the floor engaged in battle. Both were bare chested with a thick leather belt around each of their waists for protection along with leather arm and leg straps. The leather arm straps were wrapped around a piece of cloth on each wrist and the leg straps were wrapped up each leg to the knee. They wore sandals on their feet to get better traction in the sand, and each carried a sword and a shield.

She didn't just sneak into the fights for the entertainment, it was more than that. The gladiators fascinated her, so much so she taught herself to fight by watching every battle she could, picking up moves here and there. The fact that women were not allowed to become gladiators did not stop her in the least. If anything, it motivated her. Of course, no one besides a few of the gladiators she secretly trained with knew anything about her abilities. Gods forbid if Felix found out his future bride not only wanted to work but was training to fight.

This must be an entry level fight, Noemi thought because she didn't recognize either one of the gladiators, they had minimal battle armor on, and the weapons were of a basic nature. It was a little disappointing because she could not learn as much from the inexperienced gladiators, but it was distracting enough to keep her mind off of Felix.

She had just missed opening announcements and the introduction of all of the afternoon's fighters and would never dare ask anyone around her for their names, so she made one up for each of the men. One man, the taller of the two, had a giant scar on his right shoulder that resembled a snake, so she called him Scales. The other took her a minute to come up with a name for, as he had no distinct scars or features she could see, until he turned and she saw his eyes. They were two different colors: one a piercing blue and the other a deep brown. This man she called Ghost.

The two were now engaged in basic sword fighting. Scales feigning and stabbing while Ghost countered his moves. Moves Noemi was already familiar with.

A referee was present to see to a fair fight, and ready to interfere with his tall wooden staff if need be. The gladiator *lanistas* stood off to the side giving the men tactical advice.

Scales looked to have the upper hand. He appeared to be more agile than Ghost who seemed like more of a lug. Both men had minor cuts on their chests from being nicked by the sword, but nothing major. She knew the injuries looked worse than they actually were.

The fight was starting to pick up as the gladiators had settled into a good pace. At one point, Scales shouted something inaudible to Ghost that made Ghost hesitate for a second. In that second Scales was able to slice his right arm thus creating a devastating blow to Ghost's dominant arm making him drop his sword in the sand. The crowd roared with approval. Ghost took a few protective steps back regaining his composure, trying to calculate his next move. Scales grimaced as he knew whatever he had said had gotten under Ghost's skin.

Noemi had seen how this played out a hundred times, the referee would allow the fight to continue and Ghost would be dead in minutes. She let her mind begin to wander while she waited for the next fight, hoping it would last longer than this one.

The noise of the crowd brought her back as they started chanting, "*Ingula, Ingula*" or "Execute him, Execute him" and pointed their thumbs down. This meant Ghost must have knelt and raised his index finger to the crowd in surrender. At which point the crowd was allowed to vote whether he was to be spared or executed. However, they rarely voted for anyone to be spared.

Well, he didn't last very long, thought Noemi. She focused back in on the arena to lay eyes on the victor and to her shock it was Scales, not Ghost, kneeling in the sand awaiting his final sentencing. *But how?* she thought. Dumbfounded, she said out loud to no one in particular, "What just happened?"

A man farther down the bench she was sharing replied, "How did you miss it? The injured one feigned surrender and just as the bigger one was to deliver the final blow, the injured one charged him, picked up his fallen sword, and somehow pinned him to the ground with his sword at his neck...and all with his left arm! It was incredible."

Noemi turned back to the arena. The crowd had chosen death as usual. As a gladiator, death was not a punishment but a respected honor of your fulfillment of the role. Scales remained on his knees, accepted his defeat, raised his head, and prepared for his final assignment. Ghost looked to the referee for permission to end the battle. The referee gave the nod and Ghost ran his sword straight through Scales's chest. Scales fell to the ground and the referee raised Ghost's good arm in victory. The crowd cheered and the fight was over.

2

CATO

"Bannnnggggg, Baannnnnggg." The unmistakable sound of the gong that could be heard every morning at dawn from the Gladitorium was right on schedule. At this point in his training, Cato, along with most all of the other first year gladiators, was already awake, accustomed to the disciplined routine of the school. Dressed in his training uniform which consisted of a short tunic, leather belt, and worn sandals, Cato stood at the door to his cell awaiting the guard to unlock it. He did not have to wait long for a guard was already in his cell block.

The school guard approached the cell door and grunted out, "Manus." Cato reached both of his arms through the cell bars exposing his wrists to the guard who then placed shackles on them.

He pulled his shackled hands back through the bars and the guard unlocked the door. Cato fell in line with the other gladiators already released from their cells without so much as a word exchanged between any of the men. This had been their routine for months and there wasn't much to say anymore even if they could speak. *Discipline* echoed inside his head as it had been drilled into all gladiator's heads from day one of their training at Ludus Magnus.

The men were led to the dining hall where they were given an ample amount of food to fuel them for the grueling day of training ahead of them. Still, no one was allowed to converse, nor did they dare try for fear of being lashed by the guards.

Cato wolfed down his meal, his shackles clanging together as he moved his hands to his mouth. The shackles were mostly a mental training exercise than anything else. No one was dumb enough to try anything, especially because getting into Ludus Magnus was so difficult and quitting once you were in was unheard of. They were also not forever, only for the *novicius* year, and only while they were not training. Cato barely even noticed them anymore.

There were multiple gladiator schools throughout Rome with Ludus Magnus ranking supreme. Only the boys born of the elite or boys who showed extreme promise were allowed admission into3 Ludus Magnus. Other schools allowed prisoners and slaves to train, however, they rarely gained any fame once they graduated.

Cato was one of the lucky ones, born into a family of renowned gladiators. It was in his blood to be one of the best. The school had practically thrown itself at Cato's parents to send him there, what with his late uncle being one of Rome's sought-after gladiators turned *lanista*. Cato did not mind the notoriety one bit. He took every advantage his name brought to him. To the outside world, gladiator schools appeared as if they were prisons because of the locked doors and strict discipline. However, when it is kill or be killed in the arena, one quickly learns that the discipline and process of the schools has worked for centuries and it was wise to follow the rules and respect the honor that comes with the privilege of being a gladiator.

After completion of breakfast, the boys were moved to the practice arena outside. The guards removed the shackles as they exited the main building of the school into the outdoor training facility.

The sun already felt hot on Cato's face, a small bead of sweat started to drip down his forehead. *It was going to be another long day,* he thought.

The arena where they held all their training was designed to mimic that of the colosseum, the giant amphitheater where the battles were held. With four stories towering over the school, its massive size was a quiet and constant reminder of their future and success.

The gladiators filed in and sat on the benches circling the oval shaped arena, the sun beating down on their backs. Still in silence, they awaited what was in store for them today.

Cato watched as Magistri Cicero entered the practice arena walking to the middle of the oval shape to address his students.

"Good morning, gentlemen," Cicero greeted them looking around the arena at all the *novicius* gladiators. Magistri Cicero was one of the least liked trainers at school. He was a tall, thin man who looked like he had never fought a day in his life. Cato did not mind him, though, because he was a *lanista* like his uncle and he had never mistreated Cato.

"Today's lesson is one of great importance, probably one of the most important lessons you will ever learn during your time here at Ludus Magnus. For today you learn how to die." Cato turned his head to look at the other men who were just as confused as he was.

Die? Cato thought the goal of being a gladiator was to live and gain honor throughout the empire, the exact opposite of what Cicero was conveying. Cato could tell Magistri Cicero had gotten the reaction from the pupils that he had intended.

Cicero continued, "I know you all are thinking that your intention is not to die and how could there possibly be a proper way to do it, but I am here to tell you there is only one way to die, and that is with honor. Each one of your careers as a gladiator will end differently. Some of you will go on to gain fame while others of you will not be as fortunate. At some point you will all be scheduled to fight at the colosseum to complete your first year of training," he lectured as he pointed to the massive amphitheater towering over the school. "It is both an honor and a privilege to fight in front of the emperor and for this empire. Do not ever take that for granted. This is not some game. We are the top school in Rome and our gladiators must reflect that."

The men just looked at each other. They had heard this speech time and time again. They knew they were the best. Why else would they be here? Cato couldn't help but wonder how such a small, frail looking man had once been the top gladiator at the school. *The guy looks like he could barely lift a sword nonetheless wield it*, Cato wanted to say out loud.

Magistri Cicero then pointed to Germanus, one of the younger *novicius* gladiators at the school, and yelled, "You. On your feet. Approach the circle."

Germanus timidly got up from his seat. He looked like he had just been sentenced to execution by a lion, his face now a pale color. Germanus walked slowly to the middle of the arena where Cicero stood, the sand crunching beneath his sandals the only sound in the practice arena.

Magistri Cicero continued, addressing the other men, "Now, gentlemen, what can you tell me about what little Germanus here is doing wrong?"

Germanus's eyes widened in fear while Cicero snickered and looked at the other men to answer.

"Anybody?" Cicero jarred.

No gladiator dared to respond even if they knew the answer. Although Germanus had not been asked to do anything, Cato did not know what he was doing wrong.

"It seems as though a lesson in bravery needs to be added to your curriculum. Very well," he said, and with an ungodly speed he pulled a whip out that had been tucked in his belt and snapped it on the ground. The crack caused everyone to jump in their seats and Germanus to fall backward into the dirt.

"Get up boy!" Cicero yelled. Germanus jumped up unsure of what was about to happen next.

"Let's see," Cicero salivated as he circled Germanus looking him up and down like a predator about to finish his prey. "Posture."

The whip cracked so fast the only reason Cato knew where the target was because Germanus's ankle was now bleeding. The poor kid knelt down wincing and clutching the wound in obvious pain.

Gods, Cato thought. Sure, gladiators were injured in training all the time, but he had never heard of a trainer purposely injuring a student.

"Upon death, a gladiator must stand tall and proud. Shoulders back, boy." The whip cracked again but did not make contact with Germanus as he immediately threw his shoulders back to the point Cato thought he was going to fall backward again.

"Good. Now we are getting somewhere." Cicero smirked. Blood had begun to pool around Germanus's foot, the sand from the arena floor caking onto his ankle.

Cato could tell that he was in pain but was more scared of what was to come than the gash on his ankle.

"Confidence!" Cicero yelled and the whip cracked again, this time expertly landing on Germanus's cheek. Blood began dripping from Germanus's face covering the lower half of his jaw so it looked like he was wearing a mask. Poor Germanus did his best to keep his posture and his head up. No one envied his position.

"He doesn't seem very confident, does he?" Cicero asked mainly to himself in a sarcastic tone.

Unsure if a response was warranted, the gladiators remained silent. With nothing more he could do (except pray to the gods it would end), Germanus was a statue. Cato didn't think this lesson was going as intended. Cicero seemed to be on some weird power trip fueled by gods know what.

"Would anyone like to take his place and show me the proper way to die?" Cicero asked. Again no one moved unsure what they were signing up for and additionally trying not to make Germanus look weaker than he already was. That lesson was learned back in the first few weeks.

"Very well," Cicero continued. "Everyone up. Form a circle around this pathetic excuse for a gladiator. Since none of you were able to answer my question, you will all be punished." He spit into the sand emphasizing his disgust as the men complied.

"Everyone, take a knee." Cicero whipped the two gladiators closest to him on the back of the leg. They fell hard on their knee both trying not to wince from the sting of the whip. Cato hoped whatever was coming wouldn't actually involve death. He had never heard of a *lanista* killing a student before.

"If you are facing death in any battle, there is a reason for it. You probably have just lost a fight or maybe the emperor was displeased with your performance. Whatever the reason, know that this is what the fates have in store for you. They have cut your string of life."

Cato looked at Germanus who was starting to get woozy from all the blood loss and the heat. Cicero continued, "Now when it is your time you will take a knee as you are all doing so now. Do not bow your head, hold it up proudly, eyes open. You will not complain, you will not show fear, and you will not flinch. You will accept defeat and take a knee. Bravery. Dignity. That is what you must feel in your veins."

At that, Germanus passed out.

Cicero did not even acknowledge the lifeless body lying in a pool of his own blood. "As punishment, you will all remain on your knee until the dusk. The guards will see to it. Anyone who so much as utters a word will be the main event at tomorrow's execution. I hear there were some ghastly new beasts brought in this morning that I am sure will love to tear you to shreds." He chuckled to himself. "Have a good evening, men," he said to them all, and to no one in particular, "Oh and have this boy dealt with." At that he walked back inside the school's compound without so much as a glance back in their direction.

Cato hoped Germanus would be taken to the infirmary but did not think that's what Cicero had in mind when he said, "dealt with." He couldn't help but feel bad for Germanus. He wouldn't even get a chance to complete his first year of training. The men watched as his breathing shallowed and his color grayed. If any one of them wanted to reach out and help him, they couldn't. A guard picked up his lifeless body not long after Cicero left and carried him to a place Cato did not want to even think about.

Cato's leg hurt. It felt like every individual grain of sand was piercing his knee and that was just after the first hour. By the fourth or fifth hour, he couldn't feel his knee or his entire right side at all for that matter. He could tell everyone else was in the same boat as they tried to shift their weight to take the pressure off their knees. To pass the time, Cato mostly watched the sun slowly move toward the horizon, praying to the god Helios, whose chariot pulled the sun, to move as fast as he could.

Since it was the end of the *novicius* year of training, pretty much all of the weak gladiators had been weeded out, so the remaining ones were all well-conditioned to endurance tasks but that didn't mean it did not hurt. At exactly dusk, a guard came down to the arena to end the punishment which just entailed him saying, "Get up." Relieved, Cato tried to stand but his knee gave out when he attempted to put any weight on that leg. He fell to the ground catching himself with his hands to keep himself from face planting in the sand. Aching, he slowly pulled himself up and limped back inside the school.

After they were all shackled, they were sent to see the medical team. However beat up and bruised the gladiators got, the school did provide care for them. The school had a vested interest in seeing the gladiators succeed, and proper care was essential to that interest.

Cato could feel the blood pumping back through his leg again as the *medicus* squeezed his hands up and down it trying to get the blood moving. Cato looked around for Germanus, but did not see him anywhere. *Poor kid*, he thought. After finishing with the *medicus*, he ate his dinner with the rest of the weakened *novicius* gladiators. The school staff must have been put on notice of their punishment because no one seemed perplexed by their late dinner and extra medical attention. The food was prepared the same as if it were their regular dinner hour.

Cato did not hang around after dinner, but instead headed to his cell early. He stumbled into his room and fell onto his bed exhausted. As he lay there welcoming sleep, he replayed the day's events over in his mind. He couldn't help but think about what Magistri Cicero had said earlier in the day about death. *That was one lesson he would never learn,* he thought. For he had come too far and risked so much to even be a gladiator. The truth was, Cato had a secret. He was not at all who he claimed to be.

3

LIVIA

Livia could not believe how naïve Noemi was. Her sister did not even understand how lucky she was to be betrothed especially to someone she knew and liked. It was nauseating how aloof she was being. Livia would have done anything to be in her shoes, and all Noemi wanted to do was run around in the dirty hypogeum.

Unlike her sister, Livia wanted nothing to do with her father and his animal parade. She wanted something more in her life. It started when she was little. First, she had prayed to the gods day in and day out for years that she would be chosen to become a Vestal Virgin. When she wasn't chosen, she cried. Not just cried, sobbed uncontrollably for weeks on end. She thought that being one of Rome's elite girls would prove to her father she could do something other than take care of gross animals.

She wanted to be seen, not holed up underground in the dark like her sister. Noemi could have the drab, dirty caveman look. She was into Rome's fashion and beauty trends, none of which the hypogeum offered. Her father couldn't rely on her for any sort of help in the hypogeum or at the school so after a while he just gave up on her, making Noemi the favorite child.

Liv found herself wandering around the hypogeum on most days looking for something to occupy her time. She would tease the animals or taunt the prisoners in their cages, really anything to take her mind off not being chosen to keep Rome's flame lit. No one really paid her much mind as they knew she was Jovian's daughter, so she got away with her antics. Although everything changed one day when she found herself outside the emperor's private quarters.

Livia had taken her usual route winding through the dark corridors. Even though she did not care about the inner workings of the place, just by the pure volume of workers that day she knew a big event was happening. After her attempt at trying to get a glimpse of the handsome gladiators in their workout facility failed, she took a different corridor back toward the exit to the tunnel thinking she might avoid some of the commotion and see what was going on in the forum above as she was already bored in the hypogeum.

Side stepping past a large man carting away a corpse, she stopped herself from gagging and made her way down the empty corridor. Two of the palace guards stood outside the door to the emperor's private quarters which meant the emperor was attending the event in the arena that day. She passed by the guards, smirking at the cuter of the two when one called out to her, "Hey, girl, get back in there. No maids are to leave."

Puzzled by his words, Livia started to rebut his accusation but thought better of it. Throwing away her last chance to explain herself to the guards, Livia decided to dive right it. *Maybe she could see the emperor in person. It had to be more fun than wandering around, and what's the worst that could happen?*

"Apologies," she replied playing dumb. "I just stepped out for a moment and lost my bearings. It is like a maze down here. It is so impressive you strong men can make sense of it."

"*Intrare*," was all the guard replied as he opened the door motioning for her to enter, clearly not interested in her flattery.

Livia found herself in the emperor's private quarters. This was one of those times she wished she had paid more attention to her father's lessons instead of goofing off. She quickly went over what she knew about this part of the hypogeum in her head and it wasn't much. She knew the emperor's quarters were located right beneath his private seating area in the colosseum and were accessed by a trap door underneath his throne. She knew he exited and entered the colosseum itself through his own private tunnel that led directly to the palace so as not to be bothered by the commoners. And most importantly, exclusive parties were held there before and after each event that she was dying to be a part of.

As she entered the room, she was pelted by a blanket of smoke. Aromatic as it was, her eyes took a few seconds to adjust to the thick haze. Once she acclimated, the first thing she saw was the emperor right there in front of her! He was just lying on a plush couch with a goblet of wine in his hands admiring a few young girls sitting on the floor around him. Paralyzed by the shock of the intimacy of the gathering, she just stood there in the doorway with her mouth agape. She was hoping to see a glimpse of the emperor alright, but did not expect to be only a few yards away from him.

"Move!" a woman whispered next to her in a harsh tone. "These new girls get younger every day," she mumbled under her breath.

Livia snapped out of her trance and walked toward the woman.

"Here. Take this over to him now before he gets cranky. Go." The woman handed Livia a gold oblong platter teeming with all sorts of fruit and gave her a light shove in the direction of the emperor and his harem.

Not knowing what else to do, Livia walked toward the emperor carrying the heavy dish. *Was she supposed to give the platter to the emperor? Was she allowed to talk to him?* Panic set in as she stepped closer to the circle of girls, her brilliant idea of getting a glimpse inside his quarters was taking a very real turn.

She silently thanked the gods when another girl met her before she got too close and took the platter off her hands placing it on a table next to the couch. Unsure of what to do next, she caught the eye of the girl who took the platter from her and interpreted her fast eye movements as an invitation to sit. So, she did.

A different girl handed her a goblet of wine and she took a sip pretending like she was supposed to be there.

Well, this is something, she thought. She took a look at the girls, who were all different ages, wearing a plethora of colored silk tunics and various baubles. Her drab tunic stuck out like a sore thumb, but no one seemed to notice because the girls were all focused on the emperor and not looking at her.

Liv sat there sipping her wine listening to the emperor brag to one of his advisers about the success of the fight that must have just ended. Not wanting to draw attention to herself, Livia tried to keep her head down and mimic the actions of the other girls. As her eyes started to look down at her goblet, she accidentally locked eyes with the emperor. She could feel her heart beating fast and the sweat pour down her back from the fear. She was not allowed to be here and not one of his chosen girls. *Did he realize it?* If she was found out, it would be her locked in a cage in the arena fighting off one of her dad's lions.

Please look away, she pleaded silently, *oh please, oh please.* The emperor stopped mid conversation with the adviser upon seeing Livia.

"You!" he pointed at her.

Livia was frozen in terror, her mind racing, thinking her family would have no idea what happened to her. *What can I say to get out of this?*

But the emperor never got to finish his thought as the door was forcefully opened and a guard rushed.

"Your Highness, we need to move you back to the palace at once. It is no longer safe here. There is a disturbance above in the arena. We need to go now," he reported.

Caught completely off guard, the emperor forgot about Livia as he bounded to the door. The girls, along with Livia, scattered to the outskirts of the room not wanting to be in his way. The guards quickly escorted the emperor out of the colosseum through the tunnel to his palace. Livia watched as his rotund body caused him to stumble through the door, his guards helping to right him. If she had not been so scared, she would have laughed.

Livia and the girls were hurried out of the private quarters shortly after the emperor made his escape and sent through the long tunnel back to the palace. She thought about stepping out of the group and leaving but the prospect of seeing the palace got the better of her.

After what seemed like hours of walking, the flat path started to incline almost to the point where it was tough to walk up. The tunnel ended with a door flanked by two guards. One guard unlocked the door which led to a steep staircase. The girls filed up the stairs and emerged in a colorful frescoed hallway.

Liv smirked as she envisioned what it must look like for the fat emperor to get up those stairs. She looked around at the ornate décor and lavish surroundings with her mouth agape. This was nothing like she had ever seen before, the palace even more glamorous than she had pictured. She tried not to look so enamored as all the other girls did not even look about.

The girls continued down the long hallway passing all sorts of large rooms until one stopped at a door tucked away and opened it. In all the chaos, no one seemed to notice that Livia was out of place. At least if they did, no one said anything to her.

Livia found herself in the women's wing of the palace where the emperor's girls resided. There were beds for each girl along with trunks at the foot of each, presumably filled with clothes and many accessories. A large bathroom was attached to the bedroom along with a sitting area.

The same girl who had helped Livia back under the colosseum approached her again. "Hi. I'm Fabia. Let's get you out of those clothes and into something more suitable," she said.

"I ummm..." Livia started to speak but was cut off by Fabia, a cute, energetic girl.

"Yes, I know you don't mean to be here and are not one of the emperor's ladies but you are here now and that is that," Fabia butt in.

Confused by the girl's instant kindness, Livia decided the only thing to do was to listen to Fabia. If she ran, who knows what would happen. *Would the emperor's guards stop her and question her? Would she be punished?* All she knew was she certainly did not want to go roam around the hypogeum again, and this could be her chance at something different.

Fabia started again, "There are few rules here, ...?" she paused waiting for Livia to state her name.

"Livia."

"Like I said, Livia, there are few rules here." Fabia continued, "Rule number one is to always keep yourself clean and presentable. There are baths you can use at any time." She gestured to the large bathroom Livia had seen when she first arrived. "Rule number two is to please the emperor at all costs. Other than that, you are not required to live here, although most girls do because the lifestyle is way better than anything off Palatine Hill. If you do choose to leave, you need to be back here every day at dawn. No exceptions. Food, clothing, and a fair wage will be provided to you. Any questions?" Her instructions were brief and quick, like she had given the speech hundreds of times over.

Of course, Livia had a million questions. *Did she get to keep the clothes? How many hours is she expected to stay at the palace? What if she did not want to do this?* But, she settled on asking just one. "What exactly do you mean, please the emperor?" she timidly asked.

Fabia answered as if the question was obvious, "The emperor is a strange man. Requests can be anything under the sun. A girl to feed him, a girl to talk with, a girl to walk with him. The list goes on and on. Some girls go on to become mistresses if that is what you are really asking but let's not worry about that right now."

Fabia gave Livia a blue silk tunic to change into and told her to wash up. When she was ready, Fabia said that the emperor required a few girls to attend dinner with him. Attending dinner meant occupying a seat at the table, not eating, not drinking, and most importantly, no talking unless directly spoken to.

Livia agreed and thanked Fabia. So far, she had a brand-new tunic and an invitation to live in the lavish palace. Sitting quietly at a dinner in exchange seemed like quite the deal. She washed up, dressed, then followed the girls to dinner.

The dining hall was an enormous room with a long rectangular table gracing the center. Golden chandeliers hung from the ceiling, hundreds of candles casting their light throughout the hall. The walls were painted a deep red color with panels of mosaics scattered around. At the head of the table sat the emperor, decked out with a fresh toga.

On his right sat his wife, the empress, a beautiful woman who Livia noticed was trying every beauty trick not to show her true age. To his left was who Livia guessed must be a mistress for she was much younger than the empress. Both women were dripping in jewels and fancy clothes with the only difference being a crown on the empress's head.

The girls filed in and sat in the empty high-backed ornate wooden chairs around the table. The only bit of acknowledgment of their presence was from the slight side eye of the mistress as if she was secretly bragging to the girls about her favoritism from the emperor. Other than that, it was like they were not even there.

Livia sat at the table reminding herself to be silent. Servants brought in three plates of food for the emperor, the empress, and the mistress. The girls got nothing. The conversation, or lack thereof, consisted of the emperor bragging to himself about the success of the colosseum and the gladiators. The empress would just nod here and there while the mistress constantly smiled.

Livia could not believe she was a part of this weird charade. *The emperor has not so much as glanced at us,* Livia thought. *Fabia was right, he really was strange. Why bring us to attend a dinner if he did not want us for anything? Well, this is a joke. If this is how this goes, I am going to have it made here.* She spent the rest of the dinner watching the empress and the mistress wondering what their lives must be like.

She may not have known much about the hypogeum, but she sure knew the gossip and hierarchy of Rome's elite. It was a well-known fact throughout the empire that this emperor was unable to produce an heir. The empress had had pregnancy after pregnancy all resulting in either a miscarriage or still birth. Years ago, the empress was blamed for the lack of heir. The emperor was furious with her, threatening to take her crown away and have her thrown out of the empire. It was one of his advisers, someone partial to the empress, who suggested taking a mistress to produce an heir. So, he did. Many mistresses had come and gone, but every mistress he had was also unable to produce him an heir ultimately saving the empress from a dire fate. Now, the whispers around the empire suggested the gods *did* want to grant the emperor an heir, which increased the emperor's desire for one. Literally everyone knew a former mistress in the empire who had been executed for her failure. Livia couldn't help but wonder how much longer this mistress had left to live as she watched her plaster on a fake smile.

As the dinner concluded, the emperor announced to no one in particular he was going to retire to his chambers. He pushed his chair back and stood motioning for his wife, then his mistress to do the same. The girls remained seated, Livia following suit as it seemed that had worked well for her all day. She could not help herself from continuing to stare at the three at the head of the table. The emperor must have been able to feel her eyes on him because as he turned to leave, he locked eyes with Livia, not long, but enough to more than acknowledge her, and let her know he was aware of her. Livia shuddered, not sure if it was from fear or something else.

4

NOEMI

Not all animals can be saved. They are meant to die. Their purpose is entertainment. Let it go. Noemi's father's words replayed over and over in her head. She learned a long time ago she could not save every animal no matter how much she wanted to.

One perk of living next to the animal school was that it was easy for Jovian to always know what was happening with the beasts. They had lived there as long as Noemi could remember, in a small house attached to the school Ludus Matutinus where gladiators learned to fight beasts rather than just each other. Growing up, Noemi would sneak over to the stables at night and watch the animals while they slept or played, sometimes even taking a few of the less dangerous ones out of the stables to train from time to time. If she listened closely, she could hear the beasts in the stables from her bedroom letting the sounds of the roars and growls put her to sleep.

The amount of injured animals from the emperor's jungle execution was overwhelming, probably the most Noemi had ever seen. Her father had the majority of his staff tending to the injured beasts that morning at the stables. The pens were bustling with men doing their best to tend to every animal. She was surprised at how many animals had actually survived the slaughter.

She weaved her way around the large building making her way to the elephant stables. Noemi only saw four of the nine elephants she knew they had had from the day before. That was a huge loss for her father. Elephants were very hard to come by, not only because of their size, but the journey from deep in the continent of Africa was lengthy and treacherous, making it difficult to reach Rome. *He would be lucky to get another shipment before the year's end,* she thought. They were valuable to Jovian because they served many purposes. Elephants were easy targets for fighters as they were large and not very fast. They usually got banged up in the beginning of a battle but would live in the end because fighters tended to lose interest, leaving elephants damaged but salvageable for the next day's battle. They also could be trained rather easily to perform tricks as Jovian had discovered. Noemi remembered her father teaching a lame elephant to draw letters in the sand for her when she was little.

The four remaining elephants seemed to be in good shape as Noemi went from stall to stall assessing the damage. Most of them looked worse than they actually were, covered in the blood of other animals and the fighters. She would have to wash them off before she could see if they were actually injured. Each elephant had been tied to a large, thick wooden stake in their own stable. The walls were three times the width of some of the other stables as Jovian had found that the strength of an elephant was tremendous and a few had broken down the walls back when the elephants were first brought into the empire from Africa years ago. Elephants were actually docile creatures despite their appearance. It was their size Noemi had to worry about when helping to take care of them. It was very easy to get stepped on.

Climbing on top of one of the stable walls, Noemi got a bird's eye view of the elephants. She noticed one was lying down, a deep laceration visible on its hind leg. The wound needed to be stitched well enough so the animal could walk across the arena at a future battle without looking maimed. A lame animal was not a crowd pleaser for the gladiators or the emperor. They were too easy to kill. Noemi set to work on the elephant. First, she cleaned the wound with water. To keep the elephant from moving or kicking her, its legs were tied tautly to posts in the stable. She slowly and calmly approached the animal so as not to startle it. She knelt a distance close enough that she could work on the animal but far enough she could duck away quickly if need be. Using a thick needle with a very thin rope, she stitched a perfect zig zag pattern, the way her father had shown her that would hold the wound together and stop the bleeding. The animal winced but remained still until she was done. She lathered on a poultice over the rope and bandaged the leg.

Done, she thought. Of course, the bandage would be removed before the animal was released in the arena so no one would be any wiser of the injury. The poultice not only stopped the bleeding but numbed the injury just enough to keep the animal from limping during battle. Just one of the many tricks of the trade her father had taught her. She untied the elephant's legs and made sure it had water for the day. Lastly, she secured the stable door and thanked the gods everything had gone smoothly. She wanted to watch some of the trainers, maybe pick up a few things, but she had errands to run for her father.

Inside their home, she washed up and changed out of her dirty clothes from the stables. Livia happened to be home as well.

"Where are you off to in a clean tunic for once?" Livia asked.

"Just the market to pick up some supplies for father," Noemi replied hoping her sister would leave her be. But Noemi wasn't that lucky.

"Oooh, I could use a few things myself at the market. I'll go with you," Liv said.

Noemi had no desire to go shopping with her sister. She only wanted to get the herbs her father needed and be done with it, not stop at every bridal shop being coaxed into trying things on.

Livia came out of her room looking like royalty, everything was perfect—from the saffron used to color her eyelids to the powdered chalk to give her face a sheen. How she could make herself look that good that quickly always baffled Noemi. Noemi was lucky if she remembered to brush her hair before tying it back for the day.

She must have had an annoyed look on her face because Livia said, "What? You never know who you might run into at the market."

"Yes, I am sure your handsome prince will be waiting for you between stacks of olive oil jars, ready to ask for your hand. You might want to put some more perfume on," Noemi teased.

Livia ignored her.

The forum was the heart of the empire. Everything and anything went on there. There were temples, magistrate buildings, entertainers, merchants, etc. along with the constant traffic of people and carts. If Noemi liked it, Livia loved it. She watched her sister in her element as people could not help but ogle over her beauty as they walked by.

This was going to be a long trip, Noemi thought.

The two headed to Trajan's, the largest marketplace in the empire, located at the far end of the forum. Standing tall with five stories, it was filled with hundreds of vendors peddling their various wares and you could find anything you could imagine: food, spices, tools, pottery, jewels, wool, etc.

They had barely made it past the first shop before Livia stopped.

"Oh, my gods, Noemi, look at these veils! They are to die for. Come here so I can see which one matches your skin tone," Livia said as she held up a long white muslin veil.

The shopkeeper all but ran to them. "Which one of you ladies is the lucky bride?", he asked eyeing their purses. "Come, come. I have more fabrics in the back that I am sure you will love."

Noemi was not about to get trapped in a bridal store all day.

"Gratias tibi, domine but I am afraid we have an appointment we are already late for. We will stop back on our way home," she lied.

The shopkeeper turned away at Noemi's disinterest, already hounding other customers.

"Why did you do that?" Livia asked, clearly annoyed.

"I do not know how to be any clearer. I do not have time for all of this. My dress could be blue for all I care."

"Fine. I'll tell mother I tried my best, but it is useless with you. Go be father's little errand girl. I have other shops to visit," Livia replied.

"I'll meet you back here when I am done," Noemi said, not even acknowledging her sister's nastiness.

Noemi pulled out the list her father had written and read the herbs he needed her to get: yarrow, garlic, tarragon, and uvaursi. *It must be time for him to make more of his poultice*, she thought. She always tried to pay attention to father's lessons especially when it came to helping the animals. She knew of yarrow and garlic, everyone did, and those were easy enough to get.

Garlic was used for literally anything and everything in the empire. Trouble breathing? Garlic in your milk. Prevent a wound from getting worse? Rub garlic on it. Her father had tried to grow it years ago but some of the animals kept digging it up and it was more trouble than it was worth. The yarrow she knew helped with healing and inflammation but the uvaursi and tarragon she wasn't so sure.

The entrance of the forum was flanked by two enormous marble columns each wrapped around with green ivy décor. An enormous white marble arch connected the two giant columns. The boisterous chatter of the crowds could be heard as she entered under the arch. Noemi knew where the shops that sold herbs were located. She had gone with her father numerous times growing up.

Her favorite shop, Hippo Crats, would have what she needed. The owner, Celia, was a longtime friend of the family. Noemi gave her father's list. Celia went in the back of her shop to fill Noemi's order. She returned from the back with a pile which she placed in Noemi's bag. "Sorry, Noemi, I am out of uvaursi and have been for some time. It has been hard to come by the past few months for some reason. You could try Sock-R-Tease a few levels above us. They might have it. Give your parents my best."

Noemi thanked and paid her. She tried the other shops in and around Trajan's, but none had uvaursi. Her only other option was the market outside of the forum where slaves purchased their goods. She hated going there because it was mostly black-market goods and not so nice people, but what choice did she have? Her father needed the ingredients and she did not want to let him down. She just wouldn't tell him she went there. He would hate to know she put herself in any sort of danger for him.

Noemi walked through the winding streets and dirty back alleys to get to the slave market. Compared to the pristine streets of the forum, this area was dark, wet, and grimy. She walked at a brisk pace hoping no one would stop her. The market could be a dangerous place at times filled with crooks and lowlifes disgruntled with their caste. Not to mention thieves. Noemi was so focused on getting to the market she almost tripped over Balbina, one of the empire's well-known street beggars.

Damn the gods, Noemi thought, for Balbina was a loon of a chatterbox always distracting people with her prophesizing while trying to steal your money at the same time, and Noemi just couldn't avoid her now.

"Hello, sweet child," Balbina crooned. An older woman, her face wrinkled and weathered from what Noemi could only imagine was a hard life on the streets. Her robe was tattered and reduced to dirty rags, no longer a robe. A patterned scarf was draped on top of her head and her long black hair was plaited over her shoulder, the braid intertwined with what was once a purple ribbon, peeking out from the pleat. Her feet were blackened and her skin was covered in a layer of grime. Some say she was a witch in another life and Noemi wouldn't disagree with them.

"Gold for a story? You rarely see a girl like you in this part of the empire. Are you lost? Perhaps, I can help you find your way. It won't cost you much. What's in that bag of yours? Can I take a look? Come sit with me. The eye of the gods shines down on you, girl. See the light. See the light," rambled Balbina.

Noemi didn't have time for the gibberish from Balbina today. She had learned that if you didn't engage her, she would eventually leave you alone and move on to someone else.

"Sorry, Balbina," she said, "not today." Noemi turned to walk past when Balbina reached out and grabbed Noemi's ankle causing Noemi to almost fall. Immediately, Noemi clutched her satchel thinking this was one of Balbina's street tricks, another distraction while her money was stolen.

Balbina just laughed, a laugh so manic it made the hair on the back of Noemi's neck stand straight up. Her grip was surprisingly strong for a frail old street vagabond.

"Run girl, save him," was all she said and then Balbina released her leg. Slightly terrified, Noemi ran the rest of the way to the slave market trying to forget her encounter with Balbina and focus on getting the herbs.

The slave market was nothing like Trajan's in the forum. It was small and unorganized, a maze of baskets and wagons with no signs to point you in any sort of direction except one of confusion. Low class people dressed in plain and some dirty tunics milled about, some even giving her nasty looks as she wandered around.

Noemi did not know where to start. Shops here did not have signs with witty names like in the forum, in fact most had no signs at all. She mustered up the courage to ask what she thought was a friendly looking slave where she could find uvaursi but to no avail. The slave just ignored her and kept walking.

Deeper into the market she walked. She stopped at one place that looked promising. A young slave boy sat out front drawing in the dirt. "Excuse me," she said, "Do you carry uvaursi?"

The boy just looked at her with a blank face.

"Excuse me," she said again, a little louder.

This time the boy smiled at her, got up from the ground, and ran into the back of the stall. *Well, that was useless,* thought Noemi.

Just as she was about to turn and walk away to find another shop, she heard a soft-spoken voice say, "Wait."

Noemi turned to see a middle-aged woman walking out from the shop holding the boy's hand.

"I heard you say uvaursi," the woman said.

"Yes, I am in need of some," Noemi said.

"An ancient request not often asked for around these parts anymore. What may I ask do you need it for?" the woman asked.

"My father oversees the animals at the colosseum. He needs it for one of his treatments," Noemi answered, instantly regretting giving a stranger all that information.

"Smart man," the woman replied. "If you have any bears, save the berries for them. It is their favorite treat."

Noemi thanked the woman and was on her way. She couldn't get out of the dirty market fast enough.

Not wanting to run into Balbina again, she took a different way back to Trajan's and found Livia waiting right where she had left her, a basket full of goods at her side.

The walk back home was slightly awkward. Noemi wasn't sure what they could talk about if it wasn't wedding related, so she did not say anything. They were almost home when Livia said out of nowhere, "I was wondering if you could do me a favor."

I knew it was strange that she wanted to go shopping with me, Noemi thought. *What could she possibly want?* Noemi just looked at her, waiting for her to continue.

"Okay, so I need you to cover for me with mother and father," Livia started in. "I kind of got hired at the palace for a full-time position and may not make it home every night."

"What could you possibly be doing there, like cleaning up after the emperor?" Noemi asked.

"Umm, something like that," Livia responded.

Noemi did not care enough to divulge into her cryptic answer. "And where would you have me telling them that you are instead?" she asked.

"Just make something up, I don't care what you tell them. They will believe anything you say. You are the favorite child."

"Okay," Noemi replied, "but you owe me."

Livia was right. Their parents were a little partial to Noemi, the obedient well-mannered child.

If they only knew.

5

CATO

C ato awoke the next morning to the throbbing of his right knee painfully reminding him of yesterday's lesson. Today was his last day as a *novicius* which meant no more shackles and no more cell. He would finally have the freedom to come and go as he pleased outside of his training schedule. *One more step closer to becoming the most famous gladiator the empire has ever seen*, he thought.

He packed up what little possessions he had and waited by the cell door for his shackles to be unlocked one final time.

The day would be spent in the colosseum, or mostly under it in the gladiator training facility of the hypogeum, awaiting his end-of-year battle. The gladiators made the trek to the hypogeum through the school's tunnel, a necessity for them to avoid getting mobbed by the public. The roars and screeches of the animals in their cages echoed throughout the entire underground area, something it took him almost all *novicius* year to get used to.

Cato marveled at the idea of how much went on under the arena floor. He had only really ever seen the gladiator's area which included a small practice arena, small living quarters, and an infirmary.

Tensions were high as the gladiators grouped off with their

specific *lanista* in the training arena. Because of Cato's family, he was given one of the best trainers in the school.

"Today's battles signify the end of your *novicius* training. I hope to see all of you back at school for celebrations; however, that won't be the case. I have trained you the best way I know how. May the best gladiator win. Go with the gods," *Lanista* Quintus said. "You have been randomly paired with your opponent," he continued. Quintus then listed off the pairs for the day.

Cato did not really pay attention until he heard his name called.

"Cato Octavian Velarius versus Rufus Celsus."

Not the easiest of opponents but not the worst, Cato thought. Cato had never sparred with him, but he had seen him fight. He knew Rufus's strength was his height. It was not hard to miss the tallest gladiator in the school. He just needed to figure out how to use his strength against him and he had a good chance to win. Rufus's *lanista* must have just given him his pairing too because he was eyeing Cato from the other side of the room.

After the assignments were announced, the gladiators were given a few minutes with their *lanistas* to strategize. Every *lanista* wanted their gladiator to win. Being the trainer of a winning gladiator was just as lucrative as being a well-known gladiator. On top of that, they got paid more. Quintus was the best in the business. Once a decorated gladiator himself, Quintus had the longest and most impressive resume of trained gladiators who went on to be renowned throughout the empire. Cato was more than thrilled when he had been assigned to Quintus at the beginning of the year.

"Okay, Cato, you've got this. You are the son of Leon the Great. It is in your blood." Quintus started to pep him up. Pep talks wouldn't help him. Cato knew he had to just focus himself.

While the gladiators were getting their last-minute preparations in, the pre-battle show could be heard in the arena above. Cato had never actually seen that part, but they had learned in school that an announcer warmed up the crowd with small side performances where people acted out gladiator fights in a humorous way. Then trumpeters played the emperor's anthem and the announcer acknowledged any senators or other high government members in attendance. Announcements usually included the event's agenda and special notes like who would be fighting and their individual statistics.

Cato heard the trumpets cease and knew that was their cue to head up. The gladiators all walked up the ramp to the arena's entry-way. A messenger boy ran a scroll with a list of the day's matchups to the announcer on the stage. Talking into a hollowed-out horn to amplify his voice, the announcer proclaimed the first matchup.

"Ladies and gentlemen. The moment you have all been waiting for. Our first matchup is Gaius Hortensia versus Decebal Laelia."

The crowd clapped as the first pair entered into the arena from the entryway.

Cato stopped looking after they walked in. He didn't need to worry himself with anyone else.

The first few battles were quick. All ending in death. So, it wasn't long before his name was called. Carrying a sword and shield, he walked out with Rufus to the middle of the arena where they turned to face each other. Cato couldn't help but notice how much taller Rufus was standing right next to him. The referee dressed in an all-black tunic separated the two with a long, gnarled wooden stick.

Cato was primed. He didn't even hear what the referee said to commence the fight. He just saw the staff lift away and immediately aimed to strike Rufus.

Rufus was ready and took a step back causing Cato to completely miss his target.

Back to basics, Cato thought. He took two steps back from Rufus and decided to be more calculated. The two sparred, nicking each other here and there but causing no real damage and neither one was really winning. They were basically playing with each other. Cato knew he had to strike. He moved his sword from side to side trying to get Rufus off balance. When Cato saw him sway just a second too long, he took his shot slashing his sword at Rufus's unprotected side.

Rufus saw it coming because he blocked Cato's sword with his shield and came over the top of him slicing Cato's right arm causing Cato to drop his sword.

Cato cursed out loud. His entire right arm was gushing blood and he had little mobility. There was no way he could hold anything.

Quintus's advice was inaudible from the sidelines over the roar of the crowd.

He needed to figure it out quickly.

Okay, think. His sword was lying in the sand out of his reach. If he tried to lunge for it, Rufus would surely kill him. He would need to somehow ditch the shield and get the sword with his left hand all while avoiding Rufus's blows.

Rufus knew it was over and so did the crowd, everyone but Cato. "Use his strength against him," kept replaying in Cato's head along with Magistri Cicero's lesson in dying. He didn't want to have to be the one to take a knee. Maybe Cicero was on to something, just not the way he had originally thought. He was not sure this was going to work and it certainly wasn't traditional, but he had to give it a shot.

Silencing the crowd, Cato took a knee. His sore right knee once again on the rough sand. He did not even dare look toward Quintus whom he could only imagine was a dark shade of angry red at his cowardice.

Rufus smiled.

"Ingula, Ingula," the crowds chanted looking to the referee for an answer. The referee nodded granting the crowd's wish for death.

"Let's end this," Rufus said as he went to deliver his final blow.

But just as Rufus started to swing his sword down toward Cato, Cato picked up his shield with his good arm and dove shield first into Rufus's knees.

Losing his balance, Rufus fell on to his back.

Meanwhile, Cato had ditched the shield, rolled to his sword, picked it up with his good arm, pinning it against Rufus's neck.

The look on Rufus's face was pure shock. He had thought he had won and not been prepared for a counterattack. The crowd erupted still chanting for death, but this time for Rufus.

The pain in Cato's right arm was so bad he could barely see straight. He was only focused on the referee ending the fight. *Please, please,* he silently begged.

The referee nodded to Cato, acknowledging his victory. Rufus, still in shock, was slow to get up, reluctantly taking a knee.

Cato didn't waste any time in running his sword right through Rufus's middle. Rufus fell to the ground, dead. Cato stood there in a daze, the threat of vomit lingering in the back of his throat. The same feeling he got every time he had to kill someone. It never got any easier. He stood over Rufus's body as the crowd cheered.

Cato said a silent prayer for him and then pushed aside his doubt, remembering Rufus's death put him one step closer to his goal. He could feel his body wobbling back and forth as the noise of the crowd faded in and out. It took all his will power not to collapse right there into the bloodied sand.

Quintus ran over to Cato putting his arm around him half holding him up, half hugging him.

"*Gratulationes*, you crazy kid. You really had me there. I thought I had lost my best fighter when you took a knee," he said to Cato slapping him on the back in an approving way. "You live up to your namesake, boy. Welcome to the *tiro* year."

Cato should have been relieved he won a hard-fought battle, one that had been way too close, but he wasn't. He should have reveled in the crowd cheering his name and clapping for him, but he barely tuned in. There was so much more racing through his mind. Winning the battle wasn't the hard part, the hard part was phase two of his plan. Graduation to the *tiro* year meant the gladiators were permitted freedoms such as socialization and interactions with the outside world which should not have been a problem—if he really *was* Cato Velarius.

～

The story of where Cato actually came from and who he really was played through his mind daily. To put it simply, Cato was a slave.

Abandoned as an infant, Cato was left in one of the gardens belonging to a beautiful villa in the countryside on the outskirts of the city. Or so he was told by Alba, the woman who had found him and raised him as her own.

Alba, a slave for the villa, found Cato wrapped up in a torn tunic lying in a broken clay pot that still had remnants of olive oil in it. She claimed the pot had been placed in a large bed of wild violets when she had found him while tending to the garden. The purple color was so bright and the flowers so fragrant she called him Tyrian after the color. Not one to abandon a child, Alba brought Tyrian into the slaves' quarters in the villa. Together with the other slaves, Tyrian was taken care of.

When he grew up, Tyrian was put to work just as every other slave living at the villa. He was a large boy for his age and the many hours of physical labor hardened his body over time. He was strong and also smart thanks to Alba's teachings.

The family who owned the villa had a son. Crippled at birth, the boy could barely walk. He was bound to a reclined seat with four posts extending from it so that slaves could carry him if need be. Tyrian and the boy were the same age and became friends growing up. The boy taught Tyrian to read and write, skills unheard of for slaves. In return, Tyrian taught the boy about the different crops and how each were harvested. The two spent countless hours at knuckle-bones, played with gladiator figures, and ended up creating a brotherly-like friendship.

It wasn't until the boy's parents started to separate them that Tyrian even questioned life as a slave. He had never really thought of the drastic differences of their caste. Tyrian couldn't imagine life as a cripple and pitied the boy. Tyrian tried to plead with the boy's parents to let them play together, but they refused.

One day he overheard the boy's parents arguing about their life before the boy and about some uncle dying. Tyrian pleaded with Alba to tell him what they had meant. After begging and begging, Alba finally gave in and told him what only few knew. The boy's family came from a long line of ruthless champion gladiators. It was in their blood. Highly decorated, arrogant, infamous gladiators who achieved their fame for being foul-mouthed, nasty brutes and were good at killing other people. That is until the boy was born. Ashamed of his son's deformity, the boy's father moved his family out of their mansion in the city to a secluded villa in the countryside immediately after his birth. No one could find out that Leon the Great's son was deformed nor could he discard his first-born and only child. It just wasn't an option.

The boy's father had the midwife who aided his wife during childbirth killed so no one would ever find out about the boy's condition. Leon fabricated a story that he wanted to privately train his son until he deemed him ready to fight, leaving the city in the middle of the night and never looking back. The boy's uncle, a great *lanista* at Ludus Magnus school, had recently died. That was what all the whispering Tyrian had overheard. The uncle had been the last remaining active gladiator at the school, and any real connection the family had left besides legacy.

And with that information, phase one of Tyrian's plan was born. Tyrian was done being a slave. Sure, there were ways to be freed, but that was extremely rare and Tyrian did not have the patience for that arduous process. He had had a good life so far and was thankful for Alba and the other slaves, but he wanted more than a lifetime of manual labor. So, he decided to run, and leave the villa for good.

Discarding his slave clothes for a stolen tunic from the boy, Tyrian kissed Alba's sleeping forehead, whispered, "*Gratias tibi ago*" in her ear—one last thank you for everything she had done for him —and he was gone. He was now Cato Velarius, the only son of Leon the Great, ready to continue the champion gladiator lineage at the most prestigious gladiator school, Ludus Magnus. There was no looking back now.

Getting into the school had been easier than he had imagined. After a few tries, he managed to forge a letter to the headmaster of Ludus Magnus.

Magistri Pompeius—

It is with great pride and honor that I present to you my son, Cato

Octavian Velarius, for admission into your school, Ludus Magnus. I have no doubt that the name precedes his abilities. He is well equipped and worthy of following in my footsteps. With the news of my brother's passing, it is time for another Velarius to become a champion. The die is cast.

Alea Jacta Est.

Ipsum,

Leon Octavian Velarius

Cato then paid a young boy to deliver the letter to the Magistri and waited for a response. It wasn't long before the boy returned from the school and handed Cato a small scroll with the wax seal of the school melted onto it. Cato unrolled the scroll and read it.

Leon the Great,

We hope this finds you well. At this time, the Ludus Magnus school would be honored to accept your son, Cato Octavian Velarius, into our elite program of gladiators. We have no doubt that your legacy will be upheld. As always, first years are to report to the school following the celebration of Janus.

If it suits you, we have a need for a lanista. Maybe dust off the old sword?

Quod genus olim amico tuo, your old friend,

Pompeius

And with that, Cato showed up to the school on the first day announcing himself Cato Octavian Velarius, son of Leon the Great, and no one ever questioned him. There was no chance Leon the Great was ever coming out of hiding because he wouldn't dare risk exposing his son and there were no other living ties to the family at the school to expose Tyrian's lie. The hardest part for him would be maintaining the façade that he was some arrogant brute with no regard for anyone but himself. The game was on and he couldn't lose.

6

NOEMI

Crowds had increased twofold for the morning *venatores* ever since the emperor's jungle exposition. Noemi knew that would change once people realized the daily beast battles were not always that extravagant. In the meantime, the surge of people made her father look good. Because of the success of the jungle, the emperor had begun to demand more beasts be incorporated into the midday executions, of course making more work for Jovian to oversee.

Noemi hated to admit it, but she secretly liked that the executions involved animals as it turned the monotonous midday hangings into a spectacle she could not help herself from watching.

Finding herself with extra time after the *venatori* that morning, Noemi wound her way through the hypogeum to watch the day's executions. Her father's innovators were always coming up with new and exciting ways for people to die. It was their job to keep the crowds coming back and the last thing anyone needed was the emperor to be bored.

As much as she hated to see people die, she secretly rooted for the animals every time. The best spot for Noemi to watch the execution was through one of the trap doors. There were numerous trap doors on the floor of the arena and around the walls. Walking to one of the doors that would allow her the best view, Noemi climbed into the wooden lift and began to pull the rope. As she pulled the rope, the lift began to rise up toward the arena above.

The trap doors operated on a pulley system consisting of ropes and anchors. With each pull of the rope, the anchor would lower, causing the platform to rise, balancing the weight. When she first started to do this, she could never muster up the strength to make it to the opening at the top. But, after years of practice, she built up enough power to pull her own body weight up to the top.

She pulled the rope until she heard the platform click into place. The locking mechanism prevented the platform from falling back down into the hypogeum once she stepped off it. Knotting the rope to a wooden post, Noemi exited the platform. The trap door in the shape of an arch was currently open to the arena floor. All of the large wooden trap doors around the arena were opened midday to allow for air to circulate in the hypogeum below. Without the air flow it got very steamy down there.

Noemi sat in the opening of the doorway half in the shadows so as not to be seen by anyone. There she watched what was unfolding on the arena floor. Two men were set to be executed. Based on the green colored marks on the back of their tunics, she knew that they were thieves. Different colors meant different crimes. Yellow for treason, red for adultery, and black for murder were among the most common.

Today, each man was seated on either side of a large wooden seesaw. The seesaw was centered on a rotating platform which was anchored into the center of the arena floor. Each man was bound to the seat back with leather straps, their legs dangling over the side of the seat and their hands were free. Also tied to the post anchoring the seesaw were two bears.

Woah, he really went all out today, Noemi thought about the innovator. Noemi watched as the men teetered and tottered up and down pushing off the ground. As one man rose, the other came down where a hungry bear was waiting. Noemi had to give the innovator credit, this was exciting to watch. Neither man wanted to get eaten by a bear.

As one man teetered down, he would panic, kicking and pumping his legs to fend off the bears while trying to make solid contact with the ground so he could quickly push off and get back up in the air to safety out of the bears' reach. Once in the air, the man could take a short breather only to start his descent all over again.

To make it even harder, the seesaw apparatus rotated as the men pushed off the ground making it more difficult to get away from the bears. The men could only really kick and punch the bears to fend them off.

Noemi watched as the men became more and more exhausted from avoiding the bears. The seesaw was not going as high as it had when the execution first started. The bears mauled at the men doing their best to claw them off the seesaw taking bites out of their legs and arms. Meanwhile, the bears took a beating as the men's kicking took its toll. One bear had been kicked in the face and was blinded.

The crowd cheered when one bear bit off a prisoner's leg. Blood spewed everywhere. Noemi wondered why they even bothered putting up a fight. *Their deaths were inevitable so why play a game to avoid death, for what, a few more minutes?* She hoped this would end quickly, those bears were well trained and could be used for future events. Thieves didn't deserve to kill a bear. Noemi knew it would be over soon.

The man who lost his leg was losing a lot of blood, looking woozy on the seesaw. Both bears were waiting under his side, licking their chops, tasting the blood dripping from the man's leg. After a valiant effort of pushing the seesaw up with only one leg, the man finally gave up, his one good leg buckling under the weight of both himself and the seesaw. The bears dove at their prey, tearing him apart. They finally got their reward after fighting for it for so long.

Once the bears were satisfied, they moved away from dead man causing the seesaw to move again as what remained of the man's lifeless body was hanging from the seat while the other man came down to meet the same fate.

Glad that both bears survived, Noemi decided to see if they needed help in the infirmary since that was where the bears were headed. She got back on the platform, untied the rope, and slowly released the pulley to bring her back down to the hypogeum.

The infirmary was directly in the center of the first floor of the hypogeum. The bears had already been brought in when Noemi got there. Each bear was carefully moved into a stall with the walls short enough to reach the animals. Both bears were satiated and lethargic not putting up a fight at all. Few people had training in animal medicine, so the ones who did were coveted. Noemi was always trying to learn all she could about healing the beasts.

One bear had multiple wounds on its head and back, along with a fractured arm. They were almost done bandaging it when Noemi walked in. The bear would be moved to the second level cages for a week recovery and then readied to fight again. The blinded bear was another story. Not only was the bear blind, but it too had several wounds that needed attention. Usually, animals at that stage would be put out of their misery because they were not worth the resources to save. However, bears were smart and easy to train. A blind bear could be put to work on light duty doing warm up acts and simple tricks. It would be bandaged up and moved to the stables outside the colosseum for recovery and training. Once recovered, it would be dressed up with a hat and bells around its ankles to be seen in the arena before a battle. In the long run, it would save Noemi's father time and money from having to import new bears.

To Noemi's dismay, they didn't need help in the animal infirmary, so she decided to wander into the gladiator wing of the hypogeum. It wasn't hard to miss. The clanging of swords against armor could be heard from every tunnel sometimes even overpowering the sound of the animals. Noemi loved the gladiators almost as much as she loved animals. She found their lifestyle exceptionally unique. She thought it was crazy how they were citizens of Rome but yet allowed to have their own set of laws as if they lived in another empire.

Noemi was not authorized to be in the gladiator facilities as all areas were off limits except the infirmary, especially to women. Next to the gods and the emperor, the gladiators were renowned and well respected. Women swooned over them and men wanted to be them. It was believed that they were almost godlike and their touch had healing powers. Growing up in the hypogeum did have its advantages. Most *lanistas* and gladiator staff knew Noemi and her family. Most turned a blind eye if she was seen wandering around in unauthorized areas, mainly because she was a harmless young girl.

Noemi peeked in the gladiator infirmary. Not unlike the animal infirmary, the gladiator infirmary was always full. It consisted of around twenty beds, each occupied. Two women were assigned to tend to the wounded gladiators. They also had their own in-house doctor trained in battle injuries. After a fight, if the gladiator had not been killed, they were taken to the infirmary. If they could not walk on their own, they were put in a wooden cart and wheeled there. As long as a gladiator was breathing, they were brought to the infirmary to get the best care. They were too valuable to lose.

Noemi took one step in the infirmary doorway and stopped abruptly. A gladiator's gruesome scream bellowed through the corridors. She did not want to get in the way of a surgery or see someone in that much pain. Instead, she continued down the corridor following the sounds of swords clanging and men grunting. Noemi walked into the arena hoping to see some of the gladiators she knew. The practice area was pretty full. Noemi saw a group of guys sitting on a bench watching a few others idly mess around with swords.

Perfect, she thought spotting Titus and Rem who were some third years who knew her well.

Titus spotted her first. "Hey, Noemi," he greeted her.

Noemi waved and walked over to them.

"Interested in picking up a few moves?" Rem asked her. "Don't worry," he said following her gaze to the other gladiators in the practice arena she didn't know, "they won't mess with us third years."

Noemi loved when they asked her to practice with them. She had picked up a lot of techniques over the years. When she was young, she would sneak in the holding cell and watch the gladiators warm up. Soaking in all that she could, she would try and mimic the moves in the privacy of her bedroom each night. Women could not fight, but maybe one day that rule would change and she would be ready.

Titus handed her a wooden sword. Thinking it would not weigh much, she was surprised when the sword almost pulled her down to the ground.

Titus chuckled to himself. "These are weighted, wooden swords for warming up. The idea is that by practicing with these you will get used to the heaviness. When it comes time to use an actual sword it will feel like a feather in your hand," Titus explained.

Knowing now how heavy it was, Noemi picked up the wooden sword again and was able to hold it upright. It was a little wobbly, but she could manage.

"Okay, let's do a little wrist work. I'm going to hold my sword up and I want you to strike each side of the sword, rotating your wrists each time," Titus instructed.

Noemi was able to do what he said fairly easily although she could feel her wrists starting to get sore.

"Nice," Titus said. "Okay, now I want you to grab the hilt with your right hand and slash across my body, once it almost touches the ground, grab the hilt with both hands and stab upwards."

It was hard for Noemi to hold the weighted sword with just one hand. Her wrist was shaking under the weight of it. As she tried to swing it downwards, she lost her balance but was able to stay on her feet.

"Next time, widen your stance before you swing," Rem chimed in.

Noemi went to try again when an unfamiliar voice shouted at them from across the room. She froze with her back toward the man hoping the new voice wasn't going to come any closer. She could sense him walking toward their group. She dared not to turn around and reveal herself. It did not work because she found herself being shoved into the dirt by the guy.

There's no way to avoid this now, let's just hope he won't rat on me, Noemi thought. She picked herself up off the ground turning to face her assailant. She saw his eyes change the second he realized she was a girl and not a scrawny gladiator, but they quickly hardened again. It was clear Titus and Rem knew the gladiator, or at least knew of him. Noemi did not dare speak, waiting for her friends to take the lead.

Titus spoke up on her behalf, "Lay off man, she isn't bothering anyone."

The gladiator did not want to hear from him, that was clear. "Disgusting," he spat at her feet. "This is no place for a woman. I can't even stand the sight of you." He then went off on a rant about women and their place in the empire.

Noemi tuned him out for most of it. Arrogant gladiators like him she despised. Then, when he challenged her to a fight, she thought she must be dreaming. Tuning back in, she heard the gladiator repeat his demand, "Fight." Noemi looked to Titus and Rem for help, but they had moved away looking at her as if they wanted to say there was nothing more they could do to help. She was on her own. There was obviously no way she could beat this gladiator in a fight and they both knew that. *Ugh. Oh, why did I have to come down here,* she thought. At this point anything could happen, this guy could kill her, or worse, report her to the emperor where she would be executed in public.

Noemi's head was spinning when the gladiator demanded she arm herself with a sword and shield. Titus was right, after using the weighted sword, the real one was as light as a feather. The shield however was another story. It was heavy and not made for someone of her size. She could barely hold the weight of it on her forearm. Noemi could see the arrogant gladiator enjoy watching her struggle. She felt the anger building up inside her wishing she could just slit his throat. She knew there was no way out of this. *Her dad would probably find her corpse lying in the hypogeum on his morning rounds,* she thought. *Well, at least I should go out in a blaze of glory.*

Okay, Diana, give me all your strength, she sent up a silent prayer. Noemi thought it best to attack first. She was smaller than him. The only thing that came to her mind was to lunge at him. Not really aiming for anything she tried slashing his side but ended up falling short, the sword missing in the dirt.

The gladiator seemed shocked she actually tried to engage him in a fight. He immediately slammed his sword against her shield, the force of the blow knocking her back into the dirt. Noemi felt her whole body tremble and was sure he could tell. She was about to die. *This is it,* she thought, *the final blow. Should she kneel? Poor Felix.* Her mind continued spiraling until she felt a searing pain in her leg. He had slashed her. The pain was so intense she crumpled to the ground. She was done trying to be tough. Tears streamed down her face. Covered in blood, she looked in his eyes with nothing but pure hatred.

The gladiator started laughing maniacally. Instead of ending Noemi's life, he threw the sword down mumbling something about wasting time and left with a spring in his step.

Titus and Rem immediately ran to Noemi once he was gone. Pressing their hands on the wound, Rem tried to calm her down. "You are going to be fine. It's not as bad as it looks," he said.

Noemi could barely speak. "Animal infirmary," she mustered out, "Lin."

The guys moved quickly. They carried her out of the gladiator wing as fast as they could, mostly because they didn't want to be seen with a girl or cause anymore raucous than they already had. The boys left her in the animal infirmary with a healer named Lin and scurried back to the gladiators hoping she was okay, and hoping not to get caught.

7

CATO

The last thing Cato remembered was Quintus carrying him out of the arena into the tunnel. Coming in and out of consciousness, he could hardly recall being carted down the tunnel ramp back into the cavernous hypogeum. His eyelids were so heavy he could barely keep them open, the temptation of a blissful dream world right at his grasp. *If only he could just rest for a minute,* he thought.

As if someone was reading his mind, he heard a woman's gentle voice say, "Not just yet boy, there will be plenty of time to rest. Come on. Here you go now."

He could sense her in front of him but did not want to exert the energy to open his eyes to look at her. She must have put something under his nose because an intense sulfur smell jolted him awake.

"Easy does it," the calm-voiced woman said. "Welcome back. I'm Lea your nurse."

Cato found himself sitting in a reclined chair. Now that he was wide awake, the pain in his arm was worse than ever, throbbing so much it felt like his arm had its own heartbeat.

"Before we get to that arm, we need to do a little house keeping first," Lea continued. With that she laid his wounded arm to a spot on the chair where the dripping blood would pool in a carved out drain in the chair.

Cato winced at her touch and watched as his blood dripped down the outside of the chair into a small jar on the floor.

Lea could see the confusion on Cato's face. "In case you become like Hercules after all this is over, the blood from your first victory as a gladiator will sell for a pretty gold aureus," she said as she reached into a closed container, pulled out a few leeches, and placed them on his bloody arm.

Cato yelped in pain.

"Sorry, chew on this please," she said as she shoved what looked like a tree leaf in his mouth.

Cato chewed the leaf as instructed, slowly feeling his mouth go numb with a sort of minty spice taste.

"That will help with the pain," she said.

Cato wasn't sure if he trusted this girl, but he was too weak to argue.

She then dipped her fingers in an oil pot and rubbed the oil on his temples. The aroma from the oil smelled fruity and calmed him a little.

"Here, drink this," she said as she handed him a cup.

Expecting it to be water, Cato took a large gulp and gagged, almost spitting it out.

Lea tipped his head back and pinched his nose closed forcing him to swallow. The aftertaste was disgusting, his whole mouth coated like dirt and sewage.

"That was to help prevent any infection from the inside," she explained.

Cato wondered when the healing part of this would begin, so far it seemed like one torture after another. The blood dripping from his arm had filled the bowl almost to the top.

Lea quickly lifted his arm off the chair drain and moved it back to Cato's side.

Cato winced, but not as much as before. *Either those herbs are starting to work or I'm half dead,* he thought.

As carefully as she could, Lea pried the satiated leeches off his arm and placed them in vials containing a clear liquid. "That's that. Now, let's have a look at this arm." She first cleaned the wound by pouring warm water all down his arm.

It stung, but the warm water was a welcoming new sensation for Cato.

"This wound is very deep, I'm afraid, too deep for me to fix it. Sit tight, the doctor will be over shortly," she assured him.

Cato sat there half slumped over in an herb-ladened haze. He watched as Lea took the bowl with his blood and neatly poured it into multiple vials which she sealed with wax. She then took a thin piece of bone and carved what Cato could only guess to be his name and the date in the not yet hardened wax. She did the same thing to the vials with the leeches. His haze was broken by a sharp prick in his arm. He was so focused on Lea he had not even noticed the doctor was working on his arm with a bone needle.

"Looks like the sword just missed the bone. Your muscle is badly severed, however, I can repair it for the most part. Sit tight, this is going to be uncomfortable," the doctor told Cato matter of factly. The doctor motioned to Lea who brought over another goblet. "This is my own special mixture of warmed wine, opium, and a few other things. It will numb the pain and help you sleep," the doctor said.

Cato accepted the goblet and gulped it down as fast as he could. *The doctor was not kidding,* Cato thought. He could feel his body quickly begin to relax and numb slowly letting sleep take him away.

Cato awoke what seemed to him like years later. He was lying in a small bed still in the gladiator infirmary. The memory of the battle bringing him back from a nice dream. Lea was next to the bed checking on his bandaged wound. The pain was dulled compared to when he first got there.

"The doctor was able to tie up your muscle and stop the bleeding," were Lea's first words to him. "You will have to stay here for a few days before we can remove the plant fibers from your arm, so you can resume your training after that." While she was explaining the outcome to Cato, she began pouring oil on the rest of his body to clean him up. The warm oil felt calm and welcoming on his skin. She coated his whole body with the oil, collecting the dried blood and dirt that still remained on his body from the fight, mixing it until a dark paste formed. She then grabbed a metal strigil and gently scraped the paste and oil residue from his body disposing of it in a bucket one scrape at a time, avoiding the area around his wound.

"All clean," Lea said as she hung the sickle shaped strigil back on the hook. "Here is something to eat," she continued as she placed a tray of food at the foot of his bed. "I would suggest rest, but I know how you boys get. If you must get out of bed, some of the other wounded can be found in the practice arena down the corridor doing gods know what with their injuries. I would rather not know," she scoffed.

With that she moved on to her next patient and left Cato alone. Cato had only grunted at Lea, mostly because he was in so much pain but also because he could not bring himself to act like the rude Velarius man he was supposed to be.

She was right, Cato thought. As much as he knew he needed the rest, he needed to get back in the arena more.

The infirmary was much different than the gladiator school Cato observed. The most obvious change being his freedom. He could come and go as he pleased, no more shackles, no more cell. But with that was the loss of his sense of security with his rigorous schedule. His actions would be scrutinized and his personality would have to mimic that of a brute Velarius man. The pressure to succeed was immense. He wished he could avoid the social aspect of being a gladiator but knew he had to just dive in headfirst.

With that he went straight for the practice arena hoping to make a rude impression. He needed to set the tone with the others from the beginning so they would not think to question his identity. Cato walked into the arena looking for an easy target to bully, pushing away the pain from his arm. *Okay,* he thought, giving a little pep talk, *your father is Leon the Great, act like it.* He thought it best to bully someone he didn't know, maybe that would make it easier. A group of *veterani* were messing around with weighted wooden swords and he didn't recognize anyone he knew. This was his chance.

Yelling from across the practice arena, Cato bellowed, "Aren't you supposed to be third years? Look at you. Pathetic." He had gotten most of their attention, a few of them stopped to see who the loud-mouth was. Cato walked toward them continuing his act. "Ha! This one can barely lift a weighted sword and you call yourself a gladiator," he continued talking to a shorter guy with his back turned. Cato shoved the guy who was having trouble wielding the heavy sword into the dirt. "Look at me when I talk to you...you." Cato froze but if only for a second to gain his composure. When the guy had turned to pick himself up off the ground, Cato saw it was not a guy but a girl. *Gods,* Cato thought shocked by a female in the practice arena, but he was already in too deep. He only had one chance to make his first impression. So, he kept at it.

"Ha! A girl. In the gladiator facilities. Is this some kind of joke?" he kept on.

"Ah, come on man, she's harmless, just fooling around down here with us," one of the third years said, standing up for her.

"Gladiator law says no females in our domain." Cato paused for dramatic effect. "But, I am not one for rules. If you want to fight. Let's fight," Cato egged on. He couldn't help but notice the girl looking absolutely terrified. "And not with pretend swords, it seems as if she wants the real gladiator experience. Well far be it from me to disappoint the little lady," Cato mocked. "Grab a sword, girl," Cato said pointing to the pile of swords.

The girl looked to the third years for guidance. The outspoken one slowly nodded to her. *They must know who I am,* Cato noted.

"Let's see what you have been practicing girl. You versus me. One sword, one shield," Cato proposed. The girl grabbed the shield. Cato could tell it was way too heavy for her as she tried to pretend it was weightless. If she was scared, she did a pretty good job of hiding it he noticed. It was actually admirable.

At this point the *veterani* boys started to back off and watch. They all knew the law, punishment for a girl in the gladiator domain was certain death and they dare not chance bringing themselves into it any more than they already were.

Cato drew his sword with his non-injured arm.

The girl drew hers and quickly made a low quick lunge swiping at his ankles.

Barely avoiding the attack while hiding his surprise, Cato purposely slashed her shield, the force causing her to fall backward onto the ground. "Get up," Cato commanded.

The girl stood up trying not to look rattled.

Cato needed this to end in his favor. He now had the attention of everyone in the practice arena. *Good*, he thought.

"Your resilience is admirable if not idiotic," Cato sniveled at her. "Why don't you take a knee and we call it a day?" Cato saw her eyes widen ever so slightly at the threat.

He was going to have to injure her just enough to end it but not kill her and still make his presence as a Velarius known. He waited for her next move.

She tried to come at him straight on this time, so Cato feigned to one side dragging his sword just enough to cut her leg. The girl winced and fell to the ground, blood quickly pooling in the sand.

No one in the arena moved.

"This was getting boring anyways," Cato nonchalantly said as he tossed his sword on the pile. "I need to save my strength for a real fight." With that, he turned and walked away half holding his breath worried that his performance was believable. He willed himself not to turn around to check on how badly he had injured her. He could feel himself shaking, every part of him wanted to turn back and help the poor girl he had hopefully only maimed. But, he couldn't risk breaking character no matter how unfortunate the circumstance was.

Some of the other guys followed him, congratulating him on his earlier win. Cato knew most of them were just posturing, wanting to get on his good side because they thought he was gladiator royalty. He retired to one of the benches to hold court with his new groupies. He did not know what felt worse, pretending to be a pompous numbskull or his sliced-up arm. He told pretend stories of his pretend father to the group until he could not bear the lies anymore. When he noticed his bandage was leaking, it gave him the perfect time to make an exit back to the infirmary. He hoped the girl would have been taken there too so he could get some peace of mind that she was alright, but there was no sign of her.

8

LIVIA

Keeping her palace life separate from her real life was easier than Livia had thought. She told her parents she was working as a maid in the palace and it required her to spend almost all her time there, and she had Noemi covering for her when she did not come home at night. Hopefully her sister would keep the excuses simple as she definitely did not need to keep up with any more lies. Technically, she was working at the palace, just not as a maid, so it wasn't a complete falsehood. Instead of being upset, her parents were okay with her working there because she had stopped moping around the hypogeum and causing trouble. And they didn't have to listen to her complain about the Vestal Virgins anymore.

Livia found she was relatively good at being one of the emperor's girls and she actually enjoyed it. Her wardrobe was growing extensively what with all the tunics and silks the emperor provided the girls. She even found herself spending more and more nights in the ladies' quarters than at her home. She attended numerous important dinners and parties, drinking expensive wine and food with her new friends until all hours of the night with no responsibilities. Her lifestyle had become quite lavish and fun, for only the feeble price of accompaniment to the emperor here and there. Plus, the palace grounds were enormous and beautiful, much better than the dreary hypogeum. What wasn't to like?

A few weeks after Livia had started at the palace, news of the mistress's pregnancy spread like wildfire. Livia was in the garden making herself a floral headpiece for the next party they would attend when Delia, another one of the emperor's girls, came to tell her the news.

"Can you believe it?" Delia exclaimed. "She's so lucky. I wish I could mother the emperor's heir," she sighed.

"Umm, hello," Liv started in an annoyed tone, "correct me if I'm wrong, but weren't you the one who told me that the gods cursed all of the emperor's heirs to die? And that all of the past mistresses were executed with each failed pregnancy?"

Now it was Delia's turn to be annoyed, "Well, yes, but my child would survive, I just know it."

Livia couldn't see herself as a mother in the least and didn't feel like arguing with Delia about her foolish notions.

Fabia, who had been there the longest and was the self-appointed mother hen, was giving instructions when Livia got back to the quarters.

"Now that Antonia is with child, it is our job to comfort her and pray for a fruitful pregnancy. Tonight, there will be a special offering for the baby. Anything Antonia needs, she gets from here on out. Livia, Delia, and Martia, per the emperor's request, you will be assigned to Antonia as her handmaidens," Fabia dictated.

Livia was less than pleased. Her carefree days of wandering the palace and smiling at the emperor here and there were over. She did not want to be massaging Antonia with oil and praising some doomed baby. But, she enjoyed her new lifestyle so much she could suck it up for a few months and then get back to galivanting about once she did not have to play handmaiden.

Livia had never been to an offering of the goddess Latona before. She'd only attended offerings in the forum outside of a large temple with thousands of other people where she could barely see a thing and did not care to pay any attention to what was going on. Now she found herself front and center at a private offering unlike anything she had ever seen before.

Antonia was lying on a large satin bed dressed in a simple white tunic with her head adorned in greenery. A wreath of thorns was laid on her barely-showing belly to protect the baby. Flowers of all sorts were littered around the bed and the floor. Small candles were lit in a circle around the bed, wax dripping and pooling on the floor. The hearth was well lit and similarly adorned. A priestess from the Temple of Juno was brought in to lead the ceremony. Livia stood in line with the other girls in front of the bed watching Antonia lie there with a smile plastered on her face.

Woah, they really went all out for this, she thought.

The priestess began her incantation, "Great goddess, Latona, protector of the unborn, we hereby bring you gifts so you may see to the safe passage of this child into the world. We call on you, oh powerful one, to shield this child from harm in the womb. Look after the mother, Antonia, as she carries this blessing inside of her. We ask you to hear us and accept our offering."

Silence filled the room.

The priestess stepped out quickly only to return with two closed baskets. Livia could tell whatever was in them was definitely alive as the baskets rustled when they were set down.

The priestess opened the first basket. Reaching inside, she pulled out a mongoose, holding it by its neck. The animal screeched in terror pumping its legs trying to escape her firm hand. Livia thought for sure she was going to kill it as some sort of sacrificial offering. Instead, the priestess stroked its back, magically calming the animal into an almost sleep.

Livia watched as she placed the subdued mongoose in the ring of thorns resting on Antonia's stomach. The mongoose curled up and remained restful in the thorns as if it was an inviting, comfy nest. She then reached into the other basket and pulled out a rooster. The rooster, like the mongoose, was not pleased at being held. It kept trying to peck at the priestess's hands and its loud crow echoed throughout the room. The priestess began to hum in a slow, rhythmic pattern, increasing the volume and tempo ever so slightly until the rooster stopped fighting back and remained calm. She released her grip on the rooster and placed it on the pillow next to Antonia's head where it calmly sat down staring back at the girls. Livia could not help but smirk as she thought of the lengths her father must have gone to find a mongoose for this offering. She could just picture him panicking, reaching out to his contacts to track down this rare animal for the emperor.

The priestess continued, "A mongoose for you, great Latona, a symbol of defense and protection against evil. And a rooster, your most sacred animal, for good luck and strength."

The girls began throwing some of the flowers on the hearth as offerings, something Livia thought to be pointless. They were only instructed to do so because it looked like the girls were useful participants. The animals remained docile in their positions on the bed.

The priestess retrieved the now sleeping mongoose and returned it to the basket where it remained asleep. Livia was shocked that it was not offered to Latona in the hearth like at every other offering she had been to where there was always a sacrifice.

"We ask for life, powerful Latona, please hear us and let it be your will that this child lives," the priestess ended her incantation.

Now addressing the girls, "Thank you for your prayers." With that she took her leave thus leaving Livia to commence her duties as adult babysitter.

Antonia remained on her back resting peacefully, and, from what Liv could tell, enjoying every second of all the attention.

Livia despised being a handmaiden to Antonia. First of all, there was the rooster that was now living in Antonia's bedroom. According to Fabia, it brought strength and protection to the unborn child throughout the pregnancy and would remain with Antonia until the child was born. For Livia, the rooster was just one big, loud headache with its crowing all hours of the day.

If that wasn't enough, Antonia was milking the pregnancy for all it was worth. Livia and the girls were at her beck and call for literally everything. Her sheets were too soft, the sunlight disturbed her, or her food was too cold, the list went on and on. Some days she did not leave her room which meant Livia did not leave the room either. It was an absolute nightmare. She was no longer allowed to come and go from the palace as she had before. She told her family she was given a special assignment that required her presence inside the palace walls at all times. Her parents were less than pleased, but glad that she was showing initiative in something she seemed to enjoy. Her days of partying in the palace decked in frivolous clothes were long gone. Her new reality was everything Antonia. She could not wait for the child to be born and this assignment to end. What was worse, Martia and Delia seemed to enjoy being handmaidens, endlessly talking about the baby and asking Antonia how it felt to carry a child, hanging on her every word.

In the weeks following, Antonia started to show, her tunic clinging to her round belly, and Livia noticed a change in the emperor's demeanor. Once a doe-eyed giddy schoolboy toward Antonia, he was now hard and cross. He would send Antonia to bed early insisting she needed rest, but Livia could tell it wasn't out of concern for her well-being, more out of annoyance. He even started spending more time with the empress and doted on her.

Antonia seemed to sense his change in feelings toward her, but she seemed not to care because she was carrying his child and could not be touched. Instead of the once flirty mistress, she was now the needy, annoying pregnant woman with never-ending and absurd demands. Which of course had to be met because she carried the heir.

Dinners were about the only thing Livia looked forward to anymore, mainly because she was allowed to eat with Antonia every night at the emperor's table. Antonia usually requested Martia to hand feed her, so Livia got to eat a lavish meal in peace—until the emperor started sending Antonia to bed early and the girls had to follow. Another let down for Livia.

One particular night, Liv could sense something was different. The emperor was in a mood. Paired with the excessive wine drinking, it was a clear recipe for disaster. Livia watched as he, clearly intoxicated, sat at the head of the table. His teeth were stained with red wine along with most of his tunic from him spilling his goblet down the front of himself. The first course was not even on the table for two seconds before he threw the whole plate on the ground like a child.

"Is this what you think is worthy for the emperor to eat?" he yelled to the poor servant who brought out his meal. Not waiting for a reply, he threw his goblet at the servant who now too was covered in red wine. "Bring me another goblet, now!" he screamed.

At once another servant ran out from the kitchen with a goblet.

"Give me that!" he yelled grabbing for the goblet. He tried to pour himself the wine but most of it ended up on the table, dripping off onto the floor. Livia prayed he would dismiss Antonia so she could get out of there herself.

The emperor now tried to stand up. He swayed from side to side holding onto the table to try and keep his balance. All the women in the room held their breath hoping not to be the next victim of his drunken wrath. With the help of the table, he began walking toward Antonia. "Why don't you go take a rest, my dear," he said to her in an eerily nice way. Livia, Delia, and Martia all stood to help Antonia to her room. For once, Livia was glad to head back to Antonia's chambers.

"Ladies, not so fast, the empress can take Antonia to her room. You have taken such good care of my Antonia that you deserve a night off."

Delia, Livia, and Martia all looked at each other unsure of what he could want. They knew that one wrong move could set him off at any second. The three girls remained standing, scared to do anything else.

The emperor made his way back to his seat. "Come and sit me with girls," he crooned.

There was nothing to do but obey. "You two, come sit on my lap," he gestured to Delia and Martia.

They did.

"You," he said talking to Livia, "dance for me."

Livia could do that, at least she didn't have to be near him. She hesitantly started to sway and move her arms to the soft music of the lyre playing in the background. She didn't consider herself much of a dancer, but it seemed that whatever she was doing pleased him because he smiled at her. The music began to pick up and Livia awkwardly adjusted to the tempo. *How much longer do I have to do this*? she thought. She couldn't believe she was beginning to miss Antonia.

The emperor stood up again moving Delia and Martia off his lap. He began walking toward Livia while she danced, tripping over himself every other step. He reminded Livia of one of her father's newborn animals learning to walk for the first time.

The lyre player again changed the melody and the emperor reached out a hand to Livia as if he wanted to dance.

Livia reached her hand out in return accepting his gesture knowing she really did not have a choice. The emperor pulled her close putting one hand behind her back. *For as drunk as he was, he was surprisingly agile*, Livia thought as he spun her around the room in time to the beat of the music.

As the song ended, he whispered in her ear, "I have been watching you for weeks now." And then like nothing had happened he stumbled back to the couch with the other girls and his wine.

Chills ran up and down Livia's spine. *Did that really just happen?*

Lucky for the girls, the emperor was snoring on the couch before he could give anymore commands. One of the servants came out from the back to tell them it was okay to leave.

The girls could not have run out of there fast enough. Livia did not dare tell the other girls what the emperor had whispered to her.

He was so intoxicated there was no way he would remember any of it anyways she reasoned. Boy was she wrong.

The next morning, she awoke to small box on top of her things. Inside was a beautiful gold brooch with two snakes intertwined on it. Beneath the brooch was a note that read:

Thank you for the dance.

9

CATO

Cato spent the night in the infirmary. He knew he didn't have to but the thought of interacting with *tiros* and *veterani* as a Velarius made him nauseous. It was going to be difficult to keep up the act.

Replaying the day's event in his head, he kept coming back to the girl's face. He kept picturing her small delicate features, long brown hair tied up in a knot, and mostly her soft brown eyes. *What would a girl like that be doing playing with swords and gladiators*? Once he'd realized she was a girl, he wished he could have walked away and just let the whole thing go, but he was already in too deep. He had an audience of gladiators, and he needed to sell his story. He could not let anyone stand in his way no matter how much the real Tyrian came out. He prayed to the gods that he hadn't hurt her too badly, trying his best for only a small flesh wound.

He fell asleep with her on his mind and awoke with the foggy memory of a dream where the girl was not scared of him but could see who he really was. He tried to go back to sleep to bring her back, but it didn't work. He was awake.

Lea came to check his wound. Her callused hands surprisingly felt smooth against his skin while she changed his dressing. "Looks like you are healing nicely, Dominus Velarius," she said. "No sense in lying around all day like a lug. If I were you, I would get a little fresh air first, it will do you wonders. Take a walk. See the agora. If your arm starts to bleed come back and I will fix you up. Since almost every one of the new *tiros* were all injured in some form, the headmaster granted a few days reprieve before training begins again."

Go for a walk? Cato thought. The amount of freedom was something he had never had in his entire life. *Could he really just go where he pleased?* He tried to act like he wasn't shocked by her proposition.

"Okay, gratias," he thanked her and was off taking the tunnel up to the street. Once he was outside, the hot sun blasted him in the face, and it took a moment for his eyes to adjust to the bright light after being inside the dark hypogeum for all that time.

The streets were crowded with people. Vendors pedaling their wares, men transporting goods on carts pulled by oxen, children playing, the wealthy being carried on thrones, and so much more. He wandered around taking in civilian life, letting his mind relax and take a break from the pressure of pretending to be a Velarius.

A sweet aroma wafting from a bakery called to him. Allowing himself a treat, he purchased a small pastry, savoring the sugar as it touched his tongue. Seeing people enjoying themselves eating and drinking as he walked by the restaurants made him want to partake. He made his way to a small bar, a little off the beaten path and took a seat.

Dressed in a simple tunic, he was unlikely to be recognized as a gladiator and could go about being fairly invisible. He sat at the bar eating olives and bread with a glass of wine. The man sitting next to him tried to make some small talk, but Cato wasn't interested. His mind kept wandering back to that girl and how he could see her again.

"Interested in the fights?" the bartender asked interrupting his daydreaming.

"Sure, who isn't?" Cato responded like he thought the average civilian would respond.

The bartender continued rambling on about his nephew who

made it to his *veterani* year before he was killed and some other unin-teresting story that seemed like popular bar talk.

Cato tuned him out until he noticed the guy wiping down the area in front of him. He lifted up his goblet and placed a piece of paper under it all while continuing his story to whomever would listen and not skipping a beat. Cato looked at the guy with confusion, but the bartender did not give any indication he had just passed him a note. He covertly retrieved the note from his goblet and read it in his lap.

Back alley. 5 minuti.

Not sure this note was meant for him, he wasn't too certain how to proceed. In the end, his curiosity got the best of him. Leaving a few coins on the bar to pay for his drink, Cato found the alley and walked to the back of it.

A small man stepped out from behind some discarded stone and motioned for Cato to follow. The man moved aside a worn sheet hanging from the wall of a building revealing a small door.

Cato followed the man through the door and down a few steps into a dark passageway.

"Umm where are we going?" Cato couldn't help but ask.

The man said nothing as he quickly moved deeper into the dimly lit passage until it opened up into a large room. The man motioned for Cato to enter and turned and went back the way he had come.

The room was filled with men sitting at tables each covered with piles of money and scattered papyrus. Cato had only heard of under-ground gambling dens but had never actually seen one. One gruff older man grumbled something inaudible to him. Cato walked toward him to better hear him.

"We've got ourselves a square here, boys." The man chuckled. "What will it be, boy, three to one odds on a couple of *veterani* for the afternoon?"

Cato looked down at the man as he pushed some papyrus toward him with drawings of the third years and a few of their statistics written underneath their pictures.

Cato could not believe they were betting on gladiators still in training. Thank the gods he wasn't on the circuit yet as he would for sure be recognized, and crucified for attempting to bet as a gladiator himself.

"Not your thing?" the man continued sensing his disinterest. "Well how about the over/under on the number of executionees mauled by lions today? Or, you interested in taking the chalk of tomorrow's rhino v' bear in the early morning fight?"

This guy might as well have been speaking a completely different language. Cato didn't really want to place any bets mainly because he didn't have money to spare, but he also didn't want any trouble. By the looks of the men in the den, leaving without a wager was not going to end well for him.

The man shuffled around some more papyrus. "How about something a little more straight forward? Chariot racing? Here are the lines for the day," he handed Cato a piece of papyrus.

It didn't matter that Cato knew how to read; he did not need it to gamble. The page was filled with a bunch of numbers he didn't understand. Cato moved to the side pretending to analyze the numbers while eavesdropping on another man's wager. Following the man's lead, Cato said to the bookie, "Three aureus, race three, chariot one to win." The bookie wrote his wager in the ledger. Then quickly grabbed Cato's tunic ripping a piece off and wrapped it around the parchment with his wager written on it.

"If you win, you return here to collect. If you lose, you return here to pay. Simple as that. If you try and stiff us our dogs will find you now that we have your scent."

Cato wasn't sure what he had just done but left with a token, nonetheless. His arm had started to ooze a little and could tell a new bandage was needed. He wanted to continue exploring but could not risk his wound going sour. *I can get fixed up then go explore some more,* he thought.

The morning sun was hotter than usual and he was sweating through his tunic by the time he returned to the infirmary. The infirmary was already smelling ripe and humid from the intense heat of the day, offering him only a small relief from the sun.

Lea checked his arm, washed out the wound, and replaced the bandage. It felt good to get cleaned up, the cool water refreshing on his warm skin. Cato wanted to get back outside, the heavy, stagnant air inside making him feel dizzy.

Walking out of the infirmary, he almost barreled into the headmaster.

"Watch where you are going, boy," the headmaster said annoyed. "All of you *tiros* come to the practice arena at once."

Odd, Cato thought, *Lea said they had at least a day or two more to recover before resuming training. What was he doing in the hypogeum?*

Assembled in the arena already were the *novocius* and *veterani*. Cato and the rest of the banged up *tiros* filed in and stood with the others.

"Today's training exercise is a little unconventional," the headmaster began. "It seems the Roman Navy has run into some trouble near Carthage and needs extra sailors to be deployed. As you can all tell it is ungodly hot out today and the emperor has put in a late order for the velarium to be let down. That being said, there is no way the few sailors remaining can get the velarium down in time for the fights this afternoon by themselves. The emperor has ordered the gladiators assist the sailors. We shall use it as a strength building lesson. Lastly, *tiros*, I realize most of you are injured but you are gladiators, rise up to the occasion. Don't be soft." He then motioned toward the entrance where a few sailors began giving their instructions.

"Okay, lads," the captain began, "we don't have much time."

Cato listened as a burly man dressed in a navy tunic with long slits by the legs spoke. He wore a long sash adorned with various medals designating him as a high-ranking officer in the navy.

"Listen carefully, we are going to have to work together to get this done. I don't much care for you non-seafaring folk dealing with the ropes, but it seems I have no choice. So, here are the basics. There are two hundred and forty masts circling the top of the colosseum. Each mast houses a silk sail which, when lowered down, provides the shade the emperor needs to keep any sort of audience today for your fights. To lower the mast, each one requires two people to operate it. Now, since we don't have four hundred and forty men, you will have to work on more than one mast as quickly as you can. We will have most of you on the ground outside the colosseum where the pulleys are anchored. My men and anyone who knows a lick about ropes will be working the masts. It is all hands on deck today. If this velarium isn't lowered by the afternoon we will all be at the emperor's mercy. Let's pray to Neptune we can get this done in time," the captain instructed.

Cato had never heard of such a thing before. *Gladiators doing the work of a sailor? This was much more than a training exercise.* But who was he to question the headmaster or even the emperor for that matter. All the *tiros*, injured or not, joined the sailors. No one was dumb enough to show any weakness no matter how severe their injury.

Cato had some experience with knots from his days at the villa but there was no way he could rig the rope with only one working arm. He followed the men to the outside of the colosseum where the pulleys were located.

The captain quickly gathered them for one final instruction once they were outside. "Each pulley is anchored to the ground holding up the weight of the sail and mast. Follow the signal of your partner above. He will guide you with the rope. I cannot stress enough the weight of each mast. It will be extremely heavy, and your job is to bear the weight until your partner can rig the mast. Whatever you do, do not let go."

Cato hurried to the first pulley. Above him on the porticus, a sailor shouted down to him, "Untie the rope, mate. Slowly release a little slack, and then hold the weight until I say."

Cato quickly untied the knot. With his good arm, he grabbed the rope leading up toward the mast. The captain wasn't kidding, as soon as the knot came undone, the weight of the mast caused it to quickly unwind around the pulley. Cato could hear the sailor yelling, "Prohibere!" Cato jumped to grab a hold of the rope with both arms out of instinct, his injured arm burning from the force. It took all of his body weight to keep the rope steady; securing it with just his good arm was excruciating. Just when Cato's arm started to go numb the sailor yelled down, "Deorsum" and Cato let go of the rope. He watched as the pulley system slowly began to lower the mast down toward the arena floor, the rope that had just given him so much trouble now gently moving around the pulley. Meanwhile, the sailor raised the sail along the mast as it lowered while Cato watched, enamored with his balance and skill so high up.

Once it was completed, the sailor motioned for Cato to move on to the next pulley as he leaped over a column above to the next mast. This time Cato was ready for the weight and countered it without an issue, saving his bad arm from tearing any more than it already had.

They repeated this process five times taking them about two hours to complete their part of the velarium. Cato's hands were raw and bloody from the rope by the time they were done. The blazing Roman sun was not doing him any favors either. He had tried not to use his injured arm but that had proven impossible as he could see his bandage was a bright crimson color soaked through with blood. *Lea will not be pleased,* he thought.

It seemed as if almost all of the masts had been successfully lowered. His part of the job was done and a Velarius man would never do more work than required so he headed back toward the tunnel entrance secretly thankful that one of his pretend attributes would work in his favor.

No sooner had he reached the entrance, he heard a loud crack followed by frantic screaming. Farther down the colosseum wall he could see a *tiro* lying on the ground covered in blood while others nearby frantically ran toward him reaching for the rope unwinding at a rapid pace. His injury must have been too severe to bear the weight of the mast and he collapsed letting go of the rope.

The men stopped the rope, but it was too late. The mast had

crashed before the rope could be secured. Screams could be heard from inside the arena.

Cato hoped no one had been killed. He wanted to help out, but the new Cato needed to get his arm bandaged again and could not risk any signs of outward empathy. Although it pained him to do so, he went back to the infirmary without so much as a glance over his shoulder.

10

NOEMI

Rem was right. Noemi's injury was not as bad as it had seemed. Thanks to Lin, her father's best animal healer, she was quickly stitched up and sent out of the animal infirmary.

There is no way Felix or anyone else could find out about this, she thought. Gods strike her dead if Felix knew she was injured while fighting with a gladiator. He was already uneasy about her working with the beasts.

Lin had given her some supplies to care for her wound along with some basic instructions and the promise to keep her injury a secret. Noemi was able to dress the wound with plant leaves, ripping an old tunic to create a makeshift bandage on her thigh the same color as her own tunic. That way, if her leg was exposed at all it would be less noticeable. Putting weight on her leg was a bit of a challenge at first but with practice she was able walk without a limp.

The heat of the bright sun was beating down on the empire this morning causing a vile smell of animal excrement and death to waft through the humid hypogeum. Even the open trap doors were not making a dent in the poor airflow.

Noemi watched as extra water was being delivered to the animal stables in large jugs carried on carts. *They were going to need it*, she thought as she wiped the sweat beading up on her forehead.

One of the workers flagged her down to hand her a folded-up note.

"From Dominus Felix," he said.

Noemi accepted the note and giggled to herself, her face lighting up. Felix was always leaving her notes with riddles or clues leading her to small presents or surprises. His thoughtfulness was one of the many things she loved about him.

All right, Felix, she thought. *I'm game.* Unfolding the small piece of parchment, Noemi read:

Your knuckles are made of bones but so are mine. Come find me or I'll whine.

This was all too easy. Noemi knew the answer right away. Knucklebones was a children's game they played growing up where you roll a die and whichever number it landed on you had to scoop up that number of bones before your ball bounced on the ground a second time. The riddle was knowing where knucklebones came from. And that answer was a sheep. Noemi had helped her father save the knucklebones of the sheep that had been killed in the arena many a time. Local toy makers would collect the bones and polish them up to make game sets to sell. The sheep were not kept in the stalls, however.

Nice try, Felix. He wasn't referring to an actual sheep. It was the whiny ram they had first thought was a sheep until its horns were found once it was sheared.

Forgetting the pain in her leg entirely, Noemi walked down the ramp to the second floor where the rams were housed. It didn't take her long to spot the parchment nailed to the outside wall of the stall. Careful not to rip it as she pulled it off the nail, she read:

My roof is made of iron, but my walls are glass. I can burn and burn but never fall. What am I?

This one was admittedly trickier. Her first thought was some sort of fireplace or stove but those did not have any glass and there were not any in the hypogeum. Felix's clues were usually in the hypogeum because that is where he spent most of his time. So, she looked around. *What else has fire down here?* She laughed out loud when it came to her. The only reason she could see anything down here was because of the light coming from the fire. There hanging from the wall was a lantern. Its top made of iron with glass encasing the fire. "Clever, Felix," she said to no one.

She lifted the lantern off of its hook in the wall and saw a piece of parchment tied to the loop at the top of the lantern. Unrolling it, the paper had a map of the colosseum scrawled on it with a small "x" marking the very top of the colosseum where slaves and women sat. It would be a hike to get there and just the thought of climbing on her wounded leg made her wince. *What could Felix possibly want to do up there?*

She didn't have a ticket for entry into the arena above but that did not matter. There were multiple hidden entryways leading into the stairwells of the arena on the lower level. They were originally built before the concept of the hypogeum existed, used to access storage, but most of the stairs were sealed up so the public could not access them.

Noemi made her way to one of those forgotten doors and began her ascent. She was drenched in sweat by the time she had climbed to the top of the colosseum. Her leg hurt so bad she could feel the pulse in her thigh.

The crowd for the gladiator fight was filing in and seats were filling up quickly. It was difficult to avoid the throngs of people bumping into her and her leg. She looked around for Felix trying to spot him in the sea of humanity. Finding herself unsuccessful, she looked back at the map he had drawn and confirmed she was in the right spot.

"Where are you?" she said out loud. She heard a sharp whistle coming from the direction she was looking and raised her eyes up higher. Of course, he was not in the stands, he was sitting on top of one of the outer support columns, too high to be seen by anyone below unless you knew where to look. *If he only knew how much trouble this was to get myself up here with this leg,* she thought.

Wincing with every step, she climbed the column using the footholds that were left from when the colosseum was first built. Felix helped her up over the edge.

"Salve, mi amor," he greeted her with a kiss. "I thought it would be fun to watch the show from the best seat in the house today," he said as he pulled her into his lap. They were sitting on top of the large column that dubbed as a small rooftop where they had one of the best aerial views of the arena. "I hope my clues did not give someone like you any trouble," he teased.

"Well, I'm here, aren't I?" she teased back. She could see him watching her favor her left leg as she sat down but he did not comment on it.

Felix had brought up some wine and cheese that he had waiting for their date. She loved this romantic side of him.

"A toast," he said raising his wine-filled goblet to Noemi's, "to everlasting love and our future, many thanks to you, Bacchus for these gifts. Saluti!"

Noemi laid her head back against his chest letting her body sink into his while he kissed the top of her head. Gently kissing her ear, he began to move his lips slowly down her neck. Noemi nuzzled her head into his kisses. Tilting her head up to meet his mouth, she leaned into his long kiss. He kissed her back aggressively and she matched his passion by biting the bottom of his lip. Felix groaned in response. Noemi smiled, turned herself around to face him. Felix pulled Noemi back toward him, letting her fall on top of him as he lay down on the column. She could feel his body beneath her, wanting to melt into him. She pulled herself up and let one more kiss linger on his lips as she pushed herself off him and took a deep breath bringing things to a grinding halt.

"You know we aren't married yet, Felix," she said trying to slow her fluttering heart rate down.

Felix grinned back at her like a cat. "Yes, yes, I know, I know. We wouldn't want to upset the gods, blah blah," he answered back slightly annoyed.

"Come on, Felix don't be like that, you know my beliefs," Noemi replied completely changing the mood.

Not wanting to ruin the date, Felix changed the subject. "Look, the emperor must have given the signal for the velarium to be put up. Praise the gods it is hot today."

Sure enough, Noemi watched as the large silk sails started to come down around the colosseum to create some shade for the spectators. The emperor was cruel but not unreasonable. He knew that without spectators for his events he would not be as popular in the eyes of his people. Thus, he had an awning designed, manufactured, and installed around the arena to shade the spectators from the sun. Without the shade during a hot day, it would be impossible for anyone to sit in the direct sunlight without having a sun stroke and needing to be carried out of the colosseum.

The velarium was probably the one thing that went on in the hypogeum that Noemi's father did not have complete control over and it bothered him. Noemi could just picture her father standing aside while the grimy sailors ran in and out of the hypogeum liked they owned the place, messing with the animals and leaving their trash everywhere. Noemi's father couldn't do anything about it though, because the sailors were employed by the emperor and were the only ones with the know-how and expertise to maneuver each sail up and down.

To aggravate her father further, this seemed to be a last-minute decision. Usually, the velarium was lowered first thing in the morning if a hot day was expected. Noemi thought it was weird that now, an hour or so before the main event of the day, they just started the process. This meant the fight would be delayed until the velarium was completely lowered. That did not bother Noemi as it gave her more alone time with Felix.

Now in the shade, Noemi relaxed a little more. Her leg wasn't bothering her as much either although that could have been the wine helping. She refilled their goblets.

"What happened to your leg?" Felix questioned. Noemi, who was mid pour, spilled some of the wine because she was so caught off guard.

"What are you talking about?" she asked trying to play it cool.

"I am talking about the blood stain on your tunic that keeps getting larger by the minute." Felix replied, glaring.

Noemi immediately looked down at her leg and saw what he was talking about. *Crap...* she thought. She must have waited too long to change the dressing. Regaining her composure, she calmly came up with an answer.

"Oh that. One of the ostriches was a little too aggressive with their beak. Must have thought my leg looked like a tasty snack," she laughed a little and shrugged her shoulders hoping her nonchalant attitude was enough to fool Felix, or at the very least get him to talk about something else.

"Let me see it," Felix asked reaching for her leg. Noemi pulled away.

"No, Felix, it's fine. Trust me. I've had way worse injuries than this one. I had completely forgotten about it until you mentioned it," she said reassuringly. She hoped he would let it go. She hated lying to him, especially after he had planned this romantic afternoon for the two of them.

"I would feel better if we had Lin look at it. The fight is delayed anyways, let's just head down to the infirmary quick to..." but his plan would never be heard because suddenly a loud snap echoed throughout the colosseum causing everyone to stop what they were doing and look up toward the sound. Even Noemi was not sure where it came from and she was an expert on most everything related to the colosseum. She looked up toward the direction of the loud crack.

"Gods, Felix!" she said in a panic pointing to the sky. One of the masts of the velarium had fallen, crashing into the crowd below. People near the mast were scrambling to get away from it. Screams could be heard from where it fell. "Something must have gone horribly wrong," Noemi said stating the obvious.

Panic. That was the only word Noemi could use to describe what was going on in the stands. Nothing like this had ever happened before. Being a spectator was supposed to be safe, that was part of the magic of the colosseum. A person could be a few hundred feet from the most dangerous things and not get hurt.

"We have to try and help," Noemi urged Felix. The two climbed down from the column and started to fight their way through the crowd.

It was pure chaos. People screaming and trying to run to the exits, pushing and shoving each other, snacks and beverages strewn about.

Felix grabbed her hand, "Stay close to me," he said.

Noemi could see her father's workers running out from tunnels and trapdoors onto the arena floor toward the fallen mast. Noemi hoped no one had been killed.

It felt like forever by the time they reached the fallen mast. It was worse than she thought. She could see bodies lying under the heavy mast unclear if they were still alive but definitely not moving. Others were tangled in the now blood-stained silk sail. The sailors were trying to give orders to anyone who would listen.

"We need to lift the mast up, everyone needs to help," one sailor shouted.

By now the area had mostly cleared out except for the people trying to help and the families of the wounded and trapped screaming for their loved ones. There were about two dozen men trying to lift the mast, but it wasn't enough. Noemi could see there was at least one fatality. The mast had cleanly severed a man in half who could not get out of the way in time. The gruesome remains of his body split in half.

"We need more men to lift it. Go get some gladiators," another sailor shouted.

Noemi didn't hesitate. "I'll go." She volunteered and was off. She scaled the arena wall using the door arch as a foot hold and propelled herself to the ground landing in the sand on the arena floor. The adrenaline pumping throughout her body made her forgot her leg entirely. She raced across the arena floor into the gladiator tunnel, down the ramp, and straight into the gladiator practice facility screaming for help along the way. There were only about twenty or so gladiators there, mostly *veterani*.

Trying to catch her breath, she mustered out, "Help. Velarium. Please." The men stopped practicing at the forbidden sound of a woman's voice in their facility. "There has been an accident. People are trapped beneath the velarium and...". She was cut off before she could finish.

"Prohibere!" one of the gladiators yelled at her to get out. "Leave before we report you. This is no place for a girl."

"Please," she pleaded, picturing all the injured above.

One gladiator took a step forward. Noemi tried to mask her fear realizing it was the same one who had maimed her leg. *Gods, why does he have to be here.*

"Let's go. People need our help," he said to the rest of the men, motioning toward the ramp.

Noemi stood there with her mouth agape. She had not seen that coming. *Maybe I misjudged him?* For a split second she worried he had recognized her, but there was no time to analyze his sudden change in demeanor, so she simply said, "Gratias. Gratias! Follow me," and led them to the scene.

Not much progress had been made on moving the mast by the time she got there. Felix, some spectators, and the sailors had secured ropes around the mast in the hopes of getting some leverage to lift it. Others were tending to the wounded who were able to get free. Blood covered the mast, seats, and rescuers. Noemi counted two casualties while the gladiators moved in, taking direction from the sailors. She heard a small whimper behind her. A young girl sat hunched in the stands, tears streaming down her face. Holding a stuffed lion now covered in blood, she was shaking all alone watching the men.

Noemi ran over to her. "Are you hurt?" she asked.

The girl didn't answer Noemi, just pointed to the mast and cried, "Mamma."

"It's okay, the gladiators are going to get your mamma out. Don't worry. I'll stay with you. Come here," she sympathized with the girl. The girl nodded her head and reached for Noemi. Noemi picked up the girl and turned her away from the chaos but not before Noemi could see a woman's bloody arm covered in bracelets, not moving from under the mast. "Okay, let's go over here," Noemi said walking over to the next section of the arena to get her away from the scene. "How about I tell you a story?" Noemi asked thinking she could distract the little girl.

The girl kept trying to turn back toward her mother.

"Okay, how about this? I am going to tell you one anyways, but you don't have to listen if you don't want to, okay?" Noemi proposed.

The girl sniffled and sat still. Noemi began her tale:

"One day long, long ago there lived a very clever king. The water supply for the king's city was running dangerously low. While he was thinking about how to fix it, he saw Jupiter, king of the gods, fly over his head with something in his hands. *That is strange,* he thought. *Jupiter rarely leaves the heavens. I wonder what he is doing all the way down here?* Just then, another god flew over him. *What is going on?* the king thought.

This god stopped above the king and shouted down, "Have you seen my daughter?" Now, the king knew better than to engage with a god, but you see, he was desperate. His people were thirsty and he still didn't have a solution. So, the clever king quickly came up with a plan. "Yes, I have seen her," he shouted up at the god, "but I will only tell you what I know, if you give me what I want."

The god, in a hurry to find his daughter, quickly agreed to the king's terms. "Okay, mortal," the god replied. "What is it you desire?"

The king then said, "I need an endless fresh water supply for my kingdom."

"Done." The god hastily answered and with a wave of his hand a giant freshwater stream bubbled up from the ground.

The king smiled, "Your daughter is with Jupiter, I saw him carrying her just a few minutes ago. They went that way." The god nodded and flew off. Jupiter was furious that the king interfered, so he called on his brother Pluto, god of the Underworld, to kill the king. Well, the clever king anticipated Jupiter's wrath so he told his wife that when he died she was not to put a gold coin under his tongue as customary to pay to cross the River Styx. Death came for the king that night and he found himself in the underworld.

"Where is your gold coin for passage across the River Styx?" Pluto asked.

The king hung his head in shame and replied, "My wife is too cheap to pay for my passage."

This infuriated Pluto who did not like giving free rides. "Well, you just go back up there and teach that woman some manners," Pluto said. The king was magically transported back to earth where he was alive and well again. He had cheated death."

The girl was hanging on Noemi's every word by the time she had finished the story. Noemi looked over her shoulder and saw the mast was finally being lifted. The gladiators were able to take most of the weight off of it while the sailors used the pulleys to hoist it back up. The girl seeing the direction of Noemi's gaze, jumped up and started running toward her mother. "Wait!" Noemi yelled, but it was no use. The girl had run to her mother's body lying broken on the seats.

"No!" she sobbed, "please, mamma! No! I need you!"

Noemi grabbed the girl off of her mother so she could be tended to. The little girl yelled, "I won't put a gold coin under your tongue and Pluto will send you back. Okay?"

Noemi's eyes started to water. *This was horrible. This poor girl,* she thought. Noemi turned to the girl. "Hey," she said sweetly, why don't we see if we can go find your papa?"

"Nooo! Mammaaa!" she wailed. Noemi tried to keep the little girl from seeing her mother's body again, but she couldn't hold on to her. The girl hunched over her mother pleading with the gods to bring her back.

Noemi could not watch. It was so sad. They were going to have to pry her off of her mother's lifeless body.

"She's alive!" the little girl screamed. "She's moving!"

Sure enough, the woman's fingers started moving ever so slightly followed by her arm. The woman was moaning in pain, but she was alive.

"Quickly, get her down to the gladiator infirmary, it's the closest," someone shouted. Noemi watched as the little girl followed her injured mother being carted down the tunnel, still clutching the bloodied stuffed lion. *I will give my mother an extra hug tonight*, she thought.

Trying to shake off the melancholy feeling that had set in, Noemi looked back to the mast. She watched as the gladiators held it in place while the sailors secured it with ropes. The awning that was supposed to be attached to it was tied back as best as could be expected by the sailors. Noemi surveyed the rest of the scene. *Besides the broken seats and the blood, it did not look as bad as it was,* she thought.

She could not help but focus her attention on the gladiator who had hurt her. He was now organizing the rest of the men to assist the injured. As he went around making sure that all the hurt people were being cared for, he seemed gentle, almost like a different person. She watched him carry a wounded man down from the stands to the medical cart, her eyes accidentally locking with his for no more than a second. In that moment, she thought she saw a kindness in his soft eyes, so much so she almost forgot about what he had done to her. She should have torn her eyes away, but she couldn't for some reason, fascinated by how much she had misread him.

Lost in her thoughts, she startled when Felix came up behind her. "Noemi, are you okay?" he asked, "thank the gods not more people were not injured."

"Yeah, I know," her response a little short. She was embarrassed to have been distracted by the gladiator to give a better reply.

"Do you want to head back and wait for the fight? There is nothing more we can do here," Felix asked.

"Okay," she replied, shoving the mystery of the gladiator out of her head. She knew there was no way the emperor would agree to cancel the afternoon fight, not even for a freak accident like this. If anything, it would increase the crowds with people hoping to get a look at the scene.

The show must go on, Noemi thought.

11

CATO

"Attention," the headmaster addressed all the *tiros* fresh off of their break. He was standing on the raised platform of the practice arena with various *lanistas* and other people Cato did not recognize standing behind him. "Welcome to your *Tiro* year. While you have already completed your basic training, there is much more to learn and many opportunities that await you."

This brought a few cheers from the men.

"We realize and acknowledge that each of you has your own strengths and weaknesses as a gladiator. To capitalize on this, we allow you to choose your own fighting style and career path. From this point forward you will become more and more recognized throughout the empire. What you are recognized for is up to you."

He paused and motioned for some of his colleagues to step forward. "Your legacy as a gladiator starts today. Who will you become? Will you be like Flamma, well respected and very skillful. Or perhaps you resonate more with Commodus, an arrogant show-boat. Maybe there is a Marcus Attlius among you who will defeat countless more experienced fighters as just a young *tiro* like your-selves. The choice is yours and yours alone. A few of my colleagues will now give you a little presentation on some of your options."

With that he stepped back and Cato listened as the first *lanista* told them about his career as a Dacicus gladiator and the skill needed to wield the short, curved *sica* sword. Other *lanistas* followed him, each boasting about their own style of fighting and training trying to promote their respective programs.

The Bestiarius *lanista* interested Cato the most. A gladiator versus a ferocious beast. He could picture it now, mosaics being sold of him with a lion carcass draped over his shoulders, the crowd chanting his name, children asking for autographs...the mental list went on and on.

The Velarius family had all trained at Ludus Magnus, the largest and most prestigious school, where they became notorious for their tactical weapons usage. They were good at being brutes and not much else, so they did not join a specialty group.

Cato did not want to raise any red flags by not following in the Velarius family footsteps, but he also could not resist the opportunity to be a bestiarius.

The presentations concluded and Cato watched as most of his classmates crowded around the *lanista* from their school—the one that would most quickly make them the most well- known, with its chariots, horses and other flashy styles. Cato moved toward the *lanista* from the *Bestiarii* school where only a handful of others gravitated.

The *lanista* representing the *Bestiarii* school was not what one would expect. He was not burly and strong looking like most gladiators but appeared lankier and leaner, almost awkward at times. Cato noticed he seemed a little timid as he spoke to those interested.

"Okay. Umm. Salve everyone. Thank you for your interest. You can sign up with me now if you desire or if you want to sleep on it, that is acceptable too. Umm, we will begin lessons this week at the Ludus Matutinus school, just umm, right down the road from here. Oh, and sometimes the lessons take place off campus in the hypogeum. So, uh thanks again," he stammered.

Cato was the first to etch his name on the papyrus. He didn't care that no other Velarius man had ever done so, it was time for a change. He could still pretend to be a heartless brute, just with an added skill.

On the first day of *Bestiarii* training, Cato was a little more nervous than he cared to admit. He, along with the other nine gladiators who had signed up, made their way to Ludus Matutinus. The first thing Cato remarked about the school was its size. It was noticeably smaller than Ludus Magnus. There was no grandeur at all. A nondescript building with only a small lion's head etched into the arch of the doorway marking it. Cato wondered if this was purposeful or if Ludus Matutinus was really as prestigious as it claimed to be.

Cato and the other gladiators were met at the door by someone from the school. Immediately upon entering, the strong smell of animal excrement caught Cato off guard. Allowing his nose to adjust, he then heard a cacophony of animal noises, screeches, howls, grunts, and roars echoing throughout the school. *This was already very different.*

The gatekeeper ushered them through the entryway and into the lobby of the school. "Wait here," was all he said and then disappeared back to where Cato assumed was his post at the gate.

Unlike the front of the building, the lobby was ornately decorated with brightly colored mosaics of famous *Bestiariis*. Each mosaic had a bust of that Bestiarius's most famous kill protruding from the wall.

Cato walked up to the great Bestiarius Philo's mosaic depicting Philo prying off the thick armor-like skin of a rhinoceros with its broken horn. Cato approached the rhinoceros bust, admiring how large the creature actually was. He reached out to touch what remained of its broken horn imagining how difficult it would be to fight an animal of this size. His thoughts were interrupted by the opening of a door. It was the *lanista* from the presentation the other day, still lean and lanky but no longer timid looking.

"Welcome everyone to Ludus Matutinus. I am Jovian, the head-master of this school, but more importantly, the head of animal operations for the emperor," he introduced himself. "The school is always excited to welcome new gladiators. One of my colleagues will show you the lay of the land, and later, answer any questions you may have. I have a busy day ahead of me so there is no time to waste. Now, if you will follow me, our first lesson is going to be in one of the fields." He opened the door gesturing for the gladiators to walk through.

Cato immediately realized that the outside of the building was a complete façade for what was actually in it. A giant animal farm was the only way he could think to describe it. Outside of the lobby was an open aired field filled with hundreds of animals each corralled by various fences and walls in an organized grid pattern. Cato had never seen anything like it. Jovian walked down the long-covered hall passing the animals while the gladiators kept their heads turned at each passing corral trying to take it all in.

"Through here, please," he pointed to a large, heavy wooden door. The doors opened to a large practice arena, twice as large as the one at Ludus Magnus except in the shape of a semi- circle instead of a full circle.

Cato noticed how the arena was surrounded by gates spaced every few yards. He could see the gates led to cages where he assumed they released the animals into the arena for practice.

"Please form a line inside the arena," Jovian instructed. The gladiators did as they were told.

Cato would never admit it, but he felt a little nervous inside the new school. He was used to fighting people, not animals. He hardened his face, hoping the other gladiators could not sense his nerves.

Jovian stood in front of them with his back to the straight wall of the semicircle. "Everyone wants to be a Bestiarius for the glory of the hunt," Jovian started the lesson as he paced back and forth in front of them. "They want to be like Hercules, where everyone knows your name. Well, I can tell you from firsthand experience that Hercules did not become famous overnight. He trained here and worked hard following our methods. So, before we go any further, if you do not care to follow my protocol you may leave now."

The gladiators looked at each other. No one left.

Jovian looked around seeming like he got the result he antici-pated. "Okay then, let's begin. Before you can fight a beast, you must know everything there is to know about the animal. The gods put them on this earth. They are living, breathing creatures and deserve respect for their role in our society. When it is their turn to be sacri-ficed, we thank them and send them on their way to the afterlife." He walked to the corner of the arena and reached up to pull down a wooden lever.

Cato watched as what he thought was a wall of the arena start to slide open. It was a partition. *Interesting,* he thought. The partition made the arena even larger once it opened up.

"This is my daughter, Noemi, who will be helping me with today's lesson," he gestured to one of those gates in the arena. A girl walked backward out of the gate holding onto a whip in her left hand and a long rope in her right hand. He could not see her face, but only her long brown hair which matched her father's. She was leading out a large lion. Cato couldn't believe how nonchalantly the girl acted so close to the ferocious beast.

She walked the lion into the middle of the arena and stood her ground, her back to the gladiators. With the crack of her whip, the lion began to slowly walk around her in a circle, the girl turning with the lion as it moved.

Cato had to stifle a small gasp when he recognized the girl as she turned toward them. It was the girl who had been training with the *veterani*, the one he had injured and the one he broke his façade for to help when the velarium fell.

It had been hard enough to walk away as Cato would have when the mast collapsed, but when he saw the girl pleading for help, he caved. Maybe it was the excruciating pain in his arm combined with his guilt for injuring her, but whatever the reason he could not stand to see her upset. He risked exposing his true identity to everyone. It was harder than he thought to mask one's humanity. And now here he was for a third time crossing paths with her.

Cato couldn't help but to stare, and the girl must have recognized him as well because her eyes opened wider with the slightest bit of surprise when she saw Cato. The sight of him must have rattled her because the lion started to stray from its path and move toward the gladiators. Cato watched as she jerked back the rope quickly, correcting her mistake as the lion fell back in line.

Jovian continued his lesson. "The lion. The king of the grasslands as they say. One of the animals you will face the most as a Bestiarius. Why is that you might ask? Because these animals are smart and put on a good show. And we all know that pleasing the emperor is the goal, because without the emperor, we *Bestiariis* would not exist."

Cato was half listening with most of his attention drawn to the girl. *Well, I guess that answers why she was so familiar with the hypogeum, her father runs the entire show down there.*

Jovian's voice brought Cato's attention back to the lesson. "Beware the females, they are the hunters. The males are lazy. Age is a factor as well, you can tell an old lion by the color of its mane. The darker the mane, the older the lion. Your first instinct is going to be to run. Do not run. Again, I repeat, do not run. For one thing, the lion is much faster than you are and you will just look like a cowardly fool before you are killed. So, stand still, and observe. If the lion feels threatened, its tail will swing back and forth. If it is hunting you, the tail will be rigid in place. Now, if a lion charges you, again, don't run. More than likely the charge is mockery, a ruse to test you."

Cato felt like he needed to write some of this down. There was so much information being thrown at him all at once.

As if Jovian was in his head, Cato heard him say, "Don't worry about remembering everything I say, there will be a scroll to take with you outlining all of the information from today for you to review until our next lesson. Now, before we end for the day, each of you will have one-on-one time with the lion in the arena by yourself. We are not trying to kill it, just getting a feel for what the beast is like up close. I will warn you, it is very intimidating the first time you are near it."

Cato wasn't sure how he felt about literally being thrown to the lions on the first day.

The gladiators formed a line. Cato watched as each of his classmates entered the arena and stood their ground while Jovian's daughter released the lion from the rope. The lion would either pace and charge, or just simply charge, immediately stopping in its tracks at the command of Jovian's daughter before reaching the gladiator.

Cato couldn't help himself from staring at her. She was simply beautiful enhanced by her confidence around the beast. He wanted to get to know her, actually needed to get to know her, especially after the way she handled herself when she tried to fight him.

Before he knew it, it was his turn. Jumping down into the arena, he stood at the designated mark awaiting the lion's charge just like everyone else who went before him. Cato wasn't scared. It was clear that the lion was well trained and this was a controlled lesson. He stood tall, looking the girl in her eyes. He even gave her a slight smile, egging her on.

The girl released the lion as she had done for the others. The beast paced back and forth. Cato had seen this already and knew what came next. A full-on charge that stopped with the girl's command. The lion began to charge.

Cato stood his ground waiting for the lion to stop, but the command never came. He lost his nerve as the lion raced toward him knocking him to the ground, claws digging into his shoulders he yelled out in fear. Cato tried to get out from underneath it, but the beast was too heavy and strong, pinning him to the ground. It let out a loud roar sending vibrations throughout the whole building. This wasn't supposed to happen. Somewhere between being pinned on his back and the deafening roar, Cato could hear Jovian yelling at his daughter.

A shrill whistle from the girl led the lion to release Cato from its clutches and casually meander back to her like nothing had happened.

Cato slowly stood up, dusting himself off, looking at the girl who smiled back at him and shrugged her shoulders like she didn't mean to just humiliate him in front of everyone.

12

NOEMI

Noemi's back ached as she heaved another heavy shovelful of animal feces from the stall into a large wooden cart. This was her father's punishment for her allowing Scylla, the old training lion, to pin one of his pupils to the ground. The truth was that she had lost her balance, barely recovering, when she realized that gladiator was one of her father's students. And when it was his turn with Scylla, she had to do something to stop him from smirking at her through the whole lesson. She did not want to admit it after he had sliced her leg open, but he was actually kind of growing on her and she did not hate that they kept running into each other.

The morning was long over by the time Noemi finished cleaning out the last stall. She was covered in excrement from head to toe and smelled like Pluto himself. She could have used a long hot bath but that would have to wait. Noemi wasn't the only thing that smelled in the hypogeum. The ripe stench of body odor and decay wafted throughout the caverns. She knew that could only mean the prisons were once again overcrowded. Sometimes the emperor would get arrest happy, ordering his soldiers to incarcerate anyone and everyone for dumb, minor infractions just to remind the citizens how powerful he was. That was all fine and dandy until the overflow of prisoners found their way into the small prison within the hypogeum which was not meant for piles of people to rot on top of each other.

Her father found Noemi had completed her punishment and just as she suspected he brought up the prison. "I am sick and tired of the warden cramming the cells down here. I can't tell you how many countless scrolls I have written to his majesty's overseers," he ran his fingers through his hair defeatedly, "and after weeks of bodies piling up, I finally hear back and what is the solution?" he asked himself, "a mass execution to be orchestrated by none other than me. They want more animals and more games. Individual hangings take too long apparently." He was now pacing back and forth clearly annoyed at this extra burden placed on him and his crew. "Oh, and to top it off he wants the prisons cleared today. Today!" he repeated exasperated. "I have already started moving the animals in place but could use your help."

Noemi could see her father was stressed and as much as she needed to take a bath and rest her sore arms, she agreed without complaining.

Word must have gotten out that there would be a mass execution this afternoon instead of the regularly scheduled one to two people because the arena was already quite filled up. Her father had twenty tall stakes mounted in the arena floor, about fifty feet from each other. To make it as efficient as possible, the guards would tie each prisoner to a stake. From there a signal would be given to her father's men to release the beasts who would have a feast on the twenty souls tied to the poles. The animals would then be corralled and brought back in while the grave runners would untie what was left of the bodies and remove them as quickly as possible through the tunnel of the dead. This process would be repeated with different animals each round until the cells were empty. From the looks of it, Noemi estimated there would be at least twenty rounds.

Damn the emperor, she would be here all afternoon, she thought.

Noemi walked along the corridor lining the trap doors making sure all the animals were properly secured so there would not be any premature executions among her father's men. Each animal was tethered to strong metal rings in the walls, spaced if multiple animals needed to wait, they could not get at each other.

Loud snarls and high-pitched screeches coming from farther down the corridor caused Noemi to pick up the pace. *Now what?* she thought.

Sure enough, a tiger and a hyena had their tethers tangled together allowing the tiger to take a swipe at the hyena. The hyena was less than happy, shrieking and pulling at its chain to get away. Grabbing a large spear from one of the men before they could argue with her, Noemi lunged toward the tiger swinging the blunt end of the spear like a club at the tiger's hind knees. The tiger's back legs buckled from the blow causing it to lose its balance for a few seconds allowing Noemi the time she needed to quickly attach a new tether. Without even batting an eye she cut the tangled one loose and let it fall to the ground.

"Not yet, big guy. Save it for the prisoners," she said to the tiger and handed the spear back to the man like what she just did was a piece of cake. She walked away before the men could even react, silently cursing the emperor for causing all this mayhem with his demands.

Noemi could hear the trumpeters start to play. A long, single note held for ten seconds at a time repeated ten times, signaling that an execution was taking place. Everyone in the empire knew what that note meant. She was at the tunnel entrance when the trumpeters finished. Scowling, she could see the emperor sitting on his throne in his private box without so much as a clue to what was happening below. She threw up a prayer he would be pleased with her father's last-minute display.

Next came the lone wolf running out of the door beneath the emperor's box and across the entire arena until it stopped at the entrance to the main tunnel, sat on its haunches, and howled. The wolf reminded people of the bond between this world and the next. It was the only part of the execution ritual she enjoyed. Most people thought it was the same wolf every time, but it was really one of a pack of wolves Noemi helped raise, all trained from a young age to run and howl on command. The wolf jogged past Noemi in the tunnel to its trainer who rewarded it with a handful of meat. Noemi bent down to pet the wolf, receiving a nuzzle and lick from her long-time friend.

The announcer was finishing up reading the decree of criminals. She could hear the last few lines she had heard every single day for as long as she could remember. His booming voice echoing throughout the arena. "...and for the unforgivable crimes against your city and emperor you shall pay the ultimate price. May the underworld be as cruel to you as you were to this world, and have Pluto show you no mercy."

As his voice cut off, that was the cue for the first of the animals to be released. Four large doors simultaneously opened around the arena and Noemi watched as a large rhinoceros emerged out of each door. *A smart move by Father to slow play it, draw the audience in with the suspenseful anticipation of which one will be killed first.*

To get the rhinoceroses angry, each handler prodded them in the rear side with a spear, which sends them running mad into the arena. Two immediately ran out and gored the closest prisoners with their tusk within seconds. The crowd oohed and ahhed, cringing and cheering as the rhinos continued to charge their way through the prisoners.

Another rhinoceros rammed full speed ahead at a man, only to get his tusk stuck in the pole as the prisoner was able to swing his legs up to his tied hands avoiding the blow. The crowd loved this scenario, hooting and hollering even louder. The rhino eventually worked his tusk free taking the entire pole down while the man screamed in fear. Noemi wasn't sure what actually killed him, the impact from the fall or being trampled by the rhinoceros after the fact. His body lay still, a mangled mess, his blood mixing with the sand.

The rhinos trampled throughout the arena leaving a wake of dead bodies and poles in their path. One rhino took a run at a prisoner but missed low causing the pole to be sheared in half. The prisoner was able to free himself from the binds and run toward the closest open door the beasts had entered from. The crowd, watching him flee, cheered all the more. He actually made it to the mouth of the door only to be met with guards carrying spears who blocked his escape and prodded him back in the direction of the arena. He gave chase for a surprisingly long time before he was cornered by two rhinos and gored to death.

Round one was over. Noemi thought her father very clever. The emperor probably had no idea the rhinoceroses only ate vegetation and would not actually eat the prisoners. Her father relied on them being territorial and easily spooked. This caused them to charge, making a spectacle.

With the prisoners dead, the rhinos calmed and were corralled back to the hypogeum where they would be transported back to the farm. As they left, the undertakers carted the bodies from the arena floor down through the tunnel of the dead while the grounds crew quickly set up for the next round.

Noemi watched as twenty men pushed a giant wooden cage on wheels out through the tunnel into the center of the arena. Noemi guessed the large cage was filled with close to thirty prisoners, crammed into the cage tightly, their arms and legs protruding through the spaces between the posts of the cage. The men were scrambling around inside the cage trying to escape.

It's amazing how instinct takes over and they still try to get free even though death is imminent. Impressive that Father was able to come up with another form of execution so quickly. He must be really worried about the emperor's displeasure, Noemi thought.

Again, the announcer repeated the Decree of Criminals to this new batch of men. The men cursed and spat at the emperor's box. This caused him to enjoy what was about to happen even more, smiling at the cage from the safety of his throne. The men quieted down after looking around, wondering what was about to happen.

This time only one door opened. From it ran a large pack of hyenas directly toward the cage.

Noemi was glad the hyenas weren't near her. They were notoriously hard to tame and handle. Loud cackles and howls drowned out the men's cries for mercy. The hyenas circled the cage, some even climbing on top of it taking swipes at the prisoners through the cage, drooling at their prey. Just as the crowd began to quiet a little as if disinterested at the lack of gore, the front side of the cage came unhinged and fell to the ground as it was designed to do so. Another idea her father had come up with to prolong the deaths of the prisoners a little. The men who were moments ago trying to escape the cage were now clawing at each other to get back in.

The hyenas didn't waste any time. The pack ravaged through the men. A whirlwind of blood and body parts strewn around and in the enclosure. The few who were brave enough to run did not get very far as the pack was very good at hunting stragglers.

Round two ended and Noemi was called back down to help with the tigers. For whatever reason, the tigers were very stubborn about getting on the platforms to be raised up the trap doors. Noemi liked to think it was because they were smart enough to know what was coming. She helped lay nice juicy pieces of raw meat on the platforms to lure them on. She had worked with many of the tigers and they trusted her.

Noemi did not even watch the third round or the rest of the rounds. She was so exhausted and disgusting from earlier that she would be mistaken for a prisoner if she did not get a bath soon. Her father didn't need her help anymore, the animal portion of the executions were concluded. If any prisoners remained, they would be hanged without flair.

Noemi could not wait to get home. The halls leading to the animal infirmary would be jammed with animals and people trying to get them back to the stables for the night. Normally, she would worm her way through the chaos, but she was just so tired she decided to avoid it and take the long way out of the hypogeum past the emperor's private quarters and the now emptied prison cells. *No one would be over that way,* she thought. As she walked down the corridor, she found she was correct, not a soul was over on this side.

Lethargically, she began to walk past the prison cells, her legs heavy and her mind somewhere else, when she tripped over something and fell to the ground. Before she could even attempt to stand up, two hands were around her neck choking her. Apparently, the cells had not been thoroughly checked and someone had evaded the guards, and that someone now had his hands around Noemi's neck. Noemi struggled to breathe, her attacker cursing at her while his grip on her neck tightened even more. There was not much she could do but flail her legs through the bars to try and kick him. She tried prying his hands off her neck, but his grip was too strong. *Why couldn't I have just gone home the usual way?* This ran through her head among other useless thoughts.

As she began to lose consciousness, she thought someone was running toward her, but the hypoxia was causing her to hallucinate— her last thoughts about her poor family finding her crumpled body, all dingy on the ground. Her eyes began to close as her body could not fight the man anymore without air. As her mind drifted off, a cold blast of water in her face caused her to take a giant breath, sucking in that sweet air once again, coughing and spitting up the water she had also inhaled. She was alive somehow.

Taking a second to focus on her breath, she slowly opened her eyes. Noemi jolted upright backing up against the wall in fear and surprise, her crushed windpipe the least of her concerns as she recognized her assailant gladiator standing before her, bloodied sword in his hands.

"Woah, easy tiger," the gladiator calmly said gesturing to the pair of severed hands at her feet. Noemi looked down at the bloodied hands still clasped together and their owner, who was now a corpse, stabbed through the heart and lying in the cell. It took her a minute to realize the gladiator had just saved her life.

"I did not need your help. I was a second away from breaking free from him," Noemi pathetically lied, her heart beating fast in her chest, aware of her mortifying appearance.

"Oh, I could see that," the gladiator sarcastically replied laughing at her. "It definitely looked like I did not need to chop off his hands that were strangling you while you were limp like a rag doll. I did it just for fun."

Embarrassed she needed saving by a man, especially one she was unsure about, Noemi turned to leave but caught herself on the cell bar as her legs started to give out from exhaustion.

"You might want to catch your breath a minute before you run away," he advised. "I don't think we have ever been properly introduced. I'm Cato," he said reaching his hand out to her. "And you are? ...not one for introductions, I see," he said pulling back his extended hand.

Noemi wasn't sure if it was the lack of air, but he seemed genuine, nothing like someone who would maim her. "Noemi," she answered her throat absolutely throbbing. Noemi watched as his eyes changed like he wanted to say something more but couldn't. She turned to make another attempt at leaving and this time was so light-headed her legs actually did give out.

Cato caught her mid fall. As he held her in his arms to help steady her, she couldn't help but notice his strong hands and muscular body pressed against hers. She should have pushed him away the second he touched her and hated herself that she didn't. Felix circled in the back of her mind. On top of that she let him see her in such a vulnerable state.

"I'm fine," she said again this time determined to walk away no matter what.

"Yeah, you seem it." Cato again with the sarcasm. "What? No thank you?" he asked her as she started to walk away for the third time.

Of course, Noemi was thankful he had saved her life but the last thing she wanted to do was let him know that. She was betrothed to Felix and should not be exchanging any pleasantries with other men. "I told you I..." but she couldn't get her snide remark in because the gladiator was now kissing her. She wasn't sure if it was her exhaustion, but she found herself kissing him back. Leaning into it him actually, forgetting everything she was thinking before.

As she got closer to him, Cato chuckled under his breath a little, snapping Noemi out of whatever trance she had just been in. She awkwardly peeled herself away from him.

"Uh thanks," was all she could come up with to say and turned to finally leave. It took all of her strength not to turn around and look back at him. "What just happened?" she whispered to no one. Walking back home she did not even care that she smelled rancid or was covered in dried blood and grime. She wobbled the whole way home, her knees weak and she wasn't entirely sure it was because of the attack.

13

CATO

Cato couldn't believe he had kissed her. *What was I thinking?* He could barely concentrate on his morning drills with yesterday's events replaying nonstop in his head. He had only gone down by the prison cells to make sure they were all cleared from the executions. With the sheer volume of prisoners in the colosseum, the emperor had ordered extra guards be present, and the *tiros* were given the assignment. He hadn't even recognized the girl she was so filthy, until after he had knifed the prisoner and was waiting for her to come to.

He could have left her there unconscious and she would have never known he had saved her. But Tyrian the slave started to come out in him, and he could not leave her lying there alone in a pool of blood. The fates had put them together in unlikely places these past few weeks and he was determined to find out why.

When she came to, he even tried to keep up his hard demeanor, but it just came off like he was making fun of her. And then to top it all off his inner conscience had gotten the best of him and he even started to act like Tyrian. He found himself starting to apologize for stabbing her and who knows what else would have come out of his mouth had he not kissed her. He still wasn't sure why he went with a kiss, but she surprisingly didn't resist, and it got him out of spilling his guts to her. He had hoped she was too out of it to remember how strange he was acting.

Now, in the middle of heaving boulders, she was all he could think about. His arm had pretty much healed for the most part, only a small soreness remained when he exerted it.

"Aye, Cato, put your back into it. You are throwing like a little boy," another gladiator poked fun at him.

Crap, he thought, *I need to focus.* Dialing his mind back in, he put all his effort into the next boulder heaving it well past any of the others that day.

"What was that Matteo?" he responded looking for the acknowledgment he wasn't going soft. Matteo backed off him. He needed something to take his mind off of her, that was clear. The day's drills ended, and Cato retired to his room.

Matteo walked in noticing the filth strewn everywhere. "Wow, you really are a pig, Cato."

Cato noted that at least his purposeful lack of tidiness had not gone unnoticed.

Matteo continued, "Some of us are going across town tonight for a little pick-me-up if you get what I'm saying?"

Cato knew he was referring to the not-so-secret brothels in the slave market. He truly wasn't interested but a Velarius man would jump at the chance and maybe it would help get his mind off Noemi. "Aye, let's go!" Cato jumped up from his bed anxiously acting like he couldn't wait another second to get there.

Matteo laughed, "Look at you, Cato, my boy, can't wait to see some real women, huh?"

Cato and a group of other thrill-seeking gladiators made their way to the slave market. Technically, they were not supposed to leave the school grounds after dark as they were property of the emperor and he did not want his property harmed outside the colosseum, but if they didn't get caught then no one was the wiser.

Dressed in plain white togas, they left any garb identifying them as gladiators back at the school. Gods forbid someone recognized them in that part of the city. The gladiators made their way through the poorly kept streets of the slave market stepping around filthy water that had pooled in between the uneven broken cobblestones in the poorly lit streets.

Unlike the Market of Trajan, the slave market was unfriendly and dirty. Dealing with anyone here was a risk. Merchants could spot a non-plebeian in a second and would take advantage. They were spiteful and after any sort of gain they could get, money being at the top of the list. Just being in this area made the hair on the back of Cato's neck stand up.

Matteo led the gladiators through a maze of twists and turns, down dark alleys and side streets.

He clearly was a frequent visitor in these parts, Cato thought. Cato had to give him some credit for picking a brothel so out of the way and inconspicuous that no one would recognize them here.

The entrance to the brothel was discreet. A small entry way leading down a few steps into a sunken area with nothing but a small red ribbon wound around a piece of wood to discern it from anything. Walking down the steps, Cato first noticed the smell, a mix of strong perfumes to mask the sweaty, bodily odors that filled the inside.

The madam, a pretty but weathered looking woman, greeted them at the door. Cato watched as Matteo placed some coin in an old oil jar the madam was holding before he walked past her. He followed Matteo's lead with a few coins he had won from gambling and entered the brothel.

The men found a corner table away from the other patrons where they sat on poorly made wooden couches covered with what Cato guessed had once been a plush cushion but now was nothing more than a thin, tattered piece of fabric. On the table was a vase of wine. After tasting it Cato wasn't sure it was entirely all wine but some sort of homemade swill to get the men drunk faster.

Cato could see the madam watching them from across the room.

She gave a discreet nod to the back signaling the women it was okay to approach. Three full bodied women came out of the back room. Their chests bare, with only their long blonde hair to cover themselves while their lower halves were draped with a barely there, short worn wrap. Decorative flowers adorned their heads while their lips were painted with a seductive red color. Cato noted their efforts to resemble the goddess Venus, but it was far from accurate, especially here in this low-rent brothel.

As the women emerged from behind the curtain, the gladiators began to snicker at each other in anticipation. Every move they made was meant to be seductive. A bat of the eyes here, a lift of the skirt there had the men desiring more. They worked their way around the table giving each of the men just enough attention to keep them wanting. One woman sat herself on Cato's lap, draping her arms around his neck and massaging the muscles of his arms. Up close, the woman was not in the least bit attractive. Cato could see the vast amount of scars on her face and chest which she had tried to cover with some sort of clay paste. *Surely one of many tricks of the trade,* he thought. The girl was weathered to say the least.

He watched as one woman took Matteo's money and led him to a room through the curtain in the back. The woman on Cato's lap muttered something about following her and reached for his money belt. He did not want to seem like a prude, but this grimy place was nothing at all like he had thought it would be plus he still couldn't get Noemi out of his head. He brushed her off like he wanted to give the other men a chance with her first, helping her off his lap and guiding her in the direction of the other guys.

It didn't take her long before she had Nico following her back behind the curtain. After a time, his fellow gladiators would emerge from behind the curtain with a satisfied look on their faces. Cato watched as they sat back down relaxed and began to brag about their experience. Cato realized he could only take so much. These women were nothing more than servants just like he had been with no hope of a free life. They reminded him of his former life as a slave at the Velarius villa. He could not even feign pleasure in a place like this, finding the thick scented air suddenly suffocating. He needed some air.

The madam tried to stop him as he walked out, "Not finding anything that interests you here? Maybe try the male house down the way," she suggested to him with a wink.

Cato was too claustrophobic to react to what the madam had said. Between the mix of sweet perfume and stale sweat, he just needed to breathe some fresh air.

It was late and the streets were mainly deserted save for the occasional drunkard stumbling home. He knew enough to be vigilant while in the black market. Being a larger, strong man was obviously an advantage, but being assaulted wasn't what he was worried about.

He had the creepy feeling he was being watched; the stories he had heard about these streets did not instill confidence in him. He contemplated waiting around for the guys but thought it better not to sit around giving someone a chance to recognize him. The guys would be too inebriated to miss him anyway and assume he would be in a room with one of the women.

The moon was bright, lighting the streets up and making it easier for him to make his way back to the school. Without Matteo to guide him, it was a little harder than he thought remembering which way he had come, but he managed.

It wasn't long before he could sense eyes on him. After making a few quick turns to be sure, he knew he was being followed. Instinct told him to run, but he did not know these streets and odds were, it would get him in more trouble than he had bargained for. Instead, he turned around and shouted out to the dark, empty street behind him, "Show yourself! I know you are there. Come out now!"

The street remained quiet with nothing but the sound of water dripping onto the cobblestones from the aqueduct running high above them. No one emerged and that frightened Cato even more, for what lurked in these streets was beyond what he knew. He did not have a weapon on him, and he did not want to engage any more than was necessary—gods forbid he got into a fight and the school found out. So, instead, he quickly jogged down the streets zig zagging here and there hoping to lose his tail all while trying to remember which way he was going. He stopped when he was sure he had lost whoever had been following him.

The street he found himself on was narrow and dark with very few doors. Walking farther down the dark street seemed risky so he decided to double back. Cato took a few steps and almost tripped over what looked like a pile of dirty rags. Righting himself, he meant to continue on when the pile began to move. *A beggar,* he thought.

The woman stood up as best she could her back clearly crippled causing her to hunch as she walked. "This way, boy, to hear your fortune. Special price for such a handsome boy," she said to Cato.

He knew enough that any fortune told in these parts was a scam, for the real augurs lived in the temples where the fates spoke to them. Cato looked at the woman. She was old and frail, not much of a threat and it would give him more time to throw his followers off his scent he decided. *What the heck,* he thought. Cato nodded at the woman.

"Follow me," she instructed leading Cato through a door not far from where she was posted.

Cato thought he noticed a little spring in her step upon his agreeance.

The woman hobbled up a few steps leading him into a dreary makeshift room that from the looks of it was where she lived. The room smelled of dried fragrant herbs, mainly sage and was surprisingly chilly despite the lack of windows and airflow, with only a few candles casting a dim light around the room.

"Take a seat," she gestured to a piece of dark stone she had just hastily cleaned a few of her things off of.

Clearly, she doesn't do this very often, Cato thought. Cato sat on the stone in front of a table the woman was now clearing off.

"I'll be right back," she said.

Cato sat there taking in his surroundings. The walls of her dwelling were covered in old pieces of scrolls that looked like she had collected over the years. The ink was worn, and he couldn't make out what they said without getting closer and being obvious about his snooping. There were bushels of dried herbs hanging from the ceiling and many jars, of what Cato guessed were poultices, in heaping piles around the floor. Necklaces and other baubles over flowed baskets in the other corner which Cato noted were probably stolen. He made a mental note to watch his money belt.

The old woman returned hobbling to the table holding a loud squawking chicken by the neck. She slammed the animal on the cold stone table stunning it while she snapped its neck. Its dead body wriggled on the table like its brain did not know it was dead yet.

"Payment first. Twenty *denarii*," she said as she held out her palm.

That was a little too steep of a price for a false fortune reading but Cato paid it as he could see she needed the money.

She took a bite of one of the *denarii* confirming it was real and placed the coins in her bosom. She then handed Cato a small knife gesturing at the dead chicken.

He accepted the knife and chuckled to himself as he realized that this woman was not just pretending to be a simple fortune teller but a haruspex, a person who inspected animal entrails to predict the future. *This should be amusing,* he thought. Cato took the knife and starting at the throat slit the chicken open through the belly. Blood and some of the intestines poured out with a small wave of steam rising from its still warm body against the chilled air.

The old woman first wafted the smell of the fresh blood toward her nose. Dipping her finger into it, she rubbed the blood between her thumb and first finger, putting them in her mouth to taste. "Ahhh," she started, "the blood is thick. I can see you are very strong, stronger than most."

Cato thought any fool with eyes could take one look at his physique and tell he was strong, but he let her continue.

She reached both hands into the chicken's stomach pulling out all the entrails onto the table. She ran them through her hands in a showy like manner clearly trying to make it more dramatic. "The artery connected to the heart is strong. You are close with your parents. Your family ties are substantial," she continued.

Cato really had to bite his tongue at this one. He was an orphan and his parents were dead, she wasn't even close. He just nodded his head encouraging her to continue.

She then picked up the liver squeezing it, letting it mush through her fingers. "The liver is diseased like your love life. Complicated and tragic," she said shaking her head.

Whose wasn't?

"Now this is interesting," she went on, "the kidneys are tightly intertwined almost in a knot." She looked him in the eyes this time. "It means there are two life paths for one person. You hold a deep secret. You are not who you claim to be for you were someone else in another life," she smiled as she could see the change in Cato's relaxed demeanor.

Cato tensed, his eyes widening ever so slightly at the truth to her claim. This was the first time someone had even hinted at him not really being Cato and it was unsettling. *There was no way she could possibly know that,* he thought. He didn't care to hear any more of his fortune from this false haruspex. "On second thought, I have heard enough for one night. Gratias," he thanked her as he got up to leave.

"Don't you want to hear the rest?" she inquired trying to stop him.

"Like I said," Cato answered, "I have had enough."

Cato made his way through the dark streets back to the school. If anyone was following him, he wouldn't have known because the woman's words kept replaying over in his mind distracting him from all else.

You are not who you claim to be.

14

NOEMI

Every year as the weather began to change and temperatures started to drop, the biggest shipment of animals from deep within the African continent were brought into the Northern African port of Tunis. From there, they traveled by ship across the sea to the port of Ostia on the Tiber River less than a day's journey outside of Rome. Noemi grew up watching the many ships and had seen thousands of animals unloaded throughout the years. It was one of the days she looked forward to each year.

The trip to the port could not have come at a better time. She needed a break from the hypogeum and what better way than a trip to the water.

Of course, for Noemi's father this was one of the more stressful days of the year. The inventory alone was a massive undertaking not to mention unloading and transporting these animals from the port back to Rome. Hundreds of her father's workers traveled to the port to bring in the animals.

Felix was finished loading their wagon by the time Noemi made it to the hypogeum. She was glad to spend the entire day with him. It would be good for their relationship.

She had not seen Cato in months, thank the gods, not since he had kissed her. Although she hated to admit that she kept up on how he was faring in the battles. It wasn't like she wanted anything to do with him, it just felt sort of powerful to have a little secret. She liked the rush of adrenaline she got when she thought she saw him pass by her even though it was never him. She knew she should stop keeping tabs on him and let it go, especially because she was in love with Felix and it was not fair to him.

So, the trip was the perfect thing to distract her. The caravan of Jovian's men was impressive. Different sizes of empty wagons and carts pulled by oxen and mules wove their way out of the city. Each would return loaded with various crates of beasts from the shipment. There were no special events scheduled for the hypogeum, so Jovian left only a skeleton crew to handle anything going on.

"I was thinking we should get a place close to our parents after we are married so that you have some help with the children," Felix said. They were about a few hours into the journey when Felix caught her off guard with his thoughts.

She hadn't even thought of children yet. "Woah, aren't you moving a little fast there, pal? I was planning on taking on more responsibility at the stables with my father," she replied.

Felix just laughed. "Nomee, you know it is customary to have children and raise them at home once we wed, right? What, did you think, that you would be working in the hypogeum forever? You are always pushing the limits and that's why I love you. But, no, no wife of mine will be mucking stables."

He did have a point, Noemi thought, *it would be a dishonor to him if she continued to work.* "Yeah, you're right, I will turn in my spear at once, my lord," she joked, bowing her head to him.

He rolled his eyes at her.

Noemi did not want to think about giving up the hypogeum, so she changed the subject like she always did when Felix brought up anything uncomfortable. "Now let's get back to this game of knuckle-bones. I believe I was winning." She playfully nudged him as she took her turn rolling the die. Felix must have gotten the hint because he did not bring it up again the rest of the ride.

~

The sounds of the port could be heard as they entered into the city. The squawking of the seagulls and the ringing bells from the approaching ships were a welcoming sound. The port had a totally different feel than Rome. It was massive, a city in itself with thousands of people coming and going at all times. Hundreds of ships could be seen lining the outskirts of the half-moon-shaped harbor. Every dock was full of porters unloading cargo from all over the world and loading Rome's goods to share with other kingdoms.

Noemi loved the smell of the fresh saltwater breeze and the aromas of the various goods being unloaded from the boats. Carts with olive oil, barrels of wine, and spices were being hauled by oxen up and down the docks, spreading their delicious scent throughout the wharf. Crane ropes creaked and the oxen bellowed as they pulled their cargo where it needed to go.

The port was like its own melting pot with men and women from different lands loading and unloading goods. Papyrus from Egypt, wine from Gaul, perfumes from Syria, silk from China and so much more. There were warehouses designated for each trade item for storage until the buyer could transport it to the city. It was loud, crowded, and full of confusion at times. Noemi could hear multiple languages being spoken as traders negotiated prices with each other. It amazed her how anyone could understand what was going on.

Noemi's job was to help with inventory. Animal traders loved to skimp on the inventory in the hopes the buyers wouldn't notice or if they did notice they wouldn't care because the shipping took a long time and communication was difficult as it was. Neither was the case for Jovian.

Noemi's father knew all the scams the traders ran. From raising the negotiated price and keeping an extra profit to lying about their ship sinking to collecting insurance money. Jovian had been exposed to all kinds of trickery. If the traders tried anything, they would not receive their full payment and their name would be run through the mud never to trade with the empire again. That's how big Jovian had become in the trading world.

"See you later, my love," Felix said as he kissed the top of her head and went down to the docks to help handle the beasts.

"Be careful," she shouted after him. She watched him hop a barge to the ships waiting at the mouth of the port. Although she had never actually seen it, she had heard that the heavier ships bottomed out and got stuck if they tried to navigate the shallow port. Handlers like Felix had to move the beasts via a barge to get them safely to the docks.

Noemi did not envy the transport team that had to load the animals onto the barges. The animals could be quite unpredictable after being cooped up for such a long period of time. Each barge had a fence enclosing it so the animals that were too big to fit in crates could not walk or jump off into the water. It would be a shame for the beasts to make it through the journey only to drown after falling off the boat. Even with the muzzles for the biters, blinders for the anxious, and weighted tarps for the fidgety, there was no guarantee there would not be an incident. She just hoped that Felix would be okay.

It wasn't long before she saw the first of the barges returning from the ships. She could see the large wooden crates weighing down the flatboat, the water crashing over the sides as it slowly made its way to the dock.

The animals were starting to be unloaded and Noemi stood at the top of the dock, manifest in hand, awaiting to triage the animals. The care of the beasts during the trip was subpar at best, with most animals not receiving fresh water or food for days at a time. Sometimes the animals hurt themselves on the ship and had to live with their injuries for the two-month-long journey.

She approached the first crate. Before the porter even opened it, she could tell by the smell that the crate housed anteaters, their odor was far worse than a skunk, absolutely putrid. Noemi did not even want to open the crate. Burying her nose in her tunic trying to hold her breath, she peered over the edge of the crate to count twenty-five anteaters, two with large gashes on their elongated noses presumably from fighting. Noemi documented the anteaters and instructed that the injured two be taken to get cleaned up. Superficial injuries were bandaged and the animals were safe to make the journey to Rome the same day. She tied a green string around the crate clearing it for transport to Rome.

The next crate was larger and whatever was inside was squawking loudly. The porter opened the crate containing ostriches, Noemi's favorite animal. One was lying down with a clear broken limb. Noemi cursed the African porters for cramming them into the crate like that. The poor thing was crying out in pain. If a limb was broken and the animal could not walk, the animal was moved to the stables in the warehouse where the appendage was set and would be transported at a later date when it could bear its own weight. Noemi couldn't get too close by herself. Besides having powerful legs, they would attack with their beaks and long necks, something she found out the hard way years ago.

The animal handlers removed one ostrich at a time from the crate and placed a long harness on each of their backs to walk them back to the storehouse. The injured one would have to be carted to the stables.

Noemi motioned for the handlers and made her notes on the inventory marking the crate with a red string signifying the delay in transport.

The next crate smelled and not in a good way. It was the smell of death, Noemi's least favorite part of this job. The second the crate was opened, a ghastly odor was released into the air causing anyone near it to gag. Inside was a dead hippopotamus. The body had begun to decay so she knew it had been dead for at least a week or two. Unfortunately, this happened frequently with animals that primarily lived in water. The crates were specially designed with a bottom to hold water but many leaked and since the animals were not checked on once they were loaded on the boat many dried up and died. She noted it on the inventory sheet and tied a black string on the crate.

Noemi checked in crate after crate until there were no more left and it was time for the bigger beasts to be hauled in. She watched an elephant tentatively take its first step off of the barge—the barge almost bouncing out of the water as it was relieved of the elephant's enormous weight. The handler riding atop its back expertly guided it up the ramp safely to the dock where it was immediately hitched to a large wagon to haul back to Rome.

Noemi watched a few more large animals exit the barges, like lions and tigers that were led with ropes and baited with meat, a job she wanted but knew her father would never assign her.

The day was winding down and most of the animals had been moved to the storehouse or loaded for the trek back to Rome. Noemi's father was tying up a few loose ends with some of the traders.

Overall, the inventory had gone well for Noemi. She had minimal dead animals and minor injuries logged. As she went to give her report to her father, a blood curdling scream rang out from the docks. Noemi whipped around to see what had happened.

A leopard had somehow gotten loose from the ropes and ran up the ramp into the crowd. It didn't make it far before it attacked a sailor awaiting to board a vessel. Pinning the man down, he stood no chance as the leopard began tearing him limb from limb, gnawing on him like the starved creature it was.

The people on the dock near the sailor were screaming and running in fear hoping to not be its next victim. The porters responsible for the leopard were trying to lasso it while it ate, but the leopard was too quick and too smart. It was finally free of that ship and it was enjoying itself.

The leopard moved on farther down the dock, leaping over any obstacle in its way as the porters chased after it. Noemi's father was yelling at anyone who would listen to help capture the leopard. Some people had even jumped off the dock into the water in fear.

Now the leopard had a woman cornered in an alley. She screamed for help as she tried to scale the wall behind her to get away from the beast, but it was no use. The leopard had sunk its teeth into her and she was dead before anyone could get to her.

It continued to make its way farther down the dock. Her father's handlers had tried to block its path, but it only jumped over buildings to get around them. People ahead in its path had gotten the message one way or another about the danger and many had taken shelter.

Noemi and some of the brave crowd had started to follow the leopard at a distance to see what was happening. She had not seen Felix since this morning and hoped he was back at the storehouse out of harm's way. At this point, Jovian had no choice but to give the order to kill the animal as casualties were involved. However, even that was proving to be difficult. Jovian's men had surrounded it multiple times, grazing it with a spear but to no avail. The leopard was too fast and determined to avoid capture again. The men continued the chase all the way to Monte Testaccio, the giant one-hundred-foot hill piled full of discarded amphoras. If the leopard got over it, it would be free for sure.

There was nothing behind the large hill but open land where it could do as it pleased and Jovian would be held responsible for the casualties not to mention the loss of one of the emperor's playthings. As Noemi and the crowd got closer to Monte Testaccio, she could smell the vile odor coming off the discarded oil amphoras and she had to stop herself from gagging.

The leopard had started its ascent up the hill, broken amphoras falling down into the street as it climbed. Jovian's men tried to climb up after it getting covered with old oil and lime covered pots. The shards of the amphoras were sharp, cutting the leopard's paws as it climbed. It slowed as it made its way halfway up, its injuries stalling escape. If it weren't for the danger of a leopard on the loose in the city, Noemi would have secretly rooted for its successful liberation. Instead, she was rooting for its quick death to end this nightmare for her father's men.

As the leopard lay down, licking its wounds, Noemi gasped as she saw Felix emerge at the top of the hill armed with a spear. He leapt off the side of the hill, sliding down the mountain of amphoras until he came crashing into the leopard spear first. The leopard, along with everyone else watching from below, never saw it coming. Felix kicked the body the rest of the way down the hill where the handlers would dispose of it.

Noemi ran to the base of Monte Testaccio as Felix nonchalantly walked down the path. She jumped into his arms not caring he was covered in lime and oil and smelling like Pluto himself. "Oh, thank the gods you are all right!" Noemi exclaimed. "You could have been killed," she kissed him on the lips not caring that she had an audience.

"Eh, I thought my skin could use a quick oil treatment," he joked.

Noemi could taste the spoiled oil on her lips. "Not funny," she replied.

The wagons were loaded with all the crates they could hold ready to be transported back to Rome. The trip had been a success. Noemi resumed her position back in Felix's arms as they rode back home. This time with the additional cacophony of thousands of beasts that joined them.

15

CATO

Cato found that betting on the chariots was something he looked forward to on a weekly basis. After that first time in the underground gambler's den, he realized he had to find something more legitimate so not to ruin his reputation. After attending his first chariot race, he found he could bet on the chariots right at the Circus Maximus, not having to risk the back alley world of gladiator betting to win a few coins. It was nice to watch someone else compete and not always be the one in the spotlight. Also, he did like it when his chariot won.

Walking back through the streets after a profitable morning at the track, he basically tripped over a ratty old vagabond woman with a long ribbon braided into her hair.

"Apologies," he told her as he tried to help gather her dirty coin pot he had displaced. The woman screeched like a banshee flailing her arms in the air causing a huge scene. Cato did not want to let this ruin his day, so he threw his arms up in the air surrendering and walked off.

It was only once he was back in his room that he noticed he had been fleeced of his winnings from the track. Cato sworn under his breath, "That damn woman."

He didn't have much time to stew over his lost money for the gong was ringing signaling an assembly. The headmaster was waiting for them as the men took their seats in the practice arena.

"Men," Magistro Cicero began, "I have an unprecedented treat in store for you tonight." There was mild pompous nudging and hollering between some of the gladiators as he continued.

"Okay, Okay," he tried to quiet them down, "The emperor is hosting a banquet this evening for some very prominent rulers from other empires. He has requested the presence of his gladiators at the banquet to give them a little flavor of what goes on at the colosseum. It is very rare to get an invitation such as this for students so early in your careers." That got everyone's undivided attention.

"You are not only representing yourselves as gladiators but this school as well. I expect you to act accordingly. Please visit the baths and make yourselves look presentable. Your tunics must be clean and your hair groomed. If I deem anyone unpresentable you will remain behind. We leave here at nine. Dismissed." Cicero ended his announcement and exited the practice arena to prepare himself for the night's dinner.

The headmaster's warning was not lost on anyone. Everyone wanted to make a good impression on the emperor. Being in the emperor's good graces was one step closer to making it as one of the most well-known gladiators. *Wasn't that what everyone was fighting each other for?* Cato thought. Well at least that's what he wanted, and he was thrilled for this opportunity.

Not only was every single one of the men presentable, but every single one was on time. This was a once-in-a-lifetime invitation. The walk to the palace wasn't far from the school. The men followed in line up Palatine Hill to the gates of the palace grounds.

Cato marveled at the vast gardens leading up to the gate. Running water could be heard in the various fountains centered in almost all of the gardens, a luxury he had only heard of but never seen. The moon light reflected off the water illuminating parts of the gardens. It was peaceful and smelled of wealth. The headmaster led the men to the gate where he showed his paperwork to the guards. The gates were opened, and everyone was gathered into the foyer.

"Wait here," one of the guards told them. Cato looked around. The room was centered around a large rectangular pool with a fountain in the shape of Neptune in the middle. Exotic, brightly colored fish swam in the immaculate pool. Detailed mosaics covered the walls, floor, and ceiling. Cato had never seen such excess in all his life, and they were only just in the foyer.

An older woman dressed in a crisp toga with a blue stola entered the atrium carrying a scroll in her hand.

"Welcome gladiators. I am Saya, one of the emperor's advisers. Before I escort you to the main dining area, I want to go over a few key rules." At this, she unrolled her scroll and began to read, "Rule number one: You will remain quiet during dinner. You are not to speak as you are property of the emperor and here to be shown off. Your headmaster will speak for all of you if addressed. Rule number two: Do not make eye contact with the emperor. You are his guests, not his equals. Rule number three: Anything you hear tonight is confidential. There will be other guests of the emperor dining with you and conducting important business with him. Whatever you hear is not to be repeated whether you deem that information to be of value or not. Failure to adhere to any of these rules will get you an execution date tomorrow afternoon. No exceptions." Saya ended her reading and looked up from the scroll. She must have seen the looks on everyone's faces because she then said, "Look on the bright side, you get to eat a fancy dinner in a palace with the emperor himself and rub elbows with some elite leaders. As long as you follow the rules you will live to finish your studies. Enjoy fellas." At that she rolled up her scroll, gold bracelets jangling against each other on her wrists. "Please, follow me."

Flanked by two guards, Saya led them through dozens of what seemed like endless corridors. Each decorated with a different motif. Some corridors, Cato noticed, had paid their respects to various gods while others were ornately decorated with wall paintings. One corridor had wall paintings of the emperor's family. His wife, parents, his many favored ladies, his pets, and a blank space on the wall for an heir which was noticeably missing.

Saya paused outside the door to the main dining room. Turning to address the gladiators she said, "Here we are. When I open the door please maintain a single file line along the far wall of the room until the Emperor acknowledges you and asks you to be seated. At that time, you may make your way to your seats. You have five tables assigned to your group designated by black cushions. Remember the rules at your own risk. Welcome to the palace."

At that the guards opened the doors and Saya left them to enjoy the dinner. Cato was not sure what he expected to see, but the dining room was ten times larger than he could have ever imagined. At least fifty tables surrounded a grandiose table in the center of the room. Each table was loaded with food and pitchers of wine and surrounded by couches with various cushion colors. Hundreds of other guests were already seated indulging in the cuisine. Bronze candelabras lit the room, wax dripping on the ground from the candles suspended from the ceiling. The room smelled incredible, like warm savory spices with a hint of red wine. Soft music could be heard from women playing the lyre.

Laying on a gilded couch adorned with bright purple fabric at the head table, the Emperor was being fed by one of his many slaves. Scantily clad women danced around him giving Cato an unpleasant flashback to the brothel. The men stood against the wall waiting for the emperor's cue. He did not seem to be in any rush to acknowledge his new guests.

Cato could single out the leaders from other empires Saya had mentioned based on their outlandish outfits. Strange silk dresses and hats, and a man with his face made up like that of a woman engaged the emperor in conversation at his table. After watching the emperor devour an entire roast peacock and drink multiple goblets of wine, the gladiators remained still and silent as he finally got up to address them.

The music came to a stop and everyone was silent as the emperor spoke.

"Tonight, I have invited our empire's fiercest gladiators to dine. Feast your eyes on the bravest and strongest of Rome," he said motioning for the men to be seated. Those guests who had their backs to the wall turned to admire the men as they took their seats.

Cato was careful not to look directly at the emperor. He made sure he did not look anywhere near him while he was talking which led his eyes to wander around the room helping him avoid the temptation. Sitting down on the black couch, he looked up and his heart skipped a beat. A few tables in front of him directly in his line of sight was Noemi. As she had turned around to see the gladiators, he locked eyes with her and gave her a little knowing smirk. Her eyes widened in surprise and she snapped back to facing the table. With her back to him, she immediately engaged the man next to her in a dramatic conversation.

Cato chuckled to himself. He guessed she might have been betrothed after he did not see her again in the hypogeum. It figures that the only girl in the empire who had piqued his interest would be spoken for. It didn't matter anyways because he was not allowed to have a relationship while he belonged to Ludus Magnus and the emperor. No unwanted distractions as they say. At least he had something beautiful to stare at the rest of the dinner.

The men at his table dared not speak a word, not even to each other. The fear of the emperor was real and they all knew it. They had removed their sandals upon sitting. Slaves were assigned to each table waiting with a warm bowl of water to wash their feet so as not to dirty the couches they lay on. The spread in front of Cato was enormous. Delicacies he had only heard of, flamingo tongue, stewed snails, dormice dipped in honey and rolled in sesame seeds, camel heels, oysters, plus the lion's share of fruits, cheeses, meats, olives, and wine covered the table in abundance. Cato, along with all the other men, dug in, not wasting any time.

The gluttony of it all was not lost on Cato. He watched as the gladiators tried their best not to indulge too much as the headmaster kept looking over from his table. Their mouths were so full there was never any risk of their speaking. Cato couldn't help but focus his attention on the slaves. He wondered if any of them were like him and longed for something more, or if they were content to live in the palace, a lottery in the slave world.

The intensity of the music began to increase and the guests looked around wondering what it meant. Without warning, the large doors to the dining room opened and a wild boar ran into the dining room being chased by hunting dogs. Cato's first instinct was to run as he had dealt with boars back at the villa and knew how dangerous they could be. He was glad he hesitated because all the other guests seemed to somehow know the boar was part of the dinner and he would have made a complete fool of himself.

The boar made it to the center of the room where the dogs circled it keeping it from running away into the crowd. Then, men dressed in hunting garb consisting of tall boots and woolen tunics decorated with tapestry-woven bands with bows on their backs holding large spears entered the dining room, marching to the beat of the music. Their faces were painted with symbols of the moon and stars, a tribute to the hunting goddess, Diana. Chanting and grunting, the men formed a circle around the dogs.

Cato watched intently. They were hunting in the dining room of the palace. *This was insane.*

The huntsmen performed a tribal dance pumping their arms and chanting in rhythmic tones as they circled their prey. A shrill whistle from the one of the men stopped the others dead in their tracks before they attacked and killed the boar with their spears. Blood sprayed the men and the dogs like paint being splattered. The huntsmen placed the boar's body on a wooden stretcher parading it around the dining hall for all to see their prize kill.

Cato had to stop himself from dropping his jaw on the floor. He could see he was not the only one impressed by the spectacle. Four men then raised the stretcher in the air while the rest of the men moved to the outskirts of the room. The music changed to intense rhythmic drumming, two notes played repeatedly. One huntsman drew a long sword raising it to the crowd for all to see and slashed the belly of the dead boar.

Cato could see the stomach of the boar begin to move. *Impossible,* he thought for the boar was clearly dead.

The wound began to open and out flew dozens of fowl shrieking as they escaped their warm-blooded prison. No sooner had the birds been set free, the huntsmen that had moved to the outskirts of the room had drawn their bows. Following another chant, in a split second, each bird was simultaneously shot with an arrow. As fast as they fell, the birds didn't even hit the ground. The dogs caught them in mid air swiftly returning them to the huntsmen. The dead birds were scooped up so quickly that the few stray feathers floating in the air were the only proof of what had just happened. The guests cheered and hollered in excitement, standing and clapping for the huntsmen, even the emperor looked amused. The huntsmen fell into line and marched out of the dining room carrying their prey and with the dogs at their heels.

Cato watched as Noemi cheered along with everyone else. She must have felt his eyes on her again for she looked at him then averted her eyes back to her own table.

The men ate and drank more than their fill. There was more entertainment throughout the evening, although how anything could top the boar Cato did not know. The emperor's harem performed a seductive dance leaving every gladiator struggling not to make eye contact with the women or the emperor. Jesters came in and out making everyone laugh with their tomfoolery. There were even actors hired to pretend to be gladiators fighting in the colosseum. Between the wine and the music, Cato was in a happy mood, mostly from the wine.

At the end of dinner, guests were allowed to mingle. Mostly because the emperor was now drunk and the rules seemed to have laxed. The gladiators, still scared to engage in any sort of conversation with the threat of execution looming over their heads, remained seated. Upbeat music played and some guests were dancing to familiar songs.

Cato saw Noemi laughing and dancing with the man she came with. Her father Jovian also on the dance floor with who Cato assumed was Noemi's mother. He knew he needed to stop with the wine when he couldn't help but think of what it would be like to dance with Noemi. He pictured himself holding the small of her back while he whisked her around the dance floor, her infectious smile beaming back at him. Visions of him kissing her in the hypogeum flooded back to him. A twinge of jealousy began to mount, and he needed to excuse himself from the table.

He couldn't watch Noemi any longer without the wine trying to make him do something he would regret. He wandered out to one of the gardens to get a breath of fresh air and let the wine stupor wear off a bit. He noticed some of the other guests, including a few gladiators, had the same idea. The moon was bright, lighting up the gardens and the air crisp as Cato inhaled the freshness. He ran his fingers through the water of the fountain fascinated by how it was able to move. Sitting on a bench, he leaned back looking up at the sky thinking about the future and how he needed to keep his focus to become one of the top gladiators.

Lost in his thoughts, he almost didn't notice Noemi sitting alone in the far end of the garden. Her back was to him and she was sitting on a mossy stained marble bench staring at the stars. He knew he shouldn't, but he couldn't help himself from making contact with her, the wine giving him a little extra courage.

Cato came up behind her so as not to scare her. He didn't know what he was going to say, but had this compulsion to talk, being completely drawn to her. Suppressing the voice in his head warning him about blowing everything he had worked so hard for, he walked toward her.

"I see we can't stop running into each other?" he said. *Smooth,* he thought, embarrassed by how he came off.

At the sound of his voice, Noemi jumped and turned her head to look at him.

"You again," she replied in disgust. "Can't you take a hint." And she turned her back on him.

This wasn't what he had envisioned her response would have been. She was clearly not interested in him and not afraid to let him know it. "Well, it's good to see that you are still alive since you can't seem to refrain from a life of peril," he tried to be humorous. He wanted so much for her to give him something more than a cold shoulder. A look or smirk, anything.

She just looked at him annoyed and responded, "Can you just leave me alone? Why don't you go bother someone else?"

He wasn't sure what he was trying to accomplish here except he felt the overwhelming need for her to like him and bothering her was not the way to get that done. So instead, he bent down to whisper in her ear, "see you around." He had meant it to be sweet maybe even flirtatious, but he just felt like a creep. *Ugh*, he thought, *why was he being so awkward?*

Noemi did not even turn to look back at him, making him wish he had listened to himself and not tried to risk anything since it was all for naught. He needed to get back to the dining room anyways, he had been gone a little too long. As he headed back inside, he saw what he assumed was her boyfriend milling around the entryway to the garden. Cato nodded to him as he walked by, a surprising urge somewhere deep inside him wanting to fight the guy, but that wasn't the battle he needed to worry about tonight.

16

NOEMI

The dinner at the emperor's palace had been nothing short of awful. Noemi had been thrilled at first when her father had told her that all of the emperor's top men and their families were invited to a special dinner. She even borrowed one of Livia's fancy togas she found hidden in her room.

The night had started out great. She was excited Felix was able to go with her and they were having fun as her father's guests. But then, the gladiators walked in and she spotted Cato and the night changed. Her thoughts were immediately brought back to the kiss and as much as she tried to pretend she had not been rattled by seeing Cato again after all that time, she was not successful.

Felix had noticed something was off about her and was not buying her story that she did not feel well. He demanded to know why she was acting so strange and Noemi dared not say. So instead, they fought the whole night. Of course, when she went outside to get away from Felix for a minute, Cato just happened to find her. She felt bad about being so short with him, but she found her heart racing just from hearing his voice and she needed him to leave before Felix came out to find her and saw them together. The night could not have ended any faster for her. But it was behind her now, and she and Felix were in a good place.

~

The season had started to change, you could feel it in the air. The dog days of the Roman summer had ended, and the harvest season was upon them. Noemi was glad to be a few months closer to her wedding.

There was a scrap of torn parchment paper lying on the windowsill of Noemi's room when she woke up. From her bed, she could see her name written at the top of the paper. Fresh off a fun romantic night with Felix, she leapt out of bed excited to see what he had written her. She hoped it was another scavenger hunt.

Meet me outside the dead tunnel at high noon.

–C

P.S. you aren't so tough when you are asleep.

Noemi dropped the letter like it was on fire. Any butterflies she had had lingering from last night with Felix were gone in an instant.

The letter wasn't from Felix, it was from Cato. And he knew where she lived. He had seen her sleeping. *And in my tunic no less,* Noemi thought. For the sake of her betrothal to Felix and for her own mental sake, she had pushed him out of her mind since that night she last saw him at the palace. But now that anxious feeling in the pit of her stomach was back.

"What's that?" Livia said, walking into her room.

Noemi quickly threw the parchment in the hearth feeling like a criminal destroying evidence. "None of your business. Shouldn't you be at the palace scrubbing floors?" Noemi replied.

"It doesn't look like nothing. Might it have something to do with that gladiator I saw you talking with at the palace?" Livia said, a knowing smile on her face.

Noemi couldn't hide her surprise, her entire body tensing as the panic bubbled up inside her.

Livia, sensing she hit a nerve, kept on. "I kept my distance from the dining room that night, obviously not wanting to run into Mother and Father, and happened to see you in the gardens with a very handsome gladiator whispering in your ear."

Noemi did not feel she owed her sister any explanation. "I don't know what you are talking about."

"I wonder if Felix would be interested in knowing what goes on behind his back?" Livia threatened.

Noemi did not think she would really tell Felix anything. He wouldn't believe her anyway since she was always stirring up trouble. Now it was Noemi's turn to catch her sister off guard, "Mother and Father are starting to get suspicious about your whereabouts. I might have implied that you had taken up residence at a certain brothel on the outskirts of the city," she lied, knowing that would scare her a bit.

"You wouldn't," Livia said, her face hardening with anger.

Noemi just shrugged her shoulders in reply, not confirming or denying anything. It worked, because Livia stormed off to find her mother to try and clear things up, completely dropping the subject of Cato.

With Livia gone, Noemi turned her attention back toward the hearth. As she watched the note burn, aside from the obvious questions of how he knew where she lived and how he knew where her room was, Noemi couldn't help but wonder what he wanted. It had been months since she had seen him and now, he was back on her mind again. She felt guilty for even having any sort of feelings toward him. As the last of the parchment turned to ash, she took a deep breath and pushed all thoughts of Cato aside.

Felix met her at the forum later that morning. She leapt into his arms as he planted a hunger-stricken kiss on her lips. Those butterflies crept back in Noemi's stomach. Felix twirled her around and laughed as he set her down.

"Aren't you a sight for sore eyes," he grinned, "I don't have much time. I have to drop off this scroll to one of the senators. Something about trying to get more animals shipped in from the south. See you for the evening fight?" he asked.

Bummed that they couldn't spend the morning together, Noemi

answered, "I wouldn't miss it!" She kissed him again—reactivating those butterflies—and said goodbye.

Noemi ran a few errands the rest of the morning and found herself aimlessly wandering the city. There were tons of shipments today which meant tons of carts clogging up the main roads. She took a few back alleys and zig zagged her way back to the colosseum. She followed the stench of the dead being piled outside the tunnel and knew she was close.

The gongs rang in the distance calling out the noon hour. As the last sound of the gong echoed into the distance, Noemi found herself at the tunnel of the dead at high noon. Recalling the note from this morning and laughing to herself, she turned to go in the opposite direction to avoid Cato. She hadn't taken but one step away from the tunnel when she heard a shrill whistle. Noemi instinctively turned around and instantly wished she hadn't. Emerging from the shadows of the colosseum like a serpent was Cato. Everything in her body told her to turn and walk away but one small part of her wanted to know what he wanted. Curiosity got the best of her and she locked eyes with him.

"Well, well, well," Cato said. "I thought it would be much harder than this to get you to accept a date with me."

"A date?!" Noemi responded in disbelief. "Don't flatter yourself, I wasn't planning on actually meeting you. I just need to get into the hypogeum through this tunnel." She rolled her eyes and began to walk away.

"Yet here you are," he said with a smirk. "Come, I have a surprise for you."

"On second thought I'd rather not," she said, her sarcasm could not be any more obvious. *What am I even still doing here?*

Cato stepped even closer to her reaching for her hand. She pulled it back. Again, he took a step toward her reaching for her arm. This time firmly grabbing it and with a smile said, "I'm not asking."

Noemi wanted to scream, she really did, but it was like one of those dreams where you scream and scream and no matter how hard you try no sound comes out. She found herself half being dragged half following him through the alleys of the city.

"Where are we going?" she asked him again and again. "You can't just grab me and drag me through the streets."

"Will you relax?" he finally responded. "We are here."

Noemi stopped walking and looked up. They were outside the tall, gilded gates of Circus Maximus where daily chariot races were held.

"Why are we here?" her voice nothing short of displeasure.

"Whoa, easy, you could have walked away at any time, you know. But you didn't," he chuckled at her.

He was right, she thought. He really had only held her hand guiding her through the streets, and she could have easily let go. But she didn't.

"I haven't run into you in a while and wanted to make sure you did not need any more saving. Plus, I had an extra ticket to the races today and thought maybe you would like to go," he said.

"Was I not clear at the palace? I am not interested," she replied.

Cato laughed again. "And, yet, here you still stand."

Noemi had never been to a race before. Of all the animals, horses were in a league of their own. They had the best trainers and care of any animal in the empire, something Jovian was not a part of. The last thing she wanted to do was experience the races for the first time with someone other than Felix. There was no real reason why she had never seen a chariot race before. It was one of those things that had been on her list to do but just never got around to it.

"Look. You don't even have to talk to me. Deal?" he said.

Noemi weighed her options. On one hand, she wasn't sure what Cato really wanted with her and was nervous to be seen with him. On the other hand, she always wanted to see a race and she was literally standing at the gates with an invitation to go in. She didn't even have to interact with him.

A crowd of people began rushing through the gates trying to get in before the race started. Noemi and Cato got swept up in the crowd moving them in through the gates.

Well, I guess that's decided, she thought. *I just won't talk to him or look at him.* If anything happens, she could always leave. It wasn't like she was being held captive.

Once inside the gates, Noemi looked around. The Circus Maximus was bigger than she had thought. Much bigger than the colosseum. A large, long oval track anchored the center of the arena. It was covered in sand just like the colosseum floor, except raked pristinely in a neat pattern. From there, stadium seating went all the way around the oval so every seat had a good view. Even though Noemi was only a few minutes walk from the colosseum, she felt like she was in another empire. The energy was different, happier almost, without the looming threat of death hanging over them like a cloud.

Cato pulled her along to a seat in the stands in the middle of the arena in a gentle, yet assertive way. The people were a little pushy and she was secretly glad he was holding on to her. She may have even leaned into him on purpose.

Their seats were pretty close to the track, so much so that Noemi wondered if the gladiators got preferential treatment when they visited other venues in the empire. She could tell Cato was being cautious, taking his cues from her as he sat there not saying anything. She sat next to him and that was about it.

She was so excited, taking everything in now that she was finally a spectator at Circus Maximus. Thousands of people were awaiting the race, most of them dressed in the color of their team. Some even had colored wax smeared on their faces to show support for their favorites. Red, blue, green, and white flags and banners filled the stadium. Chants and cheers supporting the teams echoed throughout the stadium. The emperor was in his box today, high above the crowds dressed in green for his favorite team, the Stallones, which she had read on multiple banners in the crowd.

Noemi was so enthralled with the atmosphere she didn't even give a thought to how she got here or who was beside her. Mouth agape, she continued to look around to figure out how everything worked. Twelve charioteers each with two horses were taking their pre-lap trot. There were three chariots per team. Each chariot along with their horses were adorned with their team colors. The horses' manes were dyed and braided with the corresponding ribbon colors. Banners were draped around the chariots. Even the plume of the charioteer's helmet was colored so there was no mistaking which team they were on.

Betting was going on all around them. Noemi could hear all sorts of wagers. "Ten quid for green," "Six on white" and others like that.

"Care to place a little wager?" Cato asked her, interrupting the silence. His voice broke the spell the Circus Maximus had on a newbie like her. She just scoffed in return not answering.

"No? Okay. I've got all my money on red today. Poe the driver is a friend of mine," Cato said.

Noemi continued to ignore him as he rambled on about his wagers and the odds. It was clear he came here often. Her focus went back to the track. In the middle of the oval was a long, tall barrier with three pillars equidistant on each end. It almost cut the track in half lengthwise but didn't, stopping just short of the ends to leave room for the chariots to go around. She wondered what it was for but didn't dare ask.

Cato must have followed her gaze and noticed the confusion on her face because he said, "That middle divider is the *spina*. The three columns that look like Cyprus trees on each end are where the chariots round the corner. The columns also protect the barrier from the chariots running into them and the ditch around the outside of the track protects the crowd from crashes."

Noemi pretended she was not interested in his knowledge but hoped he would continue as she was fascinated by the intel.

He did.

"See the figures lined up on the two crossbars of columns on either end. That's how you know how many laps remain. After each lap, an egg is removed and a dolphin is flipped over."

Sure enough, Noemi saw on one side of the *spina* there were seven golden eggs lined up on a tall slab of white marble while on the other side there were seven dolphin figures lined up in the same fashion. She knew the dolphins were a tribute to Neptune who was a patron of horses and figured that the eggs were a tribute to Castor and Pollux, patron saints of Rome who were said to be born from eggs.

Each charioteer donned a leather ensemble. They had leg and arm protectors, a mesh corset covering their ribs with a colored tunic draped over the corset to represent their team, and a bronze helmet. Noemi noticed the similarities to the gladiator garb except the charioteers were flashier with colored gems bedazzling their helmets and plumes of feathers adorning their heads. The chariots themselves looked like nothing more than a small wooden platform to stand on with a high waist guard that came around the front and sides all sitting on two spoked wheels. Each chariot had two horses hitched to it. Each driver carried only a leather whip.

Noemi watched the charioteers as they entered their respective twelve gates at the starting line marked by white chalk drawn on the sand. Two statues of Mercury flanked the gates each statue holding a chain which she could see kept the horses in their stalls. Trumpeters played a three-note salute, then someone she assumed was a magistrate dropped a bright yellow cloth into the sand signaling the beginning of the race, and the starter released the chain holding the horses in. They were off. It all happened so quickly she found herself jumping up with the rest of the crowd to see.

The crowd roared, yelling and waving their flags. The horses were so majestic to Noemi. Their strong muscles glistening in the sun as they ran down the track, sand flying up behind their hind legs. All twelve chariots were on an even keel approaching the first turn. As they rounded the turn, two chariots careened out of control and were thrown into the wall. Fragments of the chariots flew everywhere, and the charioteers were tossed to the ground while the horses neighed in protest still tethered to what remained of the chariots. The two drivers scrambled to pull themselves and their horses off the track before they got trampled. Both made it, scurrying through one of the numerous gates around the track.

As the chariots completed the first lap, Noemi watched as a man climbed a tall ladder to remove an egg from the marble pillar. Laps two, three, and four were uneventful. As the fourth dolphin was flipped over, a green chariot purposely collided with a white chariot causing both to overturn. The white charioteer was able to get off the track safely while the green charioteer was dragged down the track by the horses, for the reigns had been tied to his hands.

Noemi gasped.

Cato, noticing her discomfort said, "Don't worry, watch."

The green charioteer was being dragged so hard it was no wonder he didn't lose a limb. Just when she thought he was going to get trampled by the rest of the chariots turning the corner behind them, he pulled a small knife from the leather arm protector and feverishly cut away at the reins until they severed. The horses kept running, the chariot long since smashed on the side, and the green charioteer hobbled his way off the track.

Noemi was clutching the seat in front her, she was so nervous for the charioteer. Out of the corner of her eye, she could see Cato laughing at her reaction. She kept her eyes forward.

The race continued. Only four chariots were left now, two blues, a red and a green. Noemi was impressed with the crew that ran out from the *spina* to remove the chariot debris before the remaining racers lapped. A few times some of the wheels even caught fire after a crash. The first time it happened she thought the whole place would go up, but she watched as a group of slaves with buckets of water expertly ran out on the track dodging chariots to extinguish the flames and remove the debris.

The final lap was here. The two blue chariots got on either side of the red chariot and pinned it between them. The red charioteer seemed calm, too calm for Noemi's nerves as it looked like there was no way he could win. As they hit the home stretch, the red charioteer reached for his knife and cut his horses loose.

"What is he doing?" Noemi yelled into the crowd, her voice lost among the thousands. The horses, now free of the weight of the chariot galloped ahead of the rest and ran across the finish first. The crowd erupted, red banners and flags being tossed onto the arena floor.

What just happened? Apparently only the horses needed to cross the finish line, the charioteer did not. That was all she could think of without bringing herself to ask Cato. He was on his feet, standing on the bench clapping and whistling for the red team. Noemi found herself cheering too, it was hard to suppress her excitement after such an exhilarating race.

Upon winning the race, the horses were draped with blankets of palm leaves and the red charioteer was given a crown of palms, money, and gold necklaces. She clapped even louder as the red charioteer passed by her during his victory lap. Her eyes then rose to the emperor in his box who was sure to be upset his team had lost. As expected, he was yelling and stomping around madder than a wet hen. Noemi laughed at the sight of him.

Some fans trickled out while others planned to stay and see the next race. As much as Noemi wanted to see more races, she definitely didn't want to spend any more time with Cato and send him the wrong message.

"Well, this has been such a blast. I'll be going now," she said sarcastically. There was no way in hell she was letting him know that she actually enjoyed herself and wanted to stay.

"You should try wiping that smile off of your face before you pretend to not have enjoyed yourself. But alright, suit yourself, have a nice day. I've got a date with a bookie," he chuckled.

As they got up to leave, Cato's hand accidentally brushed her thigh or at least she thought it was an accident. She wanted to be disgusted by his touch but found her skin tingling where he had touched her. She felt her face getting flush so she turned away from him so he couldn't see it. He didn't seem to be paying attention to her or even realize he had brushed her thigh for that matter because he was waving down some bookie to collect his purse.

What is wrong with me? she thought as she snuck away into the crowd avoiding any more awkwardness. On her walk back to the colosseum, she replayed the race over in her mind trying to remember every detail. She wished she could tell Felix all about it, but there was no way she could. Her secret was getting more complex and she did not hate the feeling it gave her.

17

LIVIA

Livia had not actually known that it was a gladiator she had seen her sister with in the palace gardens the night of the party, but the look on Noemi's face confirmed it. She was actually happy her sister was not the perfect girl everyone thought her to be and that her betrothal to Felix was not what it seemed. Maybe there was a rebellious side to Noemi she had not known about. But Livia had no plans to rat out her sister. She didn't want to get caught up in any more secrets since she had enough of her own to keep track of. Plus, she needed her sister to continue to cover for her with their parents.

If any of the other girls noticed the lavish new brooch on Livia's tunic, they did not hint at it. At first, she had been hesitant to wear it, unsure of what it might lead to if she did. She thought she would be drawing unwanted attention from the emperor, skeptical of what the gift really meant. Her ostentatious nature got the best of her and she decided that it was too beautiful of a piece to let it rot in her trunk. It needed to be shown off regardless the consequences. As luck would have it, the brooch seemed to prove itself to be a simple gift and nothing more. After that night at dinner, the emperor acted like nothing had ever happened. He did not so much as make eye contact with her when present with Antonia or anywhere else. Part of her was relieved she could just hide in the shadows inside the palace again, but the other part wondered what would have happened if the emperor really did fancy her.

The months had been good to Antonia and her unborn child. Her belly was swollen and there was no doubt she was carrying the emperor's heir. Murmurs of the possibility of a healthy child had even started spreading around the palace. Livia had even stopped despising that she had to care for Antonia, if only just a little bit. Livia mostly felt sorry for Antonia, but she could not imagine being in her position.

The pressure to have a healthy baby was taking its toll on Antonia. Every time the priestess or doctor visited Antonia, she became panicked they would have bad news. She would go into hysterics, crying and shaking so much it would take the girls the rest of the day to calm her down. She wanted less and less to leave her quarters, becoming paranoid someone was trying to hurt her baby. She even went so far as having Martia try all of her food first in case someone was trying to poison her.

Livia could not really blame her for being a handful. The constant attention and pressure to produce an heir was a lot. To lift her spirits, the girls decorated Antonia's bedroom for Saturnalia. Red poinsettias were placed all around the room to brighten it up, and garlands made of cypress branches with red berries tied to them were draped over the doorways, hearth, and windows making her room smell fresh and citrusy. It was hard not to be happy during this time of year. Shouts of "Io Saturnalia" could be heard everywhere around the palace spreading cheer and warm wishes to everyone.

The palace was teaming with decorations that had transformed it into a forest filled with fragrant flowers and greenery. It was magical to walk through the halls. Livia imagined she was in another world as she walked through the palace. Pastries and sweets were abundant, their smells wafting through the palace all day long. Gifts were delivered for the emperor from all over the empire, amassing in a giant pile in the great room so tall it touched the ceiling. Everything from handmade figures of the emperor to cookies could be found in the pile of gifts. It was the most excess Livia had ever seen in her life and it just kept getting larger.

Everything was over the top during Saturnalia, no expense or detail was spared. The god Saturn was depicted everywhere possible as the festival was a tribute to him. The emperor even had a giant mosaic of Saturn commissioned on the ceiling of the dining hall to watch over them while they ate. In the great hall, cutouts of stars, suns, and moons were carved out of the ceiling allowing the light to cast through, making patterns on the floor. Candles were lit in every room with the hope that Saturn would bring back the longer days. Every visible surface was gilded. Mountains of emeralds and rubies were everywhere and Livia had to watch her step wherever she went.

Besides the excess and abundance of fanciful things, her favorite part of Saturnalia was the lack of laws. The whole empire dropped social norms and had the time of their lives for an entire week. That meant Livia was relieved of her duties with Antonia during the festival and could return to frolicking around the palace doing whatever she pleased.

Before she headed home for her family traditions, she was going to unwind with her friends for a much needed night of debauchery in the palace. It was customary during Saturnalia that the slaves traded roles with their masters. Her parents would let their slaves wear their clothes for the night while they catered to the slaves' every whim. Her parents even let the slaves keep a toga or two as a gift for Saturnalia. In the case of the emperor, it would mean he would be serving everyone. Livia certainly did not want to miss that.

The girls were all gifted emerald tunics with gold stitching to wear during the festival season. Livia twirled around the maidens' quarters with glee, thrilled she was free for the week, the Saturnalia spirit making her almost giddy. She made sure to wear her brooch because not only was it the nicest thing she owned, it made her feel like she had a secret.

Livia entered the dining room and saw the empress and emperor greeting the slaves and other palace help. She was escorted to the table by the empress herself, something so foreign to her she almost did not believe it was happening.

This was going to be the best night ever, Liv thought.

She sat at a table with some of the other girls, the empress washing the feet of each girl as they sat. In keeping up with the rest of the gilded palace, the table was adorned with a gold silk cloth while the couches had matching pillows. Garland and bows had been strung from the chandeliers throughout the dining room making it feel like she was in a wooded wonderland. Livia couldn't really picture the emperor waiting on her, but there he was dressed in a plain peasant's tunic pouring wine and replenishing food for all the people who usually served him.

The girls indulged in wine and sweets taking full advantage of the holiday. Carolers sang tunes about Saturn and good tidings throughout the dinner creating a cheering atmosphere. Liv knew everyone loved being waited on by the emperor and he was surprisingly attentive to his task. Even Antonia was out of her room laughing at the table next to her, excused from participating in the role reversal because of her pregnancy.

Lost in a fog of wine and sultry music, Liv barely noticed the emperor beginning to serve them until his large stomach bumped into the table, making the plates and goblets on it clank around. His attempts at pouring wine for the girls was mediocre at best with most of the wine ending up in a puddle on the floor. When it was Liv's turn to refill her drink, the emperor reached for her goblet placing his hand over hers while she held it. She watched as he sloppily poured her more wine all while caressing her hand with his thumb.

At first, she thought the wine had gone to her head and she was imagining his touch, but then he smiled at her in a longing way. Livia's heart started to beat faster, but not in a good way. She really did not want anything physical to do with the vile man. He was cruel and unappealing to Livia in every way. Truth be told, she was very frightened of him.

So shaken up by his behavior, she wanted to leave the dinner, but didn't want to waste the once-in-a-lifetime experience so she stayed and indulged some more, making a point to avoid the emperor. She watched as he made his rounds to some of the other girls giving them extra attention as well. This made her feel a little better that it was not just her he was interested in, but still she was cautious. Each time he neared their table, she would get up and visit another table or pretend to go relieve herself not wanting to put herself in another situation where he could touch her.

Her diversions worked well for the remainder of the dinner; she had no more interaction with him and was able to enjoy herself. As the dinner was winding down, the debauchery was just beginning. The music played louder and faster as people danced and ran around the dining hall.

Martia had the drunken idea to visit the empress's room and try on all her clothes and jewels. A few girls followed including Livia. The empress had trunks and trunks of tunics, so many that she would have to wear five a day to get through them all in a year. Livia had never seen so many colors and exotic materials. Martia draped herself in a purple satin tunic and laid herself on the throne acting like the empress pretending to give orders to the other girls.

Livia was extremely tipsy. She actually needed to relieve herself and making her way to the bathroom was a challenge. She kept stumbling and bumping into the walls on the way, giggling to herself. Her eyelids felt heavy and she kept forcing them open to see the way there. Sitting down to relieve herself was godly. She leaned her head back looking up at the ceiling realizing how tipsy she actually was as the room started to spin.

Time had gotten away from her and every other person at the party. Gathering herself, she left the bathroom to find the girls again. She had left them in the midst of removing their tunics to skinny dip in the fountains. She turned to make her way toward the gardens when someone grabbed her from the shadows. Yelling out in fear,

Livia's mouth was quickly covered with a dirty wine-soaked hand to muffle her screams as she was thrown into a wall.

Livia's eyes widened as her attacker became revealed from the moonlight peeking through a sun shaped cutout in the ceiling. It was the emperor. He had her pinned against the hall wall, holding her arms by the wrists pressing them up next to her head.

"Calm down, little Bella, you have been avoiding me all night and now I finally have you to myself," he greedily said.

Livia tried to push him off of her but between his weight and her drunken state she was trapped against the wall.

"I see you accepted my token," he said moving his eyes down toward her brooch.

Any feeling of being tipsy Livia had had moments ago in the bathroom was long gone. She could feel his hot, foul breath on her face as he spoke, "I've been watching you ever since you wandered into my chambers in the hypogeum."

Liv couldn't help but catch her breath in shock. She thought she had been blending in this whole time.

"Yes, my dear, how could I not notice someone as beautiful as you. I allowed you to stay because you intrigue me. I wondered why the daughter of the best director of *venatores* this empire has ever seen would want to be a foolish attention-seeking, degraded girl in the palace. So, then I watched you for these past months trying to figure it out and noticed you are not like the others, giggling when they are near me or hoping to catch my eye with their not-so-subtle gestures. You are smart and not interested in pettiness."

Livia could not believe what she was hearing. *He knew who I was. This whole time.* She felt like such a fool thinking no one would notice just one more girl.

"Don't worry now, I won't bite," squeezing her wrists a little tighter. Pressing her harder against the wall, he leaned in forcing his mouth on hers.

Livia tried to turn her head to keep from kissing him. It worked for a second until he released her wrists and grabbed her head with both hands to keep it in place. Again, he forced his mouth on hers jamming his tongue as far down her throat as he could.

Livia couldn't stand it, she felt so vulnerable with his slimy tongue in her mouth. She did the first thing she could think of and bit down as hard as she could. The emperor retracted his tongue and pulled away from her, slapping her face with the back of his hand. Livia reached for her face with both hands to stop the sting, eyes welling up with tears.

The emperor stood there with a small trickle of blood running out of the side of his mouth showing absolutely no remorse. He quickly ripped her hands off of her face once again pinning her against the wall.

Tears were now streaming down Livia's face, stinging ever so slightly as they ran down the spot where he had struck it.

The emperor now smiled, his teeth a crimson color covered in blood, and leaned in to whisper in her ear, "I do like a good game of cat and mouse if that is how you want to play this, my dear. Best be warned, I never lose. Apologizes for letting my temper get the best of me." He then slowly licked the side of Livia's face where he had struck her starting at her chin and ending beneath her eye.

Livia could feel the grooves in his tongue where she had bit him slide along her face, imagining the blood trail it would leave behind. She dared not move.

Looking her in the eyes now, his face so close to hers, he continued, "I am going to release you now and you can continue your foolery with the others. Tell anyone of this and I will have you eaten by one of your father's prized pets. If you try and run, I will kill your family. Io Saturnalia, Domina Livia."

With that he let go of her wrists, wiped his bloodied mouth on the sleeve of his peasant tunic, and walked off into the shadows.

Livia let herself slide down the wall and crumple to the floor pulling down garland from the walls as she did, the tears steadily falling down her face. *How could I be this stupid?* she thought. *I should have never come here. Now my family is involved and there is no way out of this.* As much as she wanted to lie in the pine scented decorations on the floor and sob, she did not want to get caught with blood on her face and it was only a matter of time before someone wandered to the bathroom. She splashed some water on her face—using her tunic to clean up as best she could—dried her eyes, and took a deep breath. She got herself into this and now she had to get herself out of it.

"Io Saturnalia," she said to no one, her voice oozing with sarcasm.

18

NOEMI

Noemi never figured out what Cato had intended by bringing her to Circus Maximus. For weeks she was on edge, half expecting him to appear out of nowhere or visit her home again. If he had, she never knew it because there was no more contact. She was relieved when the holiday season came because it took her mind off of him and stopped her from looking over her shoulder.

The winter solstice was upon them and that could only mean one thing: Saturnalia, Noemi's favorite festival of the calendar year. Noemi loved festivals in Rome, the joyful energy of the people radiated around the whole forum. Saturnalia was the best because the whole empire went on holiday closing down to celebrate the solstice. People sang in the streets, dancing and enjoying life, calling out "Io Saturnalia" to everyone. Throwing social status to the side for one week brought out many colorful outfits and unique looks. It was truly a happy time of year.

Each family had their own traditions; Noemi's family not being the exception. Her mama would prepare a beautiful breakfast spread full of candied fruits and cured meats for each day of festival. Sometimes she hid small gifts in little cakes she would bake for the girls. Special offerings of dried crops would be laid on the hearth for the hope that the next year would bring a bountiful harvest. Then they would melt wax to make cerei candles which would be given out as gifts to their friends and family to signify the return of longer days. Even the animals got a little bit of a break from the colosseum. Each day her family would bring the animals special treats and decorate the pens with greenery and holly. Even Livia was planning on spending most of the week at home away from working at the palace. Noemi loved this time of the year.

Father's loud voice interrupted her thoughts. "Noemi, the emperor has many requests for this year's Saturnalia and everyone is trying to accommodate him. He wants the animals to be more than just a spectacle but part of the crowd. Some sort of crowd immersion was how he described it," her father said.

"Part of the crowd?" Noemi questioned.

The look on her father's face told Noemi that he was not for this new idea. "He wants us to parade them around the agora and let the people play games with them or some far-fangled notion of the sort. I want you to take a tiger, leash it, and walk it around the perimeter of the agora. Make it look like the tiger is in control, but know that you are. Pack your work gear in a satchel just in case. A few of us will be out with other animals as well," her father instructed.

Noemi started to protest. This was not how she wanted to spend the beginning of Saturnalia. She wanted to spend it with her family, wandering the festival markets and enjoying the atmosphere, not parading around a tiger.

"But, Father..." Noemi started to protest when he cut her off and walked over to her putting his strong callused hand on her shoulder.

"Please don't fight me on this. I am up to my ears with the emperor's silly requests and I don't need another headache," he said.

Noemi knew better than to push her father when he was like this. She would never understand why he was so obedient to the emperor. Plus, the faster she got the tiger the faster she could enjoy the first day of Saturnalia.

"Yes, Father," she replied and turned to go pack up.

Choosing a tiger was easy. She picked one of the more feeble ones that had been in the most fights. Most importantly, it had the fewest teeth which Noemi hoped would not come into play. The tiger was not bothered by Noemi collaring and leashing it. It was familiar with her at this point because it had been in the stables for so long. Around its neck, she tied a festive collar made from greenery with a few sprigs of holly sticking out, and secured the leash to its neck. Giving it a quick pet, the tiger nuzzled her leg. "Come on, old girl," she said, "let's get this over with."

Dressed in her bright red winter cloak, walking into the agora was magical. It was almost as if she had been transported to another land she barely recognized. The decorations alone were magnificent. Every marble column had greenery wrapped around it, giant wreaths hung from the peak of every building, the ground was covered in pine needles with their fresh scent spreading through the agora as each person stepped on them, releasing their aroma into the air. And the cerei lit up the entire agora, placed in every window and on the steps of every building. You could barely get near Saturn's temple the stairs were so overloaded with offerings pouring out into the streets.

At first when Noemi walked with the tiger through the crowd, no one paid her any notion. Probably because they couldn't fathom such a dangerous beast would be allowed so near to them. She was about a third of the way into the agora when a few children first noticed the tiger, pointing and urging their parents to look. Some people quickly ran off, scurrying their children away, while most were intrigued and cautiously watched Noemi's every move.

Her father had wanted her to interact the tiger with the crowd. She couldn't really think of much other than petting the tiger and that really wasn't thrilling. She decided on an old trick they used in training. Noemi rolled up the sleeve of her cloak exposing her arm. She put her arm in front of the tiger allowing it to put her arm in its mouth. The crowd gasped holding their breath to see what was going to happen to this poor girl's arm.

Noemi feigned an injury, wincing to make it look like the tiger had bitten off her arm. *A little dramatic, but it was getting the job done,* she thought.

An audience had gathered around them now. Noemi milked it a few more minutes before gently tugging on the leash for the tiger to release her arm. She held up her uninjured arm displaying it for everyone to see and took a bow. Some people started clapping.

Whispers of sorcery and trickery could be heard.

"Who would like to try their luck with this ferocious tiger here?" Noemi asked the crowd as she prodded the tiger to give out a growl.

At first, no one stepped forward clutching their goods from the market and pushing their children behind them. She did not blame them. She felt like some cheap, desperate side show act. One man stepped forward, a slave—Noemi could tell by the way he was dressed, a black cloth adorning his tunic. He walked up to the tiger without fear, rolled up his sleeve, and put his arm in the tiger's mouth. Just like with Noemi, the tiger was calm, did not bite, and released the arm on command.

Then people started lining up, one after the other to put their arms in the tiger's mouth, cheering after each successful attempt. After a few dozen people, Noemi could tell the tiger had had enough. She didn't want to push her, so she announced that was it for today and attempted to walk away when a loud, clearly drunk man stumbled his way in front of her blocking her path.

"How's about I take a turn, little lady?" he slurred.

"Apologies, sir, we are done for the day," Noemi responded trying to get around the guy. But the man wasn't listening. He shoved his arm at the tiger's mouth completely missing it and hitting her in the face.

Noemi tried to stop the tiger, but it was too agitated after the unexpected slap and chomped down on his arm for real, using whatever teeth it had left.

The man screamed, sobriety hitting him fast, as he tried to pull his arm out of its mouth. By the time Noemi was able to get control of the tiger the damage had been done. His severed fingers lay in a small pool of blood on the ground while the rest of his hand looked mangled beyond repair.

The crowd cheered, thinking this was part of the show while the man fell to the ground from both the shock and the alcohol. Noemi had to get the tiger back before something worse happened. Not really knowing what else to do, she bowed to the crowd quickly taking her leave back to the hypogeum, leaving the drunk man in the street clutching what was left of his hand, and hoping someone would come to his aid.

If the emperor was looking for a unique animal experience, he got one, Noemi thought. She safely returned the tiger to its pen giving it a little extra meat for its obedience and quickly returned to the forum. She figured she had helped her father enough for one day. Plus, she didn't want to miss opening night of Saturnalia.

The streets were packed near the central piazza, everyone crowded around the Temple of Saturn trying to get a view of the statue. The closest she could get was the Arch of Septimius Severus. It wouldn't be the best view of the opening ceremony, but a view nonetheless. Usually, her family would spend the day together in the forum setting up a blanket in the piazza to watch the festivities. Not this year, Noemi found herself alone what with her father bidding the emperor's wishes and Livia not yet home.

She was a little melancholy that they were straying from tradition but realized things change and she should look at the positives. The ceremony started. The crowd began to light their cerei, thousands of candles held around the forum, a beautiful sight just as dusk was beginning to set.

Soft music began to play, echoing throughout the forum, as all eyes shifted to the player. A lone man, the Mock King, emerged from the temple of Saturn, a sickle in his hand ready to perform his duty of watching over the festival and breaking rules. He approached the statue of Saturn outside the temple steps where he used his sickle to cut through the woolen bonds tied around the statue's feet that had been there for the year, thus signifying the loosening of the laws for the week of Saturnalia. As the sickle cut through the last of the bonds and they fell to the ground, the music sped up to a merry tune. The crowd cheered in unison, "Io Saturnalia."

Noemi joined in, the festival spirit filling her with happiness.

Suddenly, she felt a hand on the small of her back. For a split embarrassing second, she thought it was Cato, but was relieved when it was only Felix when she turned around.

"Io Saturnalia mi amor," he greeted her with a kiss.

"Gods, Felix, you startled me! But, I'm so glad you showed up. I was beginning to think I would be spending the first night of Saturnalia alone," she said.

"Now, that would certainly be a tragedy on your last Saturnalia as an unwed woman," he said as he began to tickle her.

Noemi laughed, squirming to get away from him.

Felix stopped and pulled her to him wrapping his arms around her. "The show is starting."

They watched the depiction of Saturn's life unfold outside the temple. Thespians dressed as various forms of Saturn, reenacted the myths related to the god's life. One of Noemi's favorites was how Saturn heard a prophecy that he would be overthrown by one of his children. To prevent this from happening, Saturn ate each of his children after they were born. Noemi loved how the thespians made it look like Saturn's stomach was getting bigger with each child. The story ended with the youngest child, Jupiter, being hidden away on the island of Crete while his mother fed Saturn a large stone swaddled in cloth to trick him.

The crowd laughed as the thespian pretended to eat a swaddled stone. When Jupiter was full grown he made Saturn vomit up his siblings and together they overthrew him.

Noemi laughed when the thespian Saturn belched out each child. It was a simple story, but one well known throughout the empire.

"I can't wait to bring our children to the forum," Felix said sweetly to her.

Noemi hesitated before responding, "Me too." *There he goes with the children again.* She hated herself for even having this thought.

Felix must have noticed her hesitation. "Is everything alright with you? Do you not want children or something?" he questioned her.

"No. It's just..." she paused, unsure of how to tell him how she felt. "Don't be silly, of course I do. Let's just enjoy the festivities," she answered back trying not to ruin the mood any more than she already had. She leaned back into him giving him a reassuring kiss on the cheek.

The show ended with a sing-along; everyone knew the words of the joyous songs and sang throughout the forum, voices echoing in unison. Then came the feast. The emperor held a public banquet right in the forum for any citizen of the empire, no matter their caste. It was the one philanthropic thing he did each year for his people. The line was always so long that Noemi's family had never accepted his generosity but packed a small dinner instead to picnic after the ceremony. When they were little, Noemi and Livia had begged to wait in the line because small dolls and figures were given to the children as gifts from Saturn. Now, all grown up, she could see why her parents made sure the less fortunate got the food and gifts as her family had more than enough.

As darkness set in on the first day of Saturnalia, the paper lanterns were lit and released into the sky letting the god Sol know it was time to slow down his chariot as it carried the sun across the sky, making each day a bit longer. Noemi liked to picture Sol collecting all the lanterns and putting them in his large chariot to make the sun a little brighter and stronger for the months to come. Noemi released hers into the sky wishing for health and happiness for her family, watching it float away until she couldn't see it anymore.

The rest of the week flew by for Noemi as it did for everyone in the empire. Because there had been no executions and venators, her family had more time than ever. And with that time, it was perfect for preparing for her wedding as was customary during the holiday. It had been a whirlwind of dinners and celebrations with Felix's family the past few days. A merger of families was a big deal and her father wanted to make certain his daughter could be provided for.

Felix's family was well off, his father being a magistrate for the emperor. It would be a perfect union, with Felix's expertise in his future father-in-law's field and Jovian's direct line to the emperor's ear through his in-law. Each day during the festival, Felix had given Noemi a gift or done something special for her, and tonight was no different.

Felix knew Noemi had had her fill of meeting his family, and that she needed a little break especially with the parade the next night on the last day of the festival. It was tradition that all the engaged couples be paraded through the streets while the citizens wished them luck and happiness from their homes. Being a son of a magistrate, the parade was very important to Felix's family as they were allowed to receive a special blessing from the emperor at the end of the night, an acknowledgment showing the respect of their family name. So, when Felix announced before dinner he was stealing his future bride away for a special night out, no one objected.

"What adventure do you have in store for me tonight"? she asked him as he led her down the road toward the forum.

"Ah, but if I told you, it would ruin the surprise," he teased.

The two walked hand in hand displaying their betrothal for all to see. Not sure exactly where he was taking her, Noemi just enjoyed the walk admiring the villas so nicely decorated with various greenery on their doors and windows. She loved the white cerei lit in most windows around the city. Each window she passed she could catch a quick glimpse of the family inside. Some sitting down to dinner, some dancing and playing games, while others were placing their Saturnalia offerings on the hearth.

Before she knew it, they had walked all the way up to Palatine Hill.

"My father got permission from the emperor to be on the grounds," Felix answered the question before she could ask it.

Noemi followed his gaze. A small picnic was set up in one of the many gardens on the property. A blanket lay on the ground, tucked away in between large trees making it both private and romantic. *Felix has gone above and beyond.* "Felix," she said exhilarated at the view of the city from the hill, "this is so beautiful!"

"I thought we could have dinner and then watch tonight's

lanterns float into the sky from up here," Felix told her.

"I love it. I love you," she said as she planted a soft kiss on his lips. They shared some wine and a delicious pheasant Felix had prepared. With her stomach full, she sat there taking in the incredible view snuggled in a fur blanket next to Felix. She could see the hustle and bustle in the streets of the forum below while in the distance the still Tiber River could be seen past the buildings, with not a single boat on the water as all were docked for the festival.

"I was thinking," Felix interrupted her thoughts, "that we could exchange our *signillaria* tomorrow before the parade."

Gods, Noemi thought. She had completely forgotten to buy the terra-cotta figurine for Felix. It was tradition that on the last day of the festival week everyone gifted *signillaria* in all shapes and sizes to one other, each with special meaning to the giver and receiver. Noemi had meant to go to the sculptor and order one weeks ago for Felix, but it must have slipped her mind. Now she would have to scramble at the Saturnalia market tomorrow hoping the pre-made ones were not already picked over.

"Yes, of course," she answered trying not to sound like she didn't have anything special for him, "I can't wait for you to see yours." Ugh, why couldn't she just shut her mouth? *I had to make it worse by lying to him.* She was sure his would be extremely thoughtful. He had probably had it for months just waiting to give it to her.

The music from the forum could faintly be heard as they prepared to release the lanterns. "I have one more surprise," Felix said as he handed her tonight's lantern. On it was written their names with a large heart around it. "I thought we could release it to the gods as a little extra special blessing for our marriage next year."

Noemi didn't even need to say anything, the genuine smile on her face was enough for Felix. The two held the lantern and released it together into the sky. She fought back the tears in her eyes as she watched the lantern rise, for she did not deserve someone as thoughtful as Felix to be her husband. They then lay on the blanket, her head on his chest as they watched their lantern join the others in the sky. "Io Saturnalia," they said in unison.

19

CATO

The last few weeks of training were grueling for the second years. Between weekly battles in the colosseum and extra classes at Ludus Matutinus, Cato was worn thin. After his failed date with Noemi at Circus Maximus, he thought it best to leave her be, as it was evident she was not interested in him, and put all his effort into training.

So, when Saturnalia came, he welcomed the break with open arms. The air in his quarters had turned cool. He woke with goosebumps as the first day of Saturnalia broke. He forced himself to lie in bed a little longer until a few of the others arose making sure they noticed his laziness. He had to keep up appearances ever since he became a little more paranoid and unsettled from the old woman's fortune.

He also wanted to avoid as many gladiators as possible today so he could dodge the inevitable question of whether or not he was spending the festival week with his family. He had learned his lesson last year after being bombarded by well wishes to the Velarius family and questions about how and when he would travel back home to their villa to see them. A few *lanistas* even had written Leon the Great letters for Cato to deliver. Of course, he never went back to the

Velarius villa but instead spent the week staying hidden around the city hoping not to run into any of the other gladiators and their families.

This year he was prepared. When Matteo invited the gladiators from well-to-do families to spend a few days at his family's villa, he jumped at the opportunity. Sure, the offer wasn't entirely sincere, it was more for Matteo to show off to his father—some high up senator to the emperor—that he was acquainted with gladiators from famous family bloodlines, but Cato did not care the reason. Only Cato and another gladiator Justus ended up accepting Matteo's offer.

"Our chariot is here," Matteo shouted down the hall toward Cato's room, "and it will leave without you," he half joked. There was no way he wasn't bringing home Leon the Great's son, even if he butted heads with Cato sometimes, and Cato knew that.

He packed a small satchel with a few tunics and a more formal toga with the Velarius family crest, a giant eagle, pinned on it. He wasn't sure what to expect but anything had to be better than spending Saturnalia on edge ducking behind columns in the forum.

The chariot was out front with Matteo and Justus waiting in it when Cato came outside. Both the chariot and the horses were decked out in greenery for the festival. The horses had bells around their necks giving a festive tune to the air. *A nice touch*, he thought. He hopped in the chariot admiring the craftsmanship as he sat down. It was much larger than the ones used for racing having multiple seats available with room to spare for belongings and fur blankets to keep them warm on the journey. He had never ridden in a chariot. Before today, the only form of transportation he had ever used was hitching a ride in the back of a cart.

The chariot driver whipped the horses while whistling a merry tune and they were off to the countryside. The villas of the senators were about an hour's ride from the school in a secluded neighborhood just outside the city. Cato didn't know much about senators so he decided to use the ride to see what information he could learn. As it turns out he didn't have to do much prying, Matteo was as much a braggadocio as they came. Add to Justus's endless questions and Cato had a wealth of knowledge by the time they were halfway through the trip.

It turned out Matteo's father was in charge of hosting this year's festival gala, a true honor among the senatorial hierarchy. Only higher ups in the Senate and well-to-do Romans were invited, hence why Matteo invited Cato and Justus. Justus was a legacy just like Cato, his father was a hero for the Roman Army who died winning the battle that opened many critical trade routes to the empire. A feather in Matteo's cap for sure. Matteo went on to brag that a few senator's daughters who'd been pining for him for years would be present. Cato stifled a laugh at Matteo's confidence.

As they rode closer to the villa's grounds, the cypress trees began to line a path leading them to the home. The trees opened up into a circular drive with a grand front entrance adorned with thick greenery trimmed with crimson ribbons. A groomsman met the chariot driver to assist with the horses and lead them to the stables. A servant placed a step stool beneath the chariot to allow for their descent.

If this is how Matteo grew up it explains a lot, Cato thought.

The servant led them into the lobby of the villa. The warmth from the hearth felt welcoming after the long chilly ride.

"Your belongings will be sent to your rooms, come, let me introduce you to my father," Matteo instructed. He led them through the villa into the back gardens. Cato could not help but marvel at the vast display of wealth in the home. Exotic animal skins and busts lined many of the floors and walls respectively. He even saw a few decorative pieces that could only have come from the far east, with strange characters written on them. It was much more elaborate than the Velarius villa he was used to.

Matteo's father was seated in the garden deep in conversation with someone Cato assumed was another senator.

Matteo cleared his throat drawing attention to himself and his guests. "Pater pardon the interruption. Allow me to introduce my colleagues, Justus Agrippa and Cato Octavian Velarius." His father and his guest rose from their seated position to greet them.

Cato could see the man's attention spark a little at hearing the Velarius surname. He noted the distinct togas with the royal purple broad stripe on both men indicating their position with the emperor.

"Welcome gladiators and Io Saturnalia," Matteo's father greeted them with his orotund voice. "This is my colleague, Senator Sulla. We were just finishing up some small business discussions, nothing near as exciting as fighting in the arena, am I right?"

Cato could tell he was trying to lighten the mood, downplaying whatever they had been talking about.

"Velarius, you say?" his father, changing the subject, began walking toward Cato leading the group back toward the villa, "I was well acquainted with your uncle. Sad to hear of his death. Such a shame. He was one of the best *lanistas* there was. I hear you are destined to follow in his footsteps, what with your father's training. Leon always was the more impressive of the two when it came to that."

Cato had been afraid of this but was prepared nonetheless. "Yes, I intend to uphold the Velarius name in the arena as I was trained to do. For I was trained by the best and am the best. No one can beat me." A scripted, closed-ended answer with a little cockiness to it. It worked as Matteo's father nodded and moved on to Justus.

"Your father was a brave man, Justus, one of the empire's greatest leaders in battle. His legacy will always be remembered for many years to come. You must be so proud to be fighting under the Agrippa name."

"That I am, Senator," Justus replied his hands a little unsteady as he seemed very intimidated by Matteo's father.

"Pater," Matteo interrupted, "Cato and Justus will be attending the gala tomorrow evening. I thought it wise to invite them."

Cato had never seen this side of Matteo before, he seemed to be almost begging for his father's approval, awkward and timid in conversation.

"Yes, it will be good to have the gladiators represented, I suppose," his father half-heartedly answered. "Now, Senator Sulla," he said, completely moving on from Matteo, "let us head inside for..." the rest of his sentence couldn't be heard as they had already made their move away from the gladiators.

"Eh, so that's my father," Matteo tried to smooth things over, "a little preoccupied at the moment but that's father, always doing important work for the emperor."

Cato was not convinced.

"There is a welcome Saturnalia dinner tonight with some of the families that have arrived today. Maybe even meet a broad or two eh, Justus?" Matteo elbowed him, his tone eased back into the guy Cato knew.

Cato was interested to see how this dinner compared to the emperor's and it did not disappoint.

The feast was extraordinary, held in a large dining room with one long table in the middle. Around the table were various couches with the seating draped in festive colored silks. The table was adorned with candles of all shapes and sizes with berries and sprigs of cypress sprinkled all over the table for decoration. The food piled teaming high over the serving plates, pheasant, oysters, peacock, ostrich, and boar all creating an intoxicating smell throughout the villa. Special Saturnalia sweets were being passed around that made Cato's mouth water. Cato indulged in everything available. After a few goblets of wine, a couple of the senator's daughters made their way over to the three gladiators. With their parents in the vicinity, the girls were proper, and Cato actually enjoyed the small talk. It was easy to pretend to be pompous when the girls were hanging on his every word. The night ended quickly as everyone was tired from their travels, Cato included. He did not know how much he needed the country air until he was lying in bed unable to keep his eyes open any longer.

The next morning Cato was invited to participate in his first hunt for sport. There was a light layer of frost on the ground and everyone's breath was visible as the men gathered by the stables. A groomsman had prepared the horses for the men, a fur lined cloak for the brisk morning awaiting on each saddle.

Cato mounted the horse. Pulling the cloak over his shoulder and securing the fastener, he found a few sewn-in pockets with well-placed knives for him. *This was much different than when we would hunt for food growing up.*

"The man who kills the largest boar will be the King of Saturnalia," Matteo's father announced, a tradition Cato had only heard of but never been a part of.

The groomsman played a few high notes on a ram's horn and the hunting dogs were off. Cato galloped after the dogs, a genuine smile on his face as he needn't pretend, for he loved a competition and had not hunted in a while. The cold air whipping him in the face caused his eyes to water and nose to run, a welcomed reminder of the outdoors.

Eventually the dogs stopped and pointed at a dense thornberry bush that was concealing the boar. A few men dismounted hoping to get a jump on the boar. Cato knew better. This particular thicket was too dense, probably only a few small boars being protected by the branches. He knew the mother boar would not be far and she would be large.

The men started hollering and tossing sticks into the thicket hoping to draw out the boar. When a few smaller boars ran out in all directions, the men dove at them with their knives. As a few men made contact, the frightened squeals were almost deafening.

Cato laughed at their inexperience and circled back behind the thicket to wait. As he predicted, a giant female boar came charging out of the woods not far from the thicket to protect her young. Some of the less experienced men knew enough to stay on their horses for fear of getting gored. While some of the more experienced others saw an opportunity to win the competition.

Cato had the best position for the kill, and he knew it. He rode along next to the large boar holding his knife in one hand while balancing on the horse with the other just like he had done so many times at the Velarius villa. He nicked the boar in her hind leg causing it to squeal in pain but not deep enough that it could not continue to run. Instead of killing it, he let it run right toward the other men. As much as he wanted to win, he could not risk all the attention that would be drawn to him as the King of Saturnalia. So, he eased up on the horse. Much to his dismay he watched as two other men fought over who was going to kill the already wounded boar.

The hunt ended with a burly senator staking his claim as the winner. "I guess she was a little too big for ya, eh?" the man gloated, teasing Cato.

"Nah, I've seen bigger," Cato replied trying to sound like he did not care that he had to lose.

The hunt ended and the men rode back to the villa where the groomsman relieved them of the horses. The boar had been dragged in, attached with rope to the back of the winner's horse. It would be prepared for the gala and the winner would get the honor of carving it as was tradition.

The men were greeted with warm mulled wine to take the chill out of them from the hunt. Cato sat back with the group enjoying their camaraderie as they recapped the hunt to each other with each tale more exaggerated than the last. He felt welcomed in the group and was thoroughly enjoying himself.

After the men relaxed, they all took their leave to prepare for the evening's gala. Cato donned his yellow tunic under his crimson toga, supplied by the school for high-end events such as this. He finished his look off with the Velarius brooch he had stolen from their villa while he was a slave many years ago. He had never attended a gala before and was not accustomed to the proper practices. His plan was to follow everyone else's lead and duck out of any awkward situations.

Matteo came to get him once he was ready and they made their way to the party. "We will be introduced together," he informed Cato.

Cato just nodded, never having been formally introduced anywhere before. Justus, Matteo, and Cato entered a large ballroom.

A man holding a pristine scroll spoke into a horn as they crossed the threshold announcing, "We now welcome the gladiators represented by his host's own son, Matteo Sextus Augustus, and his comrades Justus Agrippa and Cato Octavian Velarius."

The crowd clapped and smiled at them as they walked in, clearly intrigued and impressed they were in the midst of such big-name gladiators.

Cato didn't even have to look at Matteo to know that he would be smug bringing in such valued guests. A part of Cato hoped it impressed his father for Matteo's sake for it was pitiful to watch him squirm under his father's shadow.

The gladiators shared a table with a few of the senator's daughters from the night before. *Clearly not a coincidence*, Cato thought. He first mingled with Matteo and Justus, drinking wine and enjoying oysters and flamingo tongue being passed around by a few servants. He was more interested in taking in the gala than entertaining the girls. The ceiling of the room was quite spectacular, strung with large arching garlands, draped over the beams supporting the roof. Intricately placed through the greenery were small shards of glass that reflected the various lamps around the room making it appear as if the garland was lit up. There were also small cypress trees placed around the room with the same glass tucked into the branches making them look almost as if sorcery was involved.

The guests were dressed in their Saturnalia best, bright colored tunics, cloaks, and togas flooded the room. Women were decked out in every jewel they owned, a few even wove jewelry into their hair. It was a night to show off wealth and power as people let down their guard while the government was shut down for a few days. Even if Cato did not feel the part, he looked the part with his bright colors.

After the introductions, lively music began playing. People took to dancing around the room while others enjoyed watching. In the middle of the room was the large boar killed during the hunt earlier that morning. It was dressed with fruits and vegetables and smelled delicious, making Cato's mouth water. Atop of its head lay a golden crown which the King of Saturnalia would place on his head after he carved the boar. Food was being brought out constantly from the kitchen to what seemed like no end.

Cato indulged as he had done the night before. He was feeling a little drunk and sat down at his table for a few minutes to regain his composure. His peace was short lived however as one of the senator's daughters came up behind him and began to massage his shoulders.

"Oh, my, what strong shoulders you have," the girl said in a desperate attempt to flirt with him.

Although the shoulder rub did feel nice in his drunken state, he shrugged her off. Not getting the message, the girl ran her hands down his arms feeling his biceps. "You look like a god," the girl continued.

The last thing Cato wanted to do was end up caught in some scandal with a government official's daughter. He got up, excused himself from the girl, feigning he had to relieve himself and left the table. He thought some fresh air might sober him up a little, so he headed toward the gardens only to change course when he saw the senator with the crown on his head blocking the way. *I do not want to hear him brag about his kill anymore tonight,* he thought. He snuck out a side entrance mainly used for servants and leaned against the wall of the villa.

The air was cold but felt refreshing and sobering as he stood there looking up at the moon, glad to be away from the attention. He was about to head back in and find Justus when two men hurried out the side door seemingly heading straight down the path toward the stables. Cato would not have paid it any mind except the men must have stopped to have a chat because he heard them say "Jovian" and "gladiators." Piquing his interest, he came out from the shadow of the wall and inched within earshot, hidden behind a few shrubs.

It was two senators, one voice Cato recognized was of Senator Sulla who he had met that first day. The other voice was unfamiliar to him.

"Jovian has the emperor's ear," Sulla said, "he does nothing but fill his head with ideals of a republic. Can you imagine? Elected officials?"

"He must be dealt with. We cannot let him jeopardize all we have worked for," the other man proposed.

Cato knew who they were talking about, Jovian, the headmaster of the Ludus Matutinus, Noemi's father.

"He is well protected and would be hard to eliminate," the mysterious man continued. "How about a little accident then?"

Cato could hear the deceitful tone coming out of Sulla's mouth. "A fire perhaps in his precious hypogeum? Would wipe out the emperor's precious animals and Jovian at once," Sulla proposed.

The other man started to say something, but the pair had moved farther away from Cato and out of earshot. Cato was taken aback. *Had he heard right?* He knew he was drunk, but he was pretty sure he had just overheard their plot to kill Jovian, the simple, kind headmaster who adored creatures and was the father to the girl he had kissed and couldn't get out of his head.

He slipped back inside making sure no one saw him and went to find Justus and Matteo. As much as he wanted to tell them what he had just heard he thought it best to keep it to himself, no telling what could happen. There was nothing they could do about it anyway. Interfering in any sort of senate affair no matter how shady would mean certain death if caught. Cato tried to enjoy the rest of the night but the thought of Jovian being killed hung over him like a black cloud.

The next few days were more relaxing. Most of the senators and their families had traveled home to spend the remaining festival days in their own villas. Of course, Senator Sulla remained but Cato made it a point to avoid him as much as possible. By the end of the week Cato could honestly say he was enjoying Matteo's company way more than he had ever thought and was glad he chose to come on the trip.

Justus and Cato made the journey back to the school on the last day of the festival week leaving Matteo to spend the final day with his family. Cato was actually a little sad to leave. It had been a nice escape from the reality of the gladiator world for a few days.

Upon returning to the city, Cato left his belongings back in his quarters at the school. It was a ghost town save for one or two gladiators milling about after returning from a long week like himself. He didn't have anyone to exchange *signillaria* with, so the final day of Saturnalia was a bit of a letdown. He decided to head to the market to see if he could maybe buy a last-minute figurine for himself. Pathetic, he realized, but he felt like that simple tradition would put him back in the festive spirit.

The streets were atrocious, discarded wine bottles, candle remnants, and other garbage littered the roadways from the week of tomfoolery. Cato was careful not to step in what he could make out to be the vomit of someone who must have had a little too much fun one night.

Finding anything in the market would be a challenge at this hour. Most stalls were closed for merchants to spend time with their families and the ones that were open were either rushing to close early or were out of *signillaria*. He finally found a shop on the second floor of the market that was open and had a small basket of *signillaria* left. The sign on the basket read "defectum."

Great, he thought, *only cheap, damaged ones left. No matter. They are better than nothing.* He dug through the bin passing up on figures of various gods with their limbs missing and a few animals with cracks through them. He picked up a gladiator *signillaria* and laughed to himself, the little statue's shield was cracked in half and it was missing an arm. *It's perfect,* he thought. He paid the merchant a measly, few bronze *assēs* for its worth and tipped him a few extra.

As he turned to wish the merchant "Io Saturnalia" he clumsily knocked into someone else in the shop. "Paenitemus," he apologized helping the person up from the ground. The person was obviously annoyed at him. He almost had to do a double take when he saw her face. It was Noemi.

Trying to act smooth even though he was completely caught off guard, he turned on the sarcastic charm. "I see you cannot help but stay away from me," Cato started.

Noemi's eyes widened in recognition pushing his arm off of hers.

"I can stand up on my own, thank you. You are the one who can't seem to watch where they are going," she replied annoyed.

"Shouldn't you be with your family?" Cato asked.

"Shouldn't you?" came Noemi's sharp retort.

"A valid point, animal girl," he teased her. Cato found himself lost in her dark brown eyes for a second too long. There was just something about her. He didn't want this encounter to end and he could see it was heading in that direction as she seemed as disinterested in him now as she was before. Changing the subject quickly he said, "Well, I am headed back toward the school. After your run in with that prisoner and your performance with a sword, I have to insist I accompany you home seeing as you don't seem capable of fighting off anyone on your own. Who knows who you will meet during these last lawless hours of the festival." He was hoping she would agree to his proposal. He wanted to spend some time with her alone and this was a long shot.

She looked conflicted for a few moments then begrudgingly accepted the invitation, "Only because I am headed that way, too."

Cato tried to hide his excitement. They walked through the empty streets, even the beggars were not out and had some place to celebrate. *Depressing*, he thought.

At first the silence between the two was deafening, both avoiding bringing up the kiss. "So..." Cato started in only to be interrupted by her starting to say something at the exact same time. Cato couldn't take the awkwardness any longer. He had to break the silence. "So, uh, how is your neck? You know after..."

"Yes, I think I would remember almost being choked to death," she said cutting him off. "And it's fine."

Her words were short, but he thought he could detect a hint of playfulness making him want to kiss her again all the more. They continued walking, passing the colosseum, silence clouded them again. He was dying to know what she was thinking.

"You know, I really could have made it home on my own. There is nobody even on the streets."

But just as she finished speaking, the hair on the back of his neck stood up. Cato looked around. The street was all of a sudden clean, too clean, welcoming almost as it began to narrow. *It was a trap.* Low life hooligans taking advantage of drunk and merry citizens passing through he suspected. The second they would walk through the narrow part of the street they would be cornered and robbed or worse. Cato stopped dead in his tracks reaching his arm out in front of her chest to stop her too.

"What the gods?!" she yelled at him.

He covered her mouth with his hand pulling her quickly down the alley to their right. "Be quiet!" he harshly whispered.

She obeyed immediately sensing the panic in his voice.

Cato hurriedly led her by the arm down the alley hoping they were not followed. They ran until they came to a small space between two buildings where they had to squeeze together, chests against the other just to fit. Cato could feel her rapid heart beating against his chest as they hid. He thought he felt her inch a little closer to him than she needed to. *Probably out of fear,* he thought. Cato prayed to the gods the men had given up chase and moved on to their next victims.

The minutes ticked by and no one ran by looking for them. Cato was lost in his thoughts calculating how long he should wait before emerging from the dark that he was totally caught off guard when Noemi's hands slowly moved from her sides to his shoulders pulling him down toward her. Her mouth found his in the darkness. Her lips were soft as she leaned into him even more. His attention now fully on Noemi, his thoughts silenced. The danger long forgotten, he gently grabbed her face pulling her even closer to him, wanting more. Her lips parted as he slipped his tongue inside her mouth, gentle yet demanding.

She welcomed him with a soft moan and shallow breathing. Between the adrenaline and the hormones his heart was racing as was hers. She pulled away playfully biting his lower lip then whispered in his ear, "If you wanted to kiss me, all you had to do was ask."

Cato laughed bringing himself back to reality. "Oh, is that all?" he teased, had he read the situation all wrong? She was playing hard to get this whole time. As much as he wanted to stay hidden together, they had to move before the men circled back.

"Now if you can continue to walk me home that would be much appreciated," she said. They doubled back a different way, making sure they weren't followed. Cato felt like he was walking on air the whole way. He wanted to believe she felt the same way he did about her, but her mixed signals had him confused.

As they neared her house, he realized he needed to leave her wanting more. "Hey, this way!" he said pulling her down a side street into a dark doorway, pushing her back against the stone wall.

"Have they followed us?" she said panic rising in her voice.

Cato smiled as he answered, "No, I just wanted to kiss you again and that seems to only happen after a little danger." He picked her up this time, her legs wrapping around his waist with her back on the stone doorframe. Her response was hungry, meeting his mouth while she pulled him closer with her legs. Their kisses were deep with a sense of longing Cato did not know existed in him. He kissed the small of her neck as she leaned her head back, panting as she caught her breath. He moved his mouth back to hers as her fingers ran through his hair pulling ever so slightly. Now he found himself trying not to moan. It took all his will power but this time it was him who pulled away and gently bit her lower lip.

Cato lowered her back down to the ground where he whispered in her ear, "Io Saturnalia." They found themselves giddy, laughing like children as they came around the corner. Both their hair was disheveled and their faces flush. He wanted to hold her hand as they reached her home, but she suddenly froze in her tracks, blood draining from her face like she had seen a ghost. Cato looked in the direction of her gaze. A man dressed in a colorful toga representing a betrothal stood in front of her doorway mouth agape as an ornate *signillaria* fell from his hands into the dirt.

20

NOEMI

Noemi's stomach dropped, forming a pit so large she didn't know how she could ever get rid of it. *The parade.* She had completely forgotten and lost track of time.

"Felix!" she half yelled, half sobbed moving toward him trying to quickly think up a way to explain what had happened even though she herself did not have an explanation. She had pushed away Cato's hand from her own moving toward Felix.

"I'm sorry. It's not what you think! Please wait." The apologies poured out of her as did the tears.

Felix's face went from heartbroken to anger in a matter of seconds. He turned back to yell at Noemi red in the face, eyes watering, "I knew it! I knew something was off with you for months. I just never imagined that you have been doing gods know what with some barbarian. Here I thought you were just nervous to get married."

"Felix, please," she tried to interject but didn't know what else to say. "I love you!" she blurted out. *But, did she really?* Sure, she loved him in some way or at least thought she knew what love was until she had met Cato. That was a different kind of love.

"You have a funny way of showing it," Felix scoffed.

Noemi caught up to Felix grabbing the back of his toga. "I can explain," she tried again. He grabbed her hand, ripping it off of him.

"There is no explanation in this or any other empire that will undo what you have done," Felix roared back.

The pain on his face was too much for her to bear. *What had she done?*

Felix stormed off mumbling a sarcastic "Io Saturnalia" to the sky.

Noemi fell to her knees into the dirt, releasing a loud guttural wail, as she began to sob. She had no idea how long she knelt there for, she felt as if it was impossible to move an inch and she didn't care who saw her lying outside her home in the dirt crying hysterically. She was sure Cato was long gone by now after he probably put the pieces together that she was betrothed.

She was such an idiot. She went to buy Felix a *sigillaria* and the next thing she knew she was gallivanting off with her gladiator. She had not meant for it to happen, but when they were hiding in the alley, so close to each other she felt something more between them, and everything just escalated from there. It was like she was a different person.

What would her family say? Her father loved Felix and she had dishonored the betrothal and her family.

Just when she thought she had no tears left to cry, she found Felix's *sigillaria* lying on the ground next to her. She picked it up and the tears intensified. It was a figurine of her, perfectly carved, surrounded by all her favorite animals in the hypogeum. The gift was perfect and thoughtful, and she was a terrible person.

Her mother was the one who found her numb in the street clutching the *sigillaria*. "Come inside, it's getting cold," her mother said putting her arms around Noemi as she helped her in the house. She guided her to the hearth where Noemi curled up on the rug with a blanket while her mother placed an offering on the mantle to Cupid for her and sat down beside her.

Noemi was so relieved her mother wasn't asking questions or yelling at her that she cried even more. Her mother held her, stroking her hair like when she was a toddler.

"I'm sorry," Noemi mustered out between sobs.

Her mother held her a little closer. "Love is love, Noemi. Your father and I just want you to be happy at the end of the day. We thought Felix would give that to you, but we understand if he is not the one."

"But the betrothal and the magistrate. What about our reputation?" Noemi said, worriedly.

"It will be difficult on your father's end to smooth things over with the magistrate, but there is nothing he wouldn't do for you," her mother's words were reassuring and helpful but, she wondered if she would be so consoling if she knew that her daughter was falling in love with a gladiator. If she had any inkling of the notion, Noemi could not tell.

"I know it doesn't seem like it now and there is nothing I can say to make it better, but you will be alright. Love is a powerful force. The fates have a plan for everyone and the road there is not always easy. Have hope," her mother said leaving Noemi to her tears.

Noemi lay on the floor in front of the hearth trying to close her eyes, the vision of Felix storming off burned into her mind. What could she even do now? She had created such a mess and for what, a couple of stolen kisses in an alley with someone she had no future with. She surely could not have a public relationship with a gladiator still in training. That was forbidden. Cato was the emperor's property until his training was complete and would be executed if it was found out that they were together. It was not even a real option.

She thought back to Felix who was her best friend. How could she do that to someone she cared about? There was no way to fix it with him and even if she could it would never be the same. But did she really want to? When she was kissing Cato, it had felt different than when she kissed Felix. The butterflies she felt with Felix were giant birds with Cato. There was a new sense of passion she had never felt with him.

Noemi continued crying for everything she could think of. She felt sorry for herself, she felt love and pain for Felix and their future they had always talked about, she felt sick to her stomach for putting her parents through this, and she cried for the gladiator she couldn't quite have and who probably wanted nothing to do with her anymore.

Her funk lasted about a week, moping about the house, staying in bed as long as possible. Her eyes were constantly puffy. As soon as she would stop crying, something would remind her of Felix and the tears would start again. She didn't leave the house, not even to visit the animals. She was pathetic and she knew it. She was ashamed to return to her daily routine, but mainly afraid to run into Felix in the hypogeum. For once she was the problem child and not Livia.

Noemi lay in bed wasting yet another day away. She could hear the music in the street as the children sang:

The Befana comes by night
With her shoes all tattered and torn
She comes dressed in the Roman way
Long live the Befana!

Usually she loved La Befana, the witch who brought children treats the week after Saturnalia. She was definitely way too old to believe in La Befana, but her mother still liked to leave her and Livia little treats under their beds each year. When they were little their mother would dress up as La Befana in old dirty rags and put mud on her face to make her look like an old vagrant hag. She would participate in the children's parade where she would toss treats to kids in the streets and she would dance and cackle along with all the other mothers who dressed up as well.

Now Noemi could smell the panettone baking in the kitchen. The smell brought back so many memories of her childhood, a time she wished she had again. Her parents had tried to get her to snap out of it, but her heart was broken, and she could not get past it. As much as she wanted to watch the children parade around the Befanas hoping to catch some sweet treats she did not want to go outside. So, she settled for watching out her bedroom window.

She pulled herself up to the arched cutout where there was room enough so she could sit. She couldn't really see much and started to come back down with she saw something on the sill. She picked it up and her heart fluttered back to life a little bit and she actually smiled for the first time since Saturnalia. It was a *sigillaria*, a gladiator figurine that was cheap and broken. She had seen Cato buy it in the market the last time she saw him. He must have left it on her windowsill as a gift for her. He was still thinking about her at the very least. This was the glimmer of hope she needed. Tomorrow was a new day, and she wouldn't be spending it in bed.

That night she burned a La Befana doll on the hearth with her family symbolizing the end of the year. She watched as the rag doll burned, secretly willing her fears and failures to burn along with it.

The new year always began in a busy fashion and this year was no exception. With the election of new senators, the emperor wanted to celebrate their appointments with extravagant shows. So that meant extra work for Jovian especially since the days were still short and there was less time to orchestrate everything behind the scenes. In addition to the small timeframe, the weather determined which animals were used. The nighttime temperatures in Rome in January were too cold for a few of the species that came from Africa and other warmer climates. In the past, those animals would just die when the winter came around, costing the emperor a great loss in inventory.

When Noemi's father was first put in charge, he came up with a way to keep the animals warm during the night. Using the idea from the bath houses that had hot water, he had pipes run throughout the ceiling of the second-floor animal stalls all originating from a room on the second floor. He then had the stalls on the top floor directly above the pipes lined with ceramic tiles and hollow bricks. He had a small hearth built in one of the rooms on the second floor where the hot air from the fire would run through the pipes heating the floor of the stalls above it. The heat would radiate up and the bricks and tiles would help contain that heat throughout the night so the animals could stay warm. After much trial and error, a few burns, and many broken pipes along the way he created his own hypocaust system.

Being back in the hypogeum was more comforting than Noemi thought it would be. She checked the stalls of the lions, panthers, and jaguars. They were all still alive. She could feel a little warmth still radiating from the stalls. She had thought she would have run into Felix already, but he was probably avoiding her as much as she was avoiding him. What she really wanted to do was run into Cato, but she knew it was a huge risk if they were seen together. She did not even dare go anywhere near the gladiator quarters.

Noemi checked the schedule for the day's fights and she read C. Velarius would be doing an exposition fight that afternoon. *Perfect,* she thought, *a chance to see him even though it would be from afar.* She changed her clothes from her secret compartment in the wall, wrapping an extra shawl around her neck and shoulders for warmth and to conceal her identity even more. She climbed into the stands to await the fight.

The schedule was not usually public and if it was it only listed famous names or just a name but not the kind of fight it was. If people knew it was not always fights to the death, they would not attend. But Noemi had the inside scoop. The staff in the hypogeum had to know what was going on so they could prepare for the bloodshed or lack thereof.

The fighters were brought out in groups of ten pairs at a time, spread out over the arena. She could hear a few groans from some of the regulars who realized this meant it was exhibition only. The wind whipped through the colosseum, the winter air causing Noemi to pull her shawl tightly around her. She searched the arena floor, her heart skipping a beat when she saw him. She resisted any urge to call out to him although he probably couldn't hear her anyway from the stands. She wormed her way to the front. If she got any closer she would fall into the arena.

The announcer introduced the gladiators and explained the exhibition to the crowd. The men would fight each other as if in battle except without taking a knee or being killed. The *lanistas* would referee to make sure no one was out of line. There were a few "boos" from those expecting to see bloodshed.

Noemi was secretly happy because there was no chance of Cato getting hurt. She watched him intently, his every move precise and direct. His muscles glistened as the sweat poured off of him. She thought that seeing him again would satisfy her at least a little bit but it only made her want him all the more. She found herself cheering for his every blow against his opponent no matter that it was just for practice. At one point she whooped so loud, a few people turned toward her.

During one of the breaks, she was even sure Cato had spotted her in the crowd. Reigning herself in, she needed to stop being so irrational over a guy. She needed to let him go, and move on with her life. Noemi started to feel sorry for herself again and snuck back down the ladder into the hypogeum. She put everything away and returned home.

The next morning, she got up to get ready for the day. She had left the gladiator figurine on her windowsill as a small reminder of what they had shared and what she had given up. This morning when she looked at it, there was something sticking out of the bottom. Curious, she reached out the window to grab it and saw a piece of parchment folded underneath. She could barely unfold the parchment she was so excited. Written inside was:

Don't worry, animal girl, I did not forget about you.
Thanks for cheering me on.
Know a place we can talk. Meet me at half past six
At the entrance to the forum.
—C

Noemi reread the note at least ten times. She couldn't believe Cato still wanted anything to do with her and on top of that he had noticed her in the crowd after all. It felt so good to have something to look forward to again. She wondered when he had left the note. Did he watch her sleep? Knowing he had been so close to her made her heart flutter. The rest of the day crawled by. She kept playing out the different scenarios in her head. What did he want to talk about? Would he be mad at her for not telling him she was betrothed?

Would he kiss her again? Would someone see them together? And on and on.

By the time the six bells rang, she was practically sprinting to the forum. She arrived a little early at the tall arch between two columns. She wasn't entirely sure where he was going to be, so she leaned her back against one of the columns and scanned the crowd for him. Half past six came and went. In none of Noemi's scenarios did it end up that Cato was a no show. This seemingly real possibility was now stuck in her head.

Was this just some cruel joke? she thought. *I'll give him five more minutes.* She continued to search the crowd which at this hour was mostly merchants returning home and pious citizens leaving offerings at the temples before their suppers. Nothing. Her excitement slowly started to turn to anger.

Silently cursing herself for being so foolishly optimistic, she began walking away from the entrance to the forum. She practically had to push her way through a group of men blocking her path. As she sidestepped them, a beggar hunched over in rags approached her.

"Not today," she yelled at the beggar, clearly not in the mood for annoyances. The beggar began to laugh underneath its tattered cloak.

"Well, you aren't very kind," the voice joked.

Noemi instantly recognized the voice. "Cato?!" she questioned aloud.

"Quiet!" Cato harshly whispered back, "don't blow my cover. Follow me but keep a mindful distance until I say it's okay," he instructed.

At this point, Noemi was so happy that she didn't get stood up, she would jump in the Tiber River if he told her to.

Cato half walked half limped through the forum toward the Temple of Saturn. She had no idea where he could be taking her and enjoyed watching him act like a beggar. It seemed like they were walking forever before he stopped outside the largest public bath house in all of Rome shedding his costume and righting his posture. He was now dressed in the simple tunic of a commoner. *That was all that looked common about him*, Noemi thought as his chiseled muscles were nicely outlined by the tunic.

"Nice outfit," Noemi joked.

Cato didn't acknowledge her sarcasm but told her to stay behind him. *Was he serious?* she thought. Why would he take her to the busiest bath house to talk? There was nothing private about it especially at this hour when people were bathing after work and before supper.

They walked up the stairs into the bath house entrance. Cato exchanged money with the clerk, paying for both of them because the clerk handed her a pair of wooden sandals. She removed her leather sandals and put the wooden ones on. She knew from visiting the bath houses as a child that this was to protect her feet from the heated floors.

When she was little, her parents would bring her and Livia to the bath houses frequently. Not only was it a good source of entertainment and socialization for children but it also ensured cleanliness, a necessity when they did not have an aqueduct line for water until her father got the new position at the hypogeum. Then the visits were no longer needed.

She followed behind Cato through the main room of the bath house called the *lepidarium*, the open air, extremely large rectangular pool for mixed use. Hundreds of people were relaxing in the bath. He had yet to even look at her or even turn back to make sure she was following him. It was very crowded, and Noemi had to dodge bathers on the deck to keep up.

Once through the *lepidarium*, he turned and went into a different room, this one fully enclosed. The blast of chilly air when she walked in gave her the obvious clue that this was the *frigidarium*, the cold bath. This was usually the last stop before you left the bath house. A quick dip in one of the smaller circular pools around the room closed the pores and you were on your way or so Livia had told her. Cato walked in this one and out another door.

Winding their way through a few of the long hallways, they passed a few vendors. Noemi's father once bought her and Livia each a ball to play with in the kids' pool area. They would throw them to each other and take turns swimming to the bottom to fetch it. Some days they would even eat supper there from one of the many food stalls. She had so many childhood memories here. Noemi wondered how Cato was so familiar with the layout of this massive place. Surely, it wasn't because he frequented the workout facilities or bathed with the public. The gladiators had their own private gym with elite equipment and private in-house baths. As far as Noemi knew they probably had people to bathe them over there.

He led her into another room, this one was incredibly hot and humid. Noemi immediately started to sweat upon entering the *caldarium*. The steam was so thick she couldn't see more than a foot in front of her and of course had lost sight of Cato. Her main concern now was getting her bearings so she didn't accidentally fall into the scalding water. The heat reminded her of being down in the hypogeum on a hot summer's day where it was difficult to breathe, but she wasn't used to the steam. She backtracked to the door and placed her hand on the wall deciding to follow it through the room. Hopefully, Cato would be waiting at the exit for her.

She didn't get more than halfway across the room before she was grabbed by the arm. Freezing instantly, she hoped it was Cato and not someone else trying to pickpocket her.

"This way," he whispered now holding her hand. He must have trusted that no one could see them through the steam. His touch instantly stirred up the butterflies in her stomach. He squeezed her hand slightly, reassuring her, and she squeezed back letting him know she was okay. He led her behind a large column in the corner of the room. He let go of her hand and fiddled with something on the wall.

What in the gods? she thought as he slid a large piece of marble to the side revealing a small opening. He motioned for her to go in. Without hesitation she stepped inside and down a few steps. She could see him clearly now as the steam wasn't an issue in there. He came in behind her making sure they weren't followed and quietly slid the marble slab back into place. With the echo in the room, it would be hard to pinpoint where any noise was coming from even if someone happened to hear them.

With the slab back in place, Cato waited a minute with his ear against the wall. When he was satisfied, he turned to her and smiled. His smile made her melt.

It took everything she had not to leap at him but instead made a sarcastic remark, "You know there are other ways to get my attention than yanking me into tight, dark spaces."

He laughed and she could see an almost relieved look on his face at her jovial remark. He grabbed her hand again leading her down the dimly lit stairs.

"It seems like we are going into the underworld to talk. You couldn't find any place in this realm?" Noemi said defaulting on another poor joke to hide her discomfort and avoid talking about Felix.

At the base of the stairs Cato lit a torch from the wall holding it out in front of them. Noemi could see that they were in an out-of-service room with what was once a square pool now empty of all water.

"When this bath house was first built, they realized that the *caldarium* wasn't heating well. So, rather than fill it in, they drained the pool and built a larger steam room above it with a better hypocaust system to heat it. This room is still connected to both the hypocaust and *frigidarium* systems and the airflow keeps the temperature manageable. Only a few people know it still exists," he informed her, answering her questions before she could even ask them.

"And how do you happen to be one of these select people with this knowledge?" she teased.

"The Velarius family was one of the largest donors to the project as the *caldarium* was where Leon liked to hold important meetings," he said and it was almost as if he was speaking as if he wasn't a Velarius himself. Noemi noticed but didn't pay it any more attention as he had lit a few torches around the room and was now leading her down the few steps into the empty bath. The butterflies were racing around her stomach at full speed now.

"Lie down here and close your eyes," he instructed her.

Noemi found herself weirdly trusting of this guy she literally did not know at all but here she was lying down on her back at the bottom of a dusty old bath.

Cato laid down next to her, his arm touching her arm. "Okay, now open your eyes," he said softly.

Noemi did and stifled a gasp. It was one of the prettiest things she had ever seen. Thousands of gemstones of all colors had been ornately arranged into the face of a beautiful woman on the ceiling. No detail spared. The light cast from the torches reflected off the gems casting down vibrant colors throughout the old bath house.

"Leon had it done for his wife. He wanted anyone who he had meetings with to see her beauty," Cato described. "They did not have time to recreate it in the new *caldarium,* so it goes to waste down here."

Noemi was rather touched he would share rather intimate stories about his family with her that she felt she had to bring up Felix and clear the air.

"Um listen," she started, clear hesitation in her voice, "about the last time I saw you." She paused here half hoping he would interrupt her so she wouldn't have to go on, but he was silent. "I meant to tell you that I was betrothed but then I was having such a good time, and everything happened so fast that I never really had the chance, and then I didn't think I would ever see you again," she rambled on finding that looking up at the gemstones rather than at him made it easier to pour her heart out. "I thought…" she paused then started again, "I thought you would want nothing to do with me. And I just have to say that against my better judgment I like you, and don't get me wrong I didn't at first but then when you saved my life things changed. And, I know you still have your training, and it would be impossible to be together but I just…"

Her rant was interrupted by Cato reaching over and kissing her on the lips.

"Stop. Come here." He pulled her into the crook of his arm and held her close.

She melted right into him feeling like this was right where she belonged.

"Now, it's my turn," Cato started in, his voice modulated. "I knew you were betrothed." Noemi turned her head toward him in shock propping herself up on her elbow so they were now looking at each other.

"After I injured your leg." He paused here as if he wasn't sure he should keep going. "I'm deeply sorry about that by the way. I just..." he hesitated again looking down at her leg and almost seemed defeated. "I just had no choice."

Noemi could see it was hard for him to talk about it so she let him continue although she would need a better explanation in the future about her leg.

"After the fight, I needed to make sure that you were okay, so I asked around about you. The nurses at the infirmary said they knew you and mentioned you worked in the hypogeum. I wandered parts of the hypogeum—during whatever free time I had—for days looking for you. One day I found you. You were with him and he was kissing you behind a column. I could see you were standing, and I had not crippled you, so I left. When I saw you again at the palace, you were sitting next to him at dinner dressed in betrothal colors. It wasn't until the fates brought us together two more times that I realized our lives were intertwined somehow, and when you kissed me first in the alley, I didn't stop you. As much as I didn't want to leave you crying at your doorstep that night I could not risk being recognized. I resigned to the fact that you would be getting married and unavailable, so I focused on my training and tried to forget you for weeks. But it was almost impossible. And then I heard you cheer for me at the exposition and saw you in the stands, and knew you had chosen me in a way, and I had to see you. So, you see, it is just as much my fault as it is yours."

Noemi took a moment to process what she had just heard. He had known about Felix and still wanted to be around her. She didn't know whether to laugh or cry she was so relieved. He must have taken her silence as need to further explain himself. He reached up gently pushing a stray brown hair that had fallen in front of her face behind her ear. Noemi's heart started to race. It was hard to believe that a gladiator of his nature could be so gentle.

"I have a little less than a year before my training is complete and I am released by the emperor. Any sort of relationship during my servitude to him is sure execution," he said matter of fact.

Noemi already knew this law and the thought of putting him in danger made her sick. She was thinking about how hard it would be to go almost a year without seeing him when he mischievously said, "That is, if we are caught."

Noemi smiled back at him. The fact that he was willing to risk his life to be with her told her everything she needed to know. She put all her worries aside and kissed him like her life depended on it.

21

LIVIA

In the weeks following Saturnalia, Livia tried to conspire a way to fix the mess she had created. Every plan she came up with ultimately ended with her death or the death of her family. There was just no way out that she could think of. She had almost told Noemi everything one night when she had been home, but Livia had instead been cornered by Noemi asking for a favor of her own and she couldn't bring herself to do it. On top of all that, she now had to cover for her sister while she snuck around with some gladiator.

In the meantime, Livia did her best to always be with the other girls and never be alone so she couldn't be cornered again. Because Antonia rarely left her quarters, Livia had managed to completely avoid the emperor for days. But as she thought more about it, he could have found her at any time and the fact that he had not yet made it even scarier. She found herself always looking over her shoulder for him to grab her again or stopping before she entered a room to listen for his voice. She was, as he said, a mouse, a very scared one at that. And he was a large, powerful cat waiting to pounce at any given moment.

For the emperor, their game continued, and he was good at it. The first time she saw him after the festival was in the temple on the palace grounds. Antonia had been increasingly pious as her pregnancy came to term, praying to gods and demi gods alike for a healthy child. She spent at least half the day on her knees there and therefore so did Livia, Martia, and Delia.

Although she was dreading it, Livia was almost relieved when she heard the emperor's booming voice echo throughout the temple one day, "Bona dies, ladies and peace be the gods! How is my son?" his hand rubbing Antonia's large belly.

Livia did not even have to look, she could feel his eyes on her.

"Strong, your grace. He is strong. I have prayed to the gods asking it be so," Antonia quickly responded.

The emperor kissed her stomach and turned to the other girls. "You know, Antonia, it is much too cool today for you to be out here. Have the girls take you inside. I wouldn't want you getting ill."

"Right away," Antonia obeyed.

Livia got up to help pack up Antonia's things. *The quicker the better*, she thought.

She was just about to release the breath she had been holding in when the emperor called out, "Oh wait! Livia is it? You dropped something. Come fetch it."

Livia knew for certain she did not drop anything. She turned back around wondering what he was getting at. As she walked toward him, she could see a little spark ignite in his eye. Livia looked directly at him, pushing her fear aside. Antonia's shawl was draped on his arm.

He must have grabbed it from her when he went to kiss her stomach. "You know you must be careful, we wouldn't want Antonia to be cold," he warned loudly for anyone to hear while handing the shawl to her.

As Livia went to reached for the shawl, he purposely dropped it on the ground.

"Clumsy me," he said bending down to pick it up. As he stood up, his one hand ever so slightly slid up Livia's leg stopping at the top of her thigh.

Livia froze knowing that the girls and Antonia could not see what was happening.

He handed her the shawl and whispered under his breath, "Good day, little topo."

Livia grabbed the shawl and quickly caught up with the girls, trying to act like nothing had happened.

"Don't be so careless," Antonia half-heartedly warned her.

He was cunning, I'll give him that, Liv thought.

The cat and mouse game continued like this for weeks. She tried to anticipate his next move, but he was always one step ahead of her. She became one of his playthings around the palace. A brush of the hair here and a subtle grab there, all in the presence of others and all so discreetly executed. The evenings were the worst. Under the cover of darkness, the emperor did not have to be as discreet.

One night, she returned to the girls' chambers to get some sleep. It had been a long day with Antonia, and she was exhausted and couldn't wait to go to sleep. She was so tired that she did not even notice how quiet the room was. No girls gossiping about the day's events to each other, no one fiddling in front of the mirror with their hair, no one moving about. As she went to dive into her bed, she noticed a package lying on her pillow. Inside was a beautiful gold silk shawl. Livia had never held anything this exquisite before. She ran her fingers along the soft silk lifting it to her nose to smell the clean fabric. There was no note, but Livia knew it was from him. She wanted to hate it, but it was so luxurious.

Wrapping it around her shoulders she walked to the mirror to see what it looked like on when a voice from the shadows spoke, "Beautiful, isn't it? It's amazing what the silkworm can produce."

Livia froze, the shawl slipping out of her hands down her back and onto the floor in a heap. He was in her room. She frantically looked around the room only just realizing that she was alone. The other girls were nowhere to be found.

"I had Fabia take them into the city for the evening. I wanted to see the look on your face when you opened my gift," he voiced as he stepped out from the shadows. "Now, come come little topo, don't be scared." He was now standing behind her, she could see him in the mirror, feel his breath on her back.

The game had ended. The mouse had been caught. Livia was at his mercy now, trapped. He ran the back of his fingers up and down the length of her bare arm, smiling at her in the mirror. Every hair on her body was standing straight up, her heart felt like it was going to beat out of her chest, and she started to tremble. She could tell he was enjoying this, her discomfort, her fear, eating it all up. He took a step back from her and sat on her bed.

"Put it on," he commanded pointing to the gold silk laying on the floor by her feet, "I want to see how it looks on you."

Livia hesitantly bent down to pick up the shawl. So many thoughts running through her head. She was still a virgin, awaiting the day she might get chosen to be a Vestal. That was her dream. She couldn't lose that to him, especially when she still had a chance to be selected. He already had a mistress, a very pregnant one at that. *So what happens when he gets bored with me? Will I be killed?* There was no happy ending in any scenario Livia could think of.

The emperor's voice interrupted her thoughts, "The gold really brings out your eyes, but I really want to see you only wearing that. Nothing else."

This was it, thought Livia. Her worst fear coming true. The most coveted women in all of Rome and she would no longer be eligible. The tears started coming down her face in a mix of fear and devastation. Her back was to him now. Reaching her hand to the top of her tunic, she slowly began to pull it down off her shoulder in between stifled sobs. "I can't do this," she whispered.

The tone in the emperor's voice sounded agitated, "Of course you will, or your precious family will be killed at tomorrow's execution and you will have a front row seat. Now, continue."

She thought of her family as more tears poured down her face. She untied her belt and removed the tunic from her other shoulder letting it fall to the floor. With her back still to him, she wrapped the gold shawl around her shoulders holding it together in the front with her hands. It covered her for now.

"Turn around," he commanded. She slowly turned to face him, the anger returning as she saw him lying on her bed with a lustful look in his eyes. Looking her up and down she wanted to gouge his eyes out. "On second thought, why don't you take the shawl off, too."

Closing her eyes, she took a deep breath and let go of the shawl she was holding together in front of her, exposing her entire body to him. The tears had stopped. Only intense anger remained. She just wanted to get it over with. This was her own fault for even entering the palace and now this is what she must do. She could hear him moaning pleasurably as she imagined him looking at her body. She still could not bear to open her eyes. She stood there like a statue unsure of what he would demand next. He must have gotten off her bed because she could hear him walking toward her.

"Open your eyes," he insisted. She did. He was standing in front of her licking his lips in desire like a famished wolf. Every muscle in her body was telling her to run, but her heart kept her in place knowing she had to protect her family. He slowly began to walk around her, looking her body over like a slave at an auction. Stopping in front of her again, he broke the painful silence, "I have been waiting a long time for this, topo, do not disappoint me." He gestured to her bed.

Livia shuffled to the bed, her shoulders hunched in defeat, her mind sending up silent prayers to every god she could think of for a way out of this. Her bed felt cold and unfamiliar as she lay down, her once safe place was no longer that. She lay there feeling exposed, trying to awkwardly cover herself with her arms as best she could, watching him as he fumbled with his toga caught in the folds of his fat stomach. He approached the bed, his bottom half exposed as he untied his belt enough to hike up the toga above his waist.

She closed her eyes again willing her body to be anywhere else. A wave of nausea rose up in her stomach in anticipation of what he was about to do to her. She could feel him grab her leg dragging her closer to him. She couldn't help but let out a small painful whimper as his hand made contact with her skin.

He only chuckled in amusement at her. She felt the right side of the bed lower from the weight of his knee as he climbed on the bed. She could feel her body shaking in fear, her teeth chattering as she tried to think of something, anything else, when a blood curdling scream rang throughout the entire palace startling the emperor enough that he immediately retreated off the bed, dropping his toga back over himself.

Livia didn't move.

She watched as a slave came running into the room to find him out of breath. "My lord," he began obviously panting from his run here. "It's Antonia. The baby. Quick. Follow me," he mustered out.

Livia watched as the emperor's hardened face softened in worry and fear.

Looking back at Livia on the bed he angrily shouted, "Get dressed. Antonia needs you." With that he ran after the slave to be with his mistress. Livia rolled over and threw up over the side of her bed the second he was out of sight. Curling into the fetal position, she allowed herself a few seconds to sob in relief. She had never been more thankful for Antonia.

Livia could have never prepared herself for what she ran into once in Antonia's chamber. Antonia was on her bed screaming and writhing in pain. Her dark hair wet with sweat, sticking to her pale face.

Martia and Delia were at her side, hands covered in blood, trying to comfort Antonia anyway possible.

The emperor was pacing at the foot of the bed giving useless commands to everyone and anyone in sight.

Pushing all thoughts and emotions aside from what just happened to her, Livia rushed past the emperor to Antonia.

"Where have you been?" Martia asked in a whispered panic.

Ignoring the question completely Livia responded, "Where is the priestess? The baby should not be arriving for at least another month. What is happening?"

"The priestess is on her way. She was sent for as soon as Antonia started bleeding, but I don't think she will make it in time," Delia whispered her answer back.

Livia had never seen a woman give birth, but she had been there for many animal births in the hypogeum. She figured it had to be similar and it was all they had to go on at this moment. "Okay, Antonia," Liv said in a calming tone, "the baby is coming whether you want it to or not."

Antonia moaned something inaudible in response. Blood had started to pool beneath Antonia, she was starting to lose consciousness, her eyes rolling back in her head.

"Antonia! Wake up!" Livia screamed.

Antonia's eyes barely fluttered open.

This is too much blood. She had seen this before with an elephant calf. The mother elephant had lost consciousness and her father had to cut the calf out of the mother. She did not want to have to do that. "Antonia, you are going to have to push this baby out now with all your strength. Martia, you push down on her stomach as hard as you can on the count of three. Unus, duo, tres. Now!" Livia commanded.

Antonia gave one feeble grunt before she passed out while Martia pressed down hard on her stomach. It worked just well enough that Livia was able to ease the baby out. The baby lay limp in Livia's arms, the cord wrapped around its neck. A boy. *Antonia had been correct,* Livia thought. His small body was a sickly looking, pale gray color with tiny features resembling Antonia.

Livia barely got the cord removed when the emperor came swooping in, ripping the infant from Livia's arms.

"A son!" he exclaimed his face radiant for only a moment until he realized the child was stillborn.

Livia watched as the emperor slowly sank to his knees on the blood-soaked floor, his face in total agony. With his lifeless son cradled in his arms he uncontrollably began to sob. He had lived this nightmare many times.

No one said a word. Even the rooster was silent.

At some point the priestess must have arrived to see to Antonia and stop the bleeding because she was no longer in her bed. But all Livia could do was stare at the emperor. Mesmerized by the notion that minutes ago he had been this dominant, cruel, sexual manipulator about to take away all her dignity, and now, here, he was a vulnerable, broken man looking completely defeated as he had still not produced a viable heir.

"Leave us," the emperor's voice cracked.

The last thing Livia saw as she exited the room was the emperor gently stroking his son's head repeatedly whispering, "my boy, my boy."

22

CATO

Cato was hard pressed to find that his plan of keeping his relationship with Noemi a secret was actually working. They had been at it for a few months now and Cato was completely smitten with her. At first, it was difficult coming up with a way to sneak off without being caught and planning when he would be able to do so. His colleagues would for sure notice his frequent absence in their off hours and there was really no consistent reason he could think of to leave the school.

Until it came to him one day, prayer. The gods were such a large part of everyone's life that no one would question his newfound devotion as his training was coming to completion. Every gladiator could use all the extra help they could get. So, he started actually going to the Temple of Mars Ultor several times a week to make an offering. A couple of his friends questioned where he was off to and he did not lie. An offering to Mars, the god who could give him strength in battle, was not questioned in the least. The temple was in the forum and relatively close to the bath house, so in case anyone followed him they would physically see him enter the temple and be none the wiser.

After settling into his new pious routine, he left Noemi a note on her windowsill informing her when to meet at the bath house so he could let her know of the plan. Putting notes on her windowsill in the dark was too risky so he came up with a new system. Actually, Noemi came up with it. They would use the calendar. Every time there was a feast day for any of the main gods, and there were a few a week sometimes, they would meet. That took care of any communication risk and did not create any sort of pattern someone could notice and pick up on. Noemi would tell her parents she was meeting Livia at the palace. Because Livia was never around—she actually had not seen her sister in months—she was supposed to be covering for her as well. Her parents loved the idea that their daughters were bonding and even encouraged it.

Most of the kinks worked themselves out in the first few weeks. One time Cato got caught up after training with his *lanista* who wanted him to run some extra drills and he missed the meetup. Noemi had been worried and was not sure what to do when he did not show up. So, they decided to make a general rule to wait a half hour and if the other person did not show, assume something happened and they couldn't come.

Another time, Cato left the Temple of Mars and spotted a few *lanistas* from the school entering the bath house. He waited out front to intercept Noemi. For the future, they laid a piece of stone into a small crevice in one of the columns that flanked the bath house. This warned the other person it was not safe to meet that day. They even tried to meet someplace other than the bathhouse like the market and the aqueduct, but it was way too risky and they could barely talk.

Cato could not wait for each feast day. Training on those days always seemed to take forever to finish. He couldn't stop thinking about kissing and touching Noemi. She had become his world, something other than a gladiator-dominated future to dream about. The absolute best days were the ones where he trained with Jovian because he got to see her while he trained.

Noemi had made it a point to always be around to help her father with the animal lesson so they could see each other. The most recent lesson involved large animals and tactics to use weight to their advantage. Noemi had come riding into the animal arena at the school on a large elephant. To Cato, she looked like a goddess. She had demonstrated how intelligent elephants were and how they could be used for things other than hauling heavy cargo. Jovian lectured how they were very useful in helping with small fires as their trunks could hold water and spray it at the flames. Cato had watched as she stood up on the pachyderm's back expertly balancing herself while holding on the rope around its neck.

Showoff, Cato smirked.

She gave simple commands and the elephant obeyed with tricks. At one point it drew letters and shapes in the sand with its foot. Cato and his fellow trainees could not believe what they were seeing.

Noemi would always try to include the gladiators in the lesson so she could get closer to him, and Cato loved the effort. Most of the time he missed what he was supposed to be learning because he couldn't help but ogle Noemi. He could see Jovian's pride for his daughter in the way he looked at her, and wondered what it would be like to have a parent who cared about you or was simply present in your life.

Over the months, Cato had come to not only trust Noemi but begin to open up to her. One day, he expertly smuggled in two weighted swords to help her train because she was so into fighting, which made him love her even more. He waited in the abandoned bath house until he heard her move the slab. She ran down the stairs, jumping into his arms the moment she saw him. He couldn't help but kiss her.

"Well, hi to you too!" he teased and gently put her down. "I have a surprise for you today," he said.

"Oh, really," she feigned being unimpressed, but Cato could tell she was excited. He pulled out the two training swords.

Noemi laughed, "What, you want to slice open my other leg now?" she joked.

"No, I want to make sure you are properly trained. You are surprisingly strong for a girl, but I want you to be the best in case you are ever in a position where you need to defend yourself." He felt a little awkward as he handed his girl a sword, but this would be good for them.

"Well, I haven't had time to train lately because I spend all my spare time with you, and I could use some firsthand instruction from Rome's next famous gladiator, Cato Velarius. He is such a brute. A mean, nasty man," she teased.

"Okay, okay, let's start," Cato tried changing the subject as he still had not told her the truth about his past. He was planning on it though, just waiting for the right time. "Your biggest obstacle is going to be your grip strength based mainly on the fact that your hands are smaller than any gladiator's. Maybe one day we can get you a custom sword from a blacksmith, but for now we will make do. The only way to fix this is to wield your sword with both hands as much as possible. When it is not possible make sure the sword is in your dominant hand and hold it like this." He rotated her wrist and moved her thumb to give her the best leverage. "It is going to take some getting used to, but it will keep you from getting blindsided like when I was able to knock you down."

"Thanks for the reminder," she rolled her eyes at him.

"The other thing is you have a huge tell. You telegraph your every move with your eyes. I know where you are going to attack before you even lift the sword in that direction because you look right where you intend to strike. Other than that, your fundamentals are pretty good."

They practiced for a while and she quickly picked up everything he suggested her to do. He couldn't get over her strength for her size.

"We can practice whenever you want down here," Cato said. They sat down to rest on the steps of the empty bath after a few rounds of practice.

"You know, I was thinking," Noemi said as she gently ran her fingers up and down the nape of his neck, "about what life will be like once you are a famous gladiator. You know, not always meeting in secret. I can't wait to actually hold hands in public."

Cato could not hold it in anymore. He wanted all those same things, too, and more, but with the real world came his real life and he couldn't lie to her anymore. "There's something I need to tell you," he started, with a changed tone in his voice. By the look on her face, he could tell that Noemi picked up right away that this was serious.

He told her everything, from being a slave in the villa, to stealing Cato's identity and forging a letter from Leon the Great. Everything came spilling out of him much easier than he thought it would. It was like a weight had been lifted off his shoulders when he finished telling her. He just sat there waiting for her response, half expecting her to run for the hills. When he looked at her, she had tears in her eyes.

"I'm so sorry, Cato," she said. Cato wanted to cry himself. He knew telling her would ruin everything. Why would she want to be with a slave?

But then she surprised him, she leaned over pulling him into her arms for a long embrace. She looked up at him resting her hands on both of his cheeks. "I'm so sorry that you had to go through all that. Thank you for trusting me with your secret. I want you to know that no matter if you were a slave or the emperor, I would love you just the same. I love you for who you are not what you are." And with tears streaming down her face, she kissed him, and Cato felt like he could die now and everything would be all right.

Cato wiped the tears from her eyes. "I mean, it does explain a lot," Noemi started. "Why you talk about the Velarius family as if you weren't one of them, and why you are so kindhearted and actually really nothing like a Velarius in the least." Her eyes got sad again, her voice starting to panic as she began to pace in the bottom of the bath. "Cato, by the gods, we can't even risk seeing each other down here, or anywhere for that matter, not until you graduate and are a true gladiator. I couldn't live with myself if I knew that I somehow exposed your true identity. They would find out you were really a slave, and you would never be freed. You would be executed without question. You only have a few more months. It will be hard, but we have no choice, and I will not hear your argument against it."

As much as Cato wanted to argue with her and tell her that he couldn't go that long without her, he knew that she was right. Watching her get so emotional over his well-being was something he had never experienced in his entire life and it made him feel all warm inside, something he was completely unfamiliar with. It made him love her something fierce.

"I'm serious, Cato. No communication whatsoever. No secret notes. No wandering the hypogeum outside of the gladiator training facility hoping to run into me. I won't even sneak up to the stands to watch you anymore. I'll hide and watch from below if I must. I don't even think I should help my father with lessons anymore, either. If anyone so much as gets an idea that we are together, you are done for."

Cato could not take watching her get this upset. "Come here," he said holding out his arms for her as she fell into him quietly weeping on his shoulder. He wanted to take away all her pain as he held her in his arms. "Listen, everything is going to be okay. I am going to win my final battles and graduate, freeing myself without anyone knowing that I needed freeing, and then we can start the next chapter of our lives and put this behind us. You got it?" he tried to sound optimistic for her sake, but he wasn't so sure he believed himself.

"There is something else," Cato began, "it is probably no big deal, but if I am not going to be able to talk to you for a few months I just wanted to mention it in case something happens."

Noemi looked like a wounded animal on its last breath as she listened to him.

"During Saturnalia I overheard a few of the senators talking about your father. I couldn't entirely hear every word but from the gist I got I think they mean him some sort of harm. I heard the word fire, and I didn't get the sense they were referring to terminating his position at the school. Maybe just keep a few extra buckets of water lying around the hypogeum or something. Ugh, I don't know, maybe I am reading too much into it. Just forget I even said anything." He kind of regretted even mentioning it once the words were out of his mouth. He didn't want her to think he was the dramatic type.

"This is too much talking if this is going to be our last evening together for a few months," was her response as she straddled him on the steps.

Cato knew that was just her way of avoiding any sort of contro-versy, change the subject and make light of a tough situation. But, he wasn't about to call her out for it especially when she was straddling him. He didn't want to waste any more time talking, either, pulling her into his lap.

~

The next few weeks were hard, harder than he expected. He thought he was just going to be able to bury his head in training, but that wasn't the case. Everything reminded him of Noemi. He knew she would never risk it, but he found himself looking over his shoulder as if she would magically appear or something.

When he showed up for classes with Jovian and she was no longer there it really sunk in that he wasn't going to see her. As tough as it was, he had to focus on the next few months. The rankings of the *veterani* were a precursor to the potential fame a gladiator would receive upon graduation. He had to maintain his top three ranking and not get killed in training, and he would graduate as one of the school's best with the added potential to become one of Rome's best gladiators.

Rankings were based on individual skills like sword handling and weightlifting, in addition to wins in arena battles. Cato had main-tained top billing throughout the year, but the competition was getting tight. To make the top of the list every potential graduate was buckling down now, spending extra time with their *lanistas* and addi-tional reps in the practice arena. The school even allowed for some wealthy high-ranking citizens to observe the gladiators during training as the final graduation doubled as a huge gambling scene.

Major bets were placed on which of them would finish at the top, who would die, and other things like least amount of sword use to obtain a victory, and most amount of bloodshed. Because the gambling had evolved and become so immense over the years, some of the gladiators got backed by the wealthy investors. That was huge for the gladiators as they got promoted around the city and fast tracked to fame. Cato was sure to get a sponsor especially with his name. Whenever he saw any spectators milling around, he made a point to make sure he was on top of his game and show off a little.

One day after a grueling training, Cato needed some self-care. His body had been so sore from all the work he had been putting in and it was starting to take its toll. Usually, he would head to the infirmary, but could not risk running into Noemi as much as he wanted to try. Instead, he borrowed some supplies from the healers and had been trying to take care of himself in his quarters. He was on his way there, arms and back throbbing when he almost walked straight into Senator Sulla.

"Ah, Velarius, I've got my money on you, boy. You better come through," he said trying to engage in a dialogue with Cato.

"No one even stands a chance against me," he replied flexing his muscles at the senator while trying to sound hot headed. All he really wanted to do was get some poultices on his shoulders, not showboat with this guy.

But it was the senator who brushed him off instead. "I must be one my way, urgent, eh," he paused uncomfortably, "urgent business in the...awaits," the senator said rushing by Cato.

Cato was glad to be rid of him. As soon as he got in his room and shut the door, he eased up on his perfect posture letting his body relax. Spreading some of the poultice on a cloth, he held it over the flame from the candle, warming up the medicine as the healer had shown him. Careful not to set the cloth on fire, he removed it from the heat placing it poultice side down on his neck. He then lay down on his bed, sighing as he could feel the warm treatment start to work, numbing his back. Closing his eyes, he melted into the bed willing himself to dream of Noemi. Instead, he dreamt of Senator Sulla and failure in the arena.

When he awoke from his nap, the poultice was cold, and he realized he was famished. Making his way to the kitchen, he encountered a bunch of drunk senators causing a raucous, fighting with each other about whose gladiator was the best and how much money they were going to make off of them. Cato wanted no part of it, but his stomach kept grumbling so he slipped around them into the kitchen to get something. He didn't mean to overhear their drunk conversation, but it was hard not to when they were so loud. The bragging kept escalating between the men. They covered all topics, money, whores, land, status within the empire, etc. It was exhausting to listen to.

Cato finished up his dinner readying to leave when he heard the word, "fire." Piquing his interest, he stopped to listen.

It was Senator Sulla talking, "He is going to have himself quite the surprise tonight when he goes to tuck his animals in."

Cato's dinner almost came back up when he realized Sulla was talking about Jovian.

"Once he is taken care of, I will have a clear path to the emperor's inner circle. Let's see one of you top that."

Cato did not wait to hear anymore, there was no time. They were planning to kill Jovian tonight. He had to try and do something. *There was no time to warn anybody*, he thought, *for all I know it's already too late.*

He raced through the gladiator tunnel down into the hypogeum. At this hour, no one would be down there. He made his way through the halls toward the stables looking for anything out of the ordinary, but there was nothing. No smoke, no fire, not a soul save for the animals moving about their pens.

Cato started to laugh at himself. *What an idiot I am*, he thought, *Sulla was just lying to make himself seem more important, there was never any fire.* Cato turned to head back to the school and that's when he got a faint whiff of smoke. Not wanting to be right, he made his way toward where he thought it was coming from. Sure enough, there was a giant cloud of thick smoke billowing out of the stairwell to the second level below.

Not even giving it another thought he walked down the stairs straight into the wall of smoke. He could only see about a body length in front of him, the smoke was so thick. It was incredibly hard to breathe, his entire chest cavity heaving to get air. He had no idea how he was going to find Jovian especially since he had never been down there before. He tried to call out, but he just inhaled more smoke causing him to continuously cough.

Trying to stay low, he slowly made his way animal stall by animal stall toward the heat thinking Jovian might be somewhere where the fire originated. He counted twenty stalls before the fire was so unbearably hot, he had to fall to his knees, the wall of heat forcing him to stop.

There was no way he was going to find Jovian down here. The only thing that was going to happen was him burning to death and Noemi finding his charred corpse the next day. He knew he had to go back. He started counting the stalls again crawling back toward the stairs. He made it as far as three before he started to feel extremely dizzy and had to sit down. The smoke was too thick and there was no relief. He pushed open the stall door behind him hoping to find some sort of better air or even some water.

All the animals had probably suffocated by now even though whatever animal was in there was not even on his mind as he crawled into the stall. There was still smoke but not as bad as in the hall so he could breathe a little bit more. He still could not see anything, so he crawled around blindly searching with his hands for something he could use. He felt around the stall floor until his hands were resting upon a warm, furry, very still body. Moving past the animal he felt around again this time finding a bucket of water that had been for the animal. He drank from it, the water feeling like a breath of fresh air as it hit his throat. He poured what was left of the water over himself drenching his body as much as he could. *I have to keep moving.* He made it another five stalls before he was gasping once more and needed the sweet relief of water.

Hoping every stall was equipped like the first one, he barely squeezed through the door of the next stall as the animal occupying it must have died blocking the door. Once inside, he began his search for more water. He cursed the gods as he found the bucket, but it was tipped over on the ground, completely empty. He would have to somehow try the next one. He crawled back toward the stall door pushing the animal out of the way a little so he could get by, only it did not feel like an animal.

Cato could feel sandals and a human foot. It was Jovian. Adrenaline now coursing through his body, he made his way to Jovian's chest. *Oh, please be alive*, he prayed. Cato laid his head on Jovian's chest. His breath was shallow, his chest barely rising and falling, but he was still alive. They needed water if they were going to go any further. Cato crawled to the next stall. This one had a full bucket. Taking a few gulps for himself, he pushed the bucket on the ground back to the stall with Jovian. He tried to pour some water in Jovian's mouth hoping it would wake him up, but it didn't work.

Cato could feel the heat from the fire getting closer to them. He was running out of time. Remembering a slave trick for using smoke to clear the weeds and waste in the fields during harvesting, he ripped a piece of his tunic and soaked it in the water. He then tied it around his mouth, the water felt cool on his cracked and dried-out lips. He ripped another piece, and this time tied the wet cloth around Jovian's mouth. He poured the remaining water over both of their heads, tossing the empty bucket to the side. He first tried to carry Jovian over his shoulder, but barely made it a few steps before he couldn't breathe, the weight of Jovian's body making it near impossible to move. The smoke was so thick he could not see anything, not even Jovian.

The fire was blazing through stall after stall—it was right next to them now. It felt like his skin was melting in the heat. Mustering up the last of his strength, he grabbed Jovian from behind his arms and began dragging him toward the stairs. He could not see the stalls to even count how many more he had to go. There was no more stopping for water for the second he stopped he would collapse and that would be the end of both of them. He dragged him for what felt like forever until his back heel made contact with the first step causing Cato to fall backward onto the stairs.

He had hoped someone would have noticed Jovian was missing or come to check on the animals, but he was on his own. He maneuvered Jovian up one step at a time trying to move quickly but it was almost impossible between his dead weight and the fact that he had not taken a full breath in gods knows how long. He somehow was able to drag Jovian to the top of the stairs and on to the ground of the first floor. The smoke was still pouring through the opening but at least there was air up here. Cato had used all his strength to get Jovian out, he could barely crawl out himself.

The last thing he remembered was crawling up the top step before everything went black.

23

NOEMI

Noemi had replayed Cato's story in her head thousands of times since she kissed him for the last time in the empty bath. She was in love with a slave. The idea was almost laughable the more she thought about it. She had told him they couldn't see each other until he graduated for his safety, but a small selfish part of her said it because she would have to denounce her own status or leave the empire to be with him if he was found out. She hated herself for even thinking that, but it was true. There was no way her family would approve of a marriage to a slave no matter how understanding they were. It just wasn't an option. Her father would most likely lose his position with the emperor and the family would be shunned in the community. She couldn't let that happen.

So, she made sure to keep her distance. When her father had lessons with Cato and his classmates, she found every excuse to get out of it. One week she pretended to be ill, the next she told him she had unfinished work in the hypogeum, it was excuse after excuse until he just stopped asking for her help. Her heart was heavy as she saw the let down in his face every time she dodged him, especially because their bond over the animals was the best thing they shared together and to lose that was devastating to him.

A few times she had watched Cato's fights from behind one of the trap doors in the hypogeum, but she found that seeing him and not being able to physically be with him was harder than not seeing him at all. Instead, she tried to make herself busy. She made pointless jobs for herself like washing the animals even though they would be killed soon and raking up the stalls even though the animals would trample through it.

She even went so far as to putting buckets of water in each stall, even the unused ones, in case of a fire which was now in the back of her head thanks to Cato. Fires were quite common in the hypogeum, with the lack of ventilation and the occasional extreme heat. One rogue spark from a torch could set the whole place ablaze. Her father, like most other things, had thought of everything and engineered the hypogeum to have a few fire fail safes.

The most important being the aqueduct system that ran through the hypogeum. If a fire broke out, the heat from the fire would burst the aqueduct causing water to pour out extinguishing most if not all of the fire. He even had small trenches dug at the top and bottom of each staircase that would contain the fire to one floor until it could be extinguished. Due to Jovian's preparations, there had been minimal damage with fires in the past, only a few animals lost each time. Also, there was always someone patrolling the hypogeum, even at night. So even if there was some crazy plot against her father, in her mind, a fire would not be the best attempt. Nevertheless, she needed tasks to bide her time so filling buckets was another useless job that kept her busy.

With all the extra hours she was spending in the hypogeum it was only a matter of time before she ran into Felix. Frankly, she was surprised it had not happened sooner. Of course, it had to be after she put in a full day wrestling some of the bear cubs, so she was covered in scratches and was all disheveled looking, anything but put together and attractive. The notion that she even cared about what she looked like was a little disconcerting. While checking some of the stalls on the second level, she noticed Felix working farther down the hall. There was no real avoiding each other so she mustered out the initial conversation.

"Salve," she greeted him. He looked up at her with an almost guilty look on his face that quickly turned into Felix's usual charming smile.

"Nomee! Haven't seen you in forever. How have you been?" his voice so familiar. Noemi's heart dropped into her stomach when she heard him use his pet name for her again, old feelings churning up she thought were long gone. She could not have imagined he would have been so nice upon seeing her the first time after what she had done to him.

He reached in to hug her. She lightly hugged him back, finding the familiar shape and smell of his body so comforting she had to stop herself from embracing him a little harder. She tried to keep her response calm and collected, not wanting him to see her all flustered over their encounter.

"Oh, you know same old stuff, helping my father. What about you?" she asked hoping he did not notice her nervous energy.

"Well, actually a lot has changed. Would you be interested in getting a drink and catching up?" he nonchalantly asked her.

"*Sic*, uh sure. Let's go." She found herself agreeing to spend time with him a little too quickly. It was like her head was telling her no, but her heart just couldn't put him through any more pain. By agreeing to go she felt she was mending something she had broken months ago.

They walked to a nearby bar and sat across from each other at a small table where Felix bought them each a glass of wine. It was awkward and familiar at the same time. They both knew each other so well yet there was this weird new tension between them that Noemi was unsure how to navigate. She did not expect to have these strong feelings for him.

Either Felix didn't seem to notice the new awkwardness, or he was just very good at hiding it. He told her about his new position with some high-ranking senators and how he was working less time in the hypogeum trying to focus on more political matters. They caught up on most every topic like family and gossip. They even briefly touched on the breakup, but she quickly changed the subject when a few tears started to well up. She told him about everything she had been up to leaving out any mention of Cato, of course. They talked for a few hours. Felix seemed happy as far as she could tell, and she truly enjoyed catching up with him.

When there was nothing more to talk about and it was clearly time to go, they hugged again. This time both holding onto each other a second too long, falling back into that old sense of familiarity with each other that felt so good if only for a second. If Noemi was being honest with herself it was hard to say goodbye and walk away. Not because she didn't love Cato, but because she had spent most of her life with Felix and they had grown together. She felt like she was letting part of herself go as they walked away from each other. Felix was her first love, and she would never forget him, but she had to let him go. She had already hurt him, and would not do the same to Cato. Her heart could not take it.

She spent that night longing for Cato more than she had in weeks. She cried herself to sleep wishing he was there to hold her in his arms and comfort her.

Noemi awoke well rested, her eyes still puffy from the night before with thoughts of Felix still on her mind. Wandering into the kitchen she found it strange that neither of her parents were home. She must have slept in late, after all, the day before had been pretty emotional for her.

She made her way to the hypogeum and before she was anywhere near it got a sense something was wrong. She got her first whiff of smoke at the entrance to the tunnel and began to run. Trying not to panic, she made it to the main floor of the hypogeum which was busier than usual. There was not any visible fire but the whole place reeked of smoke. The usual workers were busy moving animals for the morning *venatio* like normal, but it was all the extra people running about that concerned her.

Noemi tried to find someone she knew to ask what the gods was going on. Finally, she found a familiar face and stopped them asking, "What in Pluto is going on?!"

The boy started to brush her off when he realized it was Noemi. "Gods, Noemi, haven't you heard? There was a fire on the second level last night. Jovian was found along with another man, unconscious and badly burned," the boy recounted.

Noemi felt paralyzed. Cato had been right. She should have taken what he had said more seriously. "Where is he now?" she asked a little too aggressively.

"They took him to the gladiator infirmary."

Noemi was already racing there before he could finish his sentence. She found her father lying in a bed, her mother hovering over him softly crying. "Mama!" Noemi yelled running into her arms.

"Noemi! Thank the gods!" her mother said pulling Noemi into her arms.

"What happened?" Noemi asked, afraid to hear the answer.

"There was a fire last night. Your father was here late meeting with someone, and must have been downstairs when the fire started. That's all they really know. He was found on the main floor unconscious with a nasty head wound, barely breathing."

Noemi looked at her father, his burned body wrapped in layered white cloths with a large bandage on his head that was a dark pink color from all of the blood. He looked like his body had started the mummification process.

"The doctors said there is nothing more they can do." Tears rolled down her mother's delicate face as she delivered the grim news. "We can only wait and pray that he wakes up."

Noemi reached for her father's bandaged hand and gave it a gentle squeeze. *This cannot be happening, he's strong,* she thought. *He will wake up. He has to.* She sat with her mother for hours, both intently watching over Jovian as doctors kept checking on him periodically and hypogeum workers came in and out to visit their boss. At some point, someone brought them some food. Noemi wondered if Livia knew what had happened, although she wouldn't be able to leave the palace. A kind nurse with a soft voice suggested they go home and get some rest. Someone would be sent if there were any changes. Noemi didn't really want to leave but she could tell her mother was more than drained and could use the rest.

"Excuse me," her mother called after the nurse, "what of the man they found him with? Will he be alright? I've noticed no one has been to visit him."

The nurse turned to look at a man lying in a bed on the other side of the room. "Ah, he faired a little better than Jovian. He has been in and out of consciousness all day with a few bad burns on his hands. We have given him a little something to keep him sedated for the time being. From what we can gather, he was the one who saved Jovian from the fire. Very heroic. Not sure what he was doing down here at night, probably getting some extra practice in the gladiator arena before the final battles," the nurse explained.

Noemi stopped in her tracks, slowly turning around. *It couldn't be,* she thought. She took a few steps toward the man's bed but did not have to get very close before she recognized a face she knew all too well. Cato, her Cato, was lying unconscious in the bed, both hands bandaged, his soot-covered tunic still on. Noemi started to hyperventilate once she saw him, her body lost control as she collapsed to the ground.

"Noemi!" Her mother tried to help her up.

"There, there love," the nurse helped Noemi up, "seeing the injured is not for everyone."

Noemi stood up with help from her mother and the nurse, tears uncontrollably pouring down her face.

"Let's get you home for a little bit." Her mother had her arm around her as she led her out of the infirmary.

All Noemi could do was nod. She wanted to hold Cato in her arms until he awoke, let him know he wasn't alone. But she couldn't and it absolutely killed her inside. There was nothing she could do. She was catatonic on the walk home, her mother attributing it to seeing her father in such a state. Millions of questions ran through her head like how did he know to be in the hypogeum at that time? Will he be able to graduate and fight again? Why was he so selfless?

Her mind raced until she just couldn't bear the unknown anymore. Her mother was long asleep, exhausted from the emotional day. Noemi scrawled a note for her and left it by her bed letting her know she couldn't sleep and was gone to be with her father.

Back to the infirmary she went trying to think of how she could get near Cato without arousing suspicion. The infirmary was pretty quiet when she arrived save for a single older nurse monitoring the patients. Noemi greeted the nurse and sat down next to her father who looked the same as when she had left. She found herself shaking. She was so anxious being this close to Cato again.

"Do you mind if I sit with that man who saved my father? He has not had any visitors. It is the least I could do," Noemi asked the nurse.

"Aren't you a sweet girl," the nurse replied.

Noemi almost tripped over herself as she tried not to run over to Cato. She sat in front of his bed, his body within inches of hers. She silently sobbed as she placed her hand on his singed arm afraid to touch his bandaged hands. His skin felt surprisingly cool to her touch. She wished she could crawl in bed next to him and lie with him until he woke up. She gently squeezed his arm, her way of letting him know she was there. When his eyes slowly fluttered open for just a second, she thought she was dreaming, but then she watched as he fell back asleep. She took that as a sign from the gods he knew it was her. She smiled through her tears.

When she was sure the nurse wasn't looking, she stood up and bent over him, cradling his head with one hand while she whispered in his ear, "Te amo," and then gently leaned in and kissed his lips. She couldn't help herself.

Noemi moved back to her father's side and resumed holding his hand. She must have been more tired than she thought because she woke up half lying on the foot of his bed. She went to go check on Cato again but when she looked over at his bed, he was gone.

24

LIVIA

The days following the birth were solemn and melancholy. The palace went into mourning, shrouds of black fabric draping every room, windows covered to block the sunlight, and doors closed blocking the fresh air, making it dark and stuffy like a tomb. The emperor was clad in black along with the empress, who, in addition to a black tunic, donned a thick veil to hide her face. Livia thought she caught a glimpse of a smirk from the empress beneath the veil, probably secretly grateful she was not the only one who could not produce a living heir. Events and large dinners had been postponed along with any activity that was not prayer related. The emperor moped about the palace for days ordering offering after offering to every single god he could think of. Everyone, including his advisers, tried to steer clear of him knowing full well the wrath that could be taken out upon them when he was in this kind of mood. Rumor had it that once he got sick of offering riches and animals to the gods he would turn to humans, and no one wanted to be near if that started.

As for Antonia, she survived for now. The priestess was able to work her magic to heal her as best she could. She had been moved from her luxurious bedroom to a small room with a locked door resembling that of a prison cell. She was still very weak in addition to depressed at the loss of her son, the heir. The extreme blood loss had left her bedridden and extremely pale for days after the birth. She cried almost all day and night, her guttural wails heard throughout most of the palace. Now that she was no longer with child, Livia and the other girls were no longer required to care for her, leaving her lonely and afraid while awaiting her fate. For once the veil of mourning was lifted, Antonia would most likely be executed like all the other failed mistresses before her. It all depended on the emperor's mood which was nothing short of grim all the time.

Livia was able to resume her role as one of the emperor's girls. Although there wasn't much fun to be had without the parties and lavish events. She was able to sneak away one day to visit her family without anyone at the palace noticing, but they were not at home or the school, and she did not have the luxury of time to seek them out. Instead, she just became aggravated they were not there awaiting her surprise arrival. *Probably off celebrating Noemi or on some foolish animal errand*, she thought. She scrawled a short note with the intent to make them miss her and feel bad they had not been home.

Came home for a visit. See you have better things to do.

Not sure when I will be home next.

—Liv

Back at the palace, she was running out of things to entertain herself with. She could only wander around the gardens so many times pretending to mourn. Livia hated to even think it, but she started to miss the attention from the emperor, if only for a second. Wearing boring black tunics was getting old, she wanted to resume the party lifestyle she was now free to enjoy again.

As if the gods heard her prayers, she awoke the next day to something quite unfamiliar to her, the sun. The windows had been unblocked and opened, allowing for the sun's light to wake the girls.

Liv jumped out of bed feeling renewed. "The veil of mourning has been lifted!" she shouted to any of the other girls in the quarters who would listen. The other girls were just as excited as she was tossing their black tunics back in their trunks and pulling out their more colorful glamorous ones. Liv wondered what made the emperor finally decide to lift the veil. No one would probably ever know. He was so unpredictable like that.

"I wonder when he will take a new mistress?" Liv heard one girl say.

"I hope it's me," said another.

Livia wasn't sure why they wanted the position with what they had just witnessed Antonia go through. *They can have it*, she thought.

Fabia entered the girls' quarters all chipper, she too was ready to return to normal. "Okay, girls. Listen up. I know you are all excited to resume your duties. However, be forewarned. His mood will vary, and you may be put in new situations which I cannot predict or help you out of. Now, to ease back into the swing of things, the emperor has invited you all to accompany him to the colosseum for some much deserved entertainment."

All the girls were excited for an outing except Livia. She dreaded going back there.

"Oh, and girls," Fabia interrupted them," tomorrow is Antonia's sentencing. Let us all offer up a few prayers to the gods that she may be spared. All right then. That is all. Salve."

"Ohhh, the colosseum!" one girl cooed.

Livia did her best not to roll her eyes as she feigned her excitement. "I just love it there."

The emperor's guards led the girls through the tunnel under the palace to the hypogeum. *The last time I was in this tunnel I ended up with a whole new life*, she thought. They entered the emperor's quarters, already filled with random senators trying to get the ear of the emperor. During the veil of mourning, there had been no business conducted so these men had mountains of topics to run by him. Most of the men were enjoying the libations provided to them a little too much, Livia noticed.

The emperor was deep in conversation with his adviser when the girls showed up. When his eye caught Livia's, his whole demeanor changed. He all but dismissed the senators from the room to shift his focus to the girls.

"Welcome, ladies! Come make yourselves comfortable," he gestured to the couches near him.

Excited to be flirted with and noticed again, most of the girls practically ran to his side.

Livia made an effort to blend in more, not wanting to draw attention to herself. As she sat on the couch farthest from the emperor, she took note that the empress was not present. A few girls took to immediately wooing him, feeding the emperor by hand, fanning him, massaging his shoulders, whatever they could think of to possibly gain his favor for it was open season now that Antonia was out of the way. Livia tried to look like she was having a good time but she could feel his eyes on her as she sipped her wine and chatted with a few other girls.

"Livia," his voice was stern yet inviting, "I saved you a special seat next to me. Come, little topo."

This is new, Livia thought, he wasn't trying to be secretive anymore. He was showing outright favor for her in front of everyone. Livia stood and took a seat next to the emperor. She could see some of the other girls giving her nasty looks and whispering to each other out of pure jealousy.

The emperor began talking to Livia as if they were the only two in the room. "Ah, I have missed you these last weeks. Apologies for not finding you sooner but I have had a lot on my plate as you know. But not to worry, the gods and fates have revealed to me their plan and I will carry on with it. And you, my topo, are part of that plan."

Hearing those words, Livia looked up at him with sheer panic no doubt showing across her face. He grabbed her hand, trying to reassure her and it took all her strength not to pull it away. She could feel all eyes on them.

He stood up, kissing her hand before he let go.

Livia could hear the horns above signaling the start of the battle.

"Everyone, let's go watch the fight, I am eager for a little violence," he announced. "Everyone except you, topo. I need you to head back to the palace. Fabia is waiting for you," he said to her in a low voice.

With that, he, along with everyone else who had been enjoying themselves ascended the stairs into the emperor's private box to watch whatever was scheduled in the arena that afternoon. Livia was escorted back to the palace through the tunnel by two guards.

When she arrived back to the palace, Fabia was waiting for her with a smile on her face. "Livia, your life is about to change. It seems you now hold the emperor's fancy and the new title of 'Mistress'."

"Wait, what?!" Livia asked dumbfounded.

"Yes, the emperor had given us instructions of his wishes a while ago and everything has been arranged for you. Let me show you to your new room," Fabia made it sound like this was as normal as taking daily prayer.

Livia followed Fabia down another wing of the palace, past the gardens on the far east side of the property. *Great,* she thought, the sarcasm oozing through her brain, *completely secluded from everyone where no one would hear her screams.* Her new bedroom, if it could even be called that, was nothing short of extravagant. It was the size of a small house.

"Everything in here is yours. A gift from his majesty. You will see that your belongings have been brought here and put away," she instructed.

Livia started to look around while Fabia continued her welcome speech. "I have held this position for years and have given each mistress the same advice. You are only something until you are nothing. That is, as long as you are favored by him, you can have everything you desire. Take full advantage of your position while you can because it will not be forever. It is only a matter of time before he loses interest, or you do something to bid yourself an ill fate like Antonia. Make your time count. Congratulations, and may the fates be on your side."

"Uh, thanks, Fabia," Livia responded not having a clue how to even begin to process what she had just said.

"Okay, well if you need anything just ask anyone you see. You have a full staff appointed to you. Good luck!" She left, the sound of her shoes on the marble echoing down the hall as she walked away.

Glad she was gone, Livia explored her new quarters. She had armoires filled to the brim with tunics and togas of all different colors made to her exact size. Not to mention sandals galore. She would probably have to wear two pairs a day for a year just to get through them all. There was a whole desk with various drawers. Each filled with countless pieces of jewelry any color and shape imaginable with everything from bracelets to earrings. She had her own private walk-in bath and attendant who introduced herself to Livia along with the other five women on staff who made their introductions as well.

"Can we get you anything?" one of them asked her.

Livia's instinct was to decline, but Fabia's words in the back of her mind made her say otherwise. "I'd care to take a bath now. Oh, and I'm also famished. Bring me whatever the emperor usually eats at this time of day. And some of his best imported wine."

As she sat in the bath, she weighed her options. There really was no way out. She would have to do what she must to survive. She was going to make the best of it, alright. She spent the rest of the day playing dress up and making outrageous requests to her new staff, all of which were met without question or strife. It was not lost on her that weeks ago she was on the other side of this, catering to Antonia's every whim. Now she could see Antonia was just heeding Fabia's warning and she did not blame her for doing so. She knew the other half of this deal was going to come into play sooner rather than later, and there was nothing for her to do but accept it.

The next morning, she awoke as if she were still dreaming. There was food beside her bed and an attendant ready to help her to the chamber pot. Her outfit had been laid out for her, a sharp-looking tunic.

"The trial is this morning," a servant girl said as if reading her mind.

Gods! She had forgotten all about Antonia's fate. *To think all this was once hers. I wonder what they did with all of her custom clothes.* Livia accentuated her look with a few baubles from the drawers and was on her way, accompanied by two guards to the hall where the sentencing would take place. She was escorted to a throne on the emperor's left while the empress sat on his right. She watched the empress snicker as she noted her new position.

Livia did not care what she thought of her. She was here and she had to play along for her own life's sake.

The emperor leaned over to her and whispered, "I hope you are finding your accommodations and amenities suitable."

"They will suffice," Livia replied arrogantly.

The emperor laughed out loud at her response.

Livia knew he was used to doting, doe-eyed girls who gave him no pushback. If she was going to give herself a chance to be a long-term mistress, she would have to change it up a bit. Be unforgettable. That was her plan, anyway.

In front of her sat a row of senators, a priest, and a scribe to record everything that happened.

Antonia was brought in by two guards. Livia had to stifle a gasp upon seeing her. She was unrecognizable. Frail looking and thin, she could barely stand on her own. Her tunic was tattered and dirty. Her hair matted and messy. It was hard to believe this was the same girl Livia had catered to for months. Antonia stood in front of everyone, her head bowed looking at the ground.

A senator began speaking, "This is the trial of Antonia Helvius, former mistress to the emperor. Let the proceedings commence."

Livia listened as a laundry list of grievances against Antonia were spelled out. All of which were completely fabricated and miscon-strued, Livia noticed.

At one point Antonia was allowed to address the court. She looked up, trying hard to seem strong and confident.

She only dropped her guard for a second when she saw she had already been replaced by Livia, but regained her composure quickly. "I, Antonia Helvius, come before your majesty and court to beg your pardon for all my transgressions. I have proven that I can bear an heir. The loss of our son was that of a curse placed upon my womb by the priestess not by my own doing. I stand here now and offer my womb again to you if you would be so willing. I ask that if it may not be your will, you pardon me for I have been nothing but a loyal mistress. Praise be the gods."

The room was silent as she finished except for the sound of the scribe feverishly writing down her plea. Livia actually felt for her. The death of the baby was no one's fault but yet someone had to be blamed.

One senator approached the throne as the emperor whispered his verdict in his ear. Livia didn't have to hear it to know what it would be. There was no way she would be pardoned not when he already had moved on from her and had declared another mistress. The emperor was already over her, on to his next conquest.

The senator walked down in front of Antonia. "On behalf of his majesty and the Roman Empire, Antonia Helvius is hereby sentenced to death by execution."

Antonia fell to her knees, sobbing, covering her face with her hands.

The guards came to escort her back to her cell until the march to her death, which would happen within the hour. She begged and screamed for mercy the entire way back.

Livia thought about asking the emperor to change his mind but knew it would do no good. She had no power.

The emperor stood up. He would now attend the parade to Antonia's execution, her final farewell.

Livia was not required to be by his side for he did not want the women to witness her death. *So kind of him,* Liv thought sarcastically. Liv watched as the emperor and his court prepared his chariot. He would follow Antonia as she walked to the colosseum for her execution by whatever means had been prepared for today. Livia should have used this time to relax in her wing and enjoy the time away from the emperor; however, something had changed within her.

For whatever reason, she felt this overwhelming urge to do anything she could to help Antonia. Maybe it was the idea in the back of her head that this would one day be her fate as well, she did not know. She dressed in a plain tunic, discarding any jewels or other signs of wealth and wore a cloak fastening the hood over her head. No one would notice if she snuck out of the palace for a little bit, most everyone was at the parade and she did not have Fabia babysitting her anymore.

She left the palace through the servants' quarters and worked her way down Palatine Hill through the gardens. She hurried, hoping Antonia was walking very slowly. Luckily for her, the Temple of Vesta and more importantly the House of the Vestal Virgins was right at the bottom of the hill. She knew that the only person who could outrank the emperor was a Vestal Virgin. Her dream of becoming one was long gone but maybe she could be part of their life if only for a second.

Livia slowed her gait upon entering the sacred ground. As much as she needed to run, it would be disrespectful to the gods for her to do so. The circular temple was pristine and when you entered you could almost feel the energy created by the virgins. It took Livia's breath away the minute she walked into the sacred atrium. But, she had to get it together and quickly find Marbella.

Marbella was Noemi's age, a family friend. A few years ago, she was the lucky girl in their part of town who was chosen over Livia and everyone else to be a Vestal Virgin. Livia had spent many sleepless nights being jealous of Marbella and now here she was seeking her help. Men were not allowed to enter the women's temple and non-Vestal Virgins were not allowed in the housing areas, but Livia had no choice.

Knowing absolutely everything there was to know about the Vestal Virgins and their lifestyle, Liv made her way down the stairs behind the offering area and into the hall where the girls resided. At this hour they would be taking their midday prayers in their rooms preparing for lunch. Livia made her way room to room peeking in at the girls. All the doors were open as no one was supposed to be down there except the girls.

Liv found Marbella's room and softly knocked on the wooden door frame entering before Marbella had a chance to turn around.

"Marbella," Liv whispered, "don't be alarmed. It's me, Livia, Noemi's sister."

Marbella turned around off the kneeler, "Livia! What are you doing here, you almost gave me a fright."

"My sincere apologies, Marbella, but I would not have come if it was not urgent," Livia explained. She did not have time to catch up with Marbella for fear that the parade would pass by the temple. "I'm sorry if this is rushed, but I need your help. You are the only person in the entire empire who can help me right now. I work in the palace now and the emperor has just sentenced his mistress to death all because she gave birth to a stillborn child. She is a good person, and it is not fair she should have to die because the gods chose to take her son. I cared for her during her pregnancy and know her heart to be pure. You can save her. Please, the parade will be by soon. I beg you, Marbella, I will do anything." Livia was so overwhelmed the words flew out of her mouth so fast.

Marbella placed a calming hand on Livia's shoulder. "I can see you mean well. Your heart is in the right place and I commend your compassion for others. Unfortunately, we cannot alter what the fates have written. We are merely a vessel for the gods."

Livia looked absolutely defeated. *Why did I even bother coming down here?* It was like she wanted to prove something to herself. Part of her felt Antonia was her future and if she could somehow save Antonia, she could save her future self from the same fate. And now Antonia was going to be killed and there was nothing she could do. Surprising herself, she began to cry. She cried for Antonia and she mostly cried for the mess she had gotten herself into.

Marbella embraced her and she let her. The small act of comfort felt so good.

"Now, if I happen to find myself praying in the gardens in a few minutes and a parade goes by it might be a sign from the gods," Marbella smiled at Livia.

Livia wiped the tears from her eyes. "Really?!" she asked in complete shock.

"Quickly. You must go now before you are seen. Go in peace.

Remember, the fates may hold the strings, but you can create your destiny within the strings themselves. Don't let your destiny control you," Marbella advised her while looking in the hall to make sure the coast was clear.

"Thank you! I can never thank you enough!" Livia said overjoyed as she took her leave of the temple.

Antonia must have been walking at a snail's pace for the parade was in sight but not quite there.

Livia climbed back up part of Palatine Hill and hid behind some foliage so she could watch.

As the procession neared, Livia could see why it was taking Antonia so long. A crowd had gathered along the route throwing garbage and rocks at her as she tried to make her way to the colosseum. Her knees were bloodied from falling in the street so many times as she kept getting hit and sworn at by the crowd.

The emperor sat in his chariot behind her with a smug look on his face clearly enjoying the show.

Livia watched the Temple of Vesta's gardens for any sign of Marbella. She couldn't quite see her but trusted she would come through. Livia wished she could somehow let Antonia know she just had to make it a little further and then it would be over.

"Come on, Antonia," she urged aloud, "you are almost there."

The procession was now in front of the temple. Livia strained to see as the crowd was dense. However, they did stop their cussing and hurling of debris while in front of the most sacred building in the empire.

Livia watched as the crowd started to quickly part as if they were scared of something nearing them. And then, one by one they all began to kneel.

Marbella looked as if she had just innocently wandered into the street while gathering some herbs from the garden. The crowd was in absolute awe at the chance of being so close to the highest power in Rome. Marbella pretended to just notice Antonia lying in the street bloodied and exhausted. Antonia was probably not even aware at what was happening.

Marbella approached Antonia like a mother helping her child. "Oh, you poor girl, let me help you up," Marbella said. The second Marbella touched Antonia, the crowd began to whisper, those whispers turned into loud cheers as the crowd realized what had just happened. A touch from a Vestal Virgin pardoned all sins no matter how severe.

The emperor stood in his chariot, his face red in anger as he watched what was happening. He then sat back down as even he knew that the Vestal Virgins outranked him and were a direct hand to the gods.

The crowd clapped as Marbella helped Antonia to her feet. "Come with me, dearie. Let us clean you up."

Livia saw the moment Antonia realized what was going on. Her face broke into a large smile and a wave of relief washed over her. It was as if all her strength had been renewed. There was even a pep in her step as she walked toward the Temple of Vesta. Antonia turned back to look at the emperor, a devilish smile on her face at a new renewal on life.

Tears of happiness streamed down Livia's face. She had done it. She had helped someone and gone over the emperor's head. Although no one would ever know what she had done, she did, and that was all she needed. Antonia would most likely rejoin society and keep a low profile for the rest of her life. A life she never thought she would have. There on that hill, Livia knew what must be done to survive the emperor. It would not be easy or desirable in anyway but like Marbella said she had to mold her own destiny.

25

CATO

Cato felt like he was in a dreamworld. Every time he tried to open his eyes he was lulled back to sleep. He gave in after realizing he could not fight off whatever medicine they had given him. It made him feel like he was not in control of his body and he did not like it. His mind kept playing tricks on him. He dreamt Noemi was next to him and even kissed him. Oh, how he wished that it was real. As the medicine wore off, he slowly awoke taking in his surroundings. He was once again back in the infirmary. This time he was in much better shape. Other than the pain in both his hands, he felt fine.

He rolled over to try and see about Jovian. He hoped more than anything that he had lived. He saw him lying in a bed not far from his but more importantly, he saw Noemi sitting in a chair with her head laying on her father's bed fast asleep. He lay there on his side turned toward her willing her to just open her eyes so she could see him.

For hours she slept and for hours he lay there watching her beautiful, soft face peacefully rest. It was the most he had seen of her in months.

Interrupting his loving stare was Lea, the nurse who had treated him when his arm was badly wounded. "It's good to see you among the living again, Dominus Velarius," she joked as she removed the bandages from his hands. "Well, you were extremely lucky, these burns look worse than they are. It might be a little challenging to grip a sword or a shield, but the damage isn't permanent. Now, the real question on everyone's mind is how did you end up in the midst of a fire in the hypogeum in the middle of the night?" she asked.

Cato had prepared himself for this question and answered without hesitation. "I was getting in some extra practice while everyone was asleep. You know, if you want to be the best you have to work harder than everyone else," the lie rolling off his tongue. "I smelled some smoke and found the second floor on fire. I planned to get someone when I heard a voice calling for help down there. I went to help him, and the smoke must have gotten the best of me because I don't remember much else except for getting us out of the fire." Cato tried to make it sound like it was no big deal. "How is he doing anyways?" Cato inquired casually steering the conversation away from himself.

Lea lowered her voice, "It's really touch and go. His breathing is not very strong. He is lucky you were down there."

"Ah, well, it wasn't anything really. Uh, it's off to training for me. Gratias. Hope to not see you again for a while. Salve," Cato awkwardly tried to end the conversation and leave the infirmary. He wanted to get back to the school before he was missed.

It seemed his worrying was all for nothing because no one noticed he was even gone. Everyone was so focused on their own extra training and themselves. His hands were pretty raw but bandaging them up would only draw unwanted attention to a potential weakness for his opponents. There were less than two weeks left until the final graduation battles and it was every man for himself.

The school was making all the necessary preparations. Cato was paired with a designer to customize his wardrobe for the final battle. A short, rotund boy, no older than Cato met with him to take his measurements. The boy was awkward and sweaty as if he had just fought off a beast in the colosseum. Cato did not really care for some flashy costume but knew it was tradition for graduation. The designers tried to be as innovative as possible for if they happened to design for Rome's next top gladiator it was their look and signature that the empire would recognize forever.

"Now, I was thinking of going with some sort of winged motif what with the name Velarius and all. What are your thoughts?" the boy sounded as if it was a struggle to even talk.

Cato did not particularly have an opinion one way or another, but he could use something for his hands for extra protection. "I would like some sort of glove for my hands to be added," Cato tried to sound interested and engaged.

"Ohhh, that would be doable. I can fit that into the theme," the boy kept talking, but Cato wasn't listening, his mind was wandering back to Noemi and Jovian. *Two more weeks,* he kept reminding himself.

The first week flew by. First, there was the trials the *veterani* competed in for their final rankings of their school careers. The entire school, not to mention the potential investors, had lined the stands making it all the more nerve racking for the gladiators. Cato had tried his best to get a top rank and thought he did well overall.

The rope climb and the boulder throw were particularly difficult because they relied on grip strength. Despite his hands being weaker due to his burns, he felt he managed well. He did excel at the speed and agility test of chasing a goat around a locked pen. He caught the goat in record time thanks to all his practice corralling animals as a slave at the villa. His vertical leap was also in the top, with his chalk mark being the highest on the wall. Overall, he was confident he would be ranked in the top five with at least a few sponsor offers.

Then he had his final lesson with the animals. He was hoping to see Jovian back but one of his assistants who taught the final class only offered up that Jovian had business elsewhere and could not advise that day. Cato knew otherwise and hoped he was on the mend.

Lastly, there was the end of school year feast he attended where some of the first years performed a skit imitating and poking fun at the graduates. Of course, they spent a good amount of time roasting Cato and the Velarius family as big dumb brutes.

"Cato is so dumb he threw a rock at the ground and missed," one teased.

Cato laughed along with everyone else, enjoying the attention.

After the show, Cicero announced the final rankings. "This year we have had an abundance of talent, some of the best we have seen at this school in years. For that, you should be proud of yourselves. I am confident many of you will be successful in your careers as gladiators. Now with that, the rankings. In fifth place, Justus Agrippa," Cicero announced.

Cato clapped for his friend, knowing that if Justus had ranked fifth, he was definitely top five. He held his breath as more rankings were revealed waiting for his name.

"Now, for this year's top gladiator. I must say that this was not even close. There was a clear difference between our top two gladiators, one of the highest scores that I have ever seen. Congratulations, Cato Octavian Velarius on the honor of being this year's top gladiator."

Cato smiled as his fellow classmates and *lanistas* cheered for him. His hard work paid off immensely as he was the most coveted gladiator of his peers. All he had to do now was win his final battle and he was golden.

His excitement was short lived as it was now time for the most uncomfortable tradition, the presentation of the swords and the helmets. The school had helmets and swords forged for each graduate entering the final battle with personal touches adorning each. Some swords had a colored gem on the hilt or a family crest engraved on the blade. The helmets were similar, some with colorful plumes and others with inscriptions on the back representing something special for each gladiator. Traditionally, if the gladiator had a family member who was an alumnus the family member would present the graduate with the sword and helmet. For everyone but Cato, this was a special and proud moment.

Of course, it would be expected that Leon the Great would present his son with his helmet and sword especially since he was the top ranked gladiator, the highest honor. Cato knew this was just one of the last lies he had to tell until he was freed after his final battle. He'd done a lot of groundwork prior to this, planting seeds for weeks that his father was having doubts about traveling for the ceremony due to his mother's recent illness. Now he waited in line and watched as some of the other gladiators got to share the honor with their families, something he knew he would never have.

Magistri Cicero presented Cato with his sword and helmet, "Sorry to hear about your mother," he said as he handed Cato his sword. "May Apollo heal her. And please give your father my regards."

"Thank you. I will," Cato said pleased the lie had worked. *That was easier than I thought it would be.* He was then able to enjoy the rest of the ceremony knowing he just had to get through one more week and the deception would not matter once he graduated. His status as a gladiator would absolve any past transgressions.

Because of his prestigious ranking posted all over the empire, Cato's celebrity status intensified. People whispered and pointed wherever he went. He heard a lot of "that's him" and "there he is" when he went out in public. He was assigned a security detail if he happened to leave school grounds, two burly men escorted him wherever he went. Anything could happen at this point, a jealous opponent could put out a hit on him or a crazed fan might try attacking him. It was strange for Cato to receive all this attention, but he knew it came with the success of his plan he had put in motion years ago at the villa. The only thing he had not accounted for was falling in love. But he couldn't worry about that, he needed to focus on what he had set out and risked everything to do.

As the highest ranked gladiator, Cato was given the privilege of lighting the ceremonial flame representing the three years of training for all the gladiators. It was the week before the final battle and the first time the gladiators would wear their newly designed gear to present to the empire. Cato's was laid out in his room with a note attached from his designer.

Fly high, Cato. Let these wings soar.

His gear was better than anything he could have envisioned for himself. In fact, it was perfect. Subtle but not boring. Every piece had some sort of wing etched or attached to it. The armor that draped over his shoulder was bronze laden with golden wings etched on his back as if he were some sort of god. The wrist guards had multiple wings entwined together etched into a circular pattern. Even the heels of his sandals had a small wing attached to the back. His favorite piece was the helmet. Two shiny golden wings framed his face, with so much detail the feathers looked real. A plume of feathers dyed red rested on the top of the helmet giving a striking pop of color. He would be unmistakable. He draped the golden cape with a large eagle embroidered on it over his shoulders, he would not fight with it on but would wear it for the ceremonies.

He picked up his sword with his initials etched onto the hilt, the only part of his attire that was plain and that was by design. A sword was a weapon he felt, not something to be flashy. As he stood in his room, dressed in his full gear he couldn't help but smile as everything he had dreamed of was falling into place. He had gotten himself here and his hard work was being rewarded.

The rest of the gladiators were dressed for battle. All the costumes had their own flair, but none were as extraordinary as Cato's.

The men stood outside the school in a semicircle, swords pointed blade down in the dirt as they placed both hands on the hilt facing Magistri Cicero as he gave his final speech to the men. "Today you stand before me as true gladiators. The road has not been an easy one, as many have failed to get here. I commend you for your strength and perseverance thus far. Now is the time for you to shine and make Ludus Magnus proud. I would again like to congratulate Cato Velarius for his high honor of top ranked gladiator. He will lead the march to the arena to light the flame, symbolizing the end of your training and the beginning of your careers."

Cato tried to listen intently to the rest of his speech but was too busy soaking in the moment of his success being recognized. He refocused in when Cicero got to the pairings announcement. As was custom the pairings for the final battle went according to rank. Cato being the highest rank would face the lowest ranked gladiator, a fight that would be quick and easy for him. Each gladiator called in the pairing went up on stage with their opponent to ceremoniously cross swords. They held their position while the artist quickly sketched them for the school records. Then it was the parade to the arena led by Cato.

Walking through the streets of the city, he was elated as crowds gathered to see and cheer them on as they passed by. People shouted his name, a feeling he didn't think he would ever quite get over. Nothing could bring him down. The parade wound through the streets ending at the gates to the colosseum. The crowd roared as the gladiators entered getting their first glimpse at each one's costume. In a few days, merchandise would be sold for the final battle. Cato imagined children in the stands with eagle figurines and wooden wings on their backs cheering for him.

Cato led them into the middle of the arena, the sand feeling fresh and crisp under his feet. He was handed a lit torch which he accepted and carried up a small ramp at the end of the arena. He touched the torch to the end of a long piece of fabric that hung down from the flame at the top of a large pole. The fire burned up the string of fabric until it reached the basin. The flame started off small circling the basin and then began to roar into the sky. The crowd cheered.

Cato closed his eyes for a second wanting to remember this moment for the rest of his life. The master of ceremonies introduced all the competing gladiators for the crowd including all their stats. Some lucky members of the crowd were allowed to come down on the arena floor to meet the gladiators in person. They asked all kinds of questions and wanted autographs from the men. Cato had a line of fans waiting to meet him. As much as he should have played the part of a Velarius brute and been dismissive of the fans he just couldn't bring himself to be mean. He had never had this much adoration in his entire life and it felt good, really good.

The ceremony ended shortly after and the men exited through the gladiator tunnel back to the school. The whole way back all the men were joking with each other about who had more fans and whooping on a high from all the excitement. Cato couldn't believe his fortune. He sent up hundreds of prayers to the gods in thanks.

When he got back to the school, he noticed Magistri Cicero giving orders to some of the emperor's guards. *Probably briefing them on the itinerary for the final battle,* he thought. He didn't pay them much attention. In fact, when Magistri Cicero called him over he thought they were also fans who wanted to meet and congratulate him. Cato smiled as he approached the guards. It was the look in Magistri Cicero's eyes that made Cato realize something was wrong.

Immediately the guards grabbed Cato knocking him to the ground and shackling his hands and feet. Cato tried to fight back but it was no use, he had been totally caught by surprise.

"What is the meaning of this?!" Cato yelled. "Don't you know who I am? There must be some mistake! Magistri Cicero tell them who I am!" Cato's pleas fell on deaf ears. No one answered him, instead they all remained silent as they hauled him to the hypogeum and locked him in a prison cell.

26

NOEMI

One more week. That was it. That was all that stood between her reunion with Cato. It was all Noemi could think about. She fantasized about what they would do and where they would go together. She dreamt about their wedding and their children and anything the future might bring. She had seen the gladiator rankings posted, everyone had. She cheered out loud when she saw Cato's name at the top of the list posted in the forum. She half thought about taking the list home so she could look at it all day long, but people would stare. Her heart filled with pride when she overheard random people in the forum saying that they were rooting for Cato and talking about him like he was Hercules.

She even found herself joining in on the rhetoric. "I heard he is the emperor's favorite going into the final battle," she said to the crowd then smiled to herself as she could hear the rumor spreading. She couldn't help herself. Her spirits were high not just because she could see Cato again, but her father had woken up a week after the fire and was regaining strength every day.

When he was well enough, he was moved back to his house to continue his recovery. The doctor said he would always have issues with breathing because of the smoke, but he should regain full mobility and strength. Everyone was thrilled to hear the news. Of course, the question on everyone's mind was what had happened that night. Unfortunately, there were not many answers. Her father said that the last thing he remembered was that he went to check the second floor and then felt a large blow to the back of his head.

So, someone had it out for him, but without him remembering anything it was hard to pin the blame on anyone. His team had managed to hold the daily animal spectacles together without the emperor noticing a shift in leadership. The fire had only damaged part of the second level and had already been cleaned and rebuilt. For the most part, people seemed to move on from it and did not want to dwell on how or why it happened.

Noemi wished it were different but to push the matter would only bring about scrutiny into her own life and threaten Jovian's position. All she could do was keep in the back of her mind that Cato was right and there were some people in the government who had it out for her father and they needed to be careful. Noemi planned to tell her father all of this when he was back to work but until then he needed to rest, and she didn't want to hinder his recovery.

While her father recovered, Noemi had thrown herself even more into organizing and coming up with ideas for new shows. That morning she was overseeing an idea she had gotten from the bath house. She had a pit dug in the center of the arena about the length of an elephant. On top of the pit a thick net was held taut by small wooden picks nailed into the ground. Her idea was that the *venatores* would make a spectacle of running the animals around the arena then lead them over the pit where they would get tangled in the net and fall in leaving the *venator* victorious. This way, she was still able to put on a good show with minimal harm to the animal as the spectators would envision the animal's death when it was really landing safely in the pit to be later returned to the stables.

Noemi was at the main arena entrance watching her idea come to fruition when Felix came up behind her readying a cheetah for the next *venatio*. Noemi hadn't thought of him since their meet up a few months ago. She had been so busy with her new responsibilities and her father's recovery.

"Salve," Felix said to her.

Noemi waved back noticing he looked gaunt and run down. She turned her attention back to the *venatio* hoping the net would fall perfectly.

"Salve," Felix said again this time in more of a forceful tone.

Noemi waved again, annoyed he couldn't take a hint that she was working.

Felix came up behind her mumbling something inaudible. He was really acting strange, but Noemi needed to focus.

"Felix, I really need to see this through. Can you not?" she said with a more aggressive tone than she had intended. That must have been just the opening he was waiting for because he proceeded to start a conversation.

"You know I love you, Noemi, and you hurt me in a way that was unforgivable," Felix started in, pacing back and forth behind her.

Noemi was only half listening, this wasn't really the place for a heart to heart.

"I even tried to forgive you for a time thinking I must have been mistaken or misunderstood what had happened. I went so far as to follow you for a while trying to see if you were as hurt as I was."

This got Noemi's attention.

Felix continued, never skipping a beat, "You didn't seem sad or even lonely from what I could see. Your aura was light, and you had a spring in your step. I thought, how was this possible? My Nomee not even shedding a tear over the life we built together. And then it came to me, the only thing that would make you get over us would be someone else."

The hairs on the back of Noemi's neck stood straight up. He had her full attention, but she dared not turn around for fear her face would confirm everything he was saying.

He kept talking. "Now, here is where I give you a lot of credit." His voice sounding confident and menacing. "I followed you for months and could spot nothing out of the ordinary save for a few more baths than usual. You would have fooled me too had it not been for how well I know you."

Noemi's fingernails were now digging into the wax tablet she held.

"It's a shame it took your father's, umm shall we say 'accident' for you to slip up. You see, I just happened to walk into the infirmary and saw you sitting with one of the other injured men. This intrigued me, as you can imagine, so I hid around the corner where I watched you the entire time. Even without seeing you kiss him, I knew. He was the someone else."

Tears began to well up behind Noemi's eyes.

Felix continued. "At first, I was a little relieved to be honest. My instincts had not failed me after all. Then the anger set in and boy did it ever. I plotted my revenge several times."

Noemi noticed the sarcastic change in his tone.

"But as you know, Nomee, I am a reasonable fellow and a loyal citizen of this empire. So, when I saw what I perceived to be a clear infraction of the gladiator code, well, frankly, I just had to report it to the emperor," at this he paused clearly waiting to see Noemi's reaction.

Noemi whipped around and charged Felix, almost knocking him to the ground except he had been prepared for her wrath. "You did what?!" she screamed at him, her voice full of pure panic. Noemi now saw a sinister look on Felix's face, a look she was unfamiliar with. Felix was not the person she had known for all those years.

He had changed and she could see it. It seemed she had given him the response he had been looking for. "I guess it doesn't matter who your family is these days, the emperor will sentence anyone to death," Felix teased.

"You're lying!" Noemi accused him.

Chuckling, Felix responded, "No, that's only something you do, Noemi. If you don't believe me, see for yourself. He has been holed up in the prison since yesterday. Better get your goodbyes in, his execution is set for tomorrow. Oh, and cheer up, Nomee, I didn't mention who his indiscretions were with. I am not that bitter."

With that he left the tunnel not only getting in the last word, but clearly feeling satisfied with his revenge.

Noemi didn't waste any time. She couldn't tell if he was lying or not, but she had to know for sure. She ran as fast as she could to the other side of the hypogeum praying Cato wasn't there. She could kill Felix she was so mad. "Please be a cruel joke, please be a cruel joke," she said to herself as she ran.

The hallway to the prison was empty when she got there, no guards. *That was a good sign,* she thought. She started looking in the cells one by one for Cato. Her panic even started to subside a little when she didn't see him.

The cells were mostly full of slaves and thieves awaiting their execution. There were only three more cells to check. Taking a deep breath, she checked the first one. Empty. And then her stomach sank. She didn't even have to look in the next cell to know that Cato was in there. She could hear him humming their favorite tune from Saturnalia.

Noemi nearly dove through the cell bars. "Cato!" she screamed reaching for him through the bars. He was sitting with his back against the wall, dressed in rich-looking golden gladiator gear. A fancy helmet lay tossed to the side.

"Noemi?" Cato's voice was soft like he hadn't spoken in a long time as he came over to embrace her through the bars. "Are you insane? What are you doing down here? You must go. It's just some sort of misunderstanding. I should be released soon," he told her, hope still in his voice.

Noemi was shaking she was so upset and mad. "Cato," she started, her voice nearly choking, "It isn't a misunderstanding. They know."

Cato looked up at her, eyes widening with understanding. "Impossible," he said, "I have been nothing but careful. Cut all ties to my former slave life. The Velarius family would never risk exposing their son by coming out of hiding. No one knew but me."

Noemi could see Cato's mind spinning. Noemi squeezed his hands through the bars. "Cato. Stop." There was pain and fear in her voice. "Not that, us. They know about us." Noemi was sobbing now as she saw the look on Cato's face change from annoyance and angst to fear. He knew what that meant. Death.

Noemi fought through her sobs to tell him what she knew. "It was Felix. He saw me with you in the infirmary. The kiss. He ratted you out to the emperor like the snake he is. Your execution is set for tomorrow. And now..." she stopped, not wanting to finish the sentence, "I could kick myself for letting my guard down. I'm so sorry, Cato. How could I have been so foolish?"

Cato interjected, "It is not safe for you here. You must leave the empire. They will find you and you will be next."

Now Noemi was crying even harder. "No, Felix protected my identity. Seemingly, the only decent thing to come out of this."

Cato wiped the tears from her eyes with his thumb, holding her head in his hands. "Don't blame yourself, my love. I would have done the same thing had I seen you lying there. We always knew this was a possibility, but I never thought it would actually happen," Cato said tears welling up behind his eyes.

Noemi reached up on her tip toes to kiss him through the bars. He pulled her as close as he could kissing her back both knowing that this could be their last. She knew he was only putting on a brave face for her. She had to figure out a way out of this. There must be something she could do. They stood there in silence, embracing through the bars both trying to soak in the last day together. And then it came to her. It was an idea so crazy and the odds were that it probably wouldn't work, but it was worth a shot. "Wait here," Noemi said it like Cato had a choice. "I have an idea and it is your only hope so no arguing. I will be back."

Noemi took off running back down the prisoner's wing to the stables. She had a lot of work to do and fast. She had to hope that Felix was done following her now that he had his revenge, she didn't have time to be careful anymore. She had seen thousands of executions working with her father to know how they went. High profile people and crimes would get the more lavish execution saved for last. Cato would normally fall into that category but with less than a day to set the scene on the arena floor, there was no way it could be extreme like when the emperor turned the arena into a jungle. Noemi knew that when the emperor made the request for the execution, her father's men would talk the emperor into something they could manage on short notice that would seem extravagant and draw crowds but could be put together in a day. That would be a large beast execution. Releasing a few animals at a time to tire the executionee out letting him get a few small victories, then the grand finale of hundreds of animals released to finish him off. It would give the emperor the show he wanted. Noemi could control what animals were released and when.

With her knowledge of the animals and the arena, she might be able to get Cato through it and sneak him out somehow. She found a half full sack of grain for the animals and emptied its contents into a trough. She then went to the market to buy some supplies, filling the sack with food and a few tunics. Her heart sank as she saw posters already displayed advertising the "Execution of the Traitorous Cato Velarius, Top Gladiator Prospect" as well as city criers yelling throughout the streets to promote it.

There would be no way to sneak him out of the hypogeum, not with the entire city expecting to see him fight to his death. She would have to alter her plan just a little. The key to the prison cells was not hard to obtain, actually it was the exact same key as the ones used in the stables. There really was no need for separate keys because the citizens did not even know about the hypogeum in its entirety. All they knew was that the animals magically appeared and that gladiators must walk through the front gate with everyone else, so there was no real risk.

Noemi hid the sack in the wall in her hidden room then made her way back to Cato. Cato tried to play it off like he hadn't been crying in his cell, but she knew better. Seeing him upset made her die a little inside especially because it was her fault they had gotten caught. Noemi stood on her tiptoes grabbing his face with both hands looking him straight in the eyes.

"Cato Velarius. You will not like what I am about to say to you, but you have no choice in the matter. I am the reason you are here, and I am going to do everything and anything to get us out of this."

Cato actually cracked a smile probably because he had never seen her like this.

Noemi went on. "I'm serious. We don't have much time. Okay, so the emperor and all of Rome now apparently expects to see you fight to your death in the morning. So that's what we are going to give them. Sort of. I am going to take your place." Noemi put her hand up warning him against refusing. "I will wear your helmet and armor and fight the animals I know so well. I think I can fake my death and fool the emperor into thinking you really were executed long enough for me to be carted off the arena floor without him even realizing." Noemi waited for him to respond.

"No. It will never work. There is no way you will pass for me," Cato argued.

"People see what they want to see. That much I have learned from working in the shadows all my life. As long as they see your helmet and armor, they would have no reason to suspect otherwise. Trust me, the only thing anyone is looking for is a good fight that ends in with an execution."

Noemi hoped she sounded confident enough to convince him to do this.

"Say this actually works. Then what? We can't stay in Rome. What would we do?" Cato's logic resonated with Noemi.

"That seems like a welcomed problem to me because it means we are both still alive," Noemi countered. "We need to switch places before the guards do their nightly rounds," she said as she unlocked the prison door. "I have a sack stashed in the wall with food and new clothes for you in a small room at the far side of the hypogeum in the corner. Change and wait there until I come and get you."

"And if you don't come get me?" Cato asked.

"I promise. I will. I have to." Noemi wished she could actually promise him that everything would be okay.

Cato pulled her in his arms her head resting on his chest. Noemi could hear his heart beating, a sound she hoped she would hear again. Cato took a deep breath. "I don't want to spend what could be our last moments together arguing. I realize you are going to do this whether I want you to or not. I think you are insane but at the same time the fact that you are willing to risk your life for mine makes me love you more than ever. Now kiss me before I change my mind."

As Noemi's lips touched his, she tried to soak in everything about him. His smell, the way his lips felt on hers, the way his hands felt on her. Everything in case it was the last time she saw him. Noemi pulled away first knowing the guards were coming soon. "This isn't goodbye, okay? I love you more than anything, Cato Velarius. See you tomorrow. Now go." Noemi kept the tears from flowing until he left, sneaking out of the cell and closing the door behind him. She didn't want him to see that she had any doubts.

The next morning, Noemi awoke in the dark cell almost forgetting where she was. She dressed herself in Cato's golden armor. It was heavier than she had expected and a little too big. It was going to be a lot harder maneuvering in the arena with all the added weight, but she would have to make do. She placed the helmet on her head pulling the visor down over her face. *Here goes nothing.* She sent up a silent prayer to the gods.

The guards came as expected during the late morning. Two men opened the prison cell, "Prisoner. Let's go. Up," one shouted at her. The other guard shackled her hands tying a rope to the shackles and led her down the hallway.

Just as Noemi had predicted they were too preoccupied gossiping with each other to notice the awkward way she walked in the armor or the fact that she was a whole foot shorter than Cato. They led her to the main tunnel's entrance where she was put in line with all the other executionees for the afternoon, her rope tied to a metal loop in the wall to prevent escape. As guessed, she was slated to go last, the grand finale of the day.

She overheard some of the staff commenting on the size of the crowd that day and could feel eyes on her as the reason. There were eighteen executions before her, she counted the men tied up in front of her. *A nice little warmup for the crowd,* she thought. She could hear the announcer getting the crowd going, promising an exciting after-noon while teasing the spectacular death of one of the strongest glad-iators the city had ever seen.

Noemi hoped Cato was safely hidden in the room and not trying to do something stupid. There was only room for one dumb act today. The line before her dwindled down, most being executed in groups via hanging. She even saw them give two prisoners weapons to fight each other. That ended in one swiftly killing the other and then trying to escape. He was killed with an arrow by one of the guards above and dragged out of the arena with the others. To say Noemi was nervous was an understatement.

One of the guards handed her a small spear as another one unchained her from the wall and shoved her toward the tunnel open-ing. The weight of armor almost caused her to fall flat on her face as she took her first step into the arena, but she managed to right herself. She was so focused on trying to walk confidently with the armor and making sure she could see out of the helmet that she didn't even hear what the announcer said. That, on top of the deaf-ening roar of the crowd, she wasn't sure she would be able to hear anything at all.

Stepping out onto the arena floor was not what she expected. It was one thing to be there when it was completely empty, setting up for events or working with the animals. But now, she was the center of attention. Every single eye was on her as she walked into the center of the arena, she could feel them boring down into her. She stopped in the middle of the sand covered arena floor just as she had seen countless other prisoners do over the years.

Shocked that she was even given a weapon, she squeezed the spear as hard as she could trying to take her mind off the fact that her entire body was trembling with fear. If the crowd wasn't so loud, she was sure they could hear the armor clanking from the vibrations of her body.

The announcer attempted to silence the crowd before reading Cato's crimes from a scroll. "Per order of the emperor, Cato Velarius is hereby sentenced to death for crimes against his majesty," the announcer paused here to keep the crowd in suspense, "the gladiator is property of the emperor and has violated his contract. He will answer for this in front of the crowd to bear witness."

Noemi stopped listening, she knew the rest. The crowd cheered that they were acknowledged and given a role in the execution. Noemi watched as the emperor stood up, his purple toga billowing in the wind, clinging to his fat stomach. He signed the decree, a small scroll held by the announcer making the execution official, and returned to his throne with a grimace across his face like he would enjoy every second of this. Noemi could not even look at him knowing he was responsible for this mess.

She took a deep breath trying to drown out the noise and distractions of the crowd. She had to focus. Yes, she knew what was coming because she had chosen and posted the list of animals behind the scenes, but animals could be unpredictable, so it wasn't a sure thing that she was going to pull this off.

The first animal to be released was one of the older lions that had been rehabbed numerous times and was on its last leg. Of course, no one but the hypogeum crew knew that. The trap door farthest from her slowly began to open, the crowd now silent, anxiously awaiting what beast they would see. The lion charged out at a full sprint to give the illusion to the crowd that it was a ferocious, hungry beast. Noemi knew that to rile it up, it had been poked in its hind with a hot piece of metal just as the door opened.

Okay, Noemi thought, *time to put on a show.* The lion stopped halfway between Noemi and the trapdoor it was released from. Noemi took the spear in both hands waving it at the lion. This was something they did in training a lot to draw the animals to them. The lion, seeing the signal, obeyed and walked toward Noemi. She knew it appeared like she was taunting the lion, looking like the brave gladiator she was supposed to be portraying. The lion walked right up to the end of the spear, feet away from Noemi. Oddly enough, the wild animal was the only thing that wasn't scaring her in that moment. The lion had been trained to know how to follow the spear. Noemi turned in a slow circle with the spear still extended. The lion walked with its nose almost touching the spear, moving with her around in a circle. For the crowd, it looked like the lion was circling its prey, ready to strike at any moment.

So far, her plan was working. Noemi could barely see out of the helmet, it was too big and hung down over her eyes. She had to keep straining her neck to continuously lift it up on her forehead. She stopped and changed direction, the lion following the spear the other way. *One last thrill before she put the poor beast out of its misery,* she thought. She tapped the end of the spear up under the lion's chin, cuing the lion to stop in place and let out a massive roar. She said a silent prayer to Diana to deliver the animal's soul before she slit its throat mid roar, warm blood spewing from its neck as it fell into the sand.

Noemi turned to where the emperor was sitting. Standing at attention, she looked directly into his eyes as if to say, *is that all you've got?*

The crowd booed, unhappy that the lion was unsuccessful. The emperor smiled back as if to say he was just getting started.

Right on cue, two elephants were released behind her from the main tunnel. They came charging toward her bringing up a large cloud of dust as the sand flew when they ran across the arena. The thing about elephants was that they were really gentle giants, but you would never guess that from their enormous stature. To the average person, an elephant was the largest beast they had ever seen and assumed it would wreak havoc.

Noemi stood her ground, casually side stepping the elephants as they charged by. She knew they wouldn't have any interest in her considering they were herbivores. If anything, they were just scared after being prodded with a hot poker. Again, she had chosen elephants that were older with many injuries.

Saying another silent prayer to Diana, she began walking slowly and confidently toward the beasts that had stopped at the far end of the arena. She approached the first elephant, ducking out of the way for show as it swung its trunk back and forth. She tapped the ground in front of it with her spear. The elephant, recognizing the command, knelt down on its front legs resting its head down in the sand. Noemi could hear laughs from crowd as the beast looked like it was bowing down to her. She wished she could see the emperor's face as she climbed onto the elephant's head and slowly stood up. She tried not to wobble with the heavy armor as the elephant began to stand back up with her still on its head. She stood on top of the elephant like she had done so many times at the school, but this time she raised a spear high above her head and thrust it down into the back of the elephant's neck piercing its thick skin as hard as she could. The elephant let out a loud trumpet of distress as it fell on all fours, Noemi gracefully jumping off of its back as it fell and landed on her feet.

The crowd roared as they were now entertained by this skillful gladiator and the show he was putting on. Noemi jogged over to the other elephant who was trying to figure out what had happened to its companion. Noemi hated to do it, but she needed to keep the show going. She somersaulted in between the elephant's legs letting the weight of the armor propel her forward hoping that the elephant wouldn't crush her with its foot. As she came out of the somersault, she raised the tip of the spear up just enough to slice open its under-side. Its innards spilling out onto the sand as the creature collapsed. Noemi kicked sand on the elephant's body adding another dramatic flair to her show.

The crowd roared again loving what they were seeing. Animal after animal was brought out. All handpicked by Noemi herself. She easily defeated each one much to the dismay of the emperor. She found herself actually enjoying the energy of the crowd and the adrenaline pounding through her veins. She had anticipated that if she had made it to this point the emperor would be at the end of his rope, for he did not want to be made a fool and she was correct. She didn't have to be close to him to see that he was irate, pacing in front of his throne, his face a dark shade of red from shouting.

Now for the grand finale, she thought. As predicted, the emperor was signaling to the interim hypogeum director to give it everything he had. Noemi had made sure that all the animals released for this last desperate act were well fed. Her plan was to fight a few beasts, dazzling the crowd one last time, then fake her own death.

That last part was the wild card. Her hope was that the animals were quickly corralled, and her body carted off without any one the wiser. However, the emperor was unpredictable. The only thing she could do was hope he didn't stray from the typical execution pattern. Noemi took a deep breath, her body sore from carrying the armor around. She could feel the sweat pouring down her back and the wet hair sticking to her neck under the helmet. Her shoulders were raw from the ill-fitted metal continuously digging into them. She pushed all those things out of her mind and prepared to finish what she started for Cato, and for her future.

This time, multiple doors opened at the same time around the arena each releasing a different beast or beasts from the depths of the hypogeum. The beasts raced out as each one before had done, most calling out in distress from their new hide burn. The carnivores in the bunch, the tigers, hyenas, and leopards, immediately ran to the large elephant carcasses once they got a whiff of the blood. Noemi knew they wouldn't bother her with all that fresh meat readily available and their already full stomachs, so she ran around the arena making it look like she was scared as she dodged the beasts.

Some of the animals began to fight each other over territory or food, drawing the attention away from her. She had to bring the focus back to the execution in order to finish this. She decided to use the bears for the first phase of the plan. She made her way to one of the pits that had been dug from a previous execution. Tapping her spear repeatedly on the ground, she got one bear's attention. Bears were curious creatures and not vicious unless provoked. Almost all of the bears her father had were trained to do tricks for the purpose of entertaining the crowd before a fight or putting on a show at the palace. She needed this to look like she was injured.

The bear made its way over to Noemi.

Grabbing the spear in one hand, she charged the bear. The bear, uncertain of what was happening, began to walk backward toward the pit. When Noemi got too close to the bear, it playfully swiped its paw at her. Noemi fell to the side, feigning that the force of the playful swipe had knocked her down. The crowd cheered, their attention once again back to the gladiator. She stood up, pretending to limp, the bear waiting to see what she was going to do next. She took the spear and lunged for the bear, missing it on purpose. The bear, thinking it was some sort of game, swiped at her again.

Again, she fell to the side. This time deliberately slow to stand back up, using the spear as a crutch to right herself. She lunged one more time putting her arm out in front of her toward the bear's mouth. Just like during Saturnalia with the tiger, the bear opened its mouth and lightly bit down on her arm, more playful than anything. Noemi screamed, trying to keep her voice low as that of Cato's. The bear released her arm and she fell to the ground clutching it like she was in excruciating pain. *Now for one last feat of strength,* she thought. She ran at the bear again, this time when the bear backed up it fell into the netted pit where it would stay until someone caged it again later in the day.

The crowd cheered as it had looked like she had tackled the bear to its death. She crawled through the bloodied sand on her hands and knees as if she was too injured to stand. *If she made it through this, she would have to think about auditioning for a drama in the amphitheater,* she half joked to herself.

She could hear some people shouting "Get up, get up" encouraging the gladiator to keep fighting.

Noemi crawled a few more feet then slowly stood up again. She stood there clutching her arm and leaning on the spear looking as defeated as possible. Shockingly, more than a few chants from the crowd were toward the emperor, asking him for mercy for the gladiator. Of course, he would never grant mercy, that was a sign of weakness.

It was time for Noemi to end it. She just had to find the right animal to engage her. She scanned the arena for her best bet. Most of the animals were still invested in the elephant carcasses. Others were roaming around exploring their new environment. She looked for a spot in the arena with the least number of beasts and farthest from the emperor's eyes so she could pull this off. So far, everything was going as planned, just one more step left. She began to limp again, falling every now and then to keep the suspense alive.

She was just about to entice a large boar to finish her off when a piercing scream echoed throughout the arena, so loud it drowned out the beasts. Startled, Noemi turned around a little too quickly for someone who was supposed to be that injured to see where the noise was coming from.

A spectator was climbing down the wall into the arena, expertly using the cutouts that the workers used to safely scale down the wall, and jumped into the sand. This was not what Noemi needed. *Who would be crazy enough to do that with all these beasts on the loose?* Noemi wasn't sure what to do. She needed the attention on her to finish this, but everyone was looking at the person who had just jumped in.

"Gods," Noemi said out loud, it was a woman.

"Prohibere!" The woman was repeatedly screaming at the top of her lungs to stop the execution. Her voice ringing throughout the now quiet arena. Dressed in rags with wild long hair, she was clearly a street beggar. In fact, Noemi actually knew her, it was Balbina. She looked much younger somehow and sprier than the Balbina she knew from the streets.

How in the gods did she even get into the colosseum in the first place? Noemi thought. Beggars and slaves were banned from entry and even if they did manage to sneak in, they would stick to the very top where they would be least likely to be seen.

Balbina stood in the sand right below where the emperor was seated screaming directly at him.

In all her years, Noemi had never seen anything like this. Sure, sometimes people accidentally fell from the stands, but never would they enter the arena on purpose if they didn't have to. As Balbina screamed for the execution to stop, she did not seem to even notice the beasts feet away from her, many that could kill her in an instant. Her screaming even deterred the beasts as most moved away, unsure what to make of this loud woman.

The emperor signaled for her to be removed from the arena, two unlucky guards sent to remove her. He looked more than annoyed at this street beggar interfering with his spectacle. Balbina did not waver. She continued her yelling.

Noemi quickly reworked her plan. She would wait until Balbina was removed from the arena then feign another injury with another beast. It wasn't ideal to keep drawing it out, but she hadn't anticipated this interruption.

The guards made their way into arena, their steps cautious and slow, clearly terrified to be inside with all of the wild beasts.

Balbina saw them coming for her and yelled out one last plea to the emperor. Noemi did not think she heard her correctly the first time.

When Balbina repeated it, Noemi fell to her knees out of shock and disbelief. The emperor stood, first looking at his mistress seated next to him whose toga hugged her stomach tightly. There was no denying she was with child. He then stepped toward the edge of the balcony leaning over slightly to get a better look at Balbina. He gripped the edge of the wall as if to steady himself before slowly raising his hand for the execution to cease.

All while Balbina continued to yell, "He is your son. He lives."

27

NOEMI

Noemi was frozen. She knew she needed to get up from her knees, but it was as if her legs had stopped working. She tried to process what she had heard, but it wasn't making sense in her mind. She barely remembered being escorted out of the arena by the guards. Her helmet had stayed on, her identity not yet exposed. She was brought, along with Balbina, into the guard's room where they would wait until summoned by the emperor.

Noemi had so many questions for Balbina, but did not dare speak. Balbina stood in the room staring at Noemi like she wanted to reach out and touch her, a look of longing on her face. Noemi stared back at Balbina. She was young, her face was merely dirty making it look like she had many years on her. Her physique was not that of a crippled old woman at all but a fit, spry middle-aged woman. Noemi could see that beneath the rags and grime she was actually quite stunning.

The guards seemed anxious as well, pacing the room waiting for word. "Could you really be the emperor's son?" one guard asked Noemi interrupting her thoughts.

When she did not answer he reached for her helmet. Noemi tried to move away from him, but she stood no chance. He pulled the helmet off, her long brown hair falling back down on her shoulders.

"What in the gods name is this?!" the guard questioned.

The look on Balbina's face was pure shock. "Where is he?" she asked urgently, her face panic stricken.

"He is safe," Noemi replied, at least she hoped he was.

The guards started to panic. They were on the hook for bringing Cato to the emperor and any other outcome would result in their deaths as well.

"Take us to him," the guards demanded.

Noemi removed the armor first, her body breathing a sigh of relief as the heavy metal was taken off. The ruse was over and for now everyone was still alive even though things did not go as planned.

She led the guards and Balbina to her room in the hypogeum. She was assuming that Cato would be there, but what if something had happened, like he decided to run away or was caught? She realized she was holding her breath as she walked into the room. When she did not see him, her heart dropped into the pit of her stomach.

"This better not be some sort of trick," one guard said to her, clearly annoyed.

"Umm, no trick. He was supposed to be here. Maybe he left a note?" Noemi said with a thick tone of despair looking around the room for any sign of Cato.

Suddenly, the boxes in the corner began to rustle as Cato emerged from his hiding place.

"Cato!" Noemi screeched her voice dripping with delight as she jumped into his arms to embrace, clearly not caring that they had an audience as they kissed each other until they couldn't breathe anymore.

"Ahem," Balbina faked a cough, interrupting them.

Cato came up for air finally acknowledging that they were not the only two in the room, a look of complete confusion on his face when he saw Balbina with the guards.

Balbina took a few steps toward Cato with tears in her eyes. She started to reach her hand out to touch him but pulled it back at the last second deciding against it.

"Can someone please explain to me what is going on?" Cato asked to no one in particular, clearly confused at what Noemi was doing with a beggar and the emperor's guards.

"We don't have time for reunions. Let's go," a guard ordered as he grabbed Cato by the arm and began to pull him toward the door.

"I would advise against touching the only living heir of the Roman Empire," Balbina warned matter of fact.

The guard was not sure how to react, so he released him but did not move away.

Cato and Noemi looked at each other, then to Balbina for answers. Balbina casually sat down on a dusty old crate like she was at her own home and began her story. The guards did nothing but listen as they were just as intrigued by what the woman had to say and how she could make such a claim.

Noemi held onto Cato like she was never going to let go.

Balbina began. "Many moons ago, when the emperor was first coronated, I worked in the palace kitchens. It was an exciting and bustling place to be what with all the parties and royalty. I was there for his betrothal to the empress, their marriage, and their every failed attempt to produce an heir. Back then, he was not the man you see now. He was kind and thoughtful, actually pleasant to be around. I think each subsequent failed pregnancy over the years really took its toll on him."

The words poured out of Balbina like she had rehearsed this story many times before. "I did not ask for it to happen, but with each loss of a child, the emperor seemed to push his empress away more and more and take a liking to me. Over time, I became his friend and then eventually his lover. I guess you could say that I was his first mistress."

Balbina paused here to gather herself then continued. "At first, the empress was less than pleased with me as you can imagine, but over the years she realized I was not after her title or power and I made the emperor more like his old self than anything else. So, she tolerated me and thus our relationship. That is until I became pregnant." Noemi looked up at Cato, his eyes full of disbelief as he slowly put the pieces together in his mind.

Balbina continued, "The empress was furious when she found out. She threatened to have me killed and denounce the child as heir to the throne making sure everyone knew the child was to be a bastard. Frankly, I did not care about the child's title, only that it was loved. And that is where the emperor and I differed. After so many failures, he was hell bent on making sure he would have a living heir and this was his chance. He made promise after promise with the empress about the child's future and my own. He basically sold my soul and his own to make the child an heir. After countless arguments, threats, and council advice the empress agreed to make the child an official heir only until they were able to have an heir of their own. In addition, I was to be removed from the palace after my child was born and my existence never to be spoken of again.

"As you can imagine, I was beyond devastated and unwilling to comply with their resolution. I pleaded with him for months to reconsider, hoping he would come around, but, he was adamant in his decision. During the rest of my pregnancy, he was caring and I got the best treatment, but I knew it was for the sake of the child, not me. He had changed.

"The birth was long and tough, I labored for three brutal days. I had succumbed to the fact that I had to give the baby up and would never see it again. Knowing that the child would have a good life was the only thing that kept me together. When he was finally born, I instantly knew something was wrong, I could just sense it. What they say about a mother's intuition is true. The wet nurse took him immediately, giving him to the emperor to hold. The emperor rejoiced as the child was alive. His happiness was short lived however as I heard a feeble cry and saw the baby's body go limp in the emperor's arms.

"The last I saw of my child was his leg dangling lifelessly out of a golden silk blanket as they quickly took him to the healers. A heart-shaped birthmark on his shin. I knew he was gone before he even left the room. I sobbed for my son and the life he would not have. The midwife was the only one left in the room with me. I could tell she was a mother herself as the sympathy oozed from her face. She comforted me as she changed the sheets from the birth and cleaned around me. I was fearful that since the baby had not made it that I would succumb to a fate much worse than exile from the palace. As I lay in the bed, mourning my child, I began to feel an intense pain in my stomach. I clutched my belly writhing in agony as the midwife rushed to my side. I thought my body was attacking itself, some sort of retribution from the gods for bearing an unhealthy son. I watched the midwife be surprisingly calm as I was surely dying.

" 'Milady,' her voice but a whisper, 'Another child is coming.' What she had said did not quite register with me. I barely had enough time to fathom what was happening before the arduous tightening of my stomach set in and I knew she was correct. Within minutes, I was holding my second son in my arms, alive and well with the same birthmark on his shin as his brother. A real-life Romulus and Remus situation, the irony was not lost on me. The upheaval of emotions had me in such a state, I went from complete tragic loss to overwhelming joy. The midwife brought me back down from the cloud I was momentarily living in. Someone was sure to hear the baby crying and eventually check in on me. The boy was strong, a fighter, and I knew I had to be strong for him. In that moment, I realized I had a second chance.

"I had lost one son but was not about to lose another. The midwife must have read my mind, an understanding in her eyes, because she was bundling up the child as I said my quick goodbyes to my second son. Over hushed tones, we made a quick plan to sneak him out of the palace. With my fate uncertain, I put my faith in the midwife and one of my closest friends in the kitchen to get him safely out of the city, and to raise him without knowledge of where he came from. I couldn't bear to let the emperor make another decision for me and this was my small revenge. When the confirmation of the death of my first son reached me, I held on to the promise of my second son's life to get me through. As agreed, I was exiled from the palace but not without the whispers of a possible execution.

"I think I was the emperor's weak link and he hardened after me, executing mistress after mistress with each failed birth. As for me, I had no real family in the empire. I laid low for the first few months, scared that I would be followed, and my secret outed. When I became sure I was but a distant memory of the emperor, I sought out my son. My friends had gotten him safely to a villa on the outskirts of town where he was being raised by a few of the slaves there. I grappled daily with the notion of retrieving him but could never live with myself if I was ever found out. So, instead, I watched him grow up from afar. I would deliver goods to the villa from time to time to see the boy. My friends would tell me news of him and keep me updated about his upbringing. As the years went on, I came to accept my decision knowing it was in his best interest as I had no real means to provide for him.

"One day, I got word that he had left the villa he worked on, to head for the city was the best guess of his slave family. I knew I had to find him so I lived as a vagrant, moving from street to street knowing eventually I would have to run into him. It didn't take long, actually. In fact, it was quite simple. Ludus Magnus had posted the roster of their new first year class around the city complete with a sketch of each gladiator. I took a copy for myself, proud of my strong son. From there he was easy to follow, the fights were posted and free to the public if you knew how to get in. I lived in the shadows keeping a distant eye on him. That is until I heard of his execution being promoted in the forum and I had to intervene."

Balbina stopped her story as everyone knew how it ended and looked at Cato, as did the people in the small room. No one said anything as Cato slowly pulled up the bottom of his tunic exposing his leg and the heart-shaped birthmark on his shin.

"So, you see," Balbina said to the guards, "I would suggest that you treat the emperor's heir with some respect."

28

CATO

Cato must have stopped breathing at least ten times during Balbina's story. His mind could barely process what was happening. Minutes before, he had been running back to Noemi's secret room after unsuccessfully trying to watch what was going on in the arena. He was cursing himself the whole time while hiding behind a few old wooden crates thinking he had been followed when he emerged after hearing Noemi's voice. He was so happy she was still alive that it did not even register to him she was not alone. Now, the same woman that had read his fortune some many months ago in the slave market was claiming to be his mother, and that he was the heir to the Roman Empire throne. *What was going on?*

Cato was skeptical of Balbina's story. It was far-fetched and innovative, a tale a weathered vagabond would spin. That was until she referenced his birthmark. No one could have known about it. As much as he wanted to open his mind to the possibility, there was no way the emperor would believe her story, true or not. He shoved down whatever glimmer of hope her story had dredged up and put his focus back on Noemi. They were alive and together for the moment.

Cato held Noemi's hand all the way to the palace. If this was to be the last time they could be together, he was not going to let go. The guards led them, along with Balbina, through the emperor's tunnel. No one said a word the entire journey unsure of what the future held. He watched the woman confidently walk in front of him and let his mind try to open up to the possibility that there was any truth to this. *Could Alba have lied to me all those years at the villa?* he thought. He had always just assumed that his parents were dead, why else would he be an orphan? The way she had looked at him with such a deep longing —he had never experienced that from a stranger before.

Noemi squeezing his hand stopped his thoughts from wandering any further than they already had.

The palace was just as magnificent as when he was there for the dinner. The guards took them to the atrium where they were seated next to a giant circular fountain and told to wait. An official-looking woman came out shortly thereafter requesting that only Balbina follow her as the emperor wanted to speak with her alone. Before following the woman back to the throne room, Balbina reached out toward Cato, giving his hand a loving squeeze for either reassurance or something more, he did not know. He was numb to Balbina's touch, not yet willing to let down his walls.

Balbina looked at Noemi and nodded, an unspoken under-standing exchanged between the two women as if to say I respect your strength and know why you had to do what you had to do.

Noemi sat next to Cato holding on to him for dear life.

"What do you make of all this?" Noemi asked. Cato ran his fingers through his hair, a perplexed look on his face trying to process everything.

"I don't know what to think. She seems pretty convincing, but the story seems a little far-fetched for me. I mean, I am a slave, not the son of the emperor."

"But the fact that we are sitting here, both alive, has to mean something," Noemi argued. Cato pulled her in closer. "Whatever happens, I want you to know that I will never forget what you did for me today." His eyes moving to dried blood on her tunic, a result of the armor.

"I would do it again a million times over if it meant only a few more hours with you," Noemi replied, her eyes full of tears.

They waited for Balbina for what felt like an eternity until finally the throne room doors opened again.

The woman came out alone, Balbina not with her. "Gladiator," she addressed Cato, waving him to the doors.

Cato turned to Noemi and held her face in his hands wanting to remember every last feature in case this was the last time he ever saw her. He wiped the tears from her eyes. "I love you," he said, choked up himself. He kissed her then, wishing he could freeze that moment in time. Instead, he had to will himself to walk away from her into the throne room, where fate awaited.

The throne room was more grandiose than Cato could have envisioned. Almost everything was gilded, even the giant chandeliers casting light throughout the room. It seemed like he walked forever to get to the throne positioned under a purple silk canopy draped down from a giant golden crown suspended over the throne.

His footsteps echoed throughout the room. The Emperor was seated on his throne, his wife on one side, his mistress on the other. Balbina sat off to the side on a small couch, a relaxed look about her. Unsure of how to approach the emperor, he stopped a little before the throne sending up a silent prayer he would live through this.

The emperor stood up looking Cato up and down. He walked around Cato in a circle like he was a slave at an auction. Finally, the emperor broke the silence and said with a smile, "He has my chin."

Cato let go of a breath he did not realize he was holding.

"Come. Sit. We have much to discuss."

29

LIVIA

"Recte, madam," the priestess said with a smile as she covered Livia's lower half back up with the sheet, "the child's heart sounds strong and it is growing as well as can be expected. Just a few more moons and you will become a mother."

Livia repeated the word "mother" in her head. It still sounded foreign to her even after all these months. If she did not have the swollen belly constantly getting in her way, she might not have ever believed it.

She excused the priestess and allowed her servants to dress her for the day.

"I'll take my meal on the terrace," Livia said to Martia, who had been reassigned to her once she was with child.

Martia nodded and motioned to another girl for her plate.

Livia thanked Martia as she set down her food on the terrace table overlooking the massive palace gardens. After what she had been through with Antonia, she had made it a point throughout the entire pregnancy to be as friendly as possible to the girls, even though she knew they all envied her and treated her differently.

Livia sipped her tea as she watched the emperor poorly play another game of bocce ball with a few senators on one of the many well-manicured courts. His sweaty palms causing the ball to almost always slip out of his hands and never make it to the other end of the court.

She cradled her stomach and waved to him from the balcony rail, a fake smile plastered on her face. He smiled and waved back almost tripping over the edge of the court as he could barely balance his overweight body. *Fool,* she thought.

She had gotten very good over the past few months at masking her complete repulsion of the man. Once she realized the only way to spare her family's lives was to go all in with the emperor, she found it was easier than she expected to turn off her emotions and let her mind take her somewhere else when they were together. She had thanked the gods that the spoonfuls of gladiator blood she had been taking had made her very fertile, for she had not had one monthly show in her sheets since he had bedded her. Since then, every priestess and healer in the empire had been summoned to visit her, making sure that nothing was missed. She knew this baby was going to live. It just had to.

"Ignosce mihi," Martia said pulling her gaze away from the gardens, "the execution will begin shortly, and you and the empress have been ordered to go."

The execution. How could she forget. She had hoped he would have changed his mind about having her attend, especially going out in public in her condition but he had said it was an extremely important event and he needed everyone there.

"Right. I think the crimson toga with the gold stitching will be suitable," Livia said.

So far, she had kept the pregnancy a secret from her family. It was not that hard considering her father was still home recovering from the fire and Noemi was galivanting around the city with some mystery man. They were too busy with their own affairs to even notice the looser togas she had worn to hide her stomach. But now, as far along as she was, there would be no more hiding it on display next to the emperor at a public event. She just had to hope her family would not be in attendance or looking her way.

Livia had never actually watched one of the executions before and she was not keen on starting, especially since she was already nauseous from the child growing inside her. She sat on a smaller throne to the left of the emperor on a secluded platform above the arena, her posture perfect, playing the role of mistress. She tried to make eye contact with the empress, but she would not dare give her any regard. *No matter*, she thought.

She did not pay attention to what was happening below, instead she was focused on scanning the crowd for her family and friends praying she did not see them. She was not sure what was so important about this execution. As far as she could tell, a gladiator was set to be executed. It was unclear what the big deal was since they died daily in battles anyways. Livia counted the seconds until it was over and she could be back at the palace hidden away. The thought of all those eyes on her and her bulging stomach made her want to crawl beneath her throne.

It didn't help that the gladiator was taking his sweet time to die.

The emperor grabbed at her hand, rubbing his thumb gently over her fingers. "Enjoying the show, topo?"

Livia had to restrain herself from cringing at his touch. He was sweating so much that his toga was soaked through, although the temperature was nothing even close to warm.

"Yes. So much so," she said faking her enjoyment willing herself not to move her hand away from him.

The gladiator looked like he was on his last leg and her anxiety was starting to subside a little as the execution would soon be over and she could go back to hiding in the palace again until the child was born.

The screaming of a ragged, elderly woman from down in the arena unraveled any hopeful notions of escape. Livia had no idea how she had gotten into the arena, but she did not care for all she could focus on was her outlandish claim that the emperor had a living heir. Livia could feel herself pale as her hands involuntarily clutched her stomach.

~

Back in the throne room seated at the emperor's left, Livia listened intently as the vagrant woman's story unfolded. She did not miss one single detail as the woman claimed to be a former mistress who had secretly given birth to a twin, the emperor's son, whom he had sentenced to death a mere day ago. She had to stop herself from laughing out loud a few times due to how far-fetched the tale was and even felt bad for her because there was no way the emperor was going to listen to this much longer.

The fact that the emperor was even entertaining the idea of a living heir was shocking to say the least. As the woman finished her tale, Livia waited for him to have her escorted out of the palace surely to make even more of a scene. But that moment never happened. Livia looked to the emperor whose face was ashen and off color as if he had seen a ghost. Even the empress who was usually aloof and stone faced gave Livia a nod and a small smile, confirming the woman's story and taking obvious pleasure in Livia's realization.

Livia's pulse began to race, her heart beating so fast and loud she was sure it was echoing throughout the entire throne room. *This isn't happening,* she thought. *What will become of my child?* She then took a deep breath trying to calm herself down. She could not let anyone see she had been rattled.

The emperor stood up from his gilded throne and took a step toward the woman. Tripping on a stair, he had to be righted by one of the servants. The woman remained still as she let him move the hair away from her face revealing a prettier and much younger person than Livia had first thought.

"Well gods be damned. It really is you," the emperor said as he looked into her eyes.

Livia felt her throat tighten as she could see her plan falling apart before her eyes.

"Is it true?" he asked the woman. "Is my son really alive?" his words weighed heavily with hope.

"Yes. You can see for yourself," the woman said.

The emperor wasted no time. "Bring in the boy," he commanded.

Livia watched as two guards escorted a tall, muscular man dressed in everyday clothes into the throne room. *For someone who was just on the brink of being executed he did not have a scratch on him,* she noted. No one else seemed to notice his condition, or if they did, they did not say anything.

The emperor circled the boy, taking in each of his features. He stopped when he saw the heart-shaped birthmark on the man's shin and began to smile.

Livia had never seen him smile like that for anything and her heart sank.

The emperor then dismissed the empress and Livia without so much as glancing in their direction while he began to process the notion of his heir, his unborn child no longer a thought.

Livia stormed into her bedroom. Trying to stop herself from hyperventilating, she leaned back against the door and tried to take deep breaths.

"Can we get you anything?" Martia asked, her voice a little too chipper.

Livia was too distraught to even acknowledge that Martia was enjoying seeing her future falter. "No, just leave me be. I need some rest," she said as she made her way to the bed to lie down.

When she was finally alone, she got up from the bed, the weight of her stomach making it difficult to stand. She made her way to the terrace to get some fresh air. The Livia from a year ago would have cried and given up at this point, but she was way past crying. She was so close to protecting her family and getting out of the palace alive with her child.

Walking along the length of the terrace, she stopped to admire all of her plants as she tried to figure out a solution. *The heir is just a small setback,* she thought. *The problem is that there is no telling what he will do with the baby and me now. I will just have to move up my timeline and escalate things.*

She took a deep breath and holding her stomach she whispered to her unborn child, "They say women are not allowed to make their own choices, but your mama doesn't care what they say. This one is mine."

Livia picked some savory, thyme, rosemary, hyssop, and parsley like she had been doing every night as her way of contributing to the kitchen. She had found a passion in growing things outside her bedroom, neatly bundling up fresh herbs to be used in the meals made her feel useful or at least that is what she told everyone.

She had noticed the emperor fancied parsley ever since a healer had told him it would help calm his stomach after each meal. So much so that the kitchen began making him a small cup of parsley juice for after his supper. For weeks she had been slipping a small amount of hemlock in with the parsley, it looked so similar to the parsley it had been going unnoticed for months.

Livia smiled to herself as she thought of the poison taking its effect on the emperor with his constant sweating, his new onset clumsiness, and his pale coloring. She found herself humming an upbeat tune as she replaced all the parsley in tonight's bundle with hemlock. There was no need to wait until the child was born now. She was not going to let a man, especially one so vile, control her. Her destiny would be her own.

30

NOEMI

Noemi sat in the atrium of the palace with her eyes closed gently rocking from side to side in between crying and trying to remember what Cato's lips felt like. Watching him walk into the throne room alone, most likely to his death, had been gut wrenching for Noemi. Her thoughts kept spiraling to a tremendous number of uncertainties mostly centered on her never seeing him again. *Was that their final kiss? Would she ever look into his soft brown eyes again?* She wasn't sure how long she was actually sitting there, hours she guessed, before she saw someone else besides the guards.

A servant girl no older than she was walking through the atrium with a stack of linens. Not sure whether she should remain silent or ask her if she knew anything, Noemi went with the latter.

"Umm, excuse me," she said to the girl who looked a little startled to be addressed by anyone. "Do you happen to know anything of the gladiator who was brought in earlier this morning?" Noemi held her breath as she waited for a reply.

"Gladiator?" she said. "Oh, you must mean the heir. Sorry, it has been a little hectic around here trying to get ready for the ball tonight in his honor."

Noemi was not sure she heard her correctly. "Ball?" she said questioning the girl.

"Oh, why yes, the emperor is introducing his son to the empire tonight. It is the most exciting thing to happen here since I started. Where you have been?"

Noemi did not know whether to laugh or cry she was so relieved. *He was still alive.* She wanted to run and hug the girl she was so excited but kept calm, unsure what would happen to her. The girl scurried away as there was not a second to waste leaving Noemi once again alone with the guards.

Before she could even worry about what to do next, the woman who had escorted Cato away was now walking toward her.

"Noemi, is it?" she asked her not giving her any time to answer, "sorry about the delay, but it has been rather crazy around here today as you can imagine. If you can just follow me, please."

Noemi kept silent as she followed the woman, her bracelets jangling together was the only sound of the whole walk.

Where is she taking me? she thought, for she dared not ask.

They walked down numerous halls, twisting and turning so much Noemi would not have able to find her way back even if she wanted to. Finally, the woman stopped and opened a large door motioning for Noemi to walk through. It was unclear who or what was inside the room, but what choice did she have but to go in?

She no sooner than turned the corner into the room when she saw him. Cato, dressed in a purple toga, was standing there—alive—with a giant grin on his face. Noemi had no idea what the woman was saying because she was too busy sprinting across the room leaping into Cato's arms.

"Thank the gods you are alive," she said as she buried her face into his chest, her tears saturating his new royal garb. "I thought I would never see you again."

Cato held her tightly, his strong, reassuring arms making all her anxiety disappear.

"Everything is going to be alright," he said nuzzling his face into the top of her head.

Noemi looked up at him, tears still streaming down her face, "You really are his son?" she asked.

"It's true. The emperor confirmed it himself. He did not even hesitate once he saw me." Cato said, a look of astonishment on his face.

"So, now what?" Noemi asked.

"The emperor is throwing a big celebration tonight in my honor. He exonerated me, barely even caring about my past it seems." He grabbed Noemi's hands. "The best part of all is you are welcome to live here with me and will be given royal status," he beamed.

Noemi could not believe what was coming out of his mouth. *Her? Royalty?* Just days ago, she had been elbow-deep in animal feces and now she would have servants and a title. It seemed too good to be true.

"I'm still having a hard time wrapping my head around it," Cato said.

"Here I was just hoping that somehow we made it out of this alive and now I am dating the heir to the Roman Empire?" She bowed to Cato in jest as she said with a laugh, "I am at your service."

Cato laughed and picked her up. Noemi wrapped her legs around him and reached up to kiss him.

Excusing the servants, he said, "Now, I think my first official duty as heir to the throne will be to have my way with you." He carried her over to the large bed in the room and gently laid her down.

Noemi had never been dressed by anyone before and found it a little strange to have someone help her do such a simple task, but here she was adorned in the most beautiful purple silk toga she had ever seen. Her hair had been braided with pieces of gold and pinned up to allow for a golden wreath to sit atop her head.

Her parents had been invited, but Jovian was still too weak to make the journey. Noemi was secretly thankful they were unable to attend as she was not ready to unload everything that had happened on them when she had not even figured out what was going on herself.

Cato held out his arm for Noemi as they stood at the entrance to the ballroom waiting to be formally introduced. Noemi could tell he was nervous and gently squeezed his arm for reassurance.

The doors opened to a full house, people packed into the room straining their necks to get the first look at the heir.

A shrill horn blew, silencing the crowd as the announcer spoke, "Dominarum et iudices, I present to you, for the first time, the one and only living heir to his royal highness."

With that, the crowd erupted, cheering and clapping for Cato as they made their way into the ballroom to their table.

To say Noemi was nervous was an understatement. She was about to meet the emperor, the man she had despised since she was old enough to know how awful he was. Yet, he was now the father of the love of her life and she was unsure how to navigate her feelings as he had welcomed them both into the palace.

The walk across the ballroom felt like it took hours, her heart beating so fast she thought she was going to faint. With each step, she was closer to seeing what fate had in store for her. They walked until they stood arm in arm in front of him, the empress, and his mistress all seated at the royal table. Even Balbina was there, giving Cato an encouraging nod from her seat at the table.

Noemi looked up, her eyes instantly widening at what she saw. But it wasn't the emperor Noemi focused on. She had locked eyes with his mistress, her sister Livia, who sat there, resting her hands on her very pregnant stomach. Noemi dug her nails into her thigh to keep from reacting. *It seems Livia had been doing a little more than working at the palace,* Noemi sarcastically thought. By the look of her shocked face, her sister was just as shocked to see Noemi as she made the connection between Noemi and the new found heir of the Roman Empire. Both trying to hide their shock, they looked away, two sisters, with their greatest secret exposed to each other without even saying a word.

Cato must have been able to feel her trembling as he pulled her even closer to him. Noemi took a deep breath, pushing down the twisted piece her sister just added to this already difficult puzzle.

Noemi watched as the emperor stood up to welcome them noting that it seemed to be difficult for him to get up from his seat at the table. He gestured for his son and Noemi to join him for their first meal together. Noemi sat down directly across from her sister. It was near impossible for her not to stare at Livia and imagine how she had gotten herself in this position. Her sister must have felt her eyes on her for she ignored Noemi the entire dinner pretending to be deep in conversation with the emperor who was clearly not interested in her anymore. All Noemi could feel was a deep sickness in her stomach for her sister. She was not sure what was going on, but she could tell that Livia had been through something awful.

Servants brought out piles upon piles of food for them to enjoy, Noemi had never seen this much excess in her life. She tried not to show her disgust as the emperor shoveled enormous amounts of food in his mouth, his face and front of his toga covered in droppings and crumbs. Her mind kept coming back to her sister, trying to figure out how she could be with such a foul man.

Throughout dinner, people Noemi assumed were important gave several toasts to the emperor and his son offering their hope for a prosperous future for the empire, each stopping before the emperor to kiss his ring after their speech.

She had only been in the man's presence for a few hours and could barely tolerate him. Despite the lifestyle, it was going to be hard to live beneath this man. Noemi could tell Cato was having similar thoughts as she looked to him, his face feigning delight. *They were alive and together,* Noemi kept telling herself.

The dinner ended and a variety of sweet fruits and cakes were brought out for dessert. Noemi was so full she could not eat another thing, so she passed on the treats watching as other indulged.

Suddenly the emperor yelled in disgust, his anger directed at Livia as she must have bumped her after dinner drink with her large stomach, which was now soaked with green liquid.

Livia did her best to try and mop up the mess, but the emperor remained displeased as he sipped his own drink from his gilded goblet.

Despite their differences, Noemi felt for her sister and wished she could get up and help her, anything to take away some of the obvious pain she was in.

Noemi cringed as the emperor yelled at yet another servant as he rose to make a speech. She was not impressed as he swayed back and forth seemingly from too much wine.

The crowd silenced as he began to speak.

"To my son," he started in, lifting his goblet in the air, "I have waited many moons for an heir to this empire and now I finally have one."

Cato squeezed Noemi's hand under the table. Noemi peeked at Livia as she held her hands protectively over her stomach while he spoke.

"From this day forward..." the emperor's speech had begun to slur. He stopped to regain his composure and started in again, "from this day forward, the entire empire shall recognize him as my successor. May Jupiter protect his reign and bring forth..." he stopped mid sentence and it was as if his mouth was trying to move but no words were coming out. He reached for his throat, his arm and the entire rest of his body was trembling with intensity. The trembles turned to convulsions as he began gasping for air and reaching for help.

Multiple servants ran toward him trying to right him as he collapsed on the floor still convulsing. As fast as they had started, the convulsions ceased leaving the emperor lying still on the floor not breathing.

A few guests shrieked out of shock.

Noemi could hear whispers of the word "dead" spread throughout the crowd like wildfire.

The royal healer was on the ground next to him, his ear to his mouth. No one moved as they all watched the panic ensuing in front of them.

The healer stood and ran his fingers through his hair clearly distraught and said, "The emperor is dead."

The entire ballroom was eerily silent, the guests not sure what was going to happen next.

Livia had thrown herself over the emperor's body, a mistress weeping over the loss of the father of her child.

Noemi furrowed her brow. Her sister had never shown compassion for anyone in her life, in fact she hid all her emotions from everyone. And now she was wailing dramatically for someone she barely knew? Noemi wasn't buying it.

One of the emperor's senior advisers broke the silence, "Long live Emperor Cato!" and with that he took to a knee.

Noemi could feel Cato squeeze her thigh beneath the table as the entire room followed the adviser's lead and knelt before him as well.

Cato looked at Noemi, his eyes full of disbelief.

Noemi smiled back at him and said, "Your Highness."

EPILOGUE

"They are waiting for you in the gardens, Empress," said a royal servant. *Empress.* Noemi could still not get used to her new title. After the coronation, Cato insisted they were to be wed immediately. For Roman standards, the ceremony was simple, and Noemi could not have been happier. She honestly would have done whatever he had asked her to do because what mattered most was that they were free, and most importantly, alive.

Noemi was so proud of her husband. After being thrown into his role as emperor, Cato was trying his best to be a better ruler than his father. He found it difficult to be somewhere in the middle of a tyrant and a benevolent emperor, while still maintaining the respect of his people. His time as both a slave and a gladiator gave him a unique perspective on life, which made his reign one of the most influential the empire had ever seen.

Noemi's new title of Empress did not stop her from doing what she loved—training beasts. As royalty, there was no way she could work in the hypogeum anymore, so she settled for the next best thing. Cato had a massive stable built on the palace grounds so she could train with the animals anytime she wanted. When she wasn't with Cato, she could be found there.

. . .

Noemi held her niece, Cornelia—Nell for short—as she sat in the gardens outside the palace overlooking the entire empire from the top of Palatine Hill. The baby had been born healthy on March thirty-first, ironically the Feast Day of Balbina. She was the spitting image of her mother, Livia. Noemi had never seen her sister happier than when she was with her daughter, whom the entire empire adored and called Nell the Younger.

"Now don't go giving her any ideas," Livia said kissing the top of Nell's head. "She will not be dressing up like a gladiator anytime soon."

Noemi laughed. "No, she seems like she is ready to train beasts with her Aunt Noemi. I'll have her taming lions before her first birthday. Isn't that right, Nell?" she joked.

Noemi watched her parents fawn over their granddaughter. It had been a long road, but Jovian had made a full recovery after the fire. Despite Cato's urging, he refused to move into the palace, insisting on living close to the beasts and overseeing the school. He did, however, retire from directing the hypogeum, giving over the reins to one of his most trusted men ensuring that he would take as much pride in the place as Jovian did.

As for Felix, he was imprisoned for life for his crimes against Roman royalty. Not only had he plotted against Cato, but he had a hand in setting up the fire that nearly killed Jovian. Both Noemi and Cato couldn't bring themselves to see him be executed no matter how much pain and suffering he had caused them.

Noemi handed Nell back to her sister who snuggled the baby into her chest. Livia still had not told her all of what went on during her time at the palace with the emperor and probably never would. Noemi knew enough not to press her and guessed that she had somehow helped the fates along to get to where she was.

Although Cato gave her wealth and status in the empire, Balbina came and went from the palace as she pleased, choosing to continue to live a simple life. Noemi enjoyed watching them get to know each other. It had taken Cato a while to get used to the idea of having a mother, and Balbina respected his initial hesitation, giving him his space when he needed it.

Noemi stood at the edge of the garden overlooking the city. Cato came up behind her, his hand finding hers as he wrapped his arms around her from behind. Noemi leaned back into him. He softly kissed the top of her head, taking in the lavender smell of her hair as he tried to get used to the idea that all of this was his. Never in his wildest dreams did he think that Tyrian, the slave, would become the most powerful person in the empire.

As the sun set in the Roman sky, they held each other wrapped up in the miracle that allowed them to be together.

NOTE FROM THE AUTHOR

After I finish reading a book, I always find myself wanting a little bit more. I love when the author adds tidbits about how he or she came up with the idea for the book. When the book is historical, I make mental notes about some of the details, wondering if they actually happened, or if the author made them up. If you are like me and want some insider information, keep reading.

I love to travel. So much so, I competed on the CBS reality television show *The Amazing Race* with my husband in 2012. The once in a lifetime experience fueled the travel bug in me and after the show we traveled as much as possible. It wasn't until 2016 on a family trip to Rome, Italy that I came up with the idea for this book.

I love history, especially interesting facts that I squirrel away in my mind for a future crossword puzzle clue or a rainy day trivia game. We toured the colosseum as everyone should do 'when in Rome' and the guide mentioned something that stuck in my mind. He said that it wasn't until the late 1990s before they discovered how the animals were moved from the hypogeum to the arena above via elevators. This concept was wild to me. I thought if they had only recently figured that out, what else haven't they discovered yet about the hypogeum? From there, the allure of a whole behind-the-scenes, unknown underground operation evolved in my mind and the story took flight. I thought everyone has heard of the gladiators and the colosseum, but what about the people who made everything happen? Like a behind-the-scenes tour at Disney World or when Mister Rogers tours the crayon factory.

Now for some fun facts.

Although all of the characters are fictional, the buildings, places, and culture in *Beneath the Sand* are real to Ancient Rome.

Hypogeum The word means underground. Everything from the tunnel system to the trap doors all existed in Roman times. The only thing I added was the multiple levels. Although possible, it is unlikely that there was more than one level due to the lack of air flow and temperature. Parts of the hypogeum have recently been restored and can be toured at the colosseum today.

Gladiator Schools Ludus Magnus and Ludus Matutinus were actual gladiator schools, 'Ludus' being the Latin word for school. There were four gladiator schools in ancient Rome. Ludus Magnus was the largest gladiator training school and had a tunnel connecting it to the colosseum. Ludus Matutinus was the school where gladiators trained to fight wild and exotic beasts. The word matutinus means 'of the morning' which was when the animal fights were scheduled. Ludus Gallicus specialized in heavily armored gladiators. Ludus Dacicus focused on training with a short, curved swords.

Lanista A gladiator trainer who gained wealth from the success of their gladiators.

Velarium A retractable awning made of canvas that protected the patrons of the colosseum from the sun. The two hundred and forty masts were operated by sailors who were familiar with sails and ropes. The awning only covered the seating, leaving the arena open to the sky so everyone could see.

Saturnalia The ancient Roman holiday honoring the god Saturn. Many of today's Christmas traditions originated from Saturnalia.

Vestal Virgins Six girls between the ages of six and ten years old were chosen to serve a thirty-year term as priestesses for Vesta, the Roman goddess of the hearth. They were responsible for keeping

Rome's eternal flame lit. During their thirty-year service, they had to remain chaste, hence 'virgins'. They held more power than the emperor. It was said that a single touch by a Vestal Virgin would pardon all sins.

Circus Maximus The ancient Roman chariot racing stadium. Each race consisted of twelve chariots pulled by a different number of horses depending on the kind of race. They had to complete seven laps which was roughly five miles. Auto racing is a modern-day equivalent.

Pharmacy I am a pharmacist by trade, so I loved learning about all the ancient medicinal remedies. To brush their teeth, Romans used powdered mouse brains and urine which was collected from the urinals at the end of each day. Cabbage and garlic were considered 'cure-alls'. Crocodile meat mixed with cyprus oil was used to combat acne and rid the face of freckles.

Strigil A metal cleaning tool used to scrape dirt, oil, and sweat off a body since there was no soap in Ancient Rome.

Knucklebones A game similar to Jacks that used the knuckle-bones of sheep as game pieces.

Trajan's Market Large five-story shopping center with hundreds of shops.

Haruspex A religious person who inspected the entrails of animals to deliver omens.

ACKNOWLEDGMENTS

I make it a point to read the acknowledgements of every single book I read, even more so now that I have written one. So, my first and most important thank you is to *you*, the reader. There would not be books without readers. Thank you for choosing to take a trip to Ancient Rome!

It took me two years to write this book. Mostly written during the kids' naptime or whenever I could get a spare minute. It was fueled by many glasses of Brunello, Barolo, and Burgundy. I got in my own way so much of the time, more than I care to admit. There was self-doubt and many insecurities that went into this process. Writing is hard. I give so much credit to all the creative authors out there.

After I had finally finished the manuscript, I had no idea what to do with it. *Was it any good? How do I get it published?* I was a fish out of water. So, a big thank you to author Alison Stone who answered all my novice questions and gave me the initial hope that I could see this through. Go check out her romance novels!

My editor, Michelle, took this book to the next level. She was very encouraging and motivating giving me an abundance of tools and guidance to get this published. Thank you!

The awesome cover design was done by Charles Leone. He is a very talented artist in Buffalo, NY, as you can see. Thank you!

I tried bouncing ideas off a few people in my family and the only person that had a good one was my sister, Kelly. She is responsible for Cato's holiday in the countryside. Thanks girl!

Special thank you to my family and friends who were my very first readers.

Huge thank you to all the bookstagrammers, book vloggers, and booktokers that took the time to spread the word about my book on social media. You are awesome!

Thank you to my parents who didn't laugh when I told them I was writing a book. Instead, they said, "I can't wait to read it!" Well Mom and Dad, I did it!

Thank you to my husband for putting up with my endless complaining about how I needed more time to work on my book.

Lastly, thank you to my daughters for giving me the purpose to write. I can't wait to teach you to read.

Read more books!

Love,

Katie

ABOUT THE AUTHOR

KATHERINE L. BICHLER is best known for her appearance on the CBS reality television show *The Amazing Race*. In her not so spare time, she continues to travel the world and watches a shameless amount of television. BENEATH THE SAND is her debut novel. She currently lives in Buffalo, NY with her husband and daughters.

For more information visit me at
www.katherinebichler.com
www.goodreads.com/katherine-l-bichler

instagram.com/Katherinebichler
twitter.com/katherinbichler
facebook.com/Katherinebichler

COVER DESIGN by Charles A. Leone

Email: chuckleone@gmail.com

Instagram: @chv.ck.leone

ISBN 978-0-578-32238-4 (hardcover)

ISBN 978-0-578-32448-7 (paperback)

ASIN B09K6S6BLT (ebook)

Lightning Source UK Ltd.
Milton Keynes UK
UKHW021310021122
411515UK00025B/861